MISSING PIECES

Sir Alistair Wilson obviously had the best office in the building, high and on the outside, but the view was still that of the asshole of Lambeth. He wedged himself against a windowsill, nodding Charlie toward a chair beside the desk. Richard Harkness sat in another, a fussily neat, striped-suited man, pearl-colored pocket handkerchief matching his pearl-colored tie.

"Your shirt collar is undone," complained Harkness.

"A pin stuck in my neck," said Charlie, in poor explanation.

"What!"

Before Charlie could respond, Wilson said impatiently, "Got an unusual one for you this time, Charlie."

Weren't they all? thought Charlie, wearily. He said, "What is it?"

"A major, international, political assassination," announced the Director simply. "It looks as if Britain is involved."

"Who?" asked Charlie.

"We don't know."

"When?"

"We don't know."

"Where?"

"We don't know."

"Who's the assassin?"

"We don't know."

"What do you expect me to do?"

Wilson looked at Charlie curiously, as if he were surprised by the question. "Find out who is to be killed and stop it happening, of course."

Fuck me, thought Charlie.

RUN AROUND

THE RUN AROUND

Brian Freemantle

BANTAM BOOKS
NEW YORK · TORONTO · LONDON · SYDNEY · AUCKLAND

This is a work of fiction. All the characters and events portrayed in this book are fictional and any resemblance to real people or incidents is purely coincidental.

THE RUN AROUND

A Bantam Book
Bantam hardcover edition / May 1989
Bantam paperback edition / July 1990

All rights reserved.
Copyright © 1989 by Brian Freemantle.
Cover art copyright © 1990 by George Tsui.

Library of Congress Cataloging-in-Publication Data

Freemantle, Brian.
   The run around / Brian Freemantle.
      p. cm.
   ISBN 0-553-28407-X
   I. Title.
PR6056.R43R84 1989
823′.914—dc19   88–47520
                       CIP

Bantam Books are published by Bantam Books, a division of Bantam Doubleday Dell Publishing Group, Inc. Its trademark, consisting of the words "Bantam Books" and the portrayal of a rooster, is Registered in U.S. Patent and Trademark Office and in other countries. Marca Registrada. Bantam Books, 666 Fifth Avenue, New York, New York 10103.

PRINTED IN THE UNITED STATES OF AMERICA

RAD   0 9 8 7 6 5 4 3 2 1

For Olive and Geoff,
supporters from the beginning

Prologue

He pulled the air into himself, panting, the effort burning his throat, grunting as he stumbled and collided with undergrowth that threatened to pull him down and tree branches that whipped his body and stung his face. The wetness, the torrential downpour, seemed to make it worse, which didn't make sense because it should actually have helped, but in his terror it was difficult to think properly about anything. Only one important thought: keep running. Had to keep running: stay ahead of them all the time. Not get caught. Terrible if he got caught. Rather be killed than be caught. He'd do that, instead of being captured: refuse to stop when they shouted the order, so that they'd shoot. What if the bullets didn't kill, only wounded? Unlikely. He knew, like he knew so much else, that the border guards carried machine pistols so it wouldn't be a single shot. A sprayed burst. People rarely survived a sprayed burst: weren't intended to. Definitely wouldn't stop, not if they got close enough positively to challenge him. Far better to be killed. Why the hell couldn't it have gone as he'd planned. Dignified. Not like this. Not running like some common criminal through some forest he didn't know toward some people he didn't know. Would he already have been listed as a criminal? That was how they'd regard him. Worse than a criminal; far worse. That's why he couldn't allow himself to be caught. He stopped, needing the wet-slimed support of a tree to stay upright, legs trembling from the unaccustomed running. The rain slapped and hissed into other trees all around him, but beyond he could hear the other noises, the shouts of those pursuing him, calling to maintain contact with each other. And worse, the barking and baying of their dogs. Thank God for the storm: wet as it was, his scent had to be confused. He was terrified of dogs. What if they didn't shoot, when he refused to stop? Set the dogs on to him instead, to bring him down? He openly whimpered at the uncertainty, pushing himself away from the tree, staggering on. Not much further: it couldn't be. Two miles, according to the map. He must have already run more than two miles. It felt like a hundred. Time was more important than distance, though. Ten o'clock: with fifteen minutes as an emergency margin. Ten-fifteen then, before they drove off. He stopped again, holding his watch close to his face but it was too dark. Dear God, please don't let it be ten o'clock yet: don't let them go and leave me. And then he saw it, the briefest on-off signal of the car headlights, away to his left. He jerked toward it, aware his strength was nearly gone. Almost at once he tripped over a tree root, crashing full length into bracken and other roots and driving what little breath was left from his body. The dogs sounded much nearer now, their movement as well as their barking, as if they'd been released. He crawled forward on his hands and knees, unable immediately to stand. The lights came again and he clawed upright against another tree, fleeing headlong toward it in a final desperate effort, knowing if he fell again he would not be able to get up, hands outstretched more in plea than for protection. The vehicle's shape formed before him and he tried to shout but it emerged only as a strained croak, so he was practically upon them before they saw him. Two men thrust from the car to catch him as he fell and with the same movement bundled him roughly into the rear seat.

It was a long time before he could speak. When he could, he said, croaking still, "Safe? Am I safe?"

"You're safe," assured a third man, who was sitting beside the driver. "Welcome to the West, Comrade Novikov."

1

He'd missed a pin. Charlie Muffin had been sure he'd got every one as he unpacked the new shirt, but now he knew he hadn't because something sharp and pointed kept jabbing into his neck, particularly if he swallowed heavily. And he'd done that a few times since entering the bank manager's office.

"An overdraft?" echoed the man. His name was Roberts and he was newly appointed, so it was the first time they'd met.

"Just the facility," said Charlie. The pin didn't hurt so much if he kept his head twisted to one side but if he did that it appeared he was furtively trying to avoid the man's eyes.

The bank manager, who was bespectacled and sparsehaired, gazed down at some papers on his desk, running a pen down several lines of figures. It seemed a long time before he looked up. There was no expression on his face. He said, "There were numerous occasions under my predecessor when you went into overdraft without any formal arrangement having been agreed."

"Never a lot," said Charlie, defensively.

"Two hundred pounds, last November," said Roberts.

The last time Harkness put him on suspension for fiddling his expenses, remembered Charlie. Why were accountants and bank managers always the same, parsimonious buggers acting as if the money they handled was personally theirs. He said, "There was a delay in the accounts department. Industrial action."

The man frowned down at Charlie's file and then up again, failing to find what he was seeking. He said, "What exactly is it that you do, Mr. Muffin?"

I'm an agent who spends too much time getting my balls caught in the vise while you go safely home every night on the 6:10, thought Charlie. Slipping easily into the prepared speech, he said, "I work for the government."

"Doing what?" persisted Roberts.

"Department of Health and Social Security," said Charlie. "Personnel." It even sounded like the lie it was.

"I suppose that could be regarded as protected employment," said the bank manager, in apparent concession.

"Very safe," assured Charlie. There had to be six occasions when he'd almost been killed, once when his own people had set him up. And then there'd been two years in jail and the time in Russia, when he'd been bait, hooked by his own side again. Bastards.

"How much?" demanded Roberts.

"Ten thousand would be nice," suggested Charlie.

The other man stared in continued blankness across the desk. There was complete silence in the room, apart from the sound of the London traffic muted by the double glazed windows. At last Roberts said, "Ten thousand pounds is always nice, Mr. Muffin."

Awkward sod, judged Charlie. If he'd called himself the chairman of some hole-in-the-wall company with a posh name and asked for ten million there would have been lunches at the Savoy and parties at Henley and Wimbledon. So far he hadn't even been offered a glass of supermarket sherry and didn't reckon he was going to be. "Just the facility, like I said," he reminded. "I doubt it would ever go that high."

Roberts made another unsuccessful search of Charlie's file and then said, "I don't see anything here about your owning your own house?"

"I live in a rented flat," said Charlie. Box would be a better description: poxy box at that.

"Insurance policies?"

It would be easier to get cover on the life of a depressed kamikaze pilot with a death wish than upon himself, Charlie guessed. He said, "There's a department plan."

"It's customary—indeed, it's a bank regulation—for overdrafts to be secured," lectured Roberts.

"The company plan is index-linked to allow for inflation," offered Charlie, hopefully.

"What exactly do you want an overdraft for?" asked the man.

There was a major reason and a lot of small ones. Harkness putting him back on the expenses stop list for not having identifiable meal receipts was one. And taxis were safer but more expensive after the pubs and the drinking clubs closed and all the street lights blurred together in a linked line. And then there was the fact he had not had a winner in weeks and the bookmaker was jumping up and down. And besides, he'd already tried to get cards from American Express and Diners and Access and MasterCard and they'd all turned him down. Searching for an acceptable reason, Charlie said, "I thought about a small car. Secondhand, of course. Maybe a new refrigerator."

"Perhaps some clothes?" suggested the man.

Cheeky bugger, thought Charlie. He'd had the suit cleaned and worked for a good thirty minutes with one of those wire brush things buffing the Hush Puppies to look better than they had for years. He knew *he* looked better than he had for years! Christ, that pin was making his neck sore. Eager to please, he said, "That sounds like a good idea."

"I'll need a reference, of course."

Of course you will, sunshine, thought Charlie. The procedure automatically meant Harkness learning about it. He offered the security-screened address and the supposed works number that routed any correspondence involving him to the Westminster Bridge Road headquarters and said, "There are a lot of divisions in the department, of course. This is the address you'll want for me."

"Thank you," said the bank manager. "I've enjoyed our meeting. I always like to try to establish some sort of personal relationship with my clients."

What about establishing it with a glass of sherry then!

Charlie said, "How long will it take for the overdraft to be arranged?"

The manager held up his hand in a halting gesture. "It would be wrong to anticipate any agreement, Mr. Muffin. First, we'll need a lot of supporting documentation from your department."

Harkness was bound to jump backward through the hoop, thought Charlie. He said, "So I haven't got it yet?"

"There's a long way to go," said the man.

There always seemed a long way to go, reflected Charlie, outside the bank. He undid his collar and, with difficulty, extracted the pin, sighing with relief. He explored his neck with his finger and then examined it, glad the damned thing hadn't actually made him bleed, to stain the collar. Stiff new shirt like this was good for at least two wearings, three if he were careful and rolled the cuffs back when he got to the office. Charlie sighed again, with resignation this time, at the prospect of returning there. He supposed he would have to confront Harkness and put up some cock-and-bull story about the expenses not having enough supporting bills, which they would both know to be precisely that, a load of bullshit, and sit straight-faced through the familiar lecture on financial honesty. What place did honesty—financial or otherwise—have in the world in which they existed? About as much as a condom dispenser in a convent lavatory.

Charlie was conscious of the security guard's awareness of what was for him an unusual appearance as he went through the regulation scrutiny check at the Westminster Bridge Road building. As the guard handed him back the pass, nodding him through, he said, "Hope it was a wedding and not a funeral."

"More like a trial," said Charlie. With a verdict that was going to be announced later. Charlie wondered how long it would take.

Charlie's office was at the rear of the building, overlooking a dusty, neglected courtyard to which there appeared no obvious access and which was gradually filling, like a medieval rubbish pit, with the detritus from the dozen anonymous, curtained, and unidentified cubicles which surrounded it. Where the wrappers and newspapers and plastic cups were most deeply piled was a pair of running shoes, arranged neatly side by side although upside down, which Charlie could not remember being there the previous day. He wondered if they were still attached to the feet of someone who'd made a suicide dive, unable any longer to stand the boredom of Whitehall bureaucracy: certainly they looked in too good a condition to have been discarded. Hardly worn in, not like his Hush Puppies were worn in. Mindful of how easily his feet became discomforted, Charlie eased them from his shoes to allow them the freedom they demanded. The socks were new, like the shirt. He'd made a bloody great effort and wanted very much to know it was going to be successful.

Charlie unnecessarily consulted his diary, blank as it had been for the past month, from the moment of his expenses suspension, and then looked through the opaque glass of his office door in the direction of Hubert Witherspoon's matching office. Witherspoon was Charlie's nemesis, the starch-knickered university entrant who knew by heart and obeyed by the letter all the regulations which Charlie dismissed as irksome, particularly when he was reminded of them by the man, which he was constantly. Witherspoon's office had been empty for a month and Charlie wondered if his were the feet in the upside down training shoes. Unlikely. If Witherspoon decided upon suicide, he'd probably choose to fall on his own knitting needles, Roman-style. At Cambridge the idiot had pranced about in a toga to attend some exclusive luncheon club. There was actually a photograph on the man's desk of the prick dressed like that at some graduation meal. Nothing changed, thought Charlie. Always boys trying to be men being boys.

He looked again at the diary, reluctantly accepting that unless he came up with some sort of story and bit the bullet with Harkness, he was going to be kept in limbo for the foreseeable future. The spy who was kept on ice, he thought. He tried to remember the name of an espionage novel with a title something like that but couldn't: he'd enjoyed the book though.

Charlie imposed his own delay, confirming the deputy director's internal extension although he already knew it and was actually stretching out for the red telephone when it rang anyway.

"You're on," said a voice he recognized at once to be that of the Director's secretary. Her name was Alison Bing and at the last Christmas party she'd said she thought he was cute, in the public school tone he'd heard used to describe garden gnomes. He'd had an affair with a Director's secretary once, recalled Charlie. And not primarily for the sex, although that had been something of a revelation, in every meaning of the word. He'd correctly guessed he was being set up as a sacrifice and had needed the protection of an inside source. So he'd got what he wanted and she'd got what she wanted, a bit of rough. He strained to remember her name, but couldn't. It seemed impolite, not being able to remember the name of a girl he'd screwed, even though they'd both been objective about the relationship.

"I'm on suspension," said Charlie.

"Not any more you're not."

"There hasn't been a memorandum rescinding it."

"Since when have you been concerned with memoranda?"

Since not wanting to drop any deeper in the shit than I already am, thought Charlie. He said, "Does Harkness know?"

"He's with the Director now."

Charlie beamed to himself, alone in his office. So Harkness was being overruled; the day was improving by the minute. At once came the balancing caution: Sir Alistair Wilson would not be taking him off suspension to supervise the controlled crossing at the diplomatic school, would he? So what the hell was it this time?

Sir Alistair Wilson obviously had the best office in the building, high and on the outside, but the view was still that of the asshole of Lambeth. Wilson's fanatical hobby was growing roses at his Hampshire home and so at least their perfume pervaded the room. There were bowls of delicate Pink Parfait on a side table and the drop front of a bookcase and a vase of deep red Lilli Marlene on the desk. Wilson stood as Charlie entered. A permanently stiffened leg from a polo accident made it uncomfortable for him to sit for any period. He wedged himself against a windowsill shiny from his use, nodding Charlie toward a chair already set beside the desk. Richard Harkness sat in another, directly opposite, a fussily neat, striped-suited man, pearl-colored pocket handkerchief matching his pearl-colored tie, pastel-pink socks coordinated with his pastel-pink shirt. Charlie was prepared to bet that Harkness could have negotiated a ten thousand pound overdraft in about five minutes flat. But not in the office of a manager who didn't serve even cheap sherry. Harkness's scene would have been the paneled dining room or library of one of those clubs in Pall Mall or St. James where all the servants were at least a hundred years old and your father put your name down for membership before announcing the birth in *The Times*.

"Your shirt collar is undone," complained Harkness, at once.

"A pin stuck in my neck," said Charlie, in poor explanation.

"What!"

Before Charlie could respond, Wilson said impatiently, "My collar's undone, too," which it was. "Got an unusual one for you this time, Charlie."

Weren't they all? thought Charlie, wearily. He said, "What is it?"

"For almost three years we've had a source directly inside the headquarters of the KGB itself, in Dzerzhinsky Square," disclosed Wilson. "Name's Vladimir Novikov. He was the senior supervisor in the cipher section; security-cleared to handle things up to and including Politburo level."

That wasn't unusual, acknowledged Charlie. That was sensational. "Was?" he queried, isolating the operative word.

"He was getting jumpy, so we agreed to his defection,"

nodded the Director. "Then he became convinced he was
under active investigation so he ran, crossing at the Finnish
border. Seems he was right because there was certainly a
chase."

"When?" asked Charlie.

"Two months ago," came in Harkness.

The timing meant other people were conducting the debriefing, realized Charlie, relieved. He had a special reason
for not liking debriefings. "How good is his information?"
he said.

"That's why you're here," said Wilson. "I know it's early
days, but so far everything he's said checks out absolutely
one hundred percent."

"So?" queried Charlie, warily.

"Something was being organized, just before he came
over. Something very big."

"What?"

"A major, international, political assassination," announced the Director simply. "It looks as if Britain is involved."

"Who?" asked Charlie.

"He doesn't know."

"When?"

"He doesn't know."

"Where?"

"He doesn't know."

"How?"

"He doesn't know."

"Who's the assassin?"

"He doesn't know."

"What do you expect me to do?"

Wilson looked at Charlie curiously, as if he were surprised by the question. "Find out who is to be killed and
stop it happening, of course."

Fuck me, thought Charlie. But then people usually did.
Or tried to, at least.

Characteristically, Alexei Berenkov was an ebullient,
flamboyant man but he was subdued now because the de-

fector had ultimately been his responsibility, as head of the KGB's First Chief Directorate. The demeanor of Mikhail Lvov was equally controlled, but then the commander of Department Eight of Directorate S, which plans and carries out ordered assassinations, was by nature a reserved and controlled man, in addition to which the meeting was being held in the office of the KGB chairman himself, which had an intimidating effect.

It was the chairman, General Valery Kalenin, who opened the discussion.

"The decision is a simple one," he said. "Do we abort the assassination? Or do we let it proceed?"

2

General Valery Kalenin was a small, saturnine man whose
life had been devoted to Soviet intelligence. He had controlled it through two major leadership upheavals in the
Politburo, which now regarded him with the respect of people well aware—because he'd made sure they were aware—
that he had embarrassing files upon all of them, like
America's J. Edgar Hoover had retained unchallenged control of the FBI with his tattletale dossiers on U.S. congressmen and presidents. Kalenin had been a young and
never-suspected overseas agent in Washington during the
last year of Hoover's reign and had been unimpressed by the
ability of the country's counterintelligence service. He'd ap-
plauded the advantage of incriminating information though
and followed Hoover's example when he had gained the ultimate promotion to Dzerzhinsky Square. Although he had
taken the precaution, Kalenin was unsure if he would ever
use it as a defense, because he found the idea of blackmail
distasteful, like he found assassination distasteful. The defection was a good enough excuse to abandon the idea but
Kalenin, a forever cautious man, thought there might also
be a good and protective reason to let it run.

Although the question had been put more to Berenkov
than to the head of the assassination division, it was Lvov
who responded. "A great deal of planning and effort has
gone into the operation," he said, an ambitious man defend-
ing something personally his.

"To how much did Novikov have access?" demanded
Kalenin.

"Certainly sufficient to know that an assassination was
being planned," said Berenkov. In contrast to Kalenin, the

head of the First Chief Directorate was a florid-faced man with a bulging stomach.

"But little more than that," argued Lvov, who was aware of the importance the Kremlin attached to the assassination and even more aware of the benefit of being recognized its creator.

"We've traced three cables which Novikov enciphered," said Berenkov. "One specifically talked of the value to be gained from a political killing."

"There was no identification of the target," insisted Lvov.

"There is in the Politburo Minute," said Berenkov. "And Novikov was security-cleared for Politburo traffic."

Kalenin, who was conscious of the differing attitudes between the two men confronting him, said, "Is there any proof of Novikov having seen the Politburo document?"

Berenkov shook his head, almost angrily. "Security in the Kremlin is a joke," he said. "There is no system, like we have here, of signature acknowledgment of handling. Maybe he did, maybe he didn't. The only way we'll ever know is to go ahead and find they're waiting for us. And then it will be too late."

"You think we should abort then?" demanded Kalenin. There was no other officer in the KGB whom Kalenin respected more than Alexei Berenkov. Like Kalenin, Berenkov had been a brilliant overseas operative—controlling five European cells under his cover as a London wine merchant—and endured English imprisonment until an exchange had been arranged, returning him to Moscow where he had proven himself to be an even more brilliant headquarters official and planner.

"I know how important the mission is regarded," said Berenkov. "I know, too, how much organization and time has gone into setting it up. But I think the risk of it being compromised outweighs every consideration."

Lvov, who had anticipated Berenkov's caution, said, "Vladimir Novikov was not the man who handled the identifying Politburo communication. . . ." He paused, offering a sheet of paper across the table to the KGB chairman.

"This is an affidavit from a man named Nikolai Perebillo," Lvov resumed, triumphantly. "He controls the entire cipher section, with absolute clearance. And he attests that only he transmitted Politburo communications naming the target."

Kalenin looked inquiringly at Berenkov.

Unimpressed, the huge man said, "Does it also attest that he's positive that Novikov, alerted by messages to which he'd already had access, didn't use his matching clearance to go through Politburo files to get more information?"

"He could have been shot for that!" tried Lvov.

"He was a traitor, leaking information to the British!" Berenkov came back. "He already risked being shot. And would have been, if he hadn't realized how close the investigation was!"

"I still consider it unthinkable that he would have tried such a thing," said Lvov. He was a small, narrow-faced man.

"It's what I would have done if I'd been about to defect and wanted to impress the people to whom I was going," admitted Berenkov.

"So it comes back to being a gamble," said Kalenin.

"Isn't it a governing principle in intelligence that gambles should be reduced to a minimum?" reminded Berenkov.

"Doesn't that depend on the stakes?" said Lvov, balancing question for question.

"And they're high," agreed Kalenin.

"They will be higher if it ends in a disaster we didn't intend," warned Berenkov.

"How long would it take to prepare for another opportunity?" Kalenin asked the head of the assassination department.

"There's no way of knowing when another such public opportunity will arise," pointed out Lvov. "Months, certainly. And there would be no guarantee that the woman would be involved again, if we aborted this time. Without her—or someone like her—it would be impossible."

"They're ready?"

"Both of them," assured Lvov. "He's an outstanding operative."

Kalenin shook his head at Berenkov and said, "I don't see we have any real alternative."

"There is," disputed Berenkov, stubbornly. "The very real alternative is to cancel and wait for another occasion, irrespective of how long it takes or how difficult it might be to manipulate."

"It's not a choice I think I have," said Kalenin.

"I don't believe Novikov saw any more than the three messages we've positively traced to him," said Lvov, recognizing the argument was tilting in his favor. "And by themselves they're meaningless. No one would be able to make any sense from them."

"I know of some who might," said Berenkov, whose British capture had been supervised by Charlie Muffin.

"We go," decided Kalenin. "I acknowledge the dangers and I don't like them and I'd personally enjoy interrogating the runaway bastard in Lubyanka until he screamed for the mercy I wouldn't give him, to learn exactly how much he's taken with him. But I think on this occasion we've got to take the gamble."

Lvov allowed himself a smile of victory in the direction of Berenkov, who remained expressionless. Berenkov said, "Let's hope, then, that it's a gamble that pays off."

The instruction center for KGB assassins is known as Balashikha. It is located fifteen miles east of Moscow's peripheral motorway, just off Gofkovskoye Shosse, and it was here in his isolated but luxury dacha that the waiting Vasili Nikolaevich Zenin received the telephone call from the head of the department, within minutes of Lvov leaving the meeting in Dzerzhinsky Square.

"Approval has been given," announced Lvov.

"When do I start?"

"At once."

Five thousand miles away, in the Libyan capital of Tripoli, Sulafeh Nabulsi left the headquarters offices of the Palestinian Liberation Organization precisely at noon, which she did every day, and headed directly toward the port area, which she also did every day, her regulated actions governed by an obedience to orders found only in absolute fanatics. At the post office close to the corner of Revolution Avenue, she made her daily check at the *poste restante* counter, feeling a jump of excitement when the letter for which she had been waiting so anxiously for so long was handed to her. Postmarked London, it consisted only of three lines, on paper headed with the name and address of a genuine English mail-order company. The catalogue about which she had inquired was being dispatched immediately, it promised. Sulafeh smiled, feeling her excitement grow. She'd known and lived among soldiers all her life but had never encountered anyone like this, someone trained specifically to kill. What did an assassin look like? she wondered.

"Names!" demanded Harkness.

"The Red Parrot, the Spinning Wheel, and the Eat Hearty," said Charlie uncomfortably. He was taking a chance, hoping they'd support the lie because he ate at all three quite a lot and they knew him.

"Why don't they print their names on their receipts!"

"I've no idea," said Charlie. "That's what they gave me when I asked for a copy."

"You know what I think these expenses are?"

"What?"

"Fraud. Criminal fraud."

"I genuinely spent the money," insisted Charlie. He supposed he should have guessed that Harkness wouldn't let the matter drop, despite the Director lifting his suspension. Vindictive bugger. What would Harkness do when the bank manager's letter arrived?

"You think you've got away with it again, don't you?"

"I don't understand what you mean."

"You understand it well enough," insisted the Deputy Director. "You haven't got away with anything. You've been assigned because the Director thinks you have some special ability for a case like this. Which I, incidentally, do not. But I am going to continue the inquiry into these expenses."

"But while I'm on assignment, I will be able to draw money, won't I?"

Harkness's face flared with anger. He said, "I want every penny properly accounted for, with receipts and bills that are verifiable."

"I always try," said Charlie. He'd have to warn the restaurants that the sneaky little sod was likely to come sniffing around.

3

Charlie Muffin had A-5 security clearance, which is the highest, and the Director's memorandum to all relevant departments within an hour of their meeting accorded the same classification to the Novikov investigation, designating it an operation of absolute priority. It also named Charlie as the agent in charge of that investigation, which allowed Charlie a moment of satisfaction as well as complete control. Hope to Christ there are a lot more such moments, he thought, and quick. He didn't mind looking for needles in haystacks, but he liked at least to know where the bloody haystack was.

The debriefing so far conducted with the Russian comprised a verbatim transcript of the automatic recordings, presented question and answer. But only Novikov was identified in the file, security precluding the naming of the interrogator even on a document with such restricted circulation. Charlie wondered in passing who the poor sod was: debriefings could take months—were *required* to take months, to drain the maximum possible from a defector—so there wasn't a chance in hell of making any money on expenses because Harkness and his abacus squad knew where you were and what you were doing every minute of the day and night.

From the raw debriefing material Charlie compiled his own notes, concentrating only on his specific inquiry, aware that others would dissect every additional scrap of information the Russian disclosed. Vladimir Andreevich Novikov claimed to have been born in Riga, to a father killed in the siege of Stalingrad during the Patriotic War and a mother who fell victim to the influenza epidemic that swept Latvia in 1964. He had graduated in 1970 from Riga University with a combined first class honors degree in electronics and mathematics, which Charlie accepted made almost automatic the approach from the KGB for the position he was later to occupy. According to Novikov the invitation actually came before the end of his course, his ability already identified by the KGB spotters installed within the university to isolate potential recruits. He had worked for three years in the cipher department at the provincial KGB headquarters, apparently improving upon two internal communication codes, and because of such ability was appointed deputy head over five people who were his superiors. His transfer to KGB headquarters in Moscow came in 1980. By which time, according to the question-and-answer sheets, Novikov was already coming to accept that Latvia was not the autonomous republic of the U.S.S.R. it was always proclaimed and supposed to be, but a despised Russian colony, although he was sure he always successfully concealed any hint of resentment during the frequent security interviews. In Moscow he married a Latvian girl, from Klaipeda, who was more forcefully nationalistic than he was. She had contact with dissident Latvian groups both in Riga and Moscow, and he had become frightened any investigation by the KGB's Second Chief Directorate—responsible for the country's internal control—would inevitably discover her links, which would have meant his automatic dismissal and possibly her imprisonment. She had been killed before either could happen. It was a hit-and-run accident, near the Moskva Bridge, and although Novikov had been a member of the KGB, with supposed influence, the driver had never been arrested, and Novikov was convinced the civilian militia hadn't bothered with a proper investigation because she had been a Latvian, someone who didn't matter.

"Latvians are second-class citizens, dispensable," was Novikov's way of expressing it, which struck a chord with Charlie who never forgot how he'd once been considered dispensable. Or forgot, either, the fallout that had contaminated so much and so many by his fighting back, creating his own personal Hiroshima.

According to the transcript, the woman's death marked

the moment of Novikov's turning traitor to Russia, doing his utmost to cause as much damage as possible to a society he finally regarded as a colonial oppressor, worse than any of the Western colonial oppressors daily criticized within the Soviet Union.

"The mind of Albert Einstein coupled with the social conscience of Mother Teresa," judged Charlie aloud in the emptiness of his refuse-viewed office. Often—and un-ashamedly—Charlie talked to himself. Sometimes he gave himself the right answers: the right answers were always the most difficult.

Charlie was disappointed in that part of the transcript devoted to the supposed assassination, although he supposed he should not have been, forewarned by the meeting with Sir Alistair Wilson just how little was available. Worse than just little, qualified Charlie. What he had here was posi-tively infinitesimal. The two cables to the Russian embassy in London were the only positive, workable facts. Still something, at least, upon which it was possible to work. Charlie continued on through the paperwork, looking ex-pectantly for the recommendation and then, with equal ex-pectation, for the confirming order, frowning in surprise when he didn't find it.

"Cunts!" he erupted angrily, speaking aloud again. Be-ing personally named as the investigatory chief and having the priority designation so clearly set out was going to prove an advantage earlier than he'd imagined. There were going to be more ruffled feathers than in a hen coop at mating time, but fuck it. It was fucking that ruffled feathers at mating time anyway.

In addition to the operation's priority coding, Charlie used the authority of Sir Alistair Wilson's name in his insis-tent messages to MI-5, Britain's counterintelligence service. In further addition he stipulated that the absolute, twenty-four-hour checks extend beyond the Kensington Palace Gar-dens embassy and the known diplomatic addresses in Edith Road and Kensington's Earl's Terrace to include the offices of every accredited Russian journalist and television com-mentator in London, the Soviet Trade Mission at West Hill, in the Highgate suburb, the Intourist and Aeroflot offices in Regent Street and Piccadilly, the Wheat Council in Charing Cross, into which the KGB had in the past infiltrated agents, and the Russian Narodny Bank on King William Street. And still remained dissatisfied. According to the Director, Novikov had been across for two months. And the assassination would have undergone planning months prior to that. So why the hell hadn't the debriefer or those analyzing what was being produced taken the most obvious and most elementary precautions!

"Cunts!" said Charlie again, more angrily than before.

With his carte blanche authorization, Charlie drew the best car available from the motor pool, a small-bodied Mercedes with a specially adapted turbo-charged engine and absolutely secured radio patch communication, waiting until he cleared the London suburbs and was actually on the highway before using it to call ahead and confirm his visit to the safe house already warned from Westminster Bridge Road of his impending visit. He took the car effortlessly up to 100 mph, knowing from the special engine it was capable of at least another 50 mph. Would he be able to get a nice secondhand little runner for the sort of overdraft he'd asked for, Charlie wondered in rare naïveté. He'd never actually bought a vehicle of his own. Edith had always had the money and purchased the cars. After the killing of his wife, in the vengeance hunt for him after he screwed British and American intelligence, Charlie, blaming himself, had refused to touch the inherited estate, placing it in an unbreakable trust for the benefit of a children's charity which had been one of Edith's favorites. Be nice to have a little car like this: run out to a country pub on Saturday lunchtimes and polish it like everyone else did in England on a Sunday morning. Might be a bit dodgy those nights when all the street lights seemed to join together though. Or parking it in the roads around his flat, where even the police cars got their radios stolen and offered back for sale. Enjoy it while you can then, he told himself. Charlie fully opened the sunroof, reclined the seat back one more notch, and stared through the tinted glass to enjoy the Sussex countryside. Sir

Archibald Willoughby, his first Director, had lived in Sussex. Not here though: on the coast, near Rye. They'd been the great days, under Willoughby. Allowed to roam, under Sir Archibald: make up his own rules. No pissing about over expenses with demands for certifiable receipts. Not that that was the fault of the present Director. Wilson was a good bloke, like Willoughby had been. Just surrounded with pricks, that's all. Which had been the problem with Willoughby, as well. Odd that there were so many comparisons: both were fanatical about rose growing. Harkness's hobby was probably reciting tables, one twelve is twelve, two twelves are twenty-four . . . Charlie didn't have the slightest doubt that the penny-pinching fart wouldn't let him off the hook without a convincing explanation about those damned receipts. If he couldn't think of one, he supposed he'd have to accept the amounts being cut off, which would be losing out. Charlie didn't like losing, certainly not fiddle expenses money. Not the biggest problem at the moment. The biggest problem at the moment was trying to find answers when he didn't even know what the questions were. Or have a clue where to find them.

His speed was reduced when he had to quit the highway for the minor road going to Pulborough but he was still ahead of the appointed time so he stopped at a pub that promised home-cooked food, deciding that if it served anything like he cooked at home, he wouldn't bother. It wasn't. Instead of his customary Islay malt, he chose beer, which was drawn from the wood, and ordered crisply baked bread and fresh pickles and tangy cheese and carried it all out to a table and bench which a craftsman had clearly spent hours fashioning to appear something that had been knocked up in minutes by a child with a Christmas gift carpentry set. All around, geraniums blazed from tubs and window boxes, and there was a dovecote for real birds that commuted between it and the thatched roof of the pub. Charlie identified it as just the sort of place to which people drove for those Saturday lunchtime sessions, wearing cravats tucked into checked shirts and cavalry twill trousers and suede shoes, and complained that the English cricket selectors didn't have a damned clue, did they? Charlie stretched his feet out before him. At least he had the suede shoes. And they looked bloody marvelous after the going-over he'd given them for the meeting with the bank manager. Last another year at least; maybe longer, if he were careful. It was always important to be careful about his Hush Puppies. Took a long time to break them in properly. They had to be molded, like a sculptor molded his clay. What was the saying about feet of clay? Charlie couldn't remember precisely, but it didn't apply to him anyway. His feet usually felt as if they were walking on that other stuff sculptors worked with, hard and sharp.

He used the car radio system to advise the gatehouse of his imminent arrival, so they were waiting for him when he pulled into the driveway of the house, about five miles outside of the town. The first man wore an unidentifiable but official-looking uniform and was posted at what appeared to be the proper gate, a huge and secured affair with a crest on top. His function—apart from simply opening the gate—was to deter casually inquiring or wrongly directed strangers. The real checks came at the guard post out of sight of the road, where the electronic surveillance began and where the guard staff was armed. Charlie presented his documentation and stood obediently for his photograph to be taken and checked by one of those electronic systems, not just against the picture on his pass but against the file records to which it was linked in London.

One of the guards, who knew Charlie from other debriefings at other safe houses, nodded to his bank manager's outfit of the previous day and said, "Dressed up for this one then?"

"I like to make an effort," said Charlie.

He continued slowly up the winding drive, locating some of the electronic checks and cameras and sensors but knowing there were others he missed. The drive was lined on either side by thick rhododendron and Charlie regretted they were not in bloom; it would have been quite a sight.

The driveway opened on to a huge graveled forecourt with a grassed centerpiece, in the middle of which was a fountain with nymphs spitting water at each other. The house was a square, Georgian structure, the front almost completely covered with creeper and ivy. Charlie parked to one side, and as he walked toward the carved oak door, he wondered what the reaction of the British taxpayer would be to knowing how much they shelled out each year, maintaining places like this. Charlie had carried out defector interviews in at least six safe houses, all in different parts of the country but all equally grand and expensive. The need for the Establishment always to be well established, he decided, particularly if some other unsuspecting bloke is picking up the bill. Shit, thought Charlie, reminded too late: he'd forgotten to get a receipt for the pub lunch.

The door opened before he reached it, but Hubert Witherspoon did not come forward to meet him.

"There you are!" greeted Charlie. "I was worried about you. Thought you'd done a fall wearing your best trainers."

"What are you talking about?" demanded Witherspoon. He was a tall, languid man who had trouble with a flick of hair that strayed permanently over his left eye. He wore an immaculate grey suit, hard-collared shirt, and a school tie. Stowe, Charlie recognized.

"Nothing," dismissed Charlie. "So you've been debriefing?"

"Took over a month ago. And very successfully," insisted the man. "I asked who was coming down today, but London didn't reply."

"Perhaps they wanted it to be a surprise."

"Are you to take over now?"

"Nope," said Charlie. "Just the assassination."

"London has got all there is on that," said Witherspoon in further insistence. "There's nothing more."

"That come out at one of your sessions?"

"I said it was a successful debrief, didn't I?"

"What did you do about it?"

"Told London immediately, of course."

"That all?"

"What else would you expect me to do?"

Not behave like a prat, thought Charlie. It wasn't worth

an argument; be unfair in fact. Instead of replying, Charlie said, "Tell me about Novikov."

"Everyone points to his being genuine," said Witherspoon. "Handled a lot of important stuff, right up to Kremlin level. And he's got a damned good recall, so he's going to be a very productive gold mine for a long time. Hates Russia, for the reason set out in the report, so he's anxious to cooperate. There's already been a request for access, from the CIA."

"I bet there has," said Charlie.

"How long do you think you'll be?" asked Witherspoon.

"How the hell do I know?" said Charlie. "As long as it takes."

"Thought I might cut away for a round of golf," said Witherspoon. "There's a jolly good course the other side of Pulborough."

"You don't want to sit in?" asked Charlie, surprised the man entrusted with the overall debrief didn't want a comparison of Novikov's earlier replies against later replies to another questioner. Charlie would have jumped at the opportunity, in reversed circumstances.

"I told you I've already covered the assassination," said Witherspoon.

"So you did."

"Unless you'd like my assistance, of course."

"I'll manage," assured Charlie. Some people were beyond help, he thought.

Vladimir Novikov was waiting in what Charlie supposed was called the drawing room. It was very large and at the side of the house, with huge windows and French doors leading out onto a paved veranda, beyond which was a view of lawns and long-ago planted trees whose branches now drooped to the ground as if they were tired from holding them out for such a long time. An intricately-patterned carpet protected most of the wood-tiled floor; the furnishings—two long couches with six easy chairs—were all chintz covered. There were flowers on two tables and an expansive arrangement in a fireplace, the mantelpiece of which was higher than Charlie's head. The Russian seemed to fit easily into such surroundings. He was tall, easily more than six feet, and heavy as well, bull-chested and thick around the waist. His size was accentuated by the thick black beard he wore in the style of the Russia he was supposed to despise, flowing to cover his neck and tufted where it had never been trimmed. The suit was clean but appeared worn, shiny at the elbows, the lapels curling inward from constant wear. His own suit had bent like that until he'd had it cleaned for the bank meeting, recalled Charlie. He guessed it would collapse again in a few days. It usually did.

The Russian stood, as Charlie moved further into the room, but from the stance Charlie decided it was more a gesture of politeness than nervousness.

"Mr. Witherspoon said I would be seeing someone else today," said Novikov.

The man's voice matched his frame, deep and resonant, but that was not Charlie's immediate thought. Witherspoon was a bloody fool, disclosing his real identity. Charlie said, "Just one or two points. Finer detail, really."

"I will do everything I can to help," said the Russian.

"So I have been told," said Charlie, gesturing the man back to the couch he'd been occupying. For himself, he chose one of the easy chairs, slightly to one side.

"What is it that particularly interests you?" asked Novikov.

Dance around a bit first, thought Charlie. He said, "You were making plans to defect, in Moscow?"

"Yes?"

"How?"

"I was leaving that to my control at the British embassy: the military attaché, George Gale. Waiting for him to tell me what to do."

Charlie wondered if that were the man's real name, as well. Silly buggers might as well hand out visiting cards, with spying listed as their occupation. He said, "Why?"

"I believed I was under suspicion."

"Why?" repeated Charlie. He decided his initial impression was correct. There was no nervousness about the man, which there usually was with defectors, caused by natural uncertainty. Novikov appeared actually confident and relaxed.

"You know I was security-cleared to the highest level?" said the man.

"Yes."

"In the last few weeks I was only allocated low level material, the sort of stuff that ordinary clerks could handle. I was not an ordinary clerk."

And I bet you never let anyone forget it, thought Charlie. He said, "But it was only suspicion? You had no actual proof?"

"If there had been any actual proof I would have been arrested, wouldn't I?"

"I suppose so," agreed Charlie, content for the man to patronize and imagine he was in the commanding role. The sessions with Witherspoon would have been something to witness. He said, "So what happened?"

"One day I was unwell, went home early. I found someone in my apartment. He went out a rear window as I opened the door. It was dismissed by the KGB militia as an attempted burglary, but I knew it was not."

"How did you know?"

"Precisely because attempted burglaries at the homes of senior KGB cipher clerks are *never* dismissed," said Novikov.

It was a convincing point, accepted Charlie. He said, "What do you think it was?"

"A search, perhaps. Or technicians installing listening devices. Most likely both."

"So what did you do?"

"I had an emergency contact system arranged with Major Gale," recounted the man. "I telephoned him at the embassy from an untraceable call box and said I could not keep our appointment—that was the code phrase, 'I cannot keep our appointment'—and that told him to go to another untraceable call box so that we could speak between the two without the risk of our conversation being intercepted. I said I had to cross at once and he agreed."

"The Finnish crossing could not have been arranged just like that," challenged Charlie at once.

"Mr. Witherspoon did not question the point."

It was automatic for this encounter, like every other, to be recorded: there was actually a simultaneous replay facility to London. If that remark got the careless little prick censured, then too bad, decided Charlie. The rules and regulations by which Witherspoon existed were no more than guidelines, like the guidelines in the weapons manuals that set out in perfect detail how to fire a bullet but failed to follow through by explaining that a well-placed bullet of sufficient caliber could separate top from bottom. And troublesome though his feet permanently were, Charlie wanted his top to remain in every way attached to his bottom. So all it took was that one careless little prick not recognizing where the trigger was. He said, "My name isn't Witherspoon."

"You didn't tell me your name," reminded Novikov.

"No, I didn't, did I?" agreed Charlie. And stopped.

There was a long moment of silence. Then Novikov said, "Is this a hostile interview?"

"No."

"What then?"

"A proper interview."

"Haven't the others been properly conducted?"

The Russian was very quick, acknowledged Charlie admiringly. It was wrong to let Novikov put questions to which he had to respond. Charlie said, "What do you think?"

"I think you doubt me. I think I made a mistake in crossing to the British. I shall go to the Americans instead," announced the Russian.

"That wasn't the answer to my question."

"I do not wish to answer any more of your questions."

"Why not, Vladimir Andreevich? What are you frightened of?"

"Mr. Witherspoon does not properly know how to use the Russian patronymic. Nor did the interrogator before him."

"Why not, Vladimir Andreevich?" persisted Charlie, objecting to what he thought was an attempted deflection but curious about it just the same.

"Neither spoke Russian properly, like you do," said the man. "Their inflection was copybook, language school stuff. From the way you instinctively form a genitive from masculine or neuter, I know you lived in Moscow. And as a Muscovite."

Charlie thought he understood at last. Not *as* a Muscovite, he thought, *with* a Muscovite. Darling, beautiful Natalia against whom he'd consciously and for so long closed the door in his mind, because it was a room he could never enter again. It had been the Russian mission, his own supposed defection, which he hadn't known was a prove-yourself-again operation until it was too late, when he'd met and fallen in love with someone he'd hoped, so desperately hoped, would replace Edith. But who had refused to come back, because of the child of another man. He said, "I am not Russian."

"What then?"

The questioning had reversed again, Charlie recognized. He said, "English."

"How is that possible?"

"There was a time when I knew Russia well," conceded Charlie. Was it right for him earlier to have thought so critically about Witherspoon and some military attaché in Moscow, disclosing details that should not have been disclosed when he was volunteering too much information himself?

"I will not be tricked."

"How can you be tricked?"

"I never want contact with a single Russian, ever again!"

"Don't be ridiculous! You know full well I am not Russian!" said Charlie. Was Novikov's anti-Sovietism overexaggerated? It would not be difficult to imagine so. But then the first principle of defector assessment was imagining nothing and only proceeding on established facts.

"Why do you doubt me, then?"

"Why shouldn't I?"

"All the information I have given is the truth."

"I hope it is."

"Everything I have told you about Major Gale can be checked."

"It will be," assured Charlie. And would have been already if other people had done their jobs properly.

"What do you want of me?"

"An answer to a point I made a long time ago," reminded Charlie. "How, when you were having to make a panicked move and when travel within the Soviet Union is so closely restricted by the need—and checks—upon internal passports, could you go at once to the Finnish border?"

Novikov smiled, in reluctant admiration. "You really have lived in the Soviet Union, haven't you?"

"We've had that routine," said Charlie, refusing another deflection.

"I had been granted travel permission to visit Leningrad before the suspicion arose," said Novikov.

"Why?"

"A vacation."

"You were planning a vacation at a time when you believed your people suspected you!"

"I did not plan it after I believed they suspected me," said Novikov. "I applied and was granted permission before I became alarmed. It was the ideal opportunity."

"Yes it was, wasn't it?" agreed Charlie. He'd achieved a great deal already, he decided, contentedly.

"You think I am a liar!" erupted Novikov, goaded by Charlie's sarcasm.

"I don't know yet whether you are a liar or not," said Charlie. "You're the defector. You have to convince me."

"I am telling the truth!"

Impatient with any continued defense, Charlie said, "Tell me how you got to the Finnish border."

"I was lucky," admitted Novikov. "The visa to visit Leningrad was already in my internal passport. I did not remind anyone in the cipher department that Friday that I was going on holiday. Nor did I go back to my apartment when I left. I went directly from headquarters to Vnukovo airport without bothering with luggage. It was late when I arrived in Leningrad. I intended to go to my hotel, the Druzhba on the Ulitza Chapygina, and not move on until the morning, but when I approached it, I saw militia cars everywhere. There was no one else they could have been looking for. I just ran. The arrangement I had made with Major Gale was to cross into Finland near a place called Lappeeranta. It's just a few miles inside their border. I caught the train to Vyborg and then walked the rest of the way, to the border. My passport was checked on the train. The visa only extended to Leningrad so I knew the alarm would be raised. They almost caught me at the border. I only just got across."

The Director had talked of a pursuit, at the moment of crossing. Charlie said, "Wouldn't you have attracted attention, trying to book into the Druzhba without any luggage?"

"You're very careful, aren't you?"

"Yes," said Charlie. "What about the luggage?"

"I had my briefcase with me, of course. It was quite large; it would have appeared sufficient."

Restricted by the clothing shortages in the Soviet Union, people frequently traveled as lightly as that, remaining for days in the same suit, remembered Charlie. Just like he did, in fact. Time to check Witherspoon's insistence upon the man's ability for recall. Charlie said, "Your memory is good?"

"It is excellent."

"I'm glad," said Charlie. "When did you start being denied access to the sort of material to which you were accustomed?"

"August."

"The precise date?"

"I think it was August 19."

"Definitely August 19? Or approximately August 19?"

Novikov hesitated. "Do you consider it that important?"

"You did," reminded Charlie. "It was the first signal you had that they were on to you."

"Definitely August 19."

"How can you be so definite?" pressed Charlie.

"I protested to the controller. Said there must have been a circulation error in giving me such inferior communication."

"Wasn't that putting yourself at risk?"

"When I made the protest, I thought it was a mistake. It was not until I was told it was intended for me that I realized the suspicion."

"So from August 19 on, everything was low level?"

"The lowest."

"Tell me now about the assassination cables."

"There were three."

"What was the first: the exact words?"

"'The need is understood that a political, public example has to be set for the maximum impact,'" quoted Novikov.

"Just that?"

"Just that."

"Dispatched or received?"

"Dispatched."

"To whom?"

"The Politburo: that's how I came to encode. I was cleared that high."

"And that was the first?"

"Yes."

"The word assassination is not there. So how did you know it involved killing?"

"The message came from Department Eight of Directorate S."

"Which is also responsible for sabotage and abduction."

"You're very knowledgeable."

"It's not my knowledge we're questioning."

"There was a marker designation on the cable."

"What's a marker designation?"

"It's like a subject reference."

"What was it?"

"*Mokrie*," said the Russian.

"*Mokrie dela*," completed Charlie. "Do they still refer to assassinations as 'wet affairs'?"

"It's a bureaucratic institution, with long-time rules," said the Russian.

"Aren't they all?" said Charlie. "Were there any other types of reference?"

"The word 'purple,'" said Novikov.

"What does that identify?" asked Charlie, who knew.

"The Politburo," replied the Russian.

"I would have expected something else," said Charlie. Novikov smiled. "'Run Around,'" he said.

"Numbered?"

Now a nod of admiration accompanied the smile. "Four," the Russian agreed.

"Who handled the first three?"

"I don't know," apologized Novikov. "There were five others in the department with clearance that matched mine."

"And you could not have asked them," said Charlie, a comment more than a question.

"Any discussion of messages sent or received is absolutely forbidden," confirmed Novikov. "Suspension and investigation is automatic."

Charlie nodded and said, "Tell me about the second."

"It said, 'You will dispatch the catalogue,'" quoted Novikov, again.

"The same references?"

"One addition," said the man. "The number seventeen."

"What did that signify?"

"The destination of the cable: the *rezidentura* in London."

"What about the other number?"

"Five."

"So you were handling the messages in sequence now," said Charlie, excited at the disclosure but not showing it.

"And I transmitted the cable numbered six, the last one," confirmed Novikov, once more.

Excellent, thought Charlie. "To where?"

"London again."

"What did it say?"

"'You will wrap the November catalogue.'"

Charlie decided there had been sufficient intensity and that Novikov needed a respite, if he weren't going to become exhausted. He smiled and said, "Wonder if we can get a drink around here?"

"I enjoy very much your Scotch whisky," said Novikov.

"So do I," said Charlie.

The man who answered the bell summons was stiffly upright, giving away the previous army service from which all the support staff at safe houses were recruited. He was someone Charlie had not encountered before but immediately agreed there was Islay malt, and when he returned with the tray, Charlie said they didn't want to bother him again, so why didn't he leave the bottle.

"Here's to the British taxpayer," toasted Charlie.

"I do not understand," said the Russian.

"Neither would they, if they knew," said Charlie.

"We are making progress?" asked Novikov. There seemed some concern in the question.

"I think so," said Charlie.

"You know why I want to hurt Russia?"

"Yes," said Charlie.

"I loved her so much," said Novikov, distantly. "So very much." He drank heavily from his glass and said, "You can't imagine what it's like to lose someone you love as completely as I loved Lydia."

I can, thought Charlie. I lost twice, not once. He wanted Novikov relaxed, but not maudlin. He added to both their glasses and said, "There are some more things I want you to help me with."

Novikov's effort to concentrate again was very obvious. He said, "What?"

"More dates," said Charlie. "You were cut off on August 19?"

"Yes."

"What was the date of that last cable, the one numbered six?"

Novikov frowned for a moment, determined upon recall, and then said, "August 12."

"And the one before that, the first to mention London?"

"August 5," said the Russian, quicker this time.

"And the first one you encoded was dated July 29?" anticipated Charlie.

Novikov frowned, head to one side. "Yes," he agreed. "How did you know?"

"I guessed," lied Charlie. "Something more about that second cable, the one mentioning catalogue? Had you ever before encoded messages from Department Eight of Directorate S?"

"Twice, both times before Lydia was killed."

"With *mokrie* as a reference?"

"Yes."

"Was the word 'catalogue' used?"

"Yes," confirmed Novikov.

Thank God and the fairies for bureaucratic rigidity, thought Charlie. He said, "Do you know what it signifies?"

"I don't *know*," said the Russian, in careful qualification.

"What do you guess it to signify?"

"The operative," said Novikov.

Charlie nodded. "That's what I think, too," he said. "One last thing: you worked from Dzerzhinsky Square?"

"Yes," agreed Novikov.

"But the cipher division is not general, is it?"

"I've never suggested it was."

"I think other people made wrong assumptions," said Charlie. "It's compartmentalized?"

"Of course. Everything is. That is the system."

Charlie nodded again, in agreement. "So, for which department of the First Chief Directorate did you work?"

"The Third," said Novikov.

Charlie sat back, satisfied, refilling both their glasses. "Of course," he said. "It had to be that, didn't it?"

"Is it significant?"

"Who knows?" said Charlie.

"Do you play chess?"

"No," said Charlie.

"I'm surprised," said the Russian. "I would have thought

with a mind like yours that you would play. I was going to suggest a game, if we meet again."

"Maybe darts," said Charlie.

"Darts?"

"It's an English game. Played in pubs."

"Maybe I could learn."

"Be quicker than me trying to learn chess," said Charlie.

"I don't think that is necessarily so," said Novikov.

Charlie encountered Hubert Witherspoon in the entrance hall, a cavernous place of wood-paneled walls around a black-and-white marbled floor. The man's face was flushed with his recent exertion, and for once his hair was stuck down, still wet from the shower.

"I got a hole-in-one and two birdies," announced Witherspoon, triumphantly.

"Terrific," said Charlie.

"That hole-in-one cost me a fortune in the bar afterward. It's tradition to treat everyone, you know."

"No," said Charlie. "I didn't know."

Witherspoon nodded in the direction of the drawing room and said, "Nothing I hadn't got, was there?"

Jesus! thought Charlie. He said, "Hardly a thing."

"Wasted journey then?"

Caught by Witherspoon's complaint at having to buy drinks in the clubhouse and remembering the forgotten lunchtime receipt, Charlie said, "You wouldn't by chance have a spare restaurant bill from anywhere around here, would you?"

Witherspoon's face colored. He said, "You don't imagine I am going to get caught up in your petty little deceits, do you?"

"No," said Charlie wearily. "Of course not."

When he got to the Mercedes, Charlie found the communication light burning permanently red, indicating a priority summons. He was patched directly through to the Director's office and recognized Alison Bing's strained-through-a-sieve voice at once.

"The bomb's gone off right beneath you," said the Direc-

areas separated according to their instructional needs, sometimes by barbed and electrified wire and occasionally with high concrete walls, the tops of which are again electrically guarded. The concrete sections are those of maximum secrecy and it was in one, located at the very center of the camp, that the contest was staged. Here there had been recreated in a vast, aircrafttype hangar a typical European city street—because Zenin was selected to operate in Europe—with shops and a cafe and apartment houses. Every part of it was monitored and surveyed by television cameras, so that the movements and behavior of both men was relayed to a control room where the panel of assessors sat.

Zenin was slightly built and small-featured with the dark coloring of a man born in Azerbaijan, which was a further reason for his being selected for the specific mission already then being planned for him. He moved with the quiet but assured confidence of someone sure—but without conceit—of his own abilities, which had been one of the first qualities isolated by the assassin division recruiters when the man had been accepted into the Kirovabad office of the KGB. He spoke four languages—English and French with a fluency that betrayed no accent—and had no moral difficulty with killing, satisfied assassination was justified because his victims were legally judged enemies of the state before he was entrusted with the responsibility of carrying out the sentence imposed upon them. The Ukrainian fitted into the same category, a criminal proven guilty of a crime.

The Ukrainian was allowed no weapon. And Zenin's instructions were that the killing had to appear to have been an accident or suicide. He was told he could have a weapon of choice or any one of the six Soviet-perfected poison-spray guns, the gas of which dissipates within thirty seconds, leaving no trace to be found in any later postmortem examination. Zenin refused anything.

The test, he was told, was timed for one hour. If the encounter had not taken place by then, he would begin losing assessment points. If twenty points were deducted, he would be dismissed from the course.

Zenin entered the hangar door low and fast, moving im-

mediately sideways, unsure what to expect, but knowing he
was an obvious target framed in the doorway. Once inside,
however, he did nothing fast, observing the basic teaching
to merge into any background, to become a wallpaper man.
The mock-up was artificially illuminated to represent natural sunlight, providing shadows, and Zenin used every one
that was available, never once disclosing himself. A constant
theme through each training session at Balashikha was self-
reliance and awareness beyond the instruction at that session, to think ahead beyond the obvious. Zenin at once
recognized the unreality of a confrontation in such a ghost-
town setting, guessing the possibility of an ambush. So he
observed another lecture, switching from hunter to hunted.
He slipped into the supposed cafe, intentionally because it
was so obvious, soft-footedly exploring the outer area and
the kitchen. Having satisfied himself they were unoccupied,
he checked the upstairs rooms. And then, back on the
ground floor again, he waited, sinking onto his haunches in
the most shadowed part of the room, his back protected by
the jut of the wall, and with a perfect view of the outside
street through the window. He had already noted a major
disparity in the cafe, guessing again that it had to have some
significance. It was complete in every respect but cutlery.
There were no knives or forks in the customer area, and
there had been no knives in the kitchen to be utilized as
weapons. It was always possible, of course, that his opponent or opponents would have been offered weapons like he
had been, but if they had been, then there would have been
no purpose in precluding them from the fake restaurant. He
decided it was a safe assumption to believe them to be unarmed. There were a lot of bottles and glasses, which could
have been broken to provide a cutting edge, but Zenin considered anything makeshift more easy to defend himself
against. Of course they were personally denied him, because
it was essential for his killing not to appear a killing at all.

The Ukrainian, whose name was Barabanov, had entered the warehouse at precisely the same time as Zenin but
through a door diametrically opposite. And like Zenin he
had gone immediately to ground, although not with so

much caution, only bothering to check the immediate room in which he concealed himself in the apartment block, careless of others around it, which Zenin would not have been.

Barabanov was a giant of a man, physically hardened by ten years of existence in the most punitive of the penal colonies in the Soviet Union and mentally reduced to animalistic violence by the need during those ten years to survive, someone who instinctively fought with boot and teeth and knee and gouging fingers, overwhelming anyone in his path. And he was determined to survive by killing whoever it was being pitted against him.

Like Zenin, he had been given the time limit of an hour for some contact to be made, although he had been told his failure would result in his return to his life sentence in Potma. Almost half an hour elapsed before uncertainty began to twitch through him. After forty minutes he decided he had to move. There were tables and chairs in the room in which he crouched. Barabanov chose one of the heavier chairs, easily splitting off a molded rear leg, hefting it in his hand, leaving a cross-spoke in place because it gave him added grip.

He took one final, hopeful look through the window onto the deserted and fake street and then carefully opened the door, not the rear one through which he had entered but one at the front, which was his first mistake.

Zenin saw him the instant he emerged. There was no fear at the man's overpowering size nor at knowing, from his awareness of Barabanov's criminal record for murder, how the man could use such obvious strength. Zenin had been graded to senior instructor level in two different styles of martial arts but decided it would still be a mistake to confront the man openly, because it was essential that he survive without any obvious mark or injury. Zenin checked the time, seeing he had twelve minutes in which to kill the man if he were not to have any points deducted. As he turned back into the cafe, Zenin shook his head in disgust at Barabanov's clumsy amateurism.

The stairway he had used earlier was to the left, curving halfway up to the next floor. From his earlier reconnaissance, Zenin knew the bathroom was the first door at the top.

He went quickly into the kitchen area and filled two of the largest copper pans with water, pleased at the obvious sound from the gas pipes when he ignited the burners under each, returning briefly to the customer area to ensure the noise was audible. Back in the kitchen he gauged the distance between the door and the stove, guessing that he would only have seconds but confident that was all he would need.

Just seven minutes left, he saw.

Back at the window, Zenin watched for Barabanov's exit from an apartment house opposite, purposely opening and quickly slamming the door leading out. Through the window he could see the man's awareness, which was the intention. As Barabanov started across the street, Zenin hurried back into the kitchen, leaving the door ajar for the gas sound to be more obvious.

He was standing by the stove, waiting expectantly, when Barabanov pushed open the door, at first cautiously but at the last moment violently, hoping to instill the fear to which he was accustomed. For a moment the two men stared at each other. And then, with the snarl of the animal he was, Barabanov hurled himself across the room, flailing with the chair leg club.

Barabanov was just feet away when Zenin hurled the boiling water directly into his face. The snarl became a scream of blinded agony. He was carried on by the force of his own impetuous lunge, so that he collided with the stove, but Zenin had moved by then. The other cauldron of boiling water, which Zenin had prepared as a safeguard against missing the man the first time, upended off the gas ring and went down the front of the man, who screamed out in fresh agony, swiping wildly with the club he still carried. Zenin carefully judged his moment, ducking beneath one swipe and bringing the heel of his hand sharply up against the point of Barabanov's chin before he could make another, hearing the distinct crack as the man's neck broke, ducking away so that he would not be hit by the man's fall. Zenin checked the time, smiling in satisfaction. There were still four minutes before the expiration of the time limit so his record was unblemished. Barabanov was very heavy, and Zenin grunted with the effort of hauling him back into the outer room. The man's head lolled, disconnected, and his face had already swollen into one huge blister. Zenin positioned the convict at the bottom of the stairs with his body coming down, as it would have done if he had stumbled and fallen from the top, and then pressed Barabanov's hand around the handle of the first water pan, the one he'd actually thrown at the man. He stepped over the body and climbed to the bathroom, covering his hand with a towel before scattering the contents of a medicine chest into the sink and on the floor, as if some frantic search for some soothing or protective cream had been made and then carried the towel downstairs again, wedging it into Barabanov's other hand.

The assessors had been unanimous in marking Zenin's performance as excellent, the highest award possible. It was the standard he intended to maintain on this, his first job.

He immediately locked the door of the Bayswater hotel, checking through every item in the suitcase that had been provided for him by KGB agents at the London embassy with which he was forbidden any direct approach, knowing any incriminating mistake in the clothing was unlikely but determined against even the slightest risk. London public transportation maps were enclosed, and using them, he traveled to Soho by underground, locating without difficulty the news agent's shop that unknowingly was going to indicate his undetected arrival and alert the London *rezidentura* to initiate the next stage of the operation. He paid four pounds to have the For Sale card advertising a six-foot dinghy displayed in a glass case crammed with other cards, telling the assistant he would call in daily for replies. From Soho he traveled by bus to the zoo in Regents Park, from which he walked to Primrose Hill, at once pleased that he had taken the reconnaissance precaution because there was a sign that bicycling in the park was illegal, about which he should have been warned. He made a mental note

to complain about the London *rezidentura* when he got
back to Moscow. It was the sort of oversight which could
have ruined everything. He lunched in a surprisingly good
bistro and afterward walked to Camden Town where he
caught an underground train back into central London. In
a Trafalgar Square cinema he saw a film about a supposed
secret agent named James Bond, which he found professionally absurd, before returning to Soho to insure that the contact message was displayed as it should have been. It was.
He was not really hungry, but he ate anyway to occupy
time. It was still early when he returned to the hotel. There
were four other guests in the television lounge but Zenin did
not join them because it was necessary to avoid any casual
contact. In his room he went directly to bed and fell at once
into a dreamless sleep.

The following day he returned to Soho, inquiring about
replies to his advertisement. The girl said one man had inquired if the boat were white, which was the arranged acknowledgment that an agent from the embassy had seen his
signal. Zenin said it was green but he wanted to withdraw
the card anyway, because he'd managed to dispose of the
boat elsewhere. She reminded him that the previous day
she'd made it clear the four pounds was not refundable, and
Zenin assured her he was not seeking one. She said they'd always be willing to put a display card in their case if he had
anything else to sell, and Zenin said he would remember.

Zenin walked unhurriedly back through Soho, isolating
four whores already plying for lunchtime trade. Would
there be any sexual involvement with Sulafeh Nabulsi, he
wondered. It was the briefest of thoughts, because he had
many other things to arrange. There was the sports gear and
the cassette-playing equipment to buy. And the bicycle
rental to be arranged. But most important, the preparation
for the false trail, in Switzerland. From a call box he telephoned Swissair advanced reservations, explaining he
wanted to accompany a friend flying from Geneva to New
York on the sixteenth but wasn't sure of the flight. When the
clerk asked for the name, he said Schmidt, but indistinctly,
in case he was out of luck. He wasn't. The girl said there

was already a Klaus Schmidt reserved in the computer for their midday flight that day and did Zenin want to confirm his seat. The Russian said he would have to call back and hung up. How useful was the universal name of Smith, he thought.

The highest secrecy accorded the assassination mission meant that all communication was absolutely restricted, with each recipient having personally to sign a receipt and any such communication having to emanate from Berenkov, whose signature accompanied and authorized every dispatch.

The notification from England of Zenin's undetected arrival in London arrived two days after Zenin's disembarkation from the trawler in Ullapool—the word catalogue again being used to describe the Russian—and after alerting the KGB chairman and the ambitious Mikhail Lvov, Berenkov sat gazing down at the incoming message, still unconvinced it was the right decision to proceed with the operation, irrespective of any political importance attached to it or the amount of time and effort already expended in its planning. Berenkov was curious that Kalenin, of whose caution he was very aware, had not taken the prudent course and abandoned the operation. Could there be a reason he didn't know? The KGB chairman was a devious man who in the past had allowed apparently straightforward missions to be run on several levels. If there was a secret reason, it would be for Kalenin's protection. What about his own?

Berenkov accepted there was at this stage very little he could attempt. But it was essential he evolve something and if necessary, in time to turn Zenin back when the assassin approached the embassy in Bern, which was the only point of necessary contact with a Soviet installation allowed him.

Berenkov took a long time preparing the instruction, wanting the checks to be made properly but without panic. The first transmission was to Switzerland and the second to England. Copies were naturally sent to both Mikhail Lvov and Valery Kalenin.

The call came from the KGB chairman the following day. "Lvov is complaining that you are unreasonably interfering," disclosed Kalenin.

"Just to you?"

"I suspect that he's going higher, but unofficially. He believes he has important friends," said Kalenin.

"What should I do?" said Berenkov, deferring to the other man's expertise in headquarters survival.

"Nothing," said Kalenin at once. "Not yet."

5

It had been late when he got back from Sussex the previous night, practically pub closing time, and so Charlie kept the car instead of returning it to the pool, which regulations required. When he got outside of his flat he saw the Mercedes insignia had been ripped off the hood.

"Shit," he said. Maybe it wasn't such a good idea after all to buy a car of his own. He wondered if the bank manager's letter had arrived yet.

The summons was for ten o'clock and Charlie intended getting to the department an hour earlier, with a lot to do beforehand, but the traffic was worse than he had expected and so he was delayed. He still hadn't finished all the Foreign Office requests by the time he should have left for the confrontation with the Director. He worked on. At fifteen minutes past, Alison Bing came on from Wilson's direct line and said, "It's no good hiding. We know you're there."

"Ten more minutes," said Charlie.

"Now!" she said.

It only took Charlie five minutes to complete the last message, to Moscow, and he left in what was for him a run, which with his feet he never normally attempted. As he went by the window, he saw that the upside-down training shoes weren't in the courtyard rubbish any more.

Sir Alistair Wilson was sitting formally behind his desk, which he rarely was, and there was none of the personal affability of which Charlie was usually aware. Harkness was in his customary chair, prim hands on prim knees, making no attempt to hide the expression of satisfaction. Charlie thought he looked like a spectator at a Roman arena waiting for the thumbs down. Attacking at once, the deputy said, "You were specifically told ten o'clock."

"One or two things came up," said Charlie. "Sorry."

"Just what the hell do you think you're doing!" erupted Wilson. The complete whiteness of his hair was heightened by his red-faced anger.

"About what, precisely?" Charlie hadn't intended the question to sound insolent, but it did, and he was aware of Harkness's sharp intake of breath.

"You have caused absolute bloody chaos," accused the Director, hands clasped for control in front of him on the desk. "In my name—but without any reference or authority from me—you've demanded . . . not politely asked, but demanded . . . MI-5 mount a massive surveillance operation on every Soviet installation in London."

"Yes," agreed Charlie, "I have."

"You any idea of the manpower involved?" said Wilson.

"Or the overtime payments?" came in Harkness, predictably.

"Quite a lot," said Charlie, answering both questions.

"MI-5 is not our service," lectured Wilson. "When we want cooperation we ask, politely. We don't insist. And we don't make requests which will tie up every watcher they've got and require extra men being seconded. Do you know what their Director said when he complained? That Britain's entire counterintelligence service was at the moment working for *us*."

"I hope they are," said Charlie.

"What are you talking about?" said Harkness.

Instead of answering the man, Charlie said to the Director, "But are they doing it?"

Wilson frowned, momentarily not replying. Then he said, "Yes. I wasn't going to cancel without knowing what was happening, but by God, you'd better have a good explanation . . . a bloody good explanation."

Charlie sighed, relieved. "I'm glad," he said.

"And not just an explanation for that," said Harkness. "We've studied the full transcript of your interview with Novikov."

"And?" lured Charlie. Come on, you penny-pinching asshole, he thought.

"Appalling," judged Harkness. "Unnecessarily antagonistic, putting at risk any relationship that might have been built up between the man and other debriefers. And absolutely unproductive."

"Absolutely unproductive?" coaxed Charlie. He didn't just want Harkness to dig a hole for himself; he wanted a damned great pit, preferably with sharpened spikes at the bottom.

"Not one worthwhile thing emerged from the entire meeting," insisted Harkness. Confident enough to try sarcasm, he said, "And for whose benefit was the whisky episode?"

"Mine," said Charlie at once. "I wanted to break his concentration. It was going so well that I didn't want to lose anything. It can sometimes happen if a defector becomes too tense." He smiled and said, "Islay malt is a favorite of mine. His, too, it seems."

There were several moments of complete silence in the room. Charlie waited, comfortably relaxed. The roses today were predominantly yellow and heavily scented.

"Going so well?" It was Harkness who spoke, his voice edged with uncertainty.

"And about time," said Charlie. "I think too many mistakes have already been made. I hope we're not too late . . ." He smiled again, directly at Wilson this time. "That's why I'm glad the Soviet surveillance is being maintained. It is something that should have been in place weeks ago. The biggest mistake of all, in fact."

"I said I wanted an explanation," complained Wilson. "I'm not getting it in a way I can understand."

Charlie recognized there was no longer any anger in the man's voice. He said, "There were a number of reasons for my being what you regarded as antagonistic. It is always necessary, in the first place, to regard any defector as a hostile plant—"

"—You'd already been told that in the opinion of other debriefers Novikov was genuine," broke in Harkness.

"I'm not interested in the opinion of other debriefers," said Charlie. "Only my own. And having read the transcripts of their sessions and seen the oversights and the errors, I didn't think their opinions were worth a damn anyway."

"So what is your opinion?" said Wilson.

"I've asked this morning for some corroboration from Moscow," said Charlie. "But provisionally, I think he's okay."

"What other reasons were there for your approach?" demanded Harkness, fully aware of the unspoken criticism of Witherspoon, who was a protégé of the man.

"Novikov is arrogant," said Charlie. "Isn't that obvious from the transcript?"

"Yes," conceded Harkness reluctantly.

"He's been handled wrongly from the start," said Charlie. "Allowed to dominate the sessions, instead of being dominated himself. I wanted him to know I didn't trust him: that he had to prove himself. Which he did."

"You said mistakes had been made?" queried Wilson.

"A lot," said Charlie. "One of the most serious is the lack of response to the word 'catalogue'. It's not in any of the debriefing guide books, but it is most frequently used by the KGB to cover an agent from their assassination department. Who will be sent in specially. That's why I mounted the surveillance: I want a comparison between their known operatives and someone we don't know. If it's not too late, that is."

Wilson nodded and said, "If you're right, I agree. But why couldn't 'catalogue' refer to the victim?"

Charlie shook his head against the qualification. "Novikov had encountered the description before," he reminded. "Both times in connection with an assassination. He refused to be absolutely positive, but his belief was that it's the code for the operative. And I think the debriefing proved that the operation does not just involve England."

"Prove?" demanded Harkness.

"Novikov agreed that the cipher division of the KGB is not a general department, that it's compartmentalized like everything else," said Charlie.

Harkness nodded, in recollection.

"The assumption by all the previous debriefers had been

that Novikov was part of some centralized system," insisted Charlie.

"Yes," said Wilson, looking directly at Harkness. "And it was a mistake."

"I wanted particularly to establish the limitations of what Novikov handled, despite the Politburo clearance," disclosed Charlie. "The numbering told me."

"Number four was his first involvement," remembered Wilson.

"I think I know what happened to the previous three," announced Charlie.

"What?" asked the Director.

"Novikov agreed with me that he worked for the Third Department, which we know from previous defectors covers England. The logical conclusion is that the previous messages, perhaps identifying the target, went through other departments," said Charlie.

"Which means the killing could be anywhere in the world!" exclaimed Wilson.

Charlie shook his head, in another refusal. He said, "I think we can narrow it down."

"How?"

"Although separate in department control, England is considered part of Europe," said Charlie. "My guess is that England is the staging post for a killing that is to be carried out somewhere in Europe."

"A guess," pounced Harkness.

"Which might have been easier to confirm if surveillance had been imposed earlier," came back Charlie.

"Why England at all, if the assassination isn't to be here?" asked Wilson.

Charlie shrugged, unable positively to answer. "It's tradecraft always to conceal the point of entry," he suggested.

"Everything is still too vague," said Harkness.

"No," disputed Charlie again. "The debriefing told us how to look. And where."

"What!" shouted Wilson.

"The dates," said Charlie. "I'm sure it's in the dates."

"Tell me how?" insisted the Director.

"The pattern fits," argued Charlie. "Novikov was cut off on August 19."

"Yes," agreed the Director. He was leaning intently across the desk.

"The last message he encoded was August 12?"

"Yes."

"Before that, August 5?"

"And you anticipated the first, July 29," remembered Harkness.

"All Fridays," said Charlie.

There was another brief silence, then Harkness said, "So?"

"The Politburo of the Union of Soviet Socialist Republics always convenes on a Thursday," said Charlie. "Novikov's first message, to the Politburo, was an acknowledgment of an instruction for a public and political assassination. The other two were outwardly transmitted messages, establishing London as a link in that planning."

Harkness shook his head in rejection. "I don't agree with that assumption," he said. "Or still understand the guide it gives us, even if I could accept it."

"Allow me the assumption," urged Charlie. "We've got three unknown messages, before Novikov was given his, numbered four in the sequence. So let's work backward from those dates. If I am right, then the assassination was discussed at three previous Politburo sessions, July 22, July 15 and July 8, with July 8 being the date of the initial concept."

"I am finding this as difficult to follow as Harkness," protested the Director. "But if I do allow you the assumption, I still don't see what we have got."

"'The need is understood that a political, public example has to be set for the maximum impact,'" quoted Charlie.

"I don't need reminding of the first cable," said Wilson.

"How about the last?" asked Charlie. "'You will wrap the November catalogue.'"

"What's the connection?"

"What political, public event, where something of maximum impact could possibly be achieved, was announced
just prior to but certainly not after July 8?" suggested Charlie. "A political, public event scheduled to take place in November?"

"Oh yes," accepted the Director, finally. "Oh yes, I
could go for that."

"It's a theory," allowed Harkness begrudgingly.

"The best we've got, after the mistakes so far," said
Charlie.

"I think so, too," agreed the Director at once.

"I'm glad," said Charlie. "I was late for this morning's
meeting because I've ordered from every British embassy in
every European capital a complete list and breakdown of
major political happenings in their countries, throughout
December as well as November just to be sure. I designated
it maximum priority, with a copy in each case to the ambassador."

"In whose name?" asked Wilson expectantly.

"Yours," said Charlie.

Harry Johnson was pissed off, right up to the back teeth.
Five weeks to go before retirement, the lump sum he'd decided to take from his pension already deposited on the holiday bungalow in Broadstairs, the extra plot negotiated to
his allotment, and this had to happen, a hands-over-your-
bum, watch-everything-that-moves red alert. It wasn't fair:
certainly the assignment wasn't fair because the buggers
had maneuvered it so he got the worst surveillance of the
lot, the one most likely to go wrong. And the last thing he
could afford was anything going wrong. Until the gold
watch that had already been selected and the insincere
speeches and the booze-up in the Brace of Pheasants, all
he'd wanted—could surely have expected!—was a quiet,
easy life, so that he could quit the service with a reasonably
good record. Not this, something that was so obviously important and even more obviously dangerous.

Johnson, who was a plump man who wore suspenders as
well as a belt and who puffed a lot when he breathed be-

cause of a tendency to bronchitis, saw the departure of Yuri Koretsky first, because Johnson was one of the most senior watchers on the squad and only ever needed the sight of a quarry once. And Koretsky, who was the KGB *rezident* in London, had to be one of the most marked quarries of the whole stupid alert. Johnson was disappointed that the younger two, Burn, who was the driver, and Kemp, who was the backup, hadn't been quicker. According to regulations, as the senior man he should have reported them but he knew he wouldn't. What was the point of being shitty, with only five weeks to go before retirement?

"There's our man," he said, alerting them for the first time.

Koretsky was in a car with a driver, which Johnson recognized at once to be significant. He said, in further warning, "This could be it."

"Why?" asked Kemp.

"Watch and learn," said Johnson. He wondered what "it" was? Throughout the majority of his MI-5 career as a professional surveillance merchant, he had followed and bugged and burgled and pried, rarely knowing the complete reason of any assignment, like he didn't know the full purpose of this one. He frequently wondered whether any of it mattered.

The Soviet car went up the Bayswater Road—ironically, within a mile of the hotel that Vasili Zenin was preparing to leave within the hour to make the collection—and went to the right at Marble Arch, clogging at once in the Park Lane traffic. Their vehicle was two cars behind and Johnson said, "Don't lose him! Close up."

The Soviet vehicle turned into Upper Brook Street to go past the American embassy but stayed to the left of Grosvenor Square, going in front of the Dorchester and then crossing Bond Street, to the next square. There the car went immediately left, to cross Oxford Street and Johnson said, "Wrong! It would have been quicker to have gone north up Edgeware Road."

"Maybe the driver made a mistake," said Burn, who frequently did.

"Maybe Santa Claus drives a snowmobile," said Johnson. He had the seniority and certainly enough reasons to depute the younger man, but instead he said to Kemp, "If he jumps, I'll follow."

"What do you want me to do?" asked the younger man.

"Stay with the car," ordered Johnson. "And don't, for Christ's sake, lose it!"

"What do we look for?" asked Burns.

"Everything there is to see."

Koretsky made his move in Oxford Street and Johnson was only yards behind him. The Russian went directly into the underground system, using the ticket line to check for pursuit. Johnson got his ticket from the dispensing machine, paying the maximum fare, and was only five people behind the Russian on the down escalator. Koretsky went to the eastbound platform, and Johnson let more people come between them to provide the buffer. He tensed at the Oxford Circus station, because of its link with the Bakerloo Line, but the Russian remained just inside the door, standing as Johnson was standing, ready for an instant departure. Koretsky darted off at the Tottenham Court Road junction, timing it practically at the moment of the doors closing, so that Johnson was only just able to get out to continue the pursuit. Koretsky used the pretense of checking the indicator map to make another surveillance check, so Johnson had to go by and fumble for change for a guitar-playing busker and be overtaken himself, to pick up the Russian's trail on to the Northern Line and actually go north. Johnson managed the adjoining car again, discarding his topcoat and turning it so that the coloring was hidden, the only change possible in his appearance. Johnson was ready at Euston Street, because of the interconnecting lines, but Koretsky didn't move, seemingly relaxed now in a seat alongside the door. Too complacent, boyo, thought the watcher. He actually moved ahead of Koretsky at Camden Town, alighting first and ascending to street level ahead of the man although keeping him constantly in view behind, in case he doubled back. He didn't. Johnson got to the exit hoping that Burn had kept close to the Soviet car if this were a pickup, feeling the jump of alarm when he failed at once to recognize their car and then relief when he couldn't see the Russian vehicle either.

Johnson let people intrude between them as much as he felt it safe to do so as they walked down Camden High Street but was almost discovered at the bus stop at which Koretsky stopped without warning. Fortunately the 74 bus was actually approaching, so there was no time for the Russian to make a proper search behind. Once again, with no idea how far they were going, Johnson took the maximum fare, more tense now than at any time because of their close proximity. He was on the rear bench and Koretsky sat on the first cross seat next to it, close enough for Johnson to have reached out to touch the man.

Alert as he was, Johnson saw the Russian begin to move as they approached Primrose Hill, so he was able to get up and away from the bus before Koretsky actually disembarked. The Russian immediately crossed the road into Albert Terrace, striding on the side where the railings edged the grassed park. Johnson followed as far back as possible and on the opposite side of the road, where the houses were. In the last house before the terrace connected with Regents Park Road, Johnson dropped his topcoat behind a low garden wall, once more trying to alter his appearance as much as possible. As he did so, he saw Koretsky enter the park through the corner gate.

It had been a mistake not to bring Kemp with him, to alternate the tail to reduce being detected by the Russian. It would be just the way his luck was going for Koretsky to pick him up and abort, making the whole business a complete waste of time. The Russian's entry into the park provided at least some minimal cover. It meant Johnson could walk parallel up Regents Park Road, keeping him in sight but not directly behind. Had he been, Johnson realized he would have been spotted, because twice Koretsky turned, making an obvious check. But even this was a mixed advantage, because the road began to bend away from the park, now putting too much distance between them, so that when it happened, Johnson almost missed it. Had he not been as experienced as he was, he would have.

The dead-letter drop was almost at the end of the avenue, along which Koretsky was walking, by a garbage can against the sixth lamppost from the beginning of the path. At the moment of approach, Koretsky flicked something to his left, not into the can but alongside it. Then the Russian paused, as if troubled with the lace of his shoe and Johnson saw the man mark the post with a smear of yellow chalk which would have looked like some failed graffiti to anyone but himself.

Johnson had already decided to abandon Koretsky, even before the Soviet car swept down Primrose Hill Road for the pickup, because Koretsky was simply part of a chain and the necessity now was to feed that chain in, to discover the next link. Then Johnson saw the car in which he had earlier traveled, grimacing as he did. The stupid bastards were far too close. If he tried to stop it, to get backup from Kemp, Johnson knew he'd be identified by association.

"Stupid fools!" he said, bitterly and aloud.

As the cars convoyed back down Regents Park Road, Johnson entered the enclosure. There were thickly leafed trees all along the pathway along which Koretsky had walked, with occasional benches. He chose the one furthest away from the drop, eyes focused on what Koretsky had delivered. It was impossible to be sure from this distance, but it appeared to be a manila envelope though bigger than that for a normal letter, maybe five inches across and eight inches deep. He wished he were able to judge its thickness, but that was impossible.

Johnson shivered, wanting the discarded topcoat but unable to risk going back even the short distance to get it. Expert that he was, Johnson knew he was observing what is called in the trade an open letter box, a deposit arrangement from which the recipient was expected to collect very quickly what had been left, to prevent its accidental discovery by some casual stranger. So close to a garbage can, the larger-than-normal envelope was very vulnerable, Johnson decided, from a foraging tramp or a conscientious garbage collector.

He focused the camera on the garbage can, guaranteeing the range, and then settled back to wait. How long? he wondered.

The specific request from Alexei Berenkov in Moscow, demanding immediate warning of increased surveillance, was waiting for Koretsky when he got back to Kensington Palace Gardens. He quickly encoded a reply, assuring Berenkov that he had remained clean that day and that the watchers had gone on a wild goose chase behind the car, which had been the intention.

6

Vasili Zenin realized there was a risk in leaving the bicycle he had rented from the Camden rental agency without enclosing the wheels in the anti-thief chain that they had demonstrated, but decided it was necessary because he couldn't waste time later, unlocking it. He hoped it was the biggest risk he was going to have to take that day.

He parked it at the junction of Elsworthy Road with Primrose Hill Road, preparing himself carefully. He positioned the earphones of the Walkman precisely in place, switching on the Tchaikovsky tape, and then fixed the sweatband with even more precision, wishing he had a mirror to insure both were as he wanted. He had been very particular about the fit of the running shoes, pleased at how comfortable they felt as he started jogging toward the park, breathing easily, arms pumping steadily as he moved. Personal fitness is naturally a priority for Balashikha graduates, and Zenin had always enjoyed the running. It was the exercise sessions there and the lectured awareness of the popularity of jogging in the West that had given him the idea in the first place.

Zenin paced into the park near the top of the hill, picking up the perimeter path furthest away from where the drop should have been made, wanting before he ventured anywhere near the marked place to make a far more thorough reconnaissance than he had on the previous occasion. There were actually three other joggers plodding around the lanes like he was, in shorts and singlet, and one was even wearing a Walkman. Zenin smiled, humming in time to the concerto, concentrating beyond them. It was emptier than he had expected from his earlier visit: a few people exercising their dogs, one or two sitting on benches, and a couple lying prostrate upon the grass practically in the act of sexual intercourse. Maybe, he thought, it heightened the pleasure to fuck in public. He turned left where the path veered to go parallel with Albert Terrace and past the sign from which he had learned bicycling was forbidden, and finally had a frontal view, although slightly to his left, of the post and the garbage can. A man was sitting on a bench about twenty feet away from the drop, and a woman with a Labrador was actually at the spot. As he looked, the animal cocked its leg against the lamp, and Zenin's face twisted in disgust at the thought that it might be fouling what he had to collect.

Johnson's concentration was entirely upon the dead letter box, and it was Zenin's snatching down immediately after the dog had urinated there—an unthinkable action because the man would have seen the animal do it—that alerted the watcher. He hadn't thought the pickup would be made by a jogger and had let Zenin merge into the background of his consciousness as the Russian went by. Johnson grabbed the camera from its concealment beneath his jacket and managed three panicked exposures and then a more sharply focused shot of Zenin spurting away before getting up himself, stumbling in pursuit. Zenin left the park through the same exit that Koretsky had used, running hard now up Primrose Hill Road.

Johnson hurried as fast as he considered he was safely able, slowing twice at Zenin's obvious backward checks, gasping because of his weak chest by the time he got to the top of the hill. He did so just in time to see Zenin mount the bicycle in Elsworthy Road, jerking the camera up for one last attempt.

"Fuck it!" said Johnson. He'd known it was going to go badly like this. Just known it! "Oh fuck it!" he said again.

Elsworthy Road is a twisting, winding thoroughfare, so by the time Johnson reached it, his quarry was completely out of sight. Expert that he was, the watcher walked its entire length, wet with the perspiration of effort and annoyance by the time he reached the junction with Avenue Road. He saw the traffic jam backed up for several hundred

yards and shook his head in bitter awareness: the fact that
he had been outprofessionaled by a professional did bugger
all to help.

A combination of normal bureaucratic delay and top
level irritation—and therefore face-satisfying obstructive-
ness—at what MI-5 considered arrogant and high-handed
surveillance demands meant it was the following day before
Charlie Muffin received Johnson's report and the developed
photographs. It took him only an hour to arrange the
meeting with the about-to-retire watcher.

"I made a balls of it, Charlie. You don't know how sorry
I am," said Johnson, after they'd talked through in every
way possible what had happened. They'd worked together
before, always well. Knowing it was Charlie's operation—
which he had not known until now—worsened Johnson's re-
morse.

"These things happen, mate," said Charlie sympatheti-
cally.

"I wanted to go out covered in glory and instead I leave
covered in odor."

"What you did get confirms a lot. I'm grateful," said
Charlie sincerely. "It could have happened to anyone."

"It happened to me," said Johnson.

"There have been worse fuck-ups already, believe me,"
said Charlie. He wondered how many more holes-in-one
Witherspoon had managed.

"Any idea who he is?"

"Not a clue."

"Or what the job is?"

"Nope." There'd been eight responses to his embassy requests, and none of them had meant a thing. Gale had replied from Moscow, too.

"Be careful, Charlie. He's good: bloody good."

"That's what frightens me," admitted Charlie.

"I'm giving the retirement party at the Brace of Pheasants," said the watcher. "Any chance of your getting along?"

"Ever known me to miss a piss-up?" said Charlie.

"I am sorry," said Johnson, again.

"A pint of beer and we're even," assured Charlie.

"I'd like to think it was as easy as that," said Johnson.

As he spoke, Vasili Zenin was entering Terminal Two at London airport with the driving license and passport which identified him as Henry Smale—and which fortunately the dog had missed peeing on—snug in his inside pocket. His ticket, however, was in the name of Peter Smith. He'd been lucky with the Swissair reservation and had decided it was an omen. He saw the pregnant woman ahead stumble, just before she fainted, and managed easily to switch to another passport line, to avoid becoming involved. Lucky again, he thought.

Because she was a member of the secretariat and therefore part of the official delegation, Sulafeh Nabulsi had a place on the platform but at the rear. The backs of those who were going to Geneva for the conference were against her, but beyond she could see the faces of the hundreds of Palestinians gathered to hear what the current speaker was describing as an historic breakthrough in their demands for an independent homeland. Fools, she sneered mentally. Worse than fools. Cowards. There was no struggle any more; no fight. Just a lot of aging men posturing in camouflage fatigues, playing at being freedom fighters and using words like the actors they were. Most of the council, at whose backs she was staring in well-concealed loathing, each had a million dollars discreetly hidden in numbered Swiss bank accounts and would find it difficult to identify the muzzle of a Kalashnikov from its butt. And most definitely didn't give a damn about the trusting idiots here whom they were deceiving at the final Tripoli assembly of the PLO with talk of a conference and a political settlement. Any more than they gave a damn about the Palestinians forgotten and rotting in the refugee camps of the Lebanon, target practice for any Shi'ite or Jew who felt like expending a bullet.

None of them had even lived in a refugee camp, not like she had. At the age of nine, in the last hours of the 1973 Six Day War, Sulafeh had seen her grandfather shot by the Israelis as a spy for Syria, which he had been. Four years later, her mother and older brother had been blown up—accidentally said the later contemptuous report—when the Jews destroyed their house in retribution for a grenade attack upon a passing Israeli patrol.

And she'd been raped in a camp. It had happened when she was fifteen, still a virgin. Her attacker had been one of the smirking clowns in a tiger uniform, like those smirking clowns in the audience in front of her, applauding and cheering every lie being told them. She'd fought as hard as she could, gouging at his face with her nails, and he'd punched her almost senseless. So finally she pretended to be unconscious when he tore at her pants and then his and drove himself into her, splitting her. And while he grunted and pumped above her, she'd taken his own knife from his belt, halfway down his thighs, and put her arms around him in what he'd thought to be belated passion, better able to stab him to death, plunging the knife into his back again and again like he'd plunged into her.

Sulafeh had an orgasm doing it. She'd never had one since: certainly never during the countless couplings that had been necessary for her to insinuate and maneuver herself into the favor of the senior hierarchy to achieve the role she now occupied. She wondered if she might know the sensation again, at the moment of what was going to happen in Geneva. It was an often longed-for feeling.

7

Four of Johnson's exposures had been possible to develop, but the face of the jogger who picked up the drop was only shown on one of them and then indistinctly, as the man half-turned to run after snatching the package. Two others showed his back view as he went toward Primrose Hill Road—in one, the logo was actually visible—and the fourth was at the moment of his mounting the bicycle, but again he was completely turned away.

"Bungled!" complained Harkness. "How the hell could it have happened?"

"Easily," said Charlie at once, in defense of a friend. "It was a brilliantly carried-out collection."

The Director was wedged as usual against the window-sill, with his back to the depressing view. The roses today were yellow-hearted Piccadilly with their pink edging, and Wilson wore one in the buttonhole of his jacket to match those arranged in the window vase. Charlie decided that the Director's tweed suit was as baggy and shapeless as his. Funny how clothes collapsed like that.

"Tell me why you think this is significant, the sort of thing you've been looking for," demanded the Director. "Why couldn't whoever it is have been an English contact of the Russians that MI-5 hasn't yet got on to?"

"It was brilliant, like I said," insisted Charlie. "So the man is a complete professional. No amateur—and an Englishman would have been an amateur suborned by the Russians, not properly trained—would have done it like this."

"What's so completely professional?" persisted Harkness.

"Becoming a jogger in the first place," set out Charlie.

"The first essential is becoming invisible, which is exactly what he did. Johnson openly admits that he'd accepted the joggers in the park that afternoon: wasn't really seeing them any more. But think of the other advantages it gave the man. He was entitled to run, because he was dressed for it. So having made the pickup, he did run, like hell, Johnson says. But that would not have looked unusual to any passerby because joggers do sprint. What it did mean is that the man could literally run away and any watcher would have disclosed himself, setting out in open pursuit: so it was an abort-or-continue test as well. He was actually looking for us!"

"I hardly consider using a bicycle professional," argued the deputy.

"It was absolutely professional," refuted Charlie. "The distance from the drop to where the bicycle was parked is just over half a mile: Johnson later carried out a positive measurement. So he would have begun to flag, after sprinting so far. But on the bicycle he could carry on running—but remain invisible to anyone he passed because he was dressed *exactly* for riding as he was for jogging—and outpace anyone trying to follow on foot."

"What about anyone in a car?" seized Wilson.

"Possibly the cleverest part," said Charlie. "Elsworthy Road runs into the Avenue. And that joins Prince Albert Road at a junction controlled by traffic lights. The change gives preference to Prince Albert Road, which means there is *always* a backup of traffic in the Avenue. And I know it is always blocked because Johnson checked it and the Metropolitan Police confirmed it when I asked them. On a bicycle he could overtake the lot, dismount, and even ignore the lights if they were red against him. While any following car would be stuck hundreds of yards back up the road, helpless to follow."

"I think you're making a lot of assumptions," said the Director doubtfully.

"Look at the picture," urged Charlie. "Not just the one showing half his face but all the rest. What—beyond the running gear—is common to them all in the disguise?"

Harkness went to the Director's side so they could study the prints together. Both did so without any sign of recognition.

"What?" asked Harkness, at last.

"There's one thing always impossible to alter in a disguise, other than by plastic surgery," reminded Charlie. "Ears. The ears always remain the same shape and size and are a marker for a trained observer. But he managed it and not just with the headset but additionally with the sweatband. It would not be obvious unless you were looking for it—which we are—but people don't usually wear a band like that, not completely encompassing the ears. But he did. And he even wore it to disarrange his hair, so that we can't be sure of any positive style."

Wilson was nodding, in growing acceptance. He said, "Do we have any identifying marks at all?"

"None," said Charlie, gesturing toward the pictures again. "I've had them blown up to the greatest possible enlargement. There's no jewelry, like a ring or a neck chain. And not one visible scar or blemish."

"What about the jogging clothes he wore?" said Harkness.

"I've had all the photographs professionally analyzed," said Charlie. "The assessment is that all the clothes were brand new, freshly bought. It's possible to detect the crease lines from the packaging in the larger pictures and to pick out the absolutely unworn tread on the soles of the shoes. We can isolate the brand name every time but it's no advantage. My guess is that he bought each piece separately, all from different shops. We could never run a trace in a hundred years because it would have been cash every time."

"And the bicycle?"

"A standard Raleigh, blue, with a three-speed attachment," said Charlie. "From the photograph the company says they think it could have been manufactured about two years ago, but they'd need to examine the machine to be sure. They say it's the sort of model most popular among rental shops."

"We haven't got a thing, have we?" said Harkness, showing his earlier anger.

"Quite a lot," disputed Charlie. "Like I said, all the shots have been professionally analyzed. Which means a complete description. He's precisely five feet ten inches tall, and from the physique that's clearly visible, he is obviously extremely fit. That was also Johnson's impression from the way and the speed with which he ran, after picking up the package. And from the style that's clear on the photographs—the way he holds himself and the measured paces—he's someone accustomed to running. The physique is confirmed by his measurements: his waist measures twenty-nine inches against a chest of thirty-eight inches. He weighs ten stone, eleven pounds, so equating his height against his measurements—and we've got biceps and calf and thigh readings, as well—he's practically all muscle. He takes a size eight shoe, slim fitting."

"We still lack any facial description," complained Harkness.

"Not entirely," said Charlie. "And what we do have might be important. He's absolutely clean shaven but although the sweatband and the headset make any hairstyle impossible to establish it can't conceal the color. It's completely black. Like his eyes, black or certainly deep brown. And there's the very definite complexion. He's dark-skinned."

"Meaning?" queried Wilson.

"Combined with another indicator that he's definitely not English, disregarding the professionalism," said Charlie.

"What indicator?"

"There was just one mistake he made. And that hardly a mistake. When he got on to the bicycle, he appeared to Johnson instinctively to ride on the right hand side of the road, not the left. It was a good hundred yards before he adjusted. He's not accustomed to traveling on our roads."

"Tenuous," insisted Harkness.

"I don't think so," said Charlie, with matching insistence.

"What's your thought about the package itself?"

"'You will dispatch the catalogue,'" said Charlie, quoting the second message Novikov had encoded. "And then 'you will wrap the November catalogue.' Johnson guessed it at five inches by eight inches and that's confirmed by the photo-analysis because it's visible in his hand, at the moment of his coming up by the street sign. Too large for any written letter then. Put together with the two messages, I'd guess a passport or a plane ticket or possibly both."

"Airports and ports?" said the Director.

"I've covered as many as I think reasonable, the full description as well as the half-face photograph," assured Charlie.

"What about major political events?" asked Wilson. "I've had the Foreign Office bitching about the time they're having to spend on that."

"Eight possibles, all in November," said Charlie. "There's a meeting of OPEC in Vienna, an IMF conference in Paris, which is also hosting the biannual gathering of African nonaligned nations. In Geneva there is the continuing arms limitation talks and again in Geneva there is the American-initiated conference for which they've finally persuaded Israel to sit at the same table as a delegation from the PLO. Jordan and Syria are also involved. In Brussels there's a Council of Ministers meeting. The United Nations is sponsoring a Foreign Ministers' assembly in Madrid to put pressure on the drug smuggling countries in Latin America—the majority of Colombian and Bolivian cocaine comes into Europe through Madrid. The American President is visiting Berlin, on the twenty-eighth. The Secretary of State will be with him, and then the Secretary goes on to the Middle East conference in Geneva. From Berlin the President is going to Venice for a NATO summit."

"Bloody hell!" said Wilson, despairingly. "With how many is Britain involved?"

"The Chancellor of the Exchequer is attending the IMF meeting in Paris, obviously," set out Charlie. "The Foreign Secretary is going to Brussels and to Madrid. And the Prime Minister is scheduled for Venice."

"When's the first meeting?" asked Harkness.

"November 2: the drug meeting in Madrid."

"That means we've got exactly three weeks," said Harkness. "That's not enough . . ." He looked at the Director and said, "I propose that we immediately issue warnings to the counterintelligence services of every country involved, with what we've got."

"That would come to thirty-two," said Charlie. "I counted."

"Then it's impractical. It would cause chaos," said the Director.

"Let's assume for a moment that the pickup was a passport," said Harkness. "What about the chaos if there is an assassination and the man is caught with a British passport in his possession? . . ." He hesitated, as the idea came to expand the argument. "That could even be part of whatever is going to happen: somehow, someway, to embarrass us with some false involvement."

"I acknowledge the risk but I don't think there is sufficient evidence to sound alarm bells yet," refused the Director. "How would we look if nothing does happen and we've got the counterintelligence services of thirty-two countries—and possibly their external agencies as well—looking under every bed they can find? We'd make ourselves the laughingstock of the century."

"I'm sure there is going to be an assassination," said Charlie. "Gale, in Moscow, responded positively to every query I sent about Novikov. If Novikov is okay, then so's the information."

"Then we've got to be the people to stop it," declared Wilson. To Charlie he said, "Are you sure enough about Primrose Hill to call off the intense surveillance of everything Russian?"

"God, no!" said Charlie. "I think Primrose Hill looks right and I think we should pull out all the stops to find whoever he is, but I'm not at the moment putting it any higher than fifty percent."

"Which is a further reason for not yet involving anyone

else prematurely," said the Director. Still addressing Charlie, he said, "What now?"

"I wish to Christ I knew," said Charlie, regretting the carelessness of the remark as soon as he'd made it, conscious of Harkness's face tightening in disgust at the blasphemy. The man was an avid churchgoer, usually three times every Sunday: it was common knowledge he'd spent his last holiday in a retreat.

They left the Director's office together, and in the antiroom outside, Harkness said, "Make an appointment to see me alone tomorrow. We have to talk about administration matters."

Over the man's shoulder, Charlie saw the Director's secretary make a grimace of sympathy. Was Alison Bing looking for a bit of rough? wondered Charlie. As the deputy turned away, Charlie grinned and winked at the girl. She winked back. Forget it love, thought Charlie. I'm old enough to be your father. Pity, though. It could have been fun.

By six o'clock in the evening, Koretsky had five confirmed and independent reports of the continuingly tightened observation and hoped he had not been too quick with his assurance to Berenkov, in Moscow. And then he relaxed, realizing how he could comply with the instruction and satisfy Dzerzhinsky Square at the same time. He set out in close detail how the cordons were being detected, around every Soviet installation in London. But then pointed out that it proved the handover had gone as well as he'd already reported. If it had been detected, the British would not still be bothering, would they?

By the time he sent the cable, Vasili Zenin had been in Switzerland for two days.

8

The Geneva mock-up had been created like all the rest at the KGB's artificial cities installation at Kuchino, but supposedly in specific and street-named detail, here like at the instruction center at Balashikha isolated behind high concrete walls to separate it from all those other less specifically detailed training recreations of Western towns. Geneva after all had Politburo priority, which supposedly again permitted no element of error. But Vasili Zenin discovered there were errors. Stupid, dangerous mistakes: like earlier there had been no warning of bicycling being forbidden by law in Primrose Hill Park. It had been a stupid, dangerous mistake, something which could have ended the entire mission before it even began.

Zenin was determined against anything endangering his first assignment, because of another, paramount determination. He had enjoyed, come to need, the accolades of Balashikha and wanted them to continue. He needed, quite simply, to be acknowledged as the foremost agent operating from Department Eight of Directorate S: to be the most successful assassin they'd ever known.

Which was why the smallest of oversights had to be guarded against. And which was why, after that late evening arrival in Geneva, he had disobeyed the final Moscow briefing instructions and not hired a car to go at once to Bern. Instead he had taken the anonymous airport bus into the city terminal and ignored taxi drivers with possibly long memories to walk through the avenues and streets until he'd found the small auberge in the side road off the Boulevard de la Tour, safely away from either of the areas of the city in which he was later to operate. He booked in as Klaus Schmidt.

It was a breakfast-only auberge, and he took the meal although he did not want to, because not to have done so might have attracted attention. It was the sort of place in which everyone was existing on the sort of budget where every meal counted. Traveling on an English passport meant he chose *The Times* and *The Independent* to hide behind, enjoying the coffee but crumbling the croissant instead of eating it, anxious to get away.

Zenin disdained any transport, public or otherwise. He got at once on to the Boulevard des Tranchees and stayed on the main and busy highways as he strode toward the lake. He crossed the Rhone, making for the area where he was to meet Sulafeh Nabulsi. And almost at once isolated the first mistake. Kuchino had shown the Quai du Mont-Blanc to be a continuous thoroughfare, without the obligatory turn into the Rue des Alpes, and there had been no indication that the Rue Phillippe Plantamour was a one-way system. It was— horrifyingly—the lack of attention to detail which could have got him trapped and caught, if he had chosen to use any sort of vehicle when he made his eventual meeting with the woman and she had been under suspicion. In a rough square that took him as high as the Notre Dame church to the Voltaire museum and then back in the direction of the lake again, Zenin encountered two more obstructive road systems. He was too highly trained to become actually emotionally angry, but as he had earlier in London, he resolved to complain about the information that had been relayed from the Bern embassy and upon which the Kuchino model would have been based.

There was a pavement cafe on the corner of the Adhemar-Fabri from which he could gaze across the water, regretting that so late in the year the Jet d'Eau had been turned off. Which had been another mistake, although not a dangerous one: the Kuchino model had shown the decorative water plume in operation. Zenin twisted in his seat, looking toward the unseen area of the Botanical Gardens. Moscow had given him estimates of walking times from various approaches but Zenin resolved to check them all himself, later. There had been too many discrepancies so far in the information provided by the embassy, so everything had to be confirmed and reconfirmed. He hoped the rented room would have the oversight that had been demanded for him to get an unobstructed shot.

Zenin was allowed to make his own choice of meeting places with the girl and chose three possibilities for the initial encounter, the first the cafe at which he was already sitting because it was on a corner with three possible escape routes. Smiling at the irony, he decided upon the other two by utilizing the oversight of the Bern embassy, choosing one restaurant on the Rue des Alpes and another on the Rue des Terreaux du Temple. The entrapping imprisonment of a one-way system could as easily be reversed into an escape route and both were restricted highways. He hoped no frantic escape would be necessary because if it was it would mean that the woman was blown and with it the operation. And failed operations—even if they were no fault whatsoever of the operative—always look bad on the record.

Precautions, of course, had to be taken. And precautions unknown to anyone but himself because Zenin only really trusted himself.

Because it was so conveniently near, actually on the quai where he was sitting, Zenin ate in the luxury of le Chat Bottee restaurant of the Beau-Rivage, seeking out a lakeside table to have the best outlook while he ate, enjoying the opportunity to relax. Briefly, fantasizing almost, he tried to imagine an escape route across the lake after the assassination, shaking his head at the idiocy of the idea. It would be easier to get trapped on the lake than in any of the one-way streets that the stupid bastards at the embassy had failed to designate. The way to escape was far easier and far less dramatic than that film he'd seen the first night in London, the name of which he could no longer remember.

At the Hertz office on the Rue de Bern he rented, for three weeks, a medium-sized Peugeot on the English driving license of Henry Smale, paying the deposit in sterling. With time to spare he drove around the immediate border towns, uncertain whether eventually to abandon it for later

discovery in Switzerland or France. Perly, in the south, was
a possibility. Or Meyrin, further north.

He got back into the city by early evening and reconnoitered by road the same area he had that morning explored
on foot. The car could certainly be parked nearby but the
first and subsequent meeting places needed to be somewhere where he had easier freedom of movement to dodge.
It was a pity the jogging and bicycle routine could not be repeated. It had worked very well in London, despite being so
unnecessary.

Zenin finished the initial reconnaissance earlier than
he'd anticipated, realizing it would be possible for him to
drive to Bern to establish himself as he should have done the
previous day. And at once abandoned the idea. It would
mean checking out unexpectedly from the auberge where
he had a reservation for two nights, and any unexpected and
identifying action had to be avoided.

Instead, because it was a cuisine with which he was not
familiar, he ate Chinese at the Auberge des Trois Bonheurs,
after which he attempted a walk along the shore of the lake
but found it too cold, so he went back to the auberge. The
clerk who had registered him was on duty again and Zenin
reminded the man that he was checking out the following
morning.

"A short stay, Herr Schmidt?" said the man.

"Off to New York in the morning," said Zenin, complet-
ing the carefully prepared false trail.

The relationship between the KGB chief and Alexei
Berenkov went beyond Dzerzhinsky Square to that of long
friendship. It had become a custom to alternate dinner invi-
tations and that night it had been Kalenin's turn, at his
bachelor Kutuzovsky apartment. He'd roasted venison with
red cabbage and served Georgian wine, because he knew
nothing about wine and had taken Berenkov's advice that it
was good: during his London posting the man had become
the connoisseur his cover required. Afterward they had
French brandy with the coffee, and then Valentina,
Berenkov's wife, cleared the table and busied herself tidying

and washing up in the kitchen because that was customary, too. The men always talked, and having been married to Berenkov for twenty years, Valentina knew precisely when to absent herself.

"There is definitely increased surveillance in London?" said Kalenin.

"No doubt about it."

"London was identifiable in the communications Novikov handled," said Kalenin. "It was to be expected."

"Not of this intensity," insisted Berenkov.

"But the embassy in Bern is adamant there is no increase there," reminded Kalenin. "There surely would have been if Novikov knew more than we believe and had been able to identify Switzerland. And if the drop had been picked up."

"I don't want to take anything for granted."

"At the moment it is insufficient to consider cancellation."

"Are you using it for some other purpose that I don't know about?" challenged Berenkov openly.

"If I'm protected, then so are you," replied Kalenin obtusely.

Berenkov allowed the pause, hoping the other man would continue but he did not. Berenkov said, "Is that your promise?"

"What else would it be?" demanded Kalenin.

"Let's build up at the Bern embassy!" urged Berenkov. "Blanket the place with additional people of our own, so that we'll detect the moment anything changes there."

"That would probably be wise," agreed Kalenin. "What about the British communication codes to their embassy here?"

"We can decipher all of them."

"Let's order a concentration on that. Build up the intercepts, as well."

"Have there been any further protests from Lvov?" asked Berenkov.

"Not to me," said Kalenin.

"What about elsewhere?"

"I've no idea."

"He could be a dangerous man," said Berenkov.
"So could I," said Kalenin.

9

Charlie Muffin was irritated for more than one reason. The most obvious cause was the forthcoming encounter with Harkness, but the greater feeling came from the frustration of not being able to do anything but sit and wait and rely on others. Charlie didn't like sitting and waiting, most definitely not on an operation like this, one with a time limit. And he never liked relying on others because it was far too easy to slip on their dropped banana peels. Which was perhaps an unfair reflection, on this particular job. He'd had rerun the one half-face picture of Primrose Hill through all the physiognomy checks possible, trying for comparisons with all known Eastern bloc agents going back for three years, using the computer system as well as human analysis. And come up with a blank, like the first time. So objectively, it was unlikely that any immigration officer or Special Branch man was going to do any better. It was a bastard; a right bastard. Maybe, ultimately, they would have to pick up Harkness's suggestion and sound a general alarm, impractical though it had seemed. Which was further cause for irritation. Charlie didn't like being unable to come up with a better idea than that prick of a deputy.

Sighing, he left his cubbyhole office in good time for the appointment, reluctant to provide the man with more grounds for complaint than he already had. Charlie was ten minutes early and was told by the stiffly coiffured secretary that he had to wait. He did so patiently, refusing to be riled any more than he already was, knowing damned well there was no reason for Harkness to delay the interview and that the man was playing his usual silly games. Charlie bet that Harkness had been one of those snotty little kids who took his bat home if he wasn't always able to have first crack at the ball.

Harkness's office was lower than the Director's and further to one side, so the vibration from the underground trains hummed up from the foundations. The man was waiting neatly behind his desk. The suit today was blue striped, the color-coded accessories pastel blue. The office was antiseptically clean, as it always was.

"Anything come in since yesterday?" said Harkness.

"Nothing," said Charlie. The man knew damned well that if there had been anything he would have been informed.

"You drew a Mercedes from the pool," announced Harkness.

"What?" said Charlie. If Harkness could play silly games, then so could he. In fact, Charlie reckoned he was better at it than the other man.

"For the Novikov debriefing you drew a Mercedes from the pool," repeated Harkness pedantically.

The deputy's pink cheeks were pinker than usual, and Charlie hoped it was anger. He said, "That was the debriefing you didn't think was any good."

"It was returned damaged," said Harkness.

"Was it?" said Charlie, in blank-faced innocence.

"The hood ornament was torn off."

"Wonder how that happened," said Charlie.

"You didn't notice it?"

"No." He wondered if the man ever farted. Probably not.

"It's directly in front of you, when you drive, man!"

Temper, temper, thought Charlie. He said, "Never noticed it. Honest."

"There were smaller, less expensive vehicles you could have chosen."

"Probably," agreed Charlie.

"So why didn't you?"

"I got the impression from the Director's briefing that there was some urgency," said Charlie. Get out of that, he thought.

Harkness couldn't. Definitely red-faced now, he said, "You drew the car on the ninth?"

"That sounds right," said Charlie, intentionally vague to irk a man to whom precise detail was everything.

"It was not returned to the pool until the tenth," persisted Harkness.

"I'm sure the pool records are accurate."

"So why did you keep it overnight?" demanded Harkness. "You know that contravenes regulations."

"I wasn't sure whether I would need it to return to Sussex the following day, to expand on anything Novikov might have told me," lured Charlie.

Harkness stepped into the very middle of the trap. "You'd been summoned for a meeting with the Director!" pounced the deputy. "So you couldn't have returned to Sussex the following day!"

"But the summons was through ..." Charlie hesitated, appearing to seek a polite route. "... through some misunderstanding about the worth of the debriefing, like I mentioned earlier," he said. "I thought it was a good interview, and it did turn out to be, didn't it? If I'd had any afterthoughts, I'd hoped the Director would have delayed our meeting. As it was, I didn't have any afterthoughts so it wasn't necessary. Bit of luck that, wasn't it?"

Harkness's mouth was in a tight line. He said, "There is a form to be filled in for damaged vehicles."

"I'm sure there is," said Charlie. The prat had probably created it.

"You'll need to complete it."

"You want me to explain the misunderstanding about the debriefing?" asked Charlie, the innocence as perfectly pitched as before.

Harkness's face was blazing now. "Just the circumstances of the damage," he said, brittle-voiced.

"Don't know the circumstances of the damage," reminded Charlie. "Never realized it had happened."

"Complete the confounded form!"

Charlie bet for once the man regretted the determination against swearing. Fucking form would have relieved the pressure much better. "Yes, sir," he said, obediently.

Harkness recognized the insolence at once: sir was a word he knew not to exist in Charlie's vocabulary, apart from occasionally when addressing the Director. He failed completely to comprehend Wilson's admiration for the grubby little jerk. Harkness said, "A letter has been channeled to me. From your bank."

Here we go, thought Charlie, everyone on the roller coaster and no one knowing where the ride would end. Cautiously he said, "Yes?"

"Are you in financial difficulties?"

"Isn't everyone?" smiled Charlie hopefully. Harkness doing the unexpected would be the biggest joke of all time.

"Do you realize this could put you in a review situation?"

"Review situation?"

"The Permanent Security Review Committee considers financial irregularity very important."

"What financial irregularity!"

"You've sought an arrangement for ten thousand pounds."

"Yes."

"Meaning you can't live within your means?"

Charlie had expected his past record—a record which Harkness could never forget or overlook—to result in suspicion like this. But the headmaster-to-difficult-pupil number was still a pain in the ass. He said, "It is an application to an English bank, not an offer to go over to the Russians."

"Like you once did!"

Charlie bet he could move his lips in anticipation of the other man's thoughts. He said, "I did not go across to the Russians; I taught a lesson to those who tried to make me sacrifice of the month."

"The Directors of American and British intelligence!"

"They were prepared for me to be seized: killed maybe. All I did was make them look stupid. Which wasn't very difficult," said Charlie. "They were only in Soviet custody for twenty-four hours anyway." Should have been longer, he thought. Assholes, all of them.

"Now you need money?"

"And that makes me a security risk?" said Charlie, answering the question with another question.

"There's precedent for it."

"Not with me," insisted Charlie. "I could have stayed in Russia last time if I'd wanted to, remember?" And still been with Natalia, he thought. He wished so much to be able to know what had happened to her; to be sure that she was safe.

"You're under pressure to repay creditors?"

"No," said Charlie. The bookmaker's demand for three hundred pounds hardly ranked with the national debt, after all.

"So why do you need the money?"

"Few improvements around the flat," ad-libbed Charlie, prepared from the encounter with the bank manager. "Thought I might get a little car, for the weekends."

"For which your salary is insufficient?"

"I've been passed over by the last two promotional boards," reminded Charlie. And he'd bet a pound to a pinch of the smelly brown stuff that Harkness had been in there blocking his upgrade.

"You realize that the security requirements—my having become involved because of this letter—are that I make a thorough investigation into your financial affairs, don't you?" said the deputy director.

Charlie wondered which would upset Harkness more, the membership fees to the three after-hours drinking clubs or the subscription to the Fantail Club, where there was a lot of fanny and tail and all of it uncovered for appreciative selection. Straight-faced, he said, "No, I didn't."

"Well, it does."

"I don't suppose I have any say in it, your having become involved?"

"None at all," said Harkness. "The procedure now is regulated."

Like the right sort of bowel movement, thought Charlie.

The bastard was enjoying himself. He said, "Regulations also say I must have complete access to your report, don't they?"

Harkness blinked, surprised at Charlie's knowledge of always disdained rules, unaware that Charlie could quote every one that was likely personally to affect or benefit him. The deputy said, "Of course."

"I'm very happy for you to make whatever inquiries you consider necessary," said Charlie, because he had to. He accepted positive vetting as a necessity of the job but was uncomfortable at this prissy little sod opening cupboard doors looking for threadbare skeletons. Harkness was more likely to encounter threadbare suits, but that wasn't the point.

"I will also require a full account, in much more detail than you've so far provided, why you require this overdraft facility," said Harkness.

"For which there is a special form?" anticipated Charlie.

"It's A/23/W98," confirmed Harkness.

"Thanks," said Charlie.

"And there's still the expenses situation, with which this could be connected," said Harkness.

No stone left unturned, thought Charlie. He said, "I'll try to complete the form this afternoon."

"I will need it for the Review Committee," began Harkness when the red internal telephone rang, the man's direct link to the Director.

"Where the hell's Muffin!" demanded Wilson.

"With me," said Harkness.

"Something's come up," announced Wilson. "Get him here."

When Harkness relayed the order, Charlie said, "Do you want me to go right away or should I fill in the form first?"

"Get out!" yelled Harkness, finally losing control.

Not bad, decided Charlie, making his way to the upper floor. In fact, quite good. He wondered how Harkness was considering the outcome. And not just now. Later.

Berenkov drafted a total of twelve Russians to form the protective screen around the Bern embassy. Six came in, all separately, by air; the rest entered Switzerland, again separately, by road and rail. Four were seconded within the legation itself but the remainder were split into two-man cells, each to monitor and watch independently.

None of the groups were told the reason for their surveillance, of course, and one ironically established itself only two streets away from the Wyttenbackstrasse, where Zenin had a room at the back, away from the street, in the Marthahaus.

It took him a day to locate and to rent in the name of Henry Smale a lock-up garage in which to hide the rented Peugeot. During that search—and afterward—he went to great lengths to avoid the Soviet embassy, only wanting to be linked with it once and then briefly. With time to spare he explored the old part of town, Spitalgasse and Marktgasse and Kramgasse and Gerechtigkeitsgasse, actually considering—and then rejecting—the idea of an early trip to the Bernese Oberland. More important to make the reconnaissance back in Geneva, from which he was intentionally distancing himself. The Oberland could wait until later, when there was a real reason. He had wondered how he'd feel, as it got closer, pleased that at the moment there was no nervousness. If there were a sensation at all, it was one of anticipation, eager anticipation.

10

Charlie chose a Mercedes again, just for the hell of it, disappointed the buildup of early rush hour traffic on the M-4 made it difficult to drive as fast as he had on his way down to Sussex. And then there had been less need for speed than there was now.

Charlie was too old and too wise to become excited ahead of time, but according to the Director, the sightings at London airport were practically positive. And not just one. Two. Trying to balance the hope, Charlie wondered how two different people were able to be anywhere near positive on the basis of such an indistinct photograph. Whatever, he thought, don't knock it; check it. The first indicator looked promising, at least. It was Terminal Two from which, with the exception of British Airways, all flights from Heathrow departed for Europe.

He sought out a parking spot near a protective pillar and used the elevated walkway to get into the building, knowing from past experience that the security offices were at the far end, beyond the banks. On Sir Alistair Wilson's instructions, the two men were waiting for Charlie in a private, inner room, where the only lighting came from a neon strip. It was a box joined to other boxes all around, and Charlie wondered why modern office planners were so stuck on the beehive style of architecture. William Cockson, the Special Branch inspector, was a grey-haired, grey-suited, anonymous sort of man, cautious in movement and manner. Edward Oliver, the immigration official, was much younger, hardly more than twenty-five. He wore a tweed jacket and rigidly pressed trousers and was blinking a lot, as if he were nervous at having committed himself to an opinion.

"This seems to be important, from the reaction," said Cockson at once.

"Maybe," said Charlie. "Maybe not." The identification was vital so it was important not to influence either man into responding as they imagined he wanted them to.

"I was supposed to be off duty an hour ago," said the policeman, someone sadly accustomed to having his private life constantly disrupted.

From his briefcase Charlie took a bigger enlargement of the Primrose Hill picture than that which had been made available for the port and airport surveillance and said, "Look at this again. Take as long as you like. Do you think this was the man?"

It was the more experienced Special Branch officer who looked up first, nodding. "I think so," he said.

Oliver raised his head soon afterward. He said, "I'm pretty sure."

Not as positive as the Director had promised, thought Charlie. He said, "When?"

"The thirteenth," said Cockson, positively.

The day of the pickup, realized Charlie. Worriedly, he said, "What time?"

"In the evening," said the young immigration man.

Johnson had timed the whole episode in Primrose Hill ending by two in the afternoon, remembered Charlie, relieved: more than long enough to get here. Nodding to the enlargement on the desk between them, Charlie said, "It's not a good picture."

"No," agreed Oliver.

"And the departure lounge was crowded?"

"It always is," said the younger man, with growing confidence.

"So how come you think you recognize him, in a crowded departure lounge from a bad photograph?"

Oliver looked sideways, deferring to the older man. Cockson said, "There was an incident . . . well, hardly an incident. Rather more something that caught the attention of us both. . . ." The policeman hesitated, imagining a further explanation was necessary. "I was on duty at Eddie's desk that evening. Right beside him. There was this girl, pretty kid, and obviously pregnant. My first thought was that she shouldn't have been traveling at all, not that far gone. There's supposed to be a time limit in pregnancy, beyond which airlines won't accept you for travel, you know?"

"I know," encouraged Charlie. "So what happened?"

"She was practically up to my desk, just one person away, when she fainted," picked up Oliver. "Went down like a log."

"So?" pressed Charlie, doubtfully.

"He walked away," said Cockson. "This man. I was looking at her, like I said. But I was aware of a someone directly behind. And when she started to sway, obviously going down, he switched lanes to another desk. If he'd caught her, as he easily could have done, she wouldn't have gone down so heavily. She started to hemorrhage, you know. Had to be taken to Middlesex Hospital, and there's still a chance she might lose the baby."

"I saw it, too," endorsed Oliver. "I thought, rude bugger, and as I thought it, Bill said it, right in my ear."

It was the avoidance of someone trained against getting caught up in the slightest sort of attention-attracting event, Charlie recognized. But also something that a lot of untrained people might have done, not wanting to get involved either. Wrong to overinterpret. He said, "You were really looking at the girl, though?"

"Yes," said Cockson, cautiously.

"And went to help her?"

"Of course," said Oliver.

"So you only had the briefest look at the man?"

"No," refused Cockson, positively. "She was obviously in a bad way, needing to lie there and not get up. When I was kneeling beside her, I looked up at the bastard, intending to say something. That's when I saw the other funny thing."

"What other funny thing?" said Charlie, patiently.

"He wasn't looking," said the policeman. "A pregnant woman falls down right in front of him, he walks away, and then when she's lying there, he doesn't even look. That wasn't right, not natural. Everyone else was looking, a lot seeing what they could do. Too many, actually. But he was staring straight ahead"—he gestured down to the photograph again—"rather like he is there, really. That side of his face, certainly."

"Did you say anything?"

"No," admitted Cockson. "The girl was the important person to worry about. She needed comforting. There wasn't any point in starting an unnecessary argument and distressing her further."

"So how long were you looking directly at him?"

"Maybe a minute," said Cockson.

To the immigration man, Charlie said, "What about you?"

"I was looking directly at him, too," said Oliver. "I couldn't get over what he'd done. Or rather, not done."

"But you didn't check him through? See the passport?" said Charlie, resigned.

"It was British," announced Oliver.

"British!" exclaimed Charlie. "How do you know?"

"That's my job, looking at passports," reminded the younger man. "He was holding it in his hand, ready to present it, so I could not avoid seeing it. And it was definitely British. I remember thinking about it. There are some people I could imagine walking away from the girl like he did, but not an Englishman."

Harkness and Witherspoon would have appreciated a remark like that, thought Charlie. He hoped to Christ the neighboring immigration official who had actually checked the man through was on duty. To Cockson he said, "You're a trained observer. Describe him to me."

The policeman hesitated and then said, "Average height, five feet ten or five feet eleven. Well built although not heavy, fit looking. Very dark hair and quite dark skinned, too."

"I remember that, as well," came in Oliver. "The skin coloring, I mean, against the British passport. Not that it means anything these days. But there was also something about the way he held himself."

"Held himself?"

"I work out a bit," said the immigration man. "Try to stay in shape. That was my immediate impression about this man: that he held himself and walked like someone who likes to keep in shape. And he does, from the photograph, doesn't he?"

"Impression formulated at the moment?" pressed Charlie, cautiously. "Or impression after you'd been shown the photograph?"

"Then," said Oliver, at once. "The bastard could have held her up with one hand if he'd wanted to."

"What time did it all happen?" asked Charlie.

"Seven," said Cockson.

"Definitely," confirmed the younger man.

"Why so certain?" demanded Charlie.

"We both came on duty at six," said the policeman. "And because I knew there would later have to be a report, by the airport police, I made a point of checking the time. It was definitely seven."

"How was he dressed?" asked Charlie, wanting to build up the description.

"Grey suit," said Cockson. "Black shoes. A colored shirt, blue, I think. I know it wasn't white. Can't remember what sort of tie it was."

"Was the suit patterned grey, check maybe, or plain grey?"

"I can't say," admitted the policeman, and Oliver shook his head, unable to go further either.

"Topcoat or mackintosh?"

"Not that I can remember," said Oliver.

"Or me," said Cockson.

"Hat?"

"No," said Cockson. The immigration official shook his head again.

"Was he carrying anything? A briefcase or a travel bag perhaps?"

"Again, not that I can recall," said Cockson.

"Or me," said the younger man.

"Newspapers or a magazine?"

Both men shook their heads this time.

"Umbrella?"

"You're trying damned hard, aren't you?" said Cockson.

"I get awarded points," said Charlie. "So was there an umbrella?"

"No," said the policeman.

"No," said the immigration man.

"Is there anything, anything at all, that you can remember about him that we haven't talked about?" persisted Charlie.

Neither man replied at once, considering the question. Then Oliver said, "I'm afraid not."

Cockson said, "I don't think we've contributed a lot."

"You've been very helpful, both of you," assured Charlie. "I'm grateful."

"What's he done?" asked Cockson.

"Nothing yet, I don't think," said Charlie. "It's what he might do."

Charlie imagined, wrongly, that he was fortunate in the other immigration man being on duty. His name was Jones. He was a balding, pot-bellied man, and within minutes of their meeting beginning, Charlie guessed correctly that Jones was counting off the days to his retirement. Jones vaguely remembered the girl collapsing although he didn't recall the date being the thirteenth or what time it was in the evening. Enough people seemed to be helping, so he'd left it to them. He shook his head at the offered picture and, when Charlie asked about the passport, demanded in return if Charlie had any idea how many British passports he examined every day. Charlie patiently recounted the physical description, adding the street clothes this time, and Jones said, "That could be anyone of a thousand men," and Charlie agreed that it could.

The contact with the Director was on an open, insecure line so the conversation had to be circumspect.

"Positive?" demanded Wilson.

"Not positive but enough to pursue."

"Know where to go?"

"No."

"Can you find out?"

"It's going to be a long job."

"Need help?"

Charlie considered the question, thinking again about relying on others and the danger of banana peels. He said, "Probably some impressive government-sounding pressure later, but at the moment I'd like to try it by myself."

"Run it your way," said Wilson supportively.

"I'm going to book into an airport hotel."

"I don't give a damn about the cost."

Charlie hoped Harkness had been in the room to hear the remark. It would ruin the deputy's day. Cautiously Charlie said, "Let's keep the other checks in place."

"They are," assured Wilson.

Charlie worked upon the assumption that the dark-skinned man would have moved with the professional expertise he had shown in Primrose Park. Which meant 7 P.M. on the thirteenth would have been a comfortable arrival for whatever flight he was catching but not too early, because tradecraft training on both sides is that a loitering person attracts attention. And a professional would not have taken that risk, even in a crowd-concealing situation like an airport departure lounge. Charlie decided three hours was the absolute maximum. Ten o'clock then. Still a haystack but at least it had a shape. He hoped.

It was a hope that faltered almost at once. Charlie realized he'd embarked upon a practically impossible task, trying alone to work out what he wanted by studying the ABC flight guide. So he sought guidance from the deputy duty officer in the control tower, confident the man's specialized knowledge would avoid banana peels. When Charlie explained what he wanted, the man shook his head in bewilderment, complaining that it would take forever but Charlie said it wouldn't, because he was concentrating only on seven European destinations. It was still very late when together they produced the final list.

Between seven and ten o'clock on the night of the thirteenth, four aircraft departed London Heathrow for Vienna, five for Paris, two for Geneva, one for Brussels, three for Madrid, two for Berlin—via Frankfurt, of course, where he could have disembarked and rerouted to any of the target cities—and three to Rome, with one internal connection to Venice.

"I wish you luck, whatever you're trying to do," said the man, when they finished.

Charlie booked into the Ariel Hotel, eased his protesting feet from his Hush Puppies and ordered turkey sandwiches and a bottle of whisky from room service, the Director's remark about expenses still clear in his mind. Eighteen aircraft, he thought. How many people made up a cabin crew? Depended on the aircraft, he supposed, but he decided to calculate using an average of ten. Which gave a maximum of a hundred and eighty people to question, if the inquiry went its full length. Like the control tower official had said, he needed luck. A lot of it.

11

President Clayton Anderson reckoned he was on stream to reverse a trend and it was about goddamned time, after Watergate and Irangate and every Cabinet member and his brother from all those previous goddamned administrations feathering their nests against their inevitable end-of-term retirement. He guessed those goddamned Ivy League eastern newspapers had tried hard enough—knew they'd tried hard, from some of their half-assed inquiries—but they hadn't come within a mile of getting an armlock on Clayton Lucius Anderson. Throughout the first four years of his presidency until now, halfway through the second term, there hadn't been a whiff of scandal anywhere, everyone who mattered keeping their trouser fly properly zipped and up front in church on Sundays, reassuring all those good folks out there in heartland America that Washington, D.C. was at last in safe hands.

He'd achieved a hell of a lot to reassure those good folks. In the first term he'd sat on inflation tighter than a man on a hog-tied calf and rallied the domestic economy with the right sort of fiscal policy that gave the farmers and domestic industry the protectionist edge they'd been demanding. Only right that domestically the polls should show him the most popular White House incumbent since Truman. So now it was time to go for the big one, the coup that was going to take him from office, remembered not just as honest Johnny Appleseed but as the international statesman who solved an insolvable problem and brought to the Middle East the peace that had defeated every world leader and every government since the creation of Israel. The International Room was already prepared at the memorial library in Austin—bigger and better than Lyndon Johnson's—and this was going to be its focal point. Which was why there couldn't be any screwup.

"Quite sure?" he demanded.

"Nothing's been overlooked, Mr. President." James Bell, the Secretary of State, replied respectfully, although the two men were old friends from Congress days. Bell's appointment had been his reward not only for successfully masterminding Anderson's election the first time but also for retaining those congressional links and associations, minimizing over the past six years any conflict between Capitol Hill and the White House.

"It's got to be more than just getting them around the same table," insisted the President, unnecessarily. "There's got to be some hard, concrete proposal at the end of it. A homeland."

"We've worked on it for a year, six months before anything leaked publicly," reminded Bell. "Jordan wants it, and Syria wants it, and Egypt wants it, and Arafat wants it, and the very fact that Israel is finally prepared to come face-to-face is proof that they want it, too."

Anderson, who was a hard-boned, heavy-featured, angular man, swung his chair around from the Oval Office desk, so that he could look out over the gardens and the Washington Monument beyond. He said, "So what about Moscow?"

"I personally sounded them out during the visit in July," reported the Secretary of State. "There wasn't any doubt. They want it settled as much as everyone else. It's gone on too long, like a running sore."

"You think we can trust them?" Anderson had a Texan's suspicion of anything communist, which had made the international gatherings during his presidency difficult. He didn't even like the color red.

"The Middle East has been draining the Soviets dry for years. Now their reforms mean they've got to divert money away from the military and military aid and into their domestic economy," said Bell. He was a shiny-cheeked, roly-poly man who didn't intend returning to his New York law practice when Anderson's term was over. He was as aware as the President how successful the administration had been, and he was already receiving approaches from businesses wanting the respect and prestige of his name on their boards. There was also the television approach and that appealed to him. Nothing tacky, of course. The sort of advisory capacity, commenting upon momentous world events, that Kissinger had. And there was the book, of course. And the lecture circuit, like Kissinger again. Bell was calculating two million dollars at least, when it all came together. It meant they could go on living in Georgetown, and he knew Martha would like that. She enjoyed Washington: the impression of being at the center of things. He'd already decided to take her to Geneva.

"I mean this to work, Jim."

"So do I, Mr. President."

"So what's our security cover?"

"I've given the CIA Director a personal briefing. Every station in every involved country is on maximum alert, for anything that might sound a bell," reported the Secretary of State.

"And Geneva itself?"

"Quite separate from the normal Secret Service cover, the CIA is sending a team of ten," said Bell. "The supervisor is a man named Giles, Roger Giles. He's their Middle East expert. Served as station chief in Amman and Cairo. Brought back to Langley two years ago to head the desk there. First-class guy."

It was unfortunate the country didn't still erect monuments to their presidents like that obelisk out there beyond the White House lawn, thought Anderson, swiveling back to face the room. He said, "You know what's a pity?"

"What?"

"That after all the work I've put into this—a whole goddamned year of background pressure and give-and-take diplomacy—that the public signings and agreements are going to be between the Arabs and Israel and the Palestinians," complained the President. "I should have been there, to be seen as the architect."

"You'll be acknowledged as such," assured the Secretary of State.

Would it be possible for him to be nominated for the Nobel Peace prize? wondered Anderson. Kissinger had shared it at the end of the Vietnam war. But with Le Duc Tho, not Nixon. He'd have to have the archives check the protocol for him: a scroll like that would look damned good as the centerpiece in Austin. Anderson said, "This is the milestone, Jim. This is the big one we're all going to be remembered by."

"That's how I see it, too, Mr. President," said the other man. Both of us remembered, he thought.

David Levy left the Foreign Minister's office inconspicuously through the side door, merging easily into the throng of people in the outside corridors of the Knesset, letting their flow carry him past the Chagall murals toward the exit.

In the forecourt outside, protected against terrorist outrage by the decorative metal fence, he hesitated in the pale sunlight, gazing out over the Jerusalem hills and the valley from which the cross of Christ was supposed to have been cut. How much blood had been shed over this land in the two thousand years since then, he thought. It seemed difficult to imagine that it would ever stop. Or that Geneva could be the final way.

Levy was a *sabra*, a Jew born in Israel without any real way of knowing what the Holocaust had truly been like, but his father had experienced it and told him how it was to exist in the Warsaw sewers, to be hunted like the rats they replaced, denied any proper home, any proper life. The old man had come to Palestine a fervent Zionist, one of Begin's first lieutenants in the *Irgun Zvai Lume* service that fought against the British in 1947 and from which the Israeli external intelligence service, the Mossad, eventually grew. It had seemed natural that Levy should follow his father. Frequently he wished the old man had lived, to see how high he had risen in the organization. Levy knew his father would have been very proud. And particularly today, although Levy supposed security would have precluded his telling the

old man. Levy had already been notified, of course, that he
would be heading the Mossad contingent to the Geneva conference. But he had not expected the Foreign Minister's appointment that put him in additional command of the
group from Shin Bet, Israel's counterintelligence organization.

But then, he reflected further, there had been a lot
about Mordechai Cohen's briefing that he had not expected.

"It's an intolerable demand!" protested Harkness. "The
Foreign Office will be furious."

"They are," confirmed Wilson, mildly. The Director was
conscious of his deputy's antipathy toward Charlie Muffin
and hoped it would not cloud Harkness's judgment about
the man's professional abilities. Someone had to clear
blocked drains and Charlie was good at it.

"What explanation can we give for demanding, through
the Foreign Ministries of seven countries, that the crew of
eighteen of their national aircraft be located wherever they
are in the world and made specifically available, as soon as
possible?"

"Drugs," said Wilson. "It was Charlie's idea. Brilliant,
isn't it? We're supposedly on the trail of a major international drug syndicate. Hundreds of millions; all that stuff.
Seem to hear about nothing else these days; makes it perfectly acceptable."

"And what if it all ends in nothing, after causing so
much trouble?" complained the deputy.

"Why don't you try to come up with an idea?" suggested
Wilson, briefly letting his irritation show.

Harkness blinked, but said nothing.

12

Vasili Zenin enjoyed the return drive to Geneva. He left
Bern with sufficient time to reach Lausanne by lunchtime,
choosing the Voile d'Or for its magnificent view of the lake
and ate trout which the menu claimed to have been caught
there. He followed the north shore of the Leman and got to
Geneva by early afternoon. Although it meant a long walk,
Zenin left the car in the park at the Cornavin railway station and walked to the Palais des Nations. It was unlikely
the vehicle would have been distinguished from any of the
hundreds of others, but he did not intend taking the risk,
and anyway, he wanted to time out, on foot, the escape
routes that had been devised at Kuchino. He paced the most
direct suggestion the first time, along the Rue de Montbrilliant and then the more circuitous roads, the Rue de Vermont and after that the Avenue Giuseppe Motta. The
schedule provided by the Bern embassy was wrong in every
case: the estimate for the Rue de Vermont, before it connected with the Vidollet, was at variance by at least fifteen
minutes and on the Giuseppe Motta, until it reached the
Rue de Servette, was off by twenty minutes.

Zenin allowed the anger this time, letting it burn
through him, determined there would be punishment when
he returned to Moscow. Of course the embassy *rezidentura*
had not been given any reason for providing the information
and obviously the stupid bastards had not taken it seriously,
dismissing it as some sort of nonsense request from Dzerzhinsky Square. And failed in one of the most vital segments
of the operation because if this section was mistimed by as
much as a minute—a few seconds even—he would be
trapped within the cordon the Swiss would throw around
the area. Bastards, he thought. Stupid, idiotic bastards!

Zenin repeated all three routes twice more, to provide an average, and on the last occasion, when he got back to the railway station, he stood for several moments looking speculatively at the baroque complex. The Kuchino planning had been for him to get away from Geneva by car, but from the reconnaissance of the immediate area he had already recognized how easy it was for the roads to become accidentally blocked, beyond the danger of official barriers. Which was further advice the embassy had failed to provide. And which was something against which he could take no precautions. So what about a train? The woman would have a detailed timetable of the conference: that was a prime although not the main reason for her involvement. So he would be able to estimate a convenient train, even buy a ticket in advance so there would be no delay. A much better proposal, the Russian thought, warming to the idea. Roads were easily closed, but the trains would not be stopped. And he could even insure against being detained in the unlikely event of that happening. There was no necessity, after all, for him to catch an international express beyond the Swiss border. All he needed was one of the local services, to get him out of the immediate area. Carouge, perhaps. Or Annemasse. Certainly no further than Thonon.

Zenin went into the concourse and found the information section, patiently joining the line. When he reached the clerk, he obtained timetables for local, internal express, and international services, as always providing himself with as wide a choice as possible.

Outside again, Zenin followed the Giuseppe Motta route, because it brought him more immediately close to the building from which he was going to have to shoot.

It was a necessarily high building, in a street just off the Colombettes road, an apparent combination of offices and apartments. Zenin knew the rooms that had been rented for the past two months were on the top floor of the northeast corner, providing a supposedly uninterrupted view from two separate windows of the grassed area where the commemorative photographs of the delegates were customarily taken. Having found fault with so much else in the local information, Zenin accepted he would have to verify that but decided against doing it today. His connection with the apartment had to be restricted to the absolute minimum, so that particular but essential confirmation would have to wait until he installed the weapon. It would also be necessary to assess properly how long it would take him to get out of the flat and descend twenty stories onto the street. The embassy gave an estimate of seven minutes, but Zenin was contemptuous now of all their timings.

Once back on to the Colombettes road, he walked up to the multilane Ferney highway, nodding appreciatively at the noise, recognizing at once and with professional awareness that the traffic roar would mask completely the muted sound of the shots and certainly make any directional fix practically impossible. Just as quickly Zenin saw an additional advantage. Vehicles flooded by in an unbroken stream: it was virtually inevitable that any security sweep, no matter how well-rehearsed and coordinated, would become snarled up in it.

Zenin went in the direction of the Palais des Nations, turning frequently to focus upon the building he would be using, easily able to isolate the corner windows through which he would be firing. He stood sideways, moving his head from the high apartment to the international area and then back up again, trying with trained marksman's expertise to visualize the trajectory. It was very difficult, as low as he was, but it appeared to be unimpeded, although there were some avenues of decorative trees about which he was unsure. They would have to remain another uncertainty that could only be resolved when he actually got into the apartment.

Zenin returned finally to the Cornavin station, more than satisfied with the visit. The next time would be to meet the girl, he reflected, as he took the Peugeot out on to the Bern road. He had the photographs, of course, because identification was essential, but he wondered again what she would be like. The pictures showed her to be very attractive. It might be an interesting diversion for their encounter to be anything but sterile.

Three of the aircraft had been short-haul airbuses, with a smaller cabin crew, so Charlie's estimate of a hundred and eighty was reduced, but not by much.

He managed to interview nine the following day, four from the Al Italia plane and five from the Austrian airline flight to Vienna. There was not even a hesitant recognition from any of them.

That night, at the hotel, Charlie sat with his diminishing whisky bottle beside him, hunched with all his information spread out on reminder sheets around his stockinged feet, the blurred print forming the centerpiece. Directly alongside was the list of European political events, the first only nine days away.

Charlie looked back to the picture and said, "Where the fuck are you, whoever you are!"

13

By the end of the third day Charlie Muffin had unsuccessfully interviewed thirty-two members of the cabin staff of six different airlines. He was also well into the second bottle of room-service whisky, and discovered the Mercedes scratched in the hotel garage. He was under increasing pressure from Sir Alistair Wilson to accept more people to conduct the hopeful photo-identification sessions, which was unnecessary because the delay in locating and bringing to England the stewards and stewardesses who had left London during those vital three hours meant there were long periods each day when there was no one even for Charlie to interrogate. And he thought the food at the airport was absolutely bloody awful. By the second day he'd had diarrhea. That night, not bothering with dinner because of the stomach upset, which he was treating with the remains of the second bottle, Charlie accepted he'd soon have to submit to the Director's insistence, pointless though it might be. He'd been in similar, cul-de-sac situations a dozen times before, and the headquarters reaction was always the same, a determination to create movement in the belief that the direction would automatically be forward. He guessed it made them feel better. He wished he did.

The demands to the European embassies had fortunately not produced any further political events, which would have meant widening the search and made it more difficult than it already was. So far the watchers had not come up with anything new. Charlie almost wished they would. He had been truthful putting this possibility no higher than fifty percent during the meeting with the Director but was by now more conscious of the upheaval his interview demands were causing than he had been at the beginning. There would be no necessity for an explanation or apology to any of the airlines if the whole thing ended as unproductively as it had so far proved to be, but Charlie knew that behind the undesignated doors of Whitehall and within the department his balls would be used for squash practice and not just for the game, either. Once—just once—it would have been nice to stand under a shower without knowing it was someone pulling the flush over his head.

And then the following morning the first person he interviewed was a senior Swissair stewardess named Eva Becker. She studied the Primrose Hill photograph with Teutonic intentness, looked up at him serious-faced, and said, "Yes."

"Yes, what?" asked Charlie cautiously.

"I think I have seen this man."

"On the thirteenth?"

"Yes," said the stewardess. "It was Flight 837."

He knew all the answers already, but it was important that everything came from her without any prompting or assumption from him. He said, "What time?"

"Twenty hundred."

One hour after the immigration episode: the timing could not be more precisely right. Charlie said, "Where does that flight go?"

"Geneva," she said.

"And then?"

"Nowhere," she said. "It terminates there."

"Why do you think it was him?"

"I thought he was rude," said the woman.

"Rude?"

"He refused any drinks. Or the food snack," she said. "When I offered again—it's customary to do so—he said he'd already told me he didn't want anything and hadn't I heard him. It was very impolite. Wilfred thought so too."

"Wilfred?"

The woman nodded behind her, and through the glass of the fishbowl office, Charlie saw a man in a Swissair uniform, waiting to follow her. She said, "We were flying together that evening. Like we are today."

The steward's full name was Wilfred Stemi. Charlie was careful to insure there was no conversation whatsoever between them when they exchanged places, from which she might have alerted the man, and Stemi identified the photograph as positively as she had done and for the same reasons. And with an acceptably minimal degree of difference from that assembled by the professional analysts he provided a satisfactory physical description of the man, just as she had done.

It had been a packed flight, without one vacant seat, and when Charlie retrieved the manifest from the Swissair passenger computer, he counted sixty English-type names likely to be traveling on British passports. There were three Smiths.

Charlie decided it was a waste of time to drive all the way into London for a secure conversation with the Director, only to have to drive back out again, so he used the open line once more, admiring the quickness with which Wilson acknowledged the guarded conversation. Charlie said he needed hurriedly to go to Geneva and asked for a replacement to carry out the job interviews, determined the photograph should go on being checked by the other aircrews from the other airlines in case this sighting was a mistake, like that in Primrose Hill could still be a mistake. He would, he said, be leaving behind a list of people whose references he wanted officially checked. Wilson said he wasn't quite sure what that meant, and Charlie said he would be when he saw the list.

"You want the Swiss firm advised of your arrival?" asked the Director.

"Definitely," said Charlie, at once. This wasn't a one-man operation, although that was normally the way he liked to work. If Geneva was the right location, it meant he had more time because neither the arms limitation session nor the Middle East conference began until the end of November, but he still needed all the help he could get from as many branches of Swiss intelligence that there were. The haystack was still about as big as Mont Blanc.

"Looking forward to a productive trip?"

"Still not considering anything more than a fifty percent return," warned Charlie guardedly.

"Anything else we can do from this end?"

"There's the hotel bill to settle."

"I'll see it's done."

"And a Mercedes to collect from the car park there."

"I'll tell the Pool."

Charlie wondered about mentioning the scratch and then decided it could be Harkness's ulcer irritant for that day.

He reached Geneva's Cointrin airport by midafternoon and made himself immediately known to the security colonel there. The man checked, as Charlie suggested, with the central intelligence unit in Bern, who confirmed his arrival that had already been signaled from London, and together they questioned the four immigration officers who had been on duty on the night of the thirteenth. One man said he thought the face in the photograph looked familiar but admitted when pressed that he could not swear to it. Hopefully, Charlie toured all the car rental desks at the airport but there was no recognition from any of them.

The colonel suggested the Beau-Rivage because it was the best hotel and Charlie, who hadn't been to Geneva before, accepted the choice. The man insisted upon driving him into the city. As they drew up outside the hotel on the Quai du Mont-Blanc, the colonel, who had not been given a reason for the order to assist Charlie in everything, said, "This man likely to cause us a lot of trouble?"

"If he's who I think he is, more trouble than you'd believe," said Charlie.

Thirty minutes later, Charlie stood at the window of his lakefront room, never to know that four days earlier Vasili Nikolaevich Zenin had enjoyed the same view from the hotel's restaurant and later strolled into the town along the quai that Charlie could see below.

Charlie turned back into the room, gazing down at the picture which was becoming bent and cracked with use. "Got something else on you," he said. "You're a rude bugger.

Silly mistake to have made, sunshine, silly mistake to have made. But thank Christ you did."

And then he remembered his own mistake and thought, Shit! He'd forgotten to ask those restaurants that knew him to agree those phony receipts were theirs when Harkness's men came around, as Charlie knew they would.

Roger Giles was grateful the marriage appeared to be ending amicably because he'd never been able to understand how people who had once loved could end up hating. And he and Barbara had loved each other once: gone as far as to talk about how sad it was that other people got divorced, never imagining it could happen to them. He still found it difficult to realize that it was happening. Or why.

It had been Barbara's suggestion they stop sleeping together, although sex had not been the problem between them. Barbara stood in the doorway of his bedroom at the Alexandria house, watching him pack.

"Any idea when you'll be back?" Like the wives of all intelligence operatives, she never talked in specifics, like she never referred openly to his being a member of the CIA or blamed the Agency for what had collapsed between them, although she considered his commitment to the Agency the reason.

"November 30," he said. "Definitely no later than December 1."

"Unusual to be so definite."

"Positive dates this time."

"I can go ahead with lawyers' appointments then?"

Giles hesitated and then said, "Sure."

"If I need to arrange anything on your behalf, can I do that too?"

"Certainly," said Giles, quicker this time. "I've settled all the bills and there's almost a thousand dollars in the checking account. Draw whatever you want."

"Thanks," said Barbara. They were going to miss each other an awful lot, she knew. Somehow it all seemed so unnecessary, like the nonsense over the bedrooms. She could not think now why she had insisted upon it.

14

Charlie met the head of Swiss counterintelligence in a tall windowed, polish-smelling office on the corner of Spitalgasse, in the cuckoo-clock part of Bern. It was a safe house away from the headquarters of the service, and Charlie admired the caution. But then, he thought, caution was a Swiss characteristic. The man's name was Rene Blom, and although he apparently had the rank of brigadier, he wore civilian clothes, a grey suit with a waistcoat that appeared tight, like a corset. Blom was a stiff, reserved man, with an unusual and almost unsettling appearance. His hair and eyebrows were completely white but naturally, not through age. Charlie guessed the man to be no more than forty years old. A pink face contributed to the impression of albino but his eyes, behind square-lensed, rimless glasses, were sharply blue.

"London marked the advisory cable highest priority," said Blom. And should have sent a senior official, he thought, offended.

"I think it is," said Charlie. He recounted the story chronologically, from the moment of Novikov's defection, going into detail about the debriefing and his assumptions from it and offering the photograph to Blom when he reached the part about the drop in Primrose Hill. Blom glanced at it, very briefly. When Charlie got to the Swissair identification at London airport, Blom asked for the names of the airline staff, noting them on a pad in front of him. There was already a notation, and Charlie wondered if it was the name of the immigration official who'd made the uncertain recognition at the airport the previous night. It would be basic tradecraft for the security chief to make what independent checks were possible of his own.

After Charlie finished, Blom sat without any response for several moments, tapping his teeth with the thin silver pencil with which he had taken his brief notes. At last he said, "Which do you think? The Middle East conference or the disarmament talks?"

"I don't have a clue," said Charlie.

Blom picked on the word. "Clues seem to be in short supply," he said. The other man's appearance, as well as inferior rank, was also offensive.

"We've got more now than we had a few days ago," said Charlie defensively. What the fuck else did the awkward sod expect, with what he'd had to work from? Miracles cost extra.

"The Middle East conference starts first," reminded Blom.

"So we've got just over two weeks," said Charlie.

"For what?"

Charlie frowned, surprised by the question. "To stop it happening, of course."

Blom nodded reflectively. He said, "Switzerland enjoys its reputation of neutrality."

And that of being the world's money box, thought Charlie; Harkness would be at home here. Unsure of the direction of the conversation, Charlie said, "I would imagine it does."

"So nothing can be allowed to endanger that neutrality."

"No," said Charlie, still cautious.

"The sort of episode you're suggesting could do just that."

Snow-head appeared very fond of stating the obvious, thought Charlie. He said, "Which is why my service gave you the warning they did, within an hour of the identification. And why I am here."

He would not be lectured by this peculiar man, thought Blom. He said, "We have already expressed our gratitude."

Charlie did not get the impression he was making much headway. He said, "There's a simple way of avoiding the problem arising."

"How?"

Charlie gestured toward the photograph. "Publish it," he suggested. "Issue prints to all the newspapers, with a story saying he's a terrorist you're hunting. Once the Soviets know we're on to them, they'll scrap the whole thing. They won't have any alternative."

For several moments Blom stared across the desk at him, wide-eyed. Then he said, obviously incredulous, "Are you serious?"

"Quite serious," said Charlie.

"Announce to the world that there's a terrorist somewhere loose in Switzerland?"

"There is, isn't there? It's as good a word as any to describe him."

"But is there?" came back the brigadier. "You've got the word of a defector, okay. But what proof—positive, unquestionable proof—have you got that this is a photograph of the man?"

"What if I'm wrong?" asked Charlie. "It still doesn't matter. We photographed him making a pickup from a Soviet drop, so he's got dirty hands. Let's use him: publish his picture whether it's the right man or not. The purpose, surely, is to stop a killing taking place on Swiss soil!"

"But what if you are wrong? What if the killing isn't going to be in Switzerland at all!" argued Blom. "You've admitted yourself there are other possible international gatherings in six European cities. Publishing the photograph here would not cause the Russians to cancel if it were in one of those other countries."

This man wasn't an intelligence expert, thought Charlie, dismayed. Brigadier Rene Blom was a politician in make-believe land. Forcing the patience, Charlie said, "I accept that you don't want to focus this sort of spotlight on Switzerland unnecessarily. But what sort of spotlight will be focused if there *is* an assassination here—an assassination we haven't been able to stop?"

Blom shifted uncomfortably. "Do you imagine I haven't been considering that from the beginning of this conversation?"

"I don't think you are considering it enough," said Charlie. Damn the impertinence.

"I think you should remember your position!" said Blom.

"I'm trying to avoid someone getting killed!" fought back Charlie. What the hell was wrong with the man!

"I concede there are grounds for some investigation," said the security chief.

A breakthrough! thought Charlie. As politely as possible, he said, "So what do you propose, sir?"

"I regard this as so important that I need to discuss it with others," announced Blom.

Buck-passer, thought Charlie, disgusted. The prat was at about the level to give out parking tickets and impose penalties for not having a dog license, but when it came to an initiative on something important, it had to be dumped onto some higher authority so the shit wouldn't be on his shoes if anything went wrong. Resigned, Charlie said, "I think it would be a mistake to allow any delay."

"So do I," agreed Blom.

Determined to remain part of it, Charlie exaggerated and said, "There will doubtless be more from Novikov."

"I would expect you to be involved throughout," accepted the counterintelligence chief.

Blom was the sort of man who would cheat on that undertaking if it suited him, recognized Charlie. But then so was he. Charlie said, "I am staying at the Beau-Rivage in Geneva."

"That is a very good hotel."

Soon the man would be recommending the best half-day tours and whether or not to take a packed lunch, thought Charlie, exasperated. He said, "When do you imagine we will be able to talk again?"

"How about tomorrow? Say ten?"

At least Blom was concerned enough to demand immediate access to whomever he was going to shift the responsibility, Charlie decided. He said, "I'll be ready, at ten." And hope to Christ you will be too, he thought.

Charlie wanted physically to shed his irritation at

Blom's attitude so he set out to walk to Thunstrasse, accepting the mistake by the time he crossed the Kirchenfeld bridge and his feet started demanding to know what the hell was going on. He found a bench, just beyond, and sat down to apologize, loosening his laces for a moment. Charlie Muffin was a man of hunches, of feelings in his water, and his instincts told him that as circumstantial as the facts were so far, the unknown jogger with the body of Mr. Atlas was definitely the man he was seeking. It felt right: the way things felt, like hunches, was something else which influenced Charlie. So how was he going to follow his hunches and his feelings? By doing nothing until ten o'clock tomorrow morning, he accepted, frustrating though it might be to sit around with his finger up his bum. It would be wrong—and worse, possibly counterproductive—to start working independently and risk antagonizing the Swiss service before he'd allowed Blom the opportunity to show whether or not the cooperation would be as the man promised. And what was he going to do if the promised cooperation was not forthcoming? At the moment Charlie didn't have an answer, but he was sure he would have if Blom started to jerk him around.

Charlie retied the Hush Puppies looser than before, but he was still walking with difficulty by the time he reached the British embassy, where his acceptance and accreditation were already waiting, authorized by a Director's cable from London. Charlie was immediately given access to a secure telephone in the Ambassador's cipher room and connected without any delay to Wilson in London. The scrambler at both ends gave a vaguely disconcerting electronic echo, like shouting into an empty tin can.

"How's it look?" demanded Wilson, at once.

"Reluctant," said Charlie.

"Explain that."

Charlie did and the Director said, "I don't think you could have expected anything different. Some of us have to live with political overlords, you know."

"Blom's nervous."

"So would I be, if I were him," said Wilson. "Remember, we're there by invitation, Charlie. No one-man vigilante stuff."

"The possibility is that it's a British passport, remember?"

"I don't need reminding of the embarrassment potential," insisted the Director. "I'm actually trying to minimize it, by warning you."

Had anyone else said it, he would have been offended, Charlie realized. He said, "Anything further from the air crews?"

"Witherspoon is handling it," disclosed the Director. "He hasn't come up with a thing."

If Witherspoon were involved, there wouldn't be a lot of point in asking in the future, thought Charlie. He wondered who had taken over the debriefing of Novikov and whether he could play chess. Charlie said, "What about the passenger manifest?"

"Too vague," said the Director. "We've been able to trace those who booked through companies or paid by credit card or check. Comes to forty-three of the likely English-sounding people, and every one of them can be verified. The other seventeen are just names on a piece of paper. You don't need addresses or even a true identity to buy a plane ticket, you know."

"I know," said Charlie. "Makes it easy, doesn't it? What about picking up Koretsky? Make out that we know more about Primrose Hill than we do and sweat the bastard?"

"I suggested it to the Joint Intelligence Committee," admitted Wilson. "The word came back that it was politically unacceptable."

"I've always thought killing someone was pretty unacceptable," said Charlie.

"That doesn't look like it's on our patch anymore, does it Charlie? Out of sight, out of mind."

"What about the passport?"

"Deniable, if it ever comes out. It's obviously a forgery or feloniously obtained, isn't it?"

"Has there been a change of heart over this?"

"Let's call it rationalization."

"Blom has promised to include me," reminded Charlie. "What's my response if he doesn't?"

"Come home," ordered Wilson.

"Come home!" Ask a silly question, get a silly answer, Charlie thought. He wasn't going to leave things in limbo like this.

"Like I said, it's not our patch anymore."

"I don't like leaving things half done."

"It's not a question of what you like or don't like," said the Director. "It's a question of following orders."

"Sure," said Charlie.

"I mean it," insisted Wilson. "Positively no one-man vigilante stuff. And that's an order."

Charlie realized he was getting boxed in, with insufficient room to plead misunderstanding. He said, "I recognize my position here. I won't upset anyone."

"I'm determined that you won't," said the Director.

"If you want me I'm staying at the Beau-Rivage," said Charlie.

There was a pause on the other end of the line. "The most expensive hotel in Geneva," acknowledged the Director.

"Very central," tried Charlie.

"Did you know, by the way, that the Mercedes was scratched at London airport?"

"I'm not having a lot of luck with cars, am I?" said Charlie.

"Harkness says there appears to have been a great deal of drinking done, too."

"Necessary hospitality," insisted Charlie. "I was making a lot of demands on the airlines and airport personnel. Considered it a good way of saying thank you."

"According to Harkness, you were very grateful."

"I was," said Charlie. "Very grateful indeed."

"Be careful, Charlie," warned the Director.

"Always," assured Charlie.

The Swiss intelligence committee met in a room in the Bundeshaus, because the federal parliament building was the most convenient for the emergency session. There were five on the committee, two parliamentarians and three permanent civil servants, and it was a civil servant, Klaus Rainer, who acted as chairman, to maintain impartiality. They listened without interruption to Blom's account, and when he finished, Rainer said, "You were quite correct in asking for this meeting."

"Should we publish the picture like the Englishman suggests?" asked Blom.

"Absolutely not!" said the younger of the two MPs, Paul Leland. As well as being a leading hotelier in Geneva, he was also deputy chairman of the national Tourist Board. He said, "Remember how Americans stopped coming to Europe after the last terrorist scare!"

"This might not be a scare," warned Blom, anxious to absolve himself completely from any later problems.

"It goes beyond tourism," said the second MP, Pierre Delon. "As you yourself have so rightly pointed out, Switzerland is a neutral country, the place where other countries that cannot agree with each other consent to meet. Everything possible must be done to preserve that image, to maintain that confidence."

"What then?" asked Blom.

"The most intensive investigation possible," insisted Leland. "But in the utmost secrecy. Nothing must become public."

"Should the Englishman be included?"

"Until it is no longer an advantage for us to cooperate," said Rainer. "The Middle East conference comes first?"

"Yes," confirmed Blom.

"I think it would be wrong to be overly alarmist with the delegations," said the permanent official. "I think America should be consulted; Israel, too. Both have excellent intelligence facilities from which we could benefit. But I do not see any purpose in extending the discussion to any of the other countries. A withdrawal by just one would wreck the conference: undermine just the sort of confidence it is necessary to sustain."

Rainer looked around the small room, to be acknowledged by nods of agreement from every member of the committee.

"It could be a false alarm, of course," said Leland. "A mistake."

"Let's hope it is," said Rainer. "Let's sincerely hope it is."

The U.S. advance party for the conference, including the entire secretariat, landed that night in Geneva, just two hours ahead of the Jewish party on the El-Al flight from Tel Aviv. The television set at the Marthahaus in Bern was in the bar. Vasili Zenin sat in its most shadowed corner, making a small beer last, and watched each arrival.

Both Roger Giles and David Levy were professionally careful against being filmed, although Zenin could not have identified either.

15

It was a safe house again, but in Geneva this time, and much larger, almost half a floor of a black-glass-and-aluminum tower block far away from the lake, on the Rue Saint Victor. The outer offices were occupied, like some sort of buffer to guard the conference suite, which was on the corner of the building with a panoramic view of the city.

Charlie arrived intentionally early, wanting the psychological advantage of being there first with his territory already established. Levy and Giles entered simultaneously, right on time. Levy was a large man, both in height and size, bulge-chested and heavy-bellied. He walked with a strange, shoulder-swinging swagger, as if it were difficult to carry so much weight. His hair was cropped very close to his head. He appeared to wear clothes for necessity, not style: the sleeves of his jacket and the legs of his trousers, behind the knee, were lined with creases. His tie was pulled down from his open collar. He dwarfed the American. Giles was small to the point of almost being petite, an impression heightened by his neatness. His tie was precisely in place, the knot clipped by a pin which secured both edges of his collar and his uncreased suit was buttoned. The red-toned brogues glistened and Charlie was glad it was so late in the year; if there had been any sunlight the reflection would have been dazzling.

The Swiss counterintelligence chief made the introductions, and as he did so, Giles put his head curiously to one side and said, "Charlie Muffin? . . . Weren't you the guy that—"

"Yes," cut off Charlie. It was best to get it out of the way as soon as possible.

"Well I'll be a son of a bitch!" said Giles.

"Do you two know each other?" asked Blom.

"No," said Charlie. "It's something that happened a long time ago." Like Edith's death, he thought. And then Natalia.

"The word was that you were back," said Giles, the surprise still showing.

"Is it something we should know about?" asked Levy. The voice, like the man, was heavy.

Charlie looked inquiringly at Giles, who turned to the other two men and said, "I don't think so. Like he told you, it was something that happened a long time ago." He looked back to Charlie and said, "But I don't understand what you're doing here."

"You will," promised Charlie.

Blom, playing the part of the uncertain host, gestured them to seats around a conference table and summoned someone from the outside offices to provide coffee, which he poured. To Levy and Giles he said awkwardly, confirming his difficulty, "Thank you both for coming."

Levy frowned and said, "Your message said it was important."

Instead of responding, the Swiss counterintelligence chief turned to Charlie and said, "I'd like you to set everything out, as you did for me."

I should have cut a long-playing record, thought Charlie. So familiar was he now with the facts that he was able to concentrate upon the reaction of the two men as he spoke. Almost at once Giles pulled forward in his chair, listening unblinkingly and again there was a contrast. Levy remained pushed back in his chair, almost slumped, occasionally sipping from his coffee cup.

When Charlie finished, the American erupted in a burst of questions, "But Geneva is only a surmise, on your part? Based on the airport identification? Nothing more than that?"

"Nothing more than that," conceded Charlie at once.

"And the surveillance hasn't been relaxed in London?"

"Not at all."

"Who specifically debriefed Novikov on the assassination?" came in Levy.

"I did," said Charlie.

"No doubts?"

"None."

"Without wishing to convey any offense, I'd like Mossad access," said the Israeli.

The man couldn't give a fuck about causing offense, Charlie knew. It was an ideal opportunity to get hold of a Soviet defector, which was always a prize. He said, "I anticipated that you would."

"And I'd like someone from our embassy in London to see him, too," said Giles hurriedly, as if he were afraid of missing out.

"I think he should be made available to my service, as well," completed Blom, wishing he'd been first instead of last.

The line was going to stretch practically to the Sussex border, thought Charlie. He said, "I'll pass on the requests."

"I'd also like the photograph and the full physical description, to run our own check," said Giles, ahead of the Israeli this time.

"Of course," assured Charlie. "I'd like to believe your records will come up with something where ours didn't, because we need the break. But I don't think they will."

"Why not?" said Blom.

"He'll be a first-timer," guessed Charlie. "Squeaky clean."

"That would be the obvious way to operate," agreed Levy.

Conscious from the State Department briefings—two from the Secretary of State himself—of the personal importance that President Anderson was attaching to the conference, the CIA man said to Blom, "I think it's wise to keep this under wraps. We're still guessing, after all."

There speaks another vested interest, thought Charlie. He said, "I'm surprised we're not including any Arab intelligence official in this discussion."

"The Arab delegations are not arriving until the next two or three days," Blom tried to avoid.

"They are going to be briefed then?" pressed Charlie.

"The view of my government is that at this stage the matter should be restricted to just us," admitted Blom reluctantly.

"I think you're taking a hell of a chance," said Charlie.

"You've already expressed your views," reminded Blom. The man was insufferable. He said, "The decision does not directly affect you."

"Low profile in everything at this stage," urged Giles.

"I agree," said Levy, at once.

Too many gaps were being left, thought Charlie. To Blom he said, "We decided upon full cooperation?"

"Yes," agreed the man cautiously.

"So what's happening here, apart from records searches?"

"I've been instructed, obviously, to carry out the most rigid counterintelligence investigation," said Blom. "Which is what I am doing. The Palais des Nations—indeed every part of the international complex—is being thoroughly swept, both visually and electronically against explosives already having been planted. Sniffer dogs are being used as well, of course. All local staff engaged there in the last three months are being questioned and their references and backgrounds reexamined. We can explain that as normal security, considering the importance of the forthcoming conference. Every hotel and auberge is being visited by officers checking registrations after the thirteenth against the photograph. Every rental car firm is being made to run through its computer the names on the manifest of Flight 837: from that we can get a registration number to make road checks." Blom paused, nodding in Charlie's direction. "Here we're maintaining the cover explanation that the British used in gathering the airline staff together: we're pursuing a major drug inquiry."

"Seems comprehensive enough," said Levy.

On superficial examination it did, agreed Charlie. But there remained more holes in that sort of investigation than in a piece of Swiss cheese. It was logical, even without the alarm, for the conference area to be swept because it was standard security practice to do so, which Blom had just admitted. Ridiculous, then, to imagine the Russians would have planted explosives at this stage for obvious discovery. Likewise it was pointless interrogating staff engaged in the last three months when they knew bloody well the man they were hunting had only arrived in the last week. And Charlie considered the rental car search a waste of time. He was prepared to bet the overdraft he didn't have and didn't expect to get that the bastard he wanted had flown into Geneva on a name quite different from that in the British passport on which he'd left London airport and that any other documentation—a driver's license, for instance— would be in a different name, too. The only thing with which he did agree was covering hotels and boarding houses. He wished to Christ that Johnson's picture had been better. Still, he thought, in optimistic balance, at least two people had found it good enough. He supposed they had to hope that the man would have attracted attention to himself by rudeness again.

"I could bring more men in from America to help your people," offered Giles.

"No!" rejected Blom, at once, seeing professional criticism in everything. Appearing to realize his brusqueness, he said more quietly, "No, thank you. This must at all times remain a Swiss inquiry."

"I was offering assistance," emphasized Giles. "I wasn't in any way suggesting that my agency should take over."

Charlie sighed, feeling very much the onlooker. He'd never known a committee operation yet that hadn't been like this, everyone staking claims and guarding their sovereignty, like virgins with their hands over the rude bits. Which was why he always insisted, whenever he could, on working absolutely alone and independently. At least that way the mistakes and oversights were his own, not somebody else's screwup to be landed with.

More diplomatically, Levy said, "Is there anything at all that my service can do to help?"

"Just run the picture and description through your records," said Blom. "That way we get the benefit of three separate services. An unprecedented check, surely?"

"I would have thought so," said Levy.

"It would be far better—and more effective—simply to publish the picture," said Charlie obstinately.

"It would endanger the conference," said Giles, almost as quickly as Blom had earlier rejected the offer of CIA assistance.

The second time the American had come out against going public, Charlie noted. It was a query worth channeling back to Washington. He said, "Someone being killed would also be a hell of a way to ruin the conference. Wouldn't do the victim a lot of good, either. Probably make his eyes water."

"Shouldn't we let your inquiry run its course in England, while we carry out our record searches?" suggested Levy.

"Publishing the picture wouldn't affect that," argued Charlie. "Of course everything should continue. And will continue."

"I think we should defer to the wishes of our host country," came in Giles supportively.

"So do I," agreed Levy.

"I appreciate your understanding," said Blom.

They were like the original models for the three wise monkeys, thought Charlie: hear no evil, see no evil speak no evil because it might be something nasty we don't want to hear, see, or talk about. It didn't make him angry; Charlie's feeling was uneasiness. And not for some poor sod who at the moment risked being dispatched to the great big stripe-trousered bureaucracy in the sky. Determinedly he said, "Okay, so what happens if the records of the Mossad and the CIA come up with nothing, which I think they will? And the Swiss investigation doesn't take us any further forward either?"

"I think we should wait until we encounter that bridge before we attempt to cross it," said Blom, satisfied with the way the conference had gone and intentionally invoking the English cliché to put the scruffy little man in his place.

"Know what bridges are for?" demanded Charlie.

"What?" said Blom, more in surprise than in response to the question.

Charlie took it the way he wanted. He said, "They're to stop people falling into the water and getting out of their depth."

"Motherfuckers!" erupted the President.

James Bell's grimace was almost imperceptible. He wondered how future historians would interpret the gross obscenity when they listened to the Oval Office tapes at the Austin memorial archive. As forcefully as possible, he said, "There's no proof whatsoever that it's the Geneva conference, Mr. President."

"I want you to call in the Soviet ambassador," said Anderson, red-faced, a vein pumping in the middle of his forehead. "You let him know. You tell him if his people try to play dirty pool, we'll break the fucking cue stick over their heads."

"We can't do that, Mr. President," said Bell.

"Why not!" demanded Anderson, happy to have someone tangible upon whom to vent his anger.

"Giles is quite clear in his cable. It's supposition on the part of the British—"

"—it looks good enough to me," stopped Anderson.

"Diplomatically I have no reason nor grounds to summon the Soviet ambassador to make any protest," said Bell.

"Do you know what I think of diplomacy?"

"What?"

"I think it's a pain in the ass."

"As do most diplomats," conceded the Secretary of State. "We need a system of guidelines."

"You make it sound like a railroad track."

"In many ways that's exactly what it is."

"Remember the phrase in Vietnam? No one being sure whether the light at the end of the tunnel was the ultimate exit or an oncoming train," demanded Anderson, who had served in those last months in 1975 and had actually piloted a rescue helicopter from the roof of the American embassy. The Purple Heart he'd been awarded, aged only twenty-two, had been his war hero's ticket into Congress.

"I remember," said Bell, who'd endured all the wartime reminiscences and couldn't understand the point of this reminder.

"I'm not going to be run down on this," announced Anderson, answering the unasked question.

"Giles has got a handle on it," assured Bell.

"He did well, keeping the cap on," remembered Anderson. "Let him know I appreciate it. Tell Langley, too, so it'll go on his record."

"He'll be grateful," assured Bell.

"Are you quite sure we can't eyeball the Soviets over this?"

"Quite sure."

"What then?"

"I think we've got to go with Giles," said the Secretary of State. "Let it run and see what happens. We've got the intelligence communities of four countries involved, after all."

Anderson was unimpressed and let it show. He said, "What have CIA records come up with?"

"Zero."

"Switzerland?"

"The same."

"England?"

"Nothing."

"Israel?"

"We're waiting to hear."

The trouble with worrying about oncoming trains was that it gave a person tunnel vision, thought Bell. He said, "How bad will it be if Geneva is a target? And there is an assassination?"

Anderson leaned forward on the table, staring at his friend. "You want me to answer that?"

"Yes, Mr. President, I want you to answer that," said the other man. It would be some years anyway before the tapes were available to historians.

"It'll be a disaster," said Anderson. "An absolute, unmitigated disaster, that's what it'll be."

"The British are allowing us access to this man Novikov," reminded the Secretary of State.

"So?"

"We'll have our own evidence of a Soviet assassination intention from a defector," continued Bell.

Anderson began to smile, in growing awareness. "Which could be made public?" he suggested.

"Which could be made public," confirmed Bell. "The way I see it, we've got insurance. If this is a false alarm—which it could easily be—then we've the chance of achieving the Middle East peace. Which was the original intention. But if there's an assassination and the conference is wrecked, we can immediately produce the evidence—evidence supported by Britain and Switzerland and Israel, all of whom have had or will have access to Novikov—to prove that Moscow was the architect."

Anderson's smile broadened. "So we can't lose?"

"Not from the way I look at it, Mr. President."

"Is that what you call diplomacy?"

"That's part of it," said Bell.

"I like it," enthused Anderson. "I like it a lot."

The diplomatic bag is rarely, in fact, a bag. The term generically describes any cargo precluded by international agreement from Customs interception or examination in the receiving or dispatching country by the appropriate designation of the embassy involved. Sometimes the diplomatic bag comprises the hold of an entire cargo plane: frequently the counterintelligence service of a country stands helplessly by as crates and boxes are loaded, knowing full well—but unable to prove—that some technological advance is being smuggled out in front of their eyes, to be lost forever.

The special American M21 sniper rifle with all its adaptations, together with the American Browning automatic and matching—but even more specially chosen—ammunition for both did not, however, need a crate when they arrived in Geneva. Both were accommodated in a small container of the sort long ago identified by the Swiss as that used by Moscow to transport embassy office furniture. Which was how it would have been described upon the counterintelligence report if one had been submitted. But no report was submitted. So many men were needed to conduct the new surveillance demands that the observation at Geneva airport was suspended. It was, after all, just routine.

16

There was a line to interview Vladimir Novikov, although it did not actually extend to the Sussex border. There should not have been, because the meetings were arranged with sufficient intervals between each. The delay was created by the Americans. They did not send someone from their London embassy to conduct the questioning but on the President's instructions flew a Russian-speaking interrogator from Washington overnight, accompanied by a polygraph team. Novikov at once displayed the arrogance that Charlie had encountered and protested at being subjected to a lie detector test, refusing to submit to it. There was a delay of two hours and a flurry of telephone calls between Whitehall, Westminster Bridge Road, and the U.S. legation in Grosvenor Square before he could be persuaded. Novikov remained hostile and it showed on the first polygraph test so the operator asked for a second, to make comparisons against his first readings, further antagonizing the defector. For the first hour of the interview he was intentionally awkward, choosing to misunderstand at every opportunity. A debriefing that had been timed for two hours took four and still ended without being as comprehensive as that which Charlie obtained.

A Mossad team followed, a man and a woman, both Russian speakers again and they capitalized upon the preceding episode, flattering Novikov by insisting they did not doubt his genuineness or honesty and asked for his cooperation instead of demanding it.

It was the better approach to a man of Novikov's ego. He consciously tried to provide more than he had for the Americans, volunteering information he thought the couple had failed to seek, which they hadn't. They just let Novikov talk himself out and then confirmed what he had provided by asking their questions in a different form.

Novikov complained of tiredness when it came to the Swiss interview, at first giving clipped answers, only expanding them properly after the initial thirty minutes when he realized that the interrogator intended persisting with the same questions until he was satisfied with replies.

The focus of each session was whether Novikov believed the assassination was planned for either of the Geneva meetings and he became irritated again, this time at the persistence about something of which he had no knowledge.

Each debriefing was, of course, automatically recorded on the electronic system installed in the Sussex house and simultaneously translated, so that complete transcripts were available to Sir Alistair Wilson and his deputy within an hour of the completion of the final meeting.

"Not a thing that Charlie didn't get, despite their having the advantage of his interview to prepare themselves in advance," judged the Director. "We'll pouch it to him with the other stuff."

"I'd like to see the detailed assessment of the analysts before committing myself," said Harkness, with his customary reluctance.

"How about the airline interviews?"

"All completed," said Harkness. "No other recognition whatsoever."

"And the watchers?"

"Nothing."

"So all we can do is go on the belief that it's Geneva," said Wilson.

"Why not let it remain there?"

"Bring Charlie home, you mean?"

"You said he should withdraw, if the Swiss remained difficult."

"What are you worried about?"

"What I'm always worried about with that man," said the deputy. "Of his doing something to damage our interests. At the moment we've got the gratitude of the intelligence agencies of three countries, America among them. That's sufficient, surely."

"We'll stay involved for a little longer," decided Wilson. "Like Charlie, I don't really like leaving things half done. I only talked about his coming home to keep him in line."

"I'd like to get him back in London," said Harkness, more directly.

"Why?"

"There are some financial difficulties to be resolved."

"They can wait, can't they?"

"There's something else."

"What?"

"He's applied for a bank overdraft. For ten thousand pounds," disclosed Harkness. "The bank referral was naturally channeled to me."

"So?"

Harkness blinked, disappointed with the Director's response. "Considering the man's history, I would have thought an apparent need for money was something with which we should concern ourselves. It's obviously necessary to bring it to the attention of the Review Board."

Wilson made clear his stifling of the laugh. "You think there's a risk of Charlie going across to the other side for thirty pieces of silver!"

"He did before."

"No, he did not," refused the Director, no longer amused.

"The point's academic."

"The point is that he won when he was supposed to lose and others lost in the process."

"We had to replace an embarrassed Director. So did the CIA."

"The embarrassment was of their making, not his. They were prepared to abandon him. The bloody fools deserved to spend a few days in Soviet captivity."

"When they were released, they both had to undergo de-lousing!" said Harkness, outraged.

"I think they deserved that, too," said Wilson. "There's actually a poetic justice to it."

Conscious of engaging in a losing battle, Harkness said, "It's covered in regulations."

"Do you intend instituting a deep investigation into Charlie Muffin's loyalty and background?"

"Yes," said Harkness, in further disclosure.

"Because of the overdraft application?"

"Yes."

"You'd better extend it," said the Director.

"Extend it?"

"There's a second charge on my place in Hampshire, to cover a fifty-thousand pound facility. I'm pretty close to the ceiling: forty-eight thousand pounds, I think."

It made practical sense for the Secretary of State to fly to Europe with the President because the Berlin visit that Anderson was making preceded by two days the Geneva Middle East conference.

"I just adore *Air Force One!*" said Martha Bell. She was a diet-trim, exercise-fit woman fifteen years younger than her husband. She'd had her bust siliconed, but discreetly, so that it was not outrageously inflated, and undergone more plastic surgery to have the cellulite removed from her thighs and butt.

"It's certainly a special way of traveling," agreed her husband.

"What should I wear?"

"You'd better check with the White House and see what Janet Anderson is going to wear," reminded Bell. "It's protocol to do so."

"It'll be something garish, like it always is. Red or orange, to brighten herself up. Why did he marry such a dowdy woman!"

"Her father was worth fifty million dollars and she was his only daughter."

"I fancy my blue suit with the muted stripe."

"You should still call the White House."

"After Geneva, we go to Venice?"

"Yes."

"Need we come straight back afterward?"

"What would you like to do?"

"Spend a few days in Paris to do some shopping. And then London. It's practically on the way home, after all, isn't it?"

"I guess we could manage that," agreed Bell. He was going to need the predicted income after he ceased being Secretary of State just to pay her bills.

"If Janet isn't wearing red, I will," declared the woman.

"I'm sure you'll look fine."

"Did I tell you about *Women's Wear Daily*?"

"No."

"They called my secretary. They want to do a feature about me being the fashion leader of Washington."

"Say no."

"I'd like to do it. It's true, after all."

"It would be a mistake, politically."

"What's politics got to do with the way I dress?"

"Everything, when it's an obvious comparison with Janet Anderson."

"We'll be photographed going aboard *Air Force One*, won't we?"

"I guess so."

"They'll make the comparison then."

"That's different; we don't have any say about that."

"Will there be caviar and champagne on the flight?"

"There usually is."

"Do you think you'll do well enough for us to have a jet of our own when you leave government? Only something small, obviously."

"Maybe," said Bell.

At that moment Sulafeh Nabulsi was disembarking from a Libyan commercial flight at Geneva airport. She had traveled in the tourist section with the rest of the support staff.

The British intelligence chief based at the embassy in Bern was a career officer named Alexander Cummings who had been on leave for Charlie Muffin's first visit to the embassy and who had hoped there would be no more. He knew of Charlie's reputation and did not want to become involved in any way with the man, reluctant even to summon him from Geneva but with no alternative because the instruction came from the Director himself.

Charlie, who sensed the reserve and wasn't interested in discovering the reason, strolled in off the Thunstrasse after lunch, and Cummings could smell the alcohol on his breath.

"Quite a lot for you in the diplomatic pouch," announced the locally-based man.

"Borrow your office then?" asked Charlie. "Hadn't better go wandering about the streets with it, had I?"

"Of course," said Cummings, tight-lipped.

Charlie studied intently the transcripts of the three different debriefings with Novikov, recognizing at once how the American team had mishandled it with their insistence upon the polygraph and smugly aware that no one had got any more than he had. The Washington embassy had replied at length to his query about the importance attached by the U.S. to the Middle East conference, from which Charlie found it easy to understand the CIA man's attitude at their meeting. In addition, there was included the CIA query to London about his personal involvement in Switzerland. Charlie sighed, easily able to understand that, too. He supposed it was obvious Giles would have alerted Langley to his being here. He tore open the last envelope, imagining it would be the Director's reply to the American agency, but it wasn't. As required by regulations, it was the official notification that a full investigation was being initiated into his affairs, with the warning that he would at some stage of the inquiry be required to undergo positive vetting.

"Fucking Harkness!" said Charlie vehemently.

Cummings, who was waiting in an outer office, looked in through the door. "Did you say something?" he inquired.

"Yes," confirmed Charlie. "I said, 'Fucking Harkness.' I often say it."

Cummings breathed in sharply, shocked. Everything that they said about this dreadful man was obviously true.

17

Sulafeh Nabulsi had been included in the Palestinian support staff because of her outstanding ability as a linguist, not just because of her willingness to sleep with whoever was necessary to achieve the appointment. She spoke fluent Hebrew, Arabic, and English and each better than the other language expert in the party, Mohammed Dajani. Their function, like that of linguists accompanying every other delegation, was to listen to the simultaneous translation during the conference to insure the official version was absolutely accurate. They were also required to attend private sessions and gatherings, to act more obviously as translators. It meant they would frequently be closer to the leading participants of the conference than their bodyguards, which was why Sulafeh was of such importance to the KGB.

The Palestinian secretariat was accommodated a long way from the international complex, on two floors of a small hotel off the Rue Barthelemy-Menn, and was bused across the city for the first day accreditation.

Sulafeh thrust on to the coach ahead of everyone else, to get a window seat so that she could see as much as possible. She did not know fully what would be asked of her by the unknown man she was to meet but was determined to be able to answer any query, not to fail him in anything.

She was aware of Dajani sitting beside her and of his thigh pressed against hers but did not turn to him, trying at once to orient herself by identifying the streets and avenues, using the lake and the Rhone as markers.

"A pretty city," he said.

"Yes," she agreed, still not looking at him. She moved her leg away.

"After the formalities of today there won't be a lot for us to do, until the conference starts," reminded Dajani.

Maybe not for you, thought Sulafeh. Disinterested in his attempted conversation, she said, "There'll be enough."

"I thought we might explore the city, you and I."

Sulafeh guessed that with his convoluted Arab chauvinism, Dajani resented her presence, as a woman with matching importance to himself, but still wanted to get her into bed. She said, "This seat seems too small for you. There are empty benches at the back."

The pressure of his thigh diminished slightly. He said, "What about it?" She'd slept with everyone else, so why not him?

She shook her head, turning back to the window, and said, "I've got other things to do." If he wanted sex, he could buy it.

"Like what?"

Sulafeh hoped the man was not going to be a nuisance. Not wanting to overly antagonize him into becoming an unwanted distraction either, she said, "Maybe I'll think about it."

The pressure resumed against her leg. "I'm sure there are many enjoyable things we could do," he said, heavily.

"Like buying a present for your wife?" she said.

Dajani remained smiling, undeterred. "That," he said. "And other things."

"We'll see," said Sulafeh, as dismissively as possible. The coach crossed a roadbridge over a skein of railway lines, and she saw the huge terminal to her left. Almost at once the bus made a right turn, following one of the routes that Vasili Zenin had paced during his earlier reconnaissance, and shortly afterward she saw the entrance to the conference area. She concentrated intently, the man beside her forgotten. There were security barriers with uniformed and armed officials checking the documentation and authority of people arriving on foot or in private cars. But the coach was acknowledged as an official vehicle and was motioned through. An important oversight, the girl thought.

In the secretariat building they formed lines at the registration desks, slowly edging forward to identify themselves against their already provided names and photographs. Sulafeh was accepted after a brief comparison with her picture and handed a plastic accreditation wallet, equipped with a clip for it to be worn on a lapel or breast pocket. Her photograph was already inside, her authority authenticated by the conference secretary. She was also handed a bulging envelope, plastic again, containing maps and explanations of all the facilities and a provisional timetable of the conference sessions. Sulafeh clamped the identification at once onto her shirtfront and hurried out, wanting to distance herself from the persistent Dajani and study everything about the main building where the delegates would be assembling in a few days' time.

The entrance was large and pillared and she halted, looking not directly at it but at the surrounding grassed area, consulting one of the maps that had been provided to establish where the commemorative photograph would be taken. To the right, she recognized, on a lawn landscaped to slope in a gentle gradient to guarantee that everyone would be clearly visible. According to the schedule, it was timed for 11 A.M. on the opening day. Sulafeh smiled briefly to herself, at her own personal joke: there was going to be more recorded for posterity than any of them could possibly guess.

Still following the guide, Sulafeh located the conference chamber at the end of a corridor that appeared practically the width of the building itself, but wasn't, not quite. Off it ran the committee rooms and offices allocated to each delegation. The Palestinian quarters were to the right, a honeycomb of boxed areas. Her desk was already designated by a nameplate. Dajani's was on the far side of the office, for which she was grateful. It might spare her at least the groping pressure the man seemed to imagine was seductive.

As she passed down the corridor, Sulafeh mentally

ticked off the offices of the Syrian, Jordanian, American, and Israeli secretariats. Diplomatically the Israeli rooms had been separated from the Arab section by placing the Americans in between. Inside the conference chamber the diplomacy was continued, by the arrangement of the table at which they would sit. The room was vast, with high, corniced ceilings picked out in gold leaf, the gold coloring continuing in the floor-to-ceiling curtains in front of the enormous French windows which opened out to gardens. The room was lighted by a series of glittering chandeliers which hung over a central but empty space. Around it, in a huge rectangle, was arranged the table, two long sides running the length of the room, with two shorter links at the top and bottom. The initial impression was that the entire rectangle was one continuous table but Sulafeh saw there was a separating gap of about a foot keeping apart the top and bottom seating arrangement from those on either side. She smiled again, contemptuously this time, sneering at the stupidity of it all. It meant that it was possible for Jew to meet Arab, with America as the mediator, but that both sides could claim with diplomatic pedantry that neither had sat at the same table. She supposed it was in this same room that a dispute over table arrangement had delayed the start of talks to end the Vietnamese war and cost an extra two thousand lives in the two months it took to resolve.

Behind the chairs at which the delegates would sit were arranged the accommodations for the support staff, seried rows of small tables already set out with notepads and blotters and a tub of pencils. The Palestinian negotiators were placed at the further end of the chamber at one of the smaller cross-tables, and the Israelis were seated as far away as possible, along the shorter section at the top of the room.

Sulafeh walked down to their area and again found a place already assigned to her. It was on the second bank of tables, directly behind the secretaries at the delegates' shoulder, positioned for immediate consultation. Sulafeh found the device upon which the translation would be made, a plastic cone fashioned to fit over her ear. Experimentally she tried it, surprised at its comfort, and twisted the selector dial clearly marked in the various languages. None, of course, was operating. She looked about and located the translation booth, a smoked-glass box impossible to see into, deciding it would be wise to make herself known in the translator's section.

In fact, it was important to make herself known to a lot of people, she realized. She went back out into the corridor, at once encountering a group of Swiss security men. Two, she thought, had been on duty at the entrance that morning, but she was not absolutely sure.

She said hello in English, and they replied in English, too. She stopped and so did they and she said she was a member of the Palestinian delegation, needlessly indicating her identification wallet. She said she guessed security was always a problem and one of the men, blond and apparently in charge, agreed it was but of particular concern for this specific gathering.

"Nothing can be allowed to cause any difficulty, now that negotiations have progressed this far," insisted Sulafeh, enjoying the sound of her apparent sincerity.

"We don't intend it to," said the man, furthering her amusement.

He asked if this were her first visit to Geneva and she admitted it was and flirtatiously the man said it was an interesting city with a lot to see and Sulafeh said she hoped to do just that and maybe find someone to show her. Dajani appeared from the door of their offices, further up the corridor, beckoning her forward and Sulafeh walked away, satisfied she had established herself in their minds just as she intended establishing recognition among as many security staff and permanent officials as possible in the lead-up to the conference, to reduce the risk of any spot-check challenge.

Dajani's summons had been for her to attend the first briefing session from the secretariat director, a man named Zeidan who had been with Arafat from the halcyon days of the PLO presence in Jordan. It was a pointless lecture, delivered only to bolster Zeidan's self-importance. He told them to orient themselves completely with the conference facilities and to minimize contact with the secretariat of any of the other delegations to avoid the slightest risk of indiscretion or compromise. He concluded by assuring them that they were present at an important moment in Palestinian history, and there was a mumble of agreement from the people assembled in offices that proved to be cramped when they were all together at the same time. Sulafeh's lack of response was undetected in the murmur of general acceptance.

"I guess we'd better discover where everything is?"

"I've already done that," refused Sulafeh.

"Why not show me then?"

"I've other things to do." From now on she slept with whom she wanted, not with whom she had to.

She'd noticed the newsstand in the secretariat building and returned to it, studying all the available street maps of Geneva and finally buying the most detailed. She ignored the waiting delegation bus, walking by it in the parking lot and twice made a point of engaging in passing conversation with groups of security guards, to extend her automatic acceptance. At the checkpoint exit she went to the main guardhouse and pretended to need help understanding her map to insure that the people on duty there would remember her.

Sulafeh used the pedestrian underpass of the Ferney highway which Vasili Zenin had already isolated as a barrier to his advantage and walked back into the city along the Rue de Montbrilliant which the Russian had also explored. The Post Office she was seeking on the obviously named Quai de la Poste was just across the Coulouvreniere bridge, but she did not go into it because the planning decreed there were still three more days before she could expect the instructions to be delivered at the *poste restante* facility. Instead she found a pavement cafe and ordered coffee, sitting relaxed with her legs stretched out before her, staring over the lake. Was the man with whom she was going to work already here in Switzerland? Or still to arrive?

And what would he be like physically? Different, she hoped, from Dajani.

Barbara Giles had chosen for a lawyer a man named Henry Harris because they'd attended high school together and even dated once or twice, but halfway through the meeting she wished she had gone instead to a stranger to handle the divorce. Although she supposed it was unavoidable, she found the probing questioning embarrassing. With difficulty she said her sex life with Roger was satisfactory, she did not believe he had a mistress, financially he provided everything she asked for, he did not drink excessively and had never, ever, hit her. They rarely even argued.

Harris, a ginger-haired, freckle-faced man whose college muscle had turned into indulged fat, looked up finally and said, "So what the hell's the problem?"

"I wish I knew," said the woman, inadequately.

"Barbara," said the lawyer encouragingly, "you've got to do better than this. So far I haven't got grounds for a divorce petition. I've got a nomination for marriage of the year!"

"We're just not interested in each other any more."

"You sure that's true?"

"Roger doesn't appear to be, at least."

"You didn't tell me what job he has."

"He works for the government," said the woman, producing the familiar cliché.

"The CIA?" recognized Harris, at once.

"I guess that's the problem," she said. "We've lived in all sorts of exciting places and now we're back here and he's got a senior grading and it should all be wonderful and it isn't. We can never talk about anything like all the other husbands and wives in the country talk about things. It's actually like he does have a mistress."

"Thought about getting guidance?"

"What can a counselor tell me that I haven't already told myself?"

"I would have thought it was worth a try. It's certainly a better idea than thinking of a divorce," said the lawyer.

"Like I said, there aren't proper grounds at the moment."

"What about disinterest?"

"From what you've said, Roger isn't disinterested," disputed Harris. "What exactly does he say about dissolving the marriage?"

"That he's willing to do whatever will make me happy."

"And will a divorce make you happy?"

Barbara Giles looked down into her lap, lower lip between her teeth. "No," she admitted.

"You've got to work it out between the two of you, and at the moment I'm not the one to help," decided Harris, positively.

"You know what I find impossible to understand?"

"What?"

"That people—ordinary people—actually believe working in intelligence is some sort of exciting job."

As Barbara Giles spoke, her husband Roger was in the code room at the American embassy at Bern, translating the series of messages coming in from the CIA headquarters at Langley. The unnecessarily repeated theme through most of them was the high presidential authority attached to the conference, which had to be protected at all costs. The last said, "Distrust all offered British help. Consider their representative, Charles Muffin, as hostile and to be treated as such at all times."

Five streets from the U.S. embassy, Vasili Zenin dispatched the meeting instructions to Sulafeh Nabulsi at the *poste restante* section of the Geneva post office she had already found.

And in Geneva itself the hotel check by Swiss counterintelligence finally reached the small, breakfast-only auberge off the Boulevard de la Tour.

"Yes," said the clerk. "I think I recognize him."

18

Although he was ahead of the time given in the unexpected summons—wanting again to be first—Charlie was in fact the last to arrive in the Geneva office suite where he'd had the initial meeting with the other intelligence officials. They all appeared relaxed and settled, coffee already set out before them, and Charlie wondered if there'd been a prior discussion between them from which he'd been excluded.

"Tried not to be late, too," he said.

"You're not," said the Swiss intelligence chief smoothly. He smiled, encompassing them all, and said, "It would seem, gentlemen, that our immediate problems are over." At once he corrected the expression of satisfaction, concentrating upon the CIA supervisor. "But that your FBI might have inherited them."

"What's happened?" asked Giles, at once.

"There's been a positive identification," declared Blom, triumphantly. "A night clerk at a small auberge in the city says the man in the picture booked in on the night of the thirteenth. He checked out on the morning of the sixteenth. His destination was New York."

Nobody else offered, so Charlie served his own coffee, noting the American's reaction. He decided it was genuine, so whatever they'd been talking about before he arrived hadn't been this. He said, "Identified by name?"

"Klaus Schmidt," disclosed Blom, at once.

"The ubiquitous Mr. Smith, although a Swiss or German variation this time," said Charlie. There'd been three Smiths on the London flight. The bastard had tried to be too clever and ended up making another mistake.

The huge Israeli chief shifted in his chair, discerning Charlie's disbelief, and said, "You don't go along with it?"

"No," said Charlie at once. "It can't be him."

"Why not?" demanded Blom, openly irritated by what appeared almost permanently sarcastic disdain.

"The passport won't support the name," said Charlie. "We know our man had an English passport, right? And can travel without it being examined from London to mainland Europe. But he couldn't go from Geneva to New York because airlines always confirm that the U.S. visa is valid. If it isn't, they get fined and stuck with the expense of repatriating the person back to his airport of origin."

"What if there's a British passport issued in the name of Klaus Schmidt?" asked Giles. He wished he'd seen the flaw as quickly as the Englishman from whom he'd been warned away.

"There won't be," said Charlie. "But if there is, we'll be in luck because British passport applications must be accompanied by a duplicate photograph, which is kept in records. And it'll be better than the one we've already got."

Levy was nodding, also admiring. "If you're right, then there's no doubt the man's a professional."

"I've never had any doubt that he was, but I don't think this is professional," said Charlie. "I think he tried something outside his training. . . ." He looked to Giles. "You'll have immigration searched, of course. And the applications?"

The American swallowed, uncomfortably. "Searched?" he said.

"Klaus Schmidt must have a U.S. visa. And those applications have duplicate photographs, too," reminded Charlie. "I guess there'll be a lot of them, but it'll give us another comparison. And an entrant into America has to give an address on the incoming flight."

Blom appeared to be deflating like a leaking balloon. He said, "I do not think this sighting should be dismissed as cursorily as you are suggesting."

Charlie frowned at the man. "The last thing I've been suggesting is that it should be cursorily dismissed," he said. "I've told you how I'm going to have it checked in Britain and suggested a similar way of doing it in America. . . ." He paused and said, "You do have a definite flight?"

"There was a Klaus Schmidt on the Swissair midday departure on the sixteenth," said Blom.

The man was already qualifying himself, Charlie recognized. He said, "What about picture comparison from the aircrew? Or from anyone at Geneva airport?"

"There has not been time yet," said Blom, in further qualification. "It is being done."

"It should be," said Charlie. "Although it'll draw a blank." He hadn't intended the remark to sound as arrogant as it did, but he'd been pissed off at Blom's attitude from the beginning and Charlie was curious to know what they had been talking about before he arrived.

"For a moment it looked as if our conference might have proceeded uninterrupted, too," said Levy.

Charlie was categorizing everyone more completely now with the benefit of this second encounter. Blom *was* obstructive. Also, to a degree, frightened and therefore clutching at the smallest straw. Possibly, too, resentful at being expected to deal on what appeared an equal footing with a subordinate, which Charlie recognized himself clearly to be. And not just a subordinate; a street-working subordinate who'd blown a fair-sized hole in what the man had obviously considered a major detection breakthrough. Charlie decided there were similarities with Giles's hand-on-the-nose attitude, which Charlie guessed from the advice that Sir Alistair Wilson had included in the diplomatic bag to be Langley's ordered response to his presence. And to which he'd become resigned, after the episode with their Director. Which left David Levy. Neither hostile nor friendly: neutral, like the country they were in was supposed to be. Except that Charlie had never considered Israel neutral in anything. His assessment was more that Levy was at this stage quite comfortable upon the fence between them, gauging advantage against disadvantage, the only consideration the benefit to David Levy and the country he represented. In matching circumstances, it was the way Charlie would have behaved. Insistently he said, "It's still got to be the most likely target."

"You've no justification at all for saying that," rejected the American. "You seem determined to substantiate a theory unsupported by any facts."

He didn't have to take any shit from the American, Charlie decided. He said, "Your people buggered up the debrief, mucking about with that silly lie detector machine. But about one thing you got the same answer, word perfect, as everyone else—Novikov insisting that the target is to be public and political." He paused, further advised by the material from London. "And the most dramatic, high profile political event in the calendar for November is the Middle East conference to which your President is personally committed, a President who seemingly just by chance is going to be here in Europe with the American Secretary of State. Just how does that look to you?"

"I'm not aware of the President's personal commitment," said Giles. He was unhappy at Langley's insistence that there should be no cooperation between them.

"Then you shouldn't be here," said Charlie, going at once for the weakness. "I'm aware of it and I'm not even a member of your service!"

If you had been—and done what I know you to have done—then you'd be six feet under in some unmarked grave, thought Giles. Anxious to escape the pressure, he said, "I'll agree to its potential."

To Blom, Charlie said, "I would like to interview the hotel clerk."

"A copy of the statement will be made available."

"Interview him myself," insisted Charlie.

In the intervening hesitation, Charlie was conscious of the look that passed between the Swiss counterintelligence chief and the CIA supervisor. Blom said, "There was a clear understanding from the outset that the Swiss service is to remain in control of this investigation."

"I am doing nothing to contravene that understanding," soothed Charlie, sure of his argument. "I've had the advantage of closely questioning the one man in our service in England actually to see the person we're seeking. There is surely an obvious advantage in my being able to compare his impressions with those of your witness."

"I would have thought so," came in Levy, supportively.

"Absolutely everything would be shared with you, of course," assured Charlie. "Exactly the same as our making Vladimir Novikov available to you."

"The Bellevue," identified Blom, reluctantly.

"Thank you," said Charlie. Although the remark appeared to be general, Charlie looked directly at the American when he continued. "And naturally I'll let you know if anything comes from the check on the passport records," he said.

"The run-through on the visa applications might take a while," said Giles, trying to obey his headquarter instructions. "Like you said, Schmidt isn't a particularly unusual name in the United States."

"But it'll be made available?" pressed Charlie.

"Yes," said Giles tightly.

"I really wish I could contribute more," offered Levy. "All I seem to be doing is sitting here taking advantage of everyone else's efforts."

"Nothing at all from your records search?"

The Israeli shook his closely shaved head. "Nothing from either the picture or the physical description that was specific enough. There was one man who looked to be a possibility for a while, but he turned out to be a Syrian terrorist we already had in custody, serving ten years."

"Are there still hotels to be questioned?" Charlie asked the Swiss.

"Some," conceded Blom. He was pink with irritation but Charlie didn't think it heightened the impression of albino this time. The man looked more like a doll badly decorated in the Christmas rush.

"And they will be?" persisted Charlie, careless of annoying the man further; he was going to remain an awkward bugger whether Blom was offended or not.

"Of course!"

"You could always publish the photograph," prodded Charlie.

"I thought I had made it abundantly clear that publication is not an option considered appropriate."

"Problem is, options are things we don't really seem to have," reminded Charlie.

Levy lingered in the foyer of the building, obviously hanging back when the American got into the waiting embassy limousine. They both watched the car merge into the traffic and Levy said, "Do you drink?"

"It's been known," said Charlie.

They found a cafe after two streets, tucked away in an alley off the Rue Alcide Jentzer. Charlie chose whisky, a brand he didn't recognize, and Levy said he'd risk it, too. It turned out to be a risk, harsh to the back of the throat.

"You didn't make any friends back there," said Levy.

"Always a problem," admitted Charlie.

"You were very quick to see what was wrong."

"It seemed obvious."

"Not to me it didn't. Or the other two."

"Fluke," dismissed Charlie. What was this hand-on-the-knee stuff all about? he wondered.

"They're talking about closing you off," revealed the Israeli. "The meeting started half-an-hour before the time you were given."

So there *had* been some earlier discussion. "They are?" said Charlie. "Not you?"

"I didn't express an opinion," said Levy honestly.

"Express one now."

"With Blom, it seems to be a matter of personality and I've always thought it juvenile to let personal feelings interfere with professional judgments," said Levy. "As far as the CIA is concerned, you can hardly be surprised by their wanting you out after what you did, can you?"

Still not an opinion, decided Charlie. But revealing nevertheless. If Levy knew what he'd done to the Americans, then the Mossad chief had run more than a check on a blurred photograph. And the Israeli records had to be more comprehensive than he'd believed them to be. He said, "What was their decision?"

"They didn't make one," said Levy. "And after today, they'd be mad to think of doing so."

"I think I'll switch to brandy," said Charlie. "What about you?"

"Probably a good idea," accepted Levy.

After the drinks were delivered, Charlie said, "You still haven't said what you're going to do."

"We wouldn't be sitting here if that wasn't obvious, would we?"

The Israeli was still on the fence, able to look into both backyards, Charlie recognized. Sneaky bastard. Charlie felt quite at home. He said, "Sounds good to me. Everything shared?"

"Between the two of us," qualified Levy. "If they want to cut you out, I don't see why they should get any feedback through me."

Levy had given the undertaking with a completely straight face, too, Charlie acknowledged. He said, "What about a feedback from them?"

"We're not going to be able to sort this out exchanging half of what's in the picture, are we?"

Levy seemed to have the habit of answering questions by asking others and therefore never openly saying anything, thought Charlie. He said, "No. And thanks."

Levy gestured to the man behind the zinc bar for more drinks. When they came, he raised his glass in a toast and said, "Here's to a working relationship."

Charlie drank. "Let's start right away. How important does Israel regard this conference?"

"Vital," said Levy at once. "Do you know the state of our economy, from having constantly to remain on a war footing? Getting rid of the Palestinian problem would be to get rid of a lot of others."

"You've warned Jerusalem about a possible outrage here?"

"Of course."

"What was the reaction?"

Levy shrugged. "I guess my people are more accustomed to outrages than most. They're concerned, obviously. But not panicking. The message came back for more proof."

"Always the same message," said Charlie, wearily.

"Something else you must expect."

"If only the bastard would make a big enough mistake!" said Charlie fervently.

"It's been almost a week," reminded Kalenin.

"I know," said Berenkov.

"And there's not been the slightest indication of any increased surveillance on the Bern embassy."

"It's time for Zenin to make the pickup," said Berenkov.

"And that's his only moment of contact," said the KGB chief, in further reminder. "We would still be able to turn him back, but it isn't any part of the training that we contact him at the Geneva apartment."

"Let's hope we don't have to," said Berenkov. "What about Lvov?"

"I hear that he's making quite a lot of the time and effort being wasted in the Bern," said the KGB chief.

"He's right," said Berenkov, objectively.

"Unfortunately he is," agreed Kalenin. Would he cut himself off from his friend, if the need for survival demanded it? He hoped he was not confronted with the choice.

19

Vasili Zenin had always acknowledged—as had every instructor at Kuchino and Balashikha—that the greatest danger of his being identified would be going to the Soviet embassy in Bern to collect the weapons. But the bulk precluded their being left safely at any dead letter drop, as the passport had been in London, and there was anyway the essential need for him to examine and approve what had been provided. His was the ultimate responsibility, overriding that of the officers at Balashikha who had packaged and dispatched them. And any immediate, on-the-spot examination would have clearly been ridiculous anywhere but in the maximum security of the KGB *rezidentura* within the building, an area forbidden even to the ambassador himself.

Like everything else it had been rehearsed until supposedly perfect in the Kuchino complex, with mock-up streets and avenues and a re-creation of the front of the building behind the protection of its gates and iron railings. KGB personnel performed the role of ordinary diplomats, tradesmen, and visitors using the embassy. Created all around were less elaborate false fronts upon which were specifically isolated spots to suggest where Swiss counterintelligence watchers might be placed. Their imagined positions had been indicated by automatic cameras triggered by remote control by watchers of the Soviet service. For a week Zenin had done nothing but attempt to enter and leave without being photographed. On the last day he had managed three unrecorded entries and two missed departures.

He'd succeeded by improvising upon the instructor training, recognizing that what he had to carry marked him more obviously than anyone else going in or out. So he prepared himself to merge with it as naturally as possible into the background, like he had earlier done by becoming a jogger at Primrose Hill. He hoped they'd remembered to pack more than just the M21 and the Browning and their ammunition.

Having had a week to study workmen on the streets of Bern and Geneva, Zenin easily found, the day before the planned pickup, a shop in the Speichergasse selling the most commonly worn type of dungarees, blue, with bib and suspenders. He bought a matching cap, as well, a pair of heavy boots and a set of rubber wedges. A comparable bag was the most difficult to locate and it was late afternoon before he discovered a store off the Munstergasse. Everything, of course, had to be kept separate from the hotel where he was staying as a supposed tourist, so he took all the packages back to the garage where he had parked the hired Peugeot. Unselfconsciously, Zenin stripped naked, putting on only the overalls, and for an hour vigorously exercised, bending and twisting to crease the newness from them and to get them as sweat-stained as possible. He dried his face with the cap, to mark that as much as he could and scuffed the boots along the floor and against the concrete sides of the garage. The bag was canvas, like that he had to collect, and he dirtied that with dust from the floor. The dungarees were damp with his perspiration when he took them off and Zenin screwed them tightly into a ball, so that they would dry further crumpled.

He approached the garage cautiously the following day, not wanting to be seen entering in a suit and emerging a workman; he waited fifteen minutes before he was satisfied the road was clear. It was more difficult to leave, because his vision was restricted by the narrowly opened door, but again he did so, sure that he was unobserved. Zenin traveled back into the center of town on a tram, confident he'd done a good job on the overalls when a woman already on the seat on which he lowered himself perceptibly moved away.

A hesitant man attracts more attention than a confident one and Zenin went assuredly along the most direct linking street into Brunnadernain, which somewhat to his surprise had been dismissed by the professional watchers at Kuchino

as being the unlikeliest to house surveillance spots. He
hoped they were right. Protectively, Zenin wore the cap
pulled low over his forehead and walked looking slightly
down. If there were observation, it would be from some el-
evation in order to avoid street level obstruction, so his face
was as hidden as it could be.

He made no stop going through the embassy gates,
someone with a right to enter, and neither did he approach
the main entrance. Instead he went to a smaller side door
not obviously marked for tradesmen deliveries, but which
was its proper purpose. And which he would have known if
he were familiar with the building. To the guard he said,
"Run Around," and was admitted immediately.

The KGB *rezidentura* was at the rear of the embassy, as
distanced as it could be from any overlooking buildings
from which directional listening devices could have been
aimed, an interlocking series of rooms absolutely divided
from the rest of the legation by a barred and locked gate behind which sat a uniformed KGB guard. Zenin gave him
the same operational identification, but before he was admitted the man verified the code with the *rezident* in
charge, Yuri Ivanovich Lyudin.

The locally-based KGB officer was striding down the
corridor, beaming, by the time the security gates thudded
closed behind Zenin.

"Vasili Nikolaevich!" greeted the *rezident*.

"Yuri Ivanovich," responded Zenin, more restrained.

Lyudin stopped some way away, still smiling, looking at
the workman's outfit. "There were many photographs from
which to recognize you today. But we weren't warned *how*
to expect you!"

"Of course you weren't," said Zenin, more than restrained. He'd memorized Lyudin's face from photographs
as well, but none had shown the man to be as fat or as flush-
faced as he was.

"It's very good concealment," praised Lyudin.

"I hope you're right," said Zenin. "Have things arrived
for me?"

"A sealed container," confirmed Lyudin.

"Which has remained sealed?"

"Of course," said Lyudin. Why had Dzerzhinsky Square been so insistent that no indication be given to this man about the additional surveillance teams that had been drafted from Moscow?

"I need an equally sealed room," demanded Zenin.

"One is set aside," said Lyudin. "But perhaps a little refreshment first? I have some excellent Polish vodka."

"It's ten-thirty in the morning," reminded Zenin.

"I waited for you before I began," sniggered Lyudin, wanting the other Russian to accept it as the joke it was intended to be.

Zenin didn't, nor did he smile. He said, "There were some requests from Moscow: detailed information about Geneva?"

Lyudin's smile became hopefully broader at the awareness of Zenin's involvement. "Which I personally responded to. Myself."

"And personally made the surveys?"

"Yes," confirmed Lyudin. "I trust it was satisfactory."

From a series of bars, guessed Zenin. It was easy to guess how Lyudin had gained the patriotic complexion. And why so much of the Geneva information had been inaccurate. The need for protest to Moscow was far more than personal now. Such a man, particularly a man in a position of command like Lyudin, represented a positive danger to the entire *rezidentura*. But more importantly to the KGB itself. Zenin said, "I've decided upon my report to Moscow."

"I am grateful, Comrade Zenin," said the other Russian, misunderstanding.

"The sealed room and the container?" reminded Zenin.

Lyudin led the way further back into the *rezidentura*, to a chamber actually within the building with no connection to any outside surface. It was so small Zenin was practically able to reach out sideways and touch either wall. There was harsh strip lighting around the four sides of the squared ceiling, and it illuminated the entire area in a glare so fierce that Zenin had to squint against it.

"This is the examination room. We were advised you would need to conduct an examination," said Lyudin.

Zenin was curious at what other things at what other times might have been examined here. Despite his profession, he'd never been into a mortuary but imagined this must be very like such a place. There was just a metal table, a single chair—metal again—and a wall-mounted telephone; there was even a smell of antiseptic cleanliness. He said, "This will do adequately."

"The container is in my personal security vault."

"I would like it now."

For a moment Zenin imagined the man was going to suggest an alternative, but instead Lyudin nodded acceptance and hurried from the room. Zenin found it oppressively hot—he supposed the heat was from the intense lighting—and claustrophobic, too. Zenin decided that such surroundings would quickly disorient a person, particularly if that person were frightened. Perhaps it was fortunate he was anything but frightened. Lyudin returned almost at once. The container appeared to be of some hardened plastic material but Zenin knew it to be stronger than that, a specialized lightweight alloy capable of withstanding an aircraft crash and any engulfing fire that might have followed. On the outside was a large combination lock activated only by a first-time operation of the correct selection of numerals, which only he possessed, memorized. Any wrongly probed sequence in an effort by an expert locksmith to discover the combination would have automatically set off the phosphorous and then acid incineration of the contents. The container was hermetically sealed so the chemical reaction of phosphorous and acid would have made a gas sufficient to create a bomb capable of destroying everybody and everything within a fifty-meter radius. In addition to the explosion, the alloy, under such pressure, would disintegrate into thousands of razor-edged shards. Its destructive capability had been tested over an additional fifty meters against gulag detainees like Barabanov, against whom Zenin had been pitted at Balashikha. There had, of course, been some survivors: twenty, each so badly maimed they were shot on the spot because they could never have recovered medically to perform any further useful function. One hundred and fifty died outright, burst apart.

"I thought at first it was a standard container, the sort we get all the time," said Lyudin inquiringly.

"It isn't," said Zenin.

"Something unusual then?"

"Get out, Yuri Ivanovich!" dismissed Zenin.

Zenin locked the door behind the departing Russian and turned back to the container, savoring its very appearance like a child knowing its most asked-for Christmas toy was beneath the wrapping. But there was no excitement shake in his hand as Zenin reached out for the combination, which moved without any perceptible click as the memorized numbers were engaged and discarded. He paused when the final one was released and then snapped open the catch. The container fell apart, either side opening like a giant mouth from its bottom hinges. It was a superbly packed Christmas toy.

The inside had been machined and socketed perfectly to receive and hold every part of the disassembled rifle and each variety of its ammunition. It occupied one entire side of the container, laid out for inspection. Which was what Zenin did, counting off from another memorized list the components that made up the 7.62 mm American M21 sniper's rifle with which he had been so diligently trained at Balashikha. It had been reconstructed especially for him by the KGB's Technical Division, measured to the millimeter to his arm length and shoulder dip, and modified further beyond the standard hand-constructed U.S. model. The stock had been replaced by a skeleton metal rest to balance the weight of the other adjustments. The most important of these was a series of attachment clasps for the elaborate harness, which went far beyond the usually fitted elbow-twist strap. The harness was again made-to-measure and of the best grade leather, once more identifiably American. It was a complete vest, the main part encompassing his body from waist to shoulders, across which went the thickest of the straps. There were four others which attached to special clamps, effectively welding the rifle to his body. The magnified sight maintained the standard design of two stadia on a horizontal graticule, but because the range was beyond the designed 300 meters, there was a heavy power ring to increase the sighting distance and this had been allowed for by strengthening the mounting. There had also been another weighting allowance for the final modification. At the bottom of the rifle side of the container was a retractable three-legged tripod upon which the weapon was to be locked by a grooved screw-nut device, which, together with the harness, made the assembly absolutely rigid. When completely tightened to fix the rifle onto the tripod, the screw-nut became parallel with two minute spring-repressing lines which compensated for the miniscule recoil. That, too, was a modification, even though the trigger pull had been taken up from its 2.15 kgs to 1.15.

Zenin ran his fingers at random over the sound suppressor and the primed gas cylinder and the piston, a craftsman encountering the favorite tool of his trade.

The Browning parabellum automatic was on the opposite wall of the case and assembled, except for the butt clip, which was fastened alongside, empty. Again there were two varieties of bullets, the Israeli hollow-nosed in a separate holder from the solid test bullets. In this section, too, was the bradawl and screws to fasten the tripod to the floor, adjoining the sockets in which were held hard metal screws and a screwdriver.

There was a metal bar upright in the center of the container, and hanging from it in separate plastic bags were the suit and shoes for Zenin to change into to alter his appearance for his departure from the embassy. At the very bottom was the duplicate bag.

Zenin stripped off the overalls, this time folding them neatly on the table beside the container and placed the workboots next to them. The suit was intentionally light colored, beige, to be as opposite as possible from what he had worn when he entered the embassy. When he finished dressing, Zenin transferred the rifle parts and the pistol to the bag, hefting it in his hands as a reminder of the weight that he had also rehearsed carrying at Kuchino, and then put the workclothes back into the container, which he closed and resealed against its specialized interior being seen by Lyudin.

The *resident* was waiting expectantly in an opposing office when Zenin opened the door. He said, "Was everything satisfactory?"

Zenin considered the question ridiculous and the man further incompetent for not making the demand he should have made. He said, "What else could it have been?"

"That drink now?"

It was still almost an hour before the lunch hour when more people than usual were arranged to make the exodus in which Zenin planned to be concealed. He said, "Why not?"

Lyudin led the way to a more spacious office further along the corridor, arranged with chairs and a couch. The bottles were set out upon a tray on top of a wall-bordering cupboard. The man splashed neat vodka into two tumblers, offered one to Zenin and made a toast with arm outstretched. "Russia!" he declared and sank the drink, Soviet fashion, in one gulp.

Zenin did not bother to respond and only sipped at his drink. He said, "Haven't you forgotten something?"

"I need a formal receipt," remembered Lyudin. He produced the form from his pocket, and Zenin completed the bureaucratic necessity. As he did so, Lyudin refilled his glass and made to top off that of Zenin, who covered the rim with his hand.

"And something else?" prompted Zenin.

From another pocket Lyudin withdrew the key to the corner apartment overlooking the Palais des Nations and said, "I hope you will be comfortable there."

Zenin wondered what the fool imagined he would be using the place for. He said, "How long have you been on station?"

"Here in Bern for two years," said Lyudin. "I am hopeful of getting Washington, upon reassignment."

Hope in vain, thought Zenin. He said, "I wish you luck."

"There have been no other instructions from Moscow," said Lyudin. "But if there is any sort of assistance you require, I am, of course, at your disposal."

The man spoke like an official report, thought Zenin. He said, "Nothing. Thank you."

"What is Moscow like under the new regime?" asked Lyudin.

"It has not affected us," said Zenin. "We are beyond government whims."

"Of course," accepted Lyudin hurriedly. "I meant among the general public."

"I have no idea what happens among the general public," said Zenin. He was bored, wishing the time would pass. Lyudin proffered the bottle again, and this time Zenin accepted.

"Is there any communication you wish transmitted to Dzerzhinsky Square?"

"You've been instructed to advise them of my being here?"

"Yes."

"That's all."

"Nothing more?"

"I would have told you if there were."

"Do you wish me to go with you from the building?"

"Don't be foolish," rejected Zenin, at once. "If Swiss counterintelligence has identified you and we were observed leaving the embassy, I would be linked by association, wouldn't I? I want no KGB officer among the group at all."

"Do you want to establish any contact procedure between us?"

"No," said Zenin.

"It is almost time," said Lyudin.

Zenin sighed, relieved. He said, "There are to be no introductions or explanations."

The diplomats and other normal embassy staff were already assembled when they reached the vestibule. As noon struck, the group moved en bloc toward the exit and Zenin eased himself into the middle, not bothering with any farewell to the other KGB man. He carried the bag in his right hand, so it would be shielded by the people around him. The majority went to the left when they emerged onto Brunnadernain and Zenin stayed with them, not splitting away until he was about three hundred meters from the building. Having separated, Zenin moved quickly to distance himself, cutting through side alleys and minor roads until he got to Marktgasse. There he caught a tram again because an attempt to follow any sort of stopping and starting public transport is more obvious than a continuously moving vehicle like a taxi. Zenin positioned himself on a rear seat, convinced after the first one hundred meters that he was not being pursued. Back at the garage, he removed the tripod, the fixture screws, the harness, and the handgun that he did not need for the test he intended, stacking them neatly in the corner beneath a piece of canvas discarded by a previous occupant. The bag he put into the trunk of the Peugeot, thrusting it as deeply as possible into the cavity created by the wheel arch.

Zenin drove hard but always within the legal limit toward the Oberland, the road running parallel with the river Aare. At Thun he skirted the lake to the south but at Interlaken swung north around the Brienzersee lake. At Brienz he put the car in a public parking lot, took the bag from the trunk and strode through the old, wooden-housed part of the town, knowing from the Kuchino instruction that it was the most direct route to the deepest of the forests.

At first the trails were wide and Zenin was concerned at the number of people who appeared to be using them. He cut once and then a second time onto smaller paths, pushing deeper among the trees, at times so tall and thick he had no sight at all of the towering Jungfrau mountain. He climbed steadily for over an hour, transferring the bag from hand to hand as the weight of the rifle began to tell, alert more to the possibility of climbers or hikers than to the sort of testing place he wanted. Zenin was high above Brienz before he found it, an abrupt clearing that overlooked a small, tree-surrounded valley.

Zenin crouched, his back against the trunk of a fir, making no immediate attempt to assemble the rifle at his feet, listening and looking for people. There was some noise from rarely seen birds and an occasional murmur of insects but that was all. Around him the forest was dark and thick and apparently empty. At last he switched his concentration.

The assassination was calculated for him to be able to fire a maximum of five undetected shots, and Zenin isolated a clump of trees ideal for the target. He carried the bag with him, unwilling to risk leaving it unattended while he set up the markers.

Throughout his long practice with the M21 at Balashikha, it had been assembled and every part so perfectly aligned that over four hundred and fifty meters his bulls-eye accuracy ran consistently at ninety-nine percent but the dismantling of the rifle would have disturbed that alignment. Zenin was determined to restore it although such a high accuracy achievement was not strictly necessary. The hollow-nose bullets he intended using flattened upon impact with a body and tore huge exit holes so death was practically automatic from shock, even if the hit itself was no more than a wounding shot.

The largest of the trees was slightly apart from the group he had selected and Zenin chose this to be the target to re-align the weapon. About six feet from the ground, he stuck a six-inch square of paper over a jutting twig, pressing it against the rough bark of the tree and then looking back between it and the spot high up in the clearing from which he intended to fire, gauging the sightlines. Satisfied, Zenin moved to the closer-together trees and arranged five more paper markers at heights dictated by convenient twigs, the highest almost to that on the first tree, the lowest just over three feet from the ground.

Back up in the clearing Zenin squatted again, opening the bag at last and bringing out the parts in the order in which he wanted to rebuild the weapon. He slid the perfectly machined barrel into the modified stock, then connected the gas cylinder, and after that, the piston. He paused at the remaining fitments, gazing intently around to search for any people. At the moment, if someone stumbled upon him, Zenin could have been mistaken for a hunter, although a rather improperly dressed one. The adapted sight and the elongated sound suppressor identified the rifle as something altogether different and Zenin with it, which was why he had left in the locked security of the garage the most obvious pieces of sniper's equipment. The forest remained dark and silent, but Zenin stayed motionless for a long time until he was sure. He screwed the power-increased sight onto the top of the M21 and finally twisted on the suppressor which extended the barrel practically half as much again, a reamed silencer that deadened the sound of the shot but in no way reduced or impaired the muzzle velocity. Zenin finally clipped in hard-nosed ammunition, not needing this time the shattering effect of the soft bullets.

Using the trunk of the tree against which he had rested as a support, Zenin focused the magnified sight on his first target, adjusting the two stadia to run either side of the paper, with the graticule at its bottom, and from the calibration was able to establish the distance precisely at three hundred and ninety meters. He took his time, snuggling the stock into his shoulder, his eye unblinking against the magnification. The sound, when he fired, was hardly audible in the vastness of the forest, the merest *phut*, and Zenin was sure it would be even less in Geneva, masked by the sound of traffic on the Ferney highway. He missed the paper completely, by at least fifteen millimeters, frowning in irritation at the sideways pull. He readjusted the sight against the extension of the barrel and tightened by half a turn the suppressor's linkage. The next shot was excellent, almost in the center of the paper, reestablishing at once his ninety-nine percent score. Cautious in everything, he fired again at the same target and again hit practically dead center, the second shot actually enlarging the penetration of the first. Zenin smiled to himself, pleased at how quickly he had recovered. For the assassination itself the rifle would be further steadied by its mounting on the tripod and his physical attachment to it by the harness.

Zenin shifted slightly, bringing himself around to the tree clump but pulling briefly away from the weapon, to establish a timing. He waited until the second sweep hand of his watch marked the twelve before hunching back into his sniper's crouch and loosing off five shots in quick succession, each time having slightly to bring himself around, to the separate pieces of paper. He hit each one, again with ninety-nine percent accuracy, and when he checked his watch, he saw it had taken one minute ten seconds, which was the timing average he had created for himself during the Balashikha training.

Zenin replaced the assembled rifle in the bag made specifically to accommodate it and walked once more across the tiny valley. Two of the pieces of paper had been blown off the trees by the force of the impact. Zenin collected them and removed the four still attached to their twigs, standing back to examine the bullet holes. Each was neatly drilled into a trunk and from a few meters was practically indiscernible to anyone not positively seeking it. Better, he decided, to leave the bullets embedded than attempt to dig them out, widening the holes to be more visible.

Zenin reclimbed the hill to the clearing for the last time, at its top finding the narrow trail that would eventually return him to Brienz. Not much longer now, he thought. And tomorrow the meeting with Sulafeh Nabulsi.

A twice-daily courier system was established between the U.S. embassy in Bern and the advanced American contingent to ferry back and forth by car the restricted contents of the diplomatic pouch, and it was on the second delivery that Roger Giles received the letter from Barbara, setting out the lawyer's opinion that there were insufficient grounds for the divorce. It was a long letter: freed from the constraining embarrassment of a personal confrontation, the woman put on paper what she had been unable so far to say. She wrote that she did not know what had brought about the disuse of their marriage but she did not want it to end. She was apportioning neither blame nor responsibility to anything or anybody, but if he had complaints about her, she would do her best to rectify them, if only they could talk instead of letting things drift, pulling them further apart.

It was a plea, which Giles recognized. And to which he

responded because he, too, found it easier to write than he
did to talk. He said that he did not want their marriage to
end, either. That he had gone along with the idea of disso-
lution because he'd imagined that was what she had
wanted. He assured her the faults weren't hers, not any of
them. The problem was his absolute and precluding ambi-
tion within the Agency, which he realized now to be wrong
and for which he apologized, in a plea of his own, asking
her to forgive him for his stupidity. He was due leave, he reminded her, and not just this year's allocation, but time he'd
refused to take the previous year because he did not want to
be away from Langley for longer than a couple of weeks.
He'd already told her the job in Switzerland had a definite
cutoff date. Why didn't she fly to Europe, and they'd take
the vacation they'd always talked about but never achieved,
driving to Italy and to France and maybe Germany, too?
Nothing planned, just handling each day as it came.

"I love you, my darling," he wrote. "Forgive me. Learn
to love me again."

There was another communication addressed personally
to him in that second delivery, official this time. It had been
easy to trace Klaus Schmidt from the arriving flight immigration form, as the Englishman had predicted. Schmidt
was a sixty-five-year-old Swiss German banker with
scarcely any head hair, but a neatly clipped and precise
beard, and he could hardly have been more different from
the picture that had been taken in London's Primrose Hill.
The man was staying at one of the larger suites at the UN
Plaza Hotel, which he customarily did during his quarterly
visit to New York for business meetings with his bank's Wall
Street division. He'd never heard of Geneva's Bellevue hotel
and certainly never stayed there.

Giles discarded the report on the table of his own hotel
suite, shaking his head at the ease with which the apparent
Swiss breakthrough had been demolished. Charlie Muffin
had been damned smart, seeing through it as quickly as he
had. A clever guy. Giles thought of his sealed and sincere
letter to Barbara, with its promises to resist in the future the
twenty-four-hour-a-day demands from the CIA. It was a

CIA demand that he reject the Englishman, he remembered: treat as hostile had been the message. Giles recognized that to be a demand he could not resist but he would like to. He thought Charlie Muffin was a funny looking son of a bitch, like a rag picker on a Calcutta rubbish tip, but the guy sure as hell appeared to know his business. If this conference was as important as Langley and the State Department kept insisting and the threat to it was as real as it could easily be, Charlie Muffin seemed to be the sort of person whom they should have taken on board with open arms, not given the bum's rush. What was past was past: Giles was concerned with the immediate future. And worried about it.

Sulafeh Nabulsi physically tingled with anticipation, walking out of the post office with the letter tight beneath her arm. She found the cafe where she had sat, legs outstretched, that first day, and she was aware of the slight shake in her hand when she opened the envelope. It was just a single, unsigned sheet of paper, with the name of another café, one on the Rue des Terreaux du Temple. Against it was the time of 3 P.M. Beside the name of her hotel 2 P.M. was listed. And there was a date, that of the following day. She stared down at it, memorizing every curve in the script, for several moments. Then, at last, she crumpled it into a ball, touched it with a lighted match advertising the place in which she sat and watched it burn into blackened ashes, which she crumbled into dust between her fingers.

20

London passport files are computerized so it took less than half a day for the response to Charlie's query, an assurance that no British document had been issued to anyone in the name of Klaus Schmidt during the preceding two years. Another bet won, thought Charlie. Pity he wasn't as good with the bloody horses. It was still useful, though, giving him an excuse, albeit slim, to seek a further meeting with the other intelligence chiefs. He wouldn't give them a reason, of course. Just hint at some additional information to keep them curious until they were all in the same room. And there was also what he hoped to achieve from the meeting with the night clerk at the hotel off the Boulevard de la Tour.

The Bellevue was a hotel small enough to miss, lost in a long and continuous block with shops and offices extending either side, the entrance no bigger than that of an ordinary house. There were four steps up into a minute vestibule, where the reception desk fronted the door. A breakfast area was to the right, an alcove of round tables and toadstoollike chairs, with a bar to the left, zinc-topped and dwarfed by the espresso machine, and incapable of accommodating more than two tables. The television had to be suspended from a supportive arm, high on the wall, to get it into the place at all. Well-chosen, judged Charlie, expertly. Discreetly inconspicuous, a hotel without regulars, none of the staff knowing the guests or guests knowing the staff.

The night clerk was a bonily thin man named Pierre Lubin, who tried his best by wearing a dark jacket with dark-striped trousers carefully brushed to hide the shine of constant use. The collar was the hard, detachable sort that enabled a shirt to be worn more than once, provided the cuffs were properly reversed.

Lubin smiled in instant recognition when Charlie produced again the photograph and said, "Drugs, isn't it? That's what the other policeman said."

Lubin was enjoying the attention, after a lifetime of being ignored, guessed Charlie. He said, "The investigation is international; that's why I'm here from England."

"Important then?"

"Very much so. I'd like you to help me all you can."

"Of course," offered the man, eagerly.

"He said his name was Klaus Schmidt?"

"Yes."

"German?"

"Certainly not Swiss-Deutsch."

"Why are you so certain?"

"I know the accent, of course; the difference."

"Definitely German, then?"

Lubin put his head to one side, doubtfully. "There was an accent," he said. "In his German, I mean. A blur in some of the words that I had not encountered before. But it was very precise, very grammatical."

"As if it were a learned, carefully studied language you mean? Not his first or natural tongue?"

"I suppose so," said the clerk. "Until you mentioned it, I hadn't thought about it."

"He signed a registration card?"

"Yes."

"With an address?"

"Yes."

"What was it?"

"I can't remember," said Lubin. "The police took it."

Another demand he could make upon Blom, thought Charlie. He said, "Tell me the system of registration?"

"System?"

"A guest has to complete a card?" said Charlie, knowing how it was done from his booking into the Beau-Rivage.

"Yes," agreed the clerk.

Knowing the answer again from his own experience,

Charlie said, "But isn't it a requirement that the passport number is given and actually lodged, here at reception, at least overnight."

Lubin trapped his lower lip between his teeth and visibly colored. "Yes," he admitted.

"But you didn't do that?"

"No," said the man, in further admission.

"Why not?"

"It was late when he arrived," said Lubin. "He complained at having traveled a long way and to be in a hurry to get to his room. And it's such a time-wasting regulation. I've always found it so pointless."

Until now, the very moment it mattered, thought Charlie. There was nothing to be gained by openly criticizing Lubin. Charlie said, "Tell me about him. What he looked like."

Lubin did so hesitantly, someone anxious to compensate for an acknowledged mistake and determined to leave nothing out. Charlie counted off the descriptive points against those he already knew, slotting one set perfectly into the other. This was the man, thought Charlie; he could smell it! Coming to the most important part of the interview, Charlie said, "I want you to take your time, don't hurry. But tell me what he was carrying."

Lubin sniggered a laugh, as if he found the question amusing. He said, "A suitcase, of course."

"Only a suitcase?"

"Yes."

"No briefcase?"

"No."

"A shoulder grip maybe?"

"Nothing more than a suitcase."

"What sort?"

"The type made from some solid plastic, to prevent any pressure on the clothes."

"What color?"

"Grey," said Lubin. "They always seem to be grey."

"How large?"

The night clerk extended his arms sideways and then

held his right hand palm down, in a measuring gesture approximately four feet by three feet and said, "Something like that."

"Quite small then?"

"Enough for maybe one suit, a change of shirt and underwear perhaps," said the man. "That's why I remembered his remark about going on to New York. I thought at the time he seemed to be traveling very light."

Charlie smiled at the irony of the other man using the word. He asked, "Who carried the bag to his room, that night when he booked in?"

"I did," said Lubin.

Charlie sighed, relieved; maybe a break at last. He said, "How heavy was it?"

Lubin shrugged. "Just a suitcase."

"Heavy? The sort of weight you'd encountered a lot before? Or light?" insisted Charlie.

Lubin considered the question, smiling again. "Actually," he recalled. "It was quite light."

Charlie let go some more held breath. "And he didn't object to your carrying it?"

"He seemed to expect it," said Lubin.

Another point, isolated Charlie. He said, "Tell me about his demeanor. He did he treat you?"

"Treat me?" Lubin appeared confused by the question.

"Did you consider him polite?"

Once more Lubin did not react at once. Then he said, "He was very direct."

"Direct?" echoed Charlie. "Would some people have considered his attitude rude?"

"Possibly," agreed the clerk. Then, with longer reflection, he added, "Yes, I suppose he could have been considered rude."

Already knowing the arrival time of the Swissair flight, Charlie said, "What time did he get here, the night he booked in?"

"It's difficult to remember accurately," qualified Lubin. "Nine-thirty, probably nearer to ten o'clock."

Which would accord close enough with Flight 837,

Charlie decided. He said, "He complained of traveling a long way?"

"Yes."

"But didn't say from where?"

"No."

"Did he look tired?"

"Not really. I didn't think so."

"Did he ask for any food?"

"No."

"Is there a room bar?"

Lubin smiled apologetically. "The hotel isn't quite of that standard."

"So did he ask for a drink?"

"No."

"Just went directly to his room and stayed there?"

"On both nights," confirmed the man.

"What about a tip, for carrying his bags?"

"It's odd that you should ask that," said Lubin.

Which was why I posed it, on the off-chance, thought Charlie. Encouragingly he said, "What was odd about the tip?"

"He was very careful about it. Gave me exactly fifteen percent. Counted it out, coin for coin. People don't often do that, not coin for coin."

"No," said Charlie. "They don't, do they?" Then he said, "Tell me, in as few words as possible, how he came across to you: the sort of man, I mean?"

There was a by now familiar pause for consideration. Eventually Lubin said, "Ready."

"Ready?" queried Charlie, curious at the man's expression.

"Even in a hotel like this, there is usually a kind of uncertainty you can detect in a person. They're away from home, in a place they don't know, a place they're unsure of. So there's an uncertainty. But with him there wasn't. That's what I mean by ready. He seemed quite confident: that he could cope with whatever difficulties he might come up against."

"He probably believes he can," said Charlie distantly.

"This drugs business?" said Lubin. "Is it very serious? Might it get in the newspapers even?"

"It's very serious," said Charlie. Again, a remark for his own benefit, he went on, "And it should get in the newspapers."

"Could I be a witness?" asked the little clerk at once, his need obvious.

"If it gets to any sort of case, I'll see that you're called," offered Charlie.

"I'd like that," said Lubin. "Thank you."

Charlie wrote his name and the 31-02-21 telephone number of the Beau-Rivage on a piece of Bellevue notepaper and said, "I want you to make me a promise. If he comes back, I want you to call me at this number. Will you do that for me?"

"Of course," undertook Lubin. "What about the Swiss authorities?"

"Did they leave a number for you to call?"

"No," said Lubin.

"You tell me and I'll tell them," said Charlie at once. For all the effort the Swiss appeared to be putting into this, the bastard could be driving around the streets in a tank with a hammer and sickle on the side and playing the Moscow Top Ten on its tape deck.

"Is he dangerous?" demanded Lubin.

"Very dangerous," warned Charlie. "If he comes back, try as hard as you can to behave quite normally. And don't call me from any of the phones here, which he might overhear. Use a public phone."

"It's very exciting, isn't it?" said Lubin enthusiastically. "Just like in the movies."

"Just like that," agreed Charlie.

He used a phone himself to call the Beau-Rivage, to be told there were no messages, and then immediately redialed Brigadier Blom. There was a protracted delay, but finally the counterintelligence chief came onto the line, the reluctance clearly obvious in his voice.

"I think there's the need for a meeting," said Charlie.

"Of everyone?" said Blom guardedly.

"We've agreed to liaise completely, haven't we?" said Charlie, extending the encouraging carrot.

Blom bit straight into it. "How about three o'clock?" he asked.

"So there was something already arranged!" seized Charlie. "I must have left the hotel ahead of your call."

There was a moment of trapped silence from the other end of the line before Blom repeated, "Three o'clock," and rang off.

Deciding he deserved a small but personal celebration, Charlie discovered a bar serving Glenfiddich, ordered a large one, and loosened his shoelaces, aware as he did so that they'd succumbed to wear again and didn't look half as posh as they'd been for the bank manager meeting. Which seemed a long time ago. The reference letters would have certainly arrived by now. What would Harkness have done? Almost a silly question, he decided. What about another one, with a more uncertain answer. Charlie scuffed across to the wall-mounted bar telephone, managing a connection at once to David Levy at the Bristol.

"Hi!" greeted Charlie, cheerfully. "How's it going?"

"This an open line?"

"I'm in a bar," confirmed Charlie.

"Tried to reach you about two hours ago," said Levy. "Didn't bother with a message."

"Been out and about," said Charlie.

"Anyone contacted you?"

"No."

"There's a meeting at three," disclosed Levy. "The American wants a daily get-together, whether there's anything to report or not."

It appeared at least as if the Israeli was playing honest Injun, and that there was a lot of heat burning out of Washington. Charlie said, "I know. I'm going."

"How did you find out?"

"I called our host."

"You weren't intended to be at the party."

"I know just how Cinderella felt," said Charlie.

"Have you got any presents?"

"Maybe. How about you?"

"Nothing."

"The others?"

"I don't think so."

"Could be a dull affair then," said Charlie. He'd carried his drink with him to the telephone, so it was finished by the time he completed the conversation. He gestured for a refill on his way back to his table, where he sat in head-bent concentration, reflecting upon what he'd discovered. Bits, he decided. Useful bits, but not enough to tell him where to go, with the speed he considered necessary to get there. One positive avenue, at least. He hoped Blom hadn't regarded that as lightly as the man appeared to be treating so much else and left it uncovered. What else? It certainly seemed Blom and Giles were determined to exclude him. Which was a bummer. But with Levy's forewarning, Charlie thought he could definitely cause them as much irritation as they were causing him, which was always important when people tried to piss him about. Charlie greatly admired the credo of America's Kennedy dynasty: don't get sore, get even. He usually managed it, although perhaps not on the scale of the Kennedys.

Charlie stopped after the third whisky and only took half a carafe of wine with a lunch of lamb and mountain wild mushrooms, congratulating himself when he left the cafe on remembering to get the all-important bill. He had quite a bunch back at the hotel in one of the hotel envelopes. Harkness was going to be pleased with him. No, thought Charlie, in immediate contradiction: Deputy Director Richard Harkness was never going to be pleased with him, not in a million years. Maybe he really did know how Cinderella felt.

For the first time he did not hurry to get to the chrome and glass building on the Rue Saint Victor. If he was going to be the uninvited guest, then he was going to make a fittingly grand entrance. Which he did. The three other men were there, and Brigadier Blom was actually moving impatiently around the room when Charlie entered.

"Late again!" he said. "Had to rearrange a couple of

things to get here. Still, better late than never: that's what I always say." He smiled around the table. Only Levy responded, an expression of curious amusement.

"You said there was a reason for us to meet?" said Blom, at once.

"But this meeting had already been arranged, so what you have is probably more important than what I have," retreated Charlie, in apparent politeness. "After you."

The redness started in Blom's face. He looked awkwardly to Giles and said, "I believe you have some information?"

"Negative, I am afraid," said the American. "Our immigration and FBI people tracked Klaus Schmidt down in New York. He's a banker: respectable as hell. Doesn't even know the Bellevue hotel."

"So Charlie was right?" said Levy.

It was an unnecessary intrusion, goading, and Charlie wondered why the Israeli was trying to irritate the other two men. Charlie said, "And there's no British passport in that name either."

"A dead end?" persisted Levy.

To Blom, Charlie said, "What about the address?"

"Address?" frowned the white-haired man.

"The man who stayed at the Bellevue put an address on the registration card, which your people apparently took," said Charlie. "Might be interesting to find out what it was?"

Blom was very red now. He snatched one of the three telephones on his desk, gave clipped instructions, and slammed the instrument down so hard that it jumped off the cradle and he had to put it back on a second time, more gently, further angering himself. He said, "So what is it that you've discovered?"

"I thought you should know about there not being any Klaus Schmidt passport," said Charlie, refusing to be hurried.

"Is that all!"

Don't get on the high horse with me, sunshine, thought Charlie. He said, "The last time we met, the supposed identification of Klaus Schmidt was being hailed as a breakthrough comparable with the discovery of penicillin! Now we've got two independent and guaranteed sources proving an attempt to lay a false trail."

"Providing, that is, that this whole episode isn't one wild goose chase," fought back Blom.

"It isn't," insisted Charlie.

"You got some additional proof?" asked Giles.

"I spent a long time with the clerk at the Bellevue," said Charlie. "The physical description he gives matches that of the man at Primrose Hill in almost every respect. He further says that the man was direct; the airline staff also considered him rude. He arrived at the Bellevue at exactly the time it would have taken him to travel in from the airport, after the arrival of Flight 837—"

The jar of the telephone broke in, cutting Charlie off. Blom listened without question to what was said and then put the telephone down, hard again. For a moment he looked back at the three questioning faces and then he said, "It was an address in the Eaux-Vives district of the city: the Rue de Mairie. A Mercedes salesroom. There is a space upon the registration form for a passport number: the one filled in has no relation to any Swiss-issued passport."

"Convinced now that you've got a Soviet illegal roaming somewhere in Geneva?" demanded Charlie.

"It would seem that something illegal is taking place."

Didn't this idiot know that with his head in the sand his ass was exposed? Charlie said, "The man at the Bellevue said he was tired after a long journey. Yet he didn't ask for anything to eat or drink."

"I don't find that significant," dismissed Blom.

"That night and the second he went directly to his room and stayed there," persisted Charlie.

"There could be a dozen reasons for his doing that," argued Giles. He wasn't as obviously resistant as Blom, but he thought it necessary to avoid viewing everything as sinister. "How about hiding away, as much as possible?"

"One of the dozen," said the American.

"He made mistakes trying to appear Swiss-Deutsch," said Charlie. "The clerk was able from his accent to know immediately that he wasn't and also to discern in his German an accent with which he was not familiar. It was the speech of someone perfectly taught, in a classroom. And he didn't know the coinage. He was very pedantic about counting out the fifteen percent. Again, someone instructed but not accustomed to living in the West."

"Circumstantial again," said Blom. "All of it."

Charlie sighed, talking directly to Levy. He said, "He carried a small suitcase, that was all. He expected the clerk to carry it to his room for him. And it was very light."

The Israeli came slightly forward in his seat, smiling again. "Really!" said Levy. "That's interesting."

Charlie looked expectantly at the American. Giles said, "Could be a lot of other explanations, apart from the obvious."

"Perhaps someone would like to explain the significance to me," complained the Swiss.

"It means at that time, six days ago, he didn't have a weapon," insisted Charlie. "No professional would risk carrying anything on an aircraft, because the electronic security checks are too good. He hadn't picked it up directly after his arrival either. The time he got to the hotel fits with the distance from the airport but it doesn't allow for any detour. But the most positive evidence of all is that he let the clerk carry the case, a case so light that the clerk remembered it. Guns are heavy, noticeably so. No professional would have let the man anywhere near it, if he'd already made a collection."

"Diplomatic pouch?" guessed Levy, more in private conversation with Charlie than in general discussion.

"It's the safest against interception, until the moment of hand-over," agreed Charlie.

"And then it's noticeably bulky," said Levy.

To the Swiss counterintelligence chief Charlie said, "You maintain watchers on the Soviet embassy, of course?"

For a moment Blom appeared reluctant to concede a piece of routine tradecraft. Then he said, "Of course."

"Did you increase the cover after the alert?"

"The alert, such as it is, meant that my personnel was stretched," complained Blom, imagining criticism.

"I offered manpower help," reminded Giles.

"So you didn't increase!" demanded Charlie, exasperated.

"The people deputed to cover the embassy are trained, experienced men who know how to react," said Blom defensively.

"Like the trained, experienced men who hadn't checked the phony address as a car salesroom until you told them to!" accused Charlie.

"Nothing unusual has been reported from the embassy as of midnight last night," assured Blom, with pedantic formality.

"That's precisely what I'm frightened of," said Charlie. "That it hasn't been reported."

"Was any special instruction issued after the alert?" demanded Giles.

"The men on such specialized duty do not need reminding what that duty is," said Blom, still stiff.

"The watcher in England had been specially warned," reminded Charlie in sad resignation. "And he knew he was sitting right on top of a drop. By the time he was aware of what was happening, it was almost all over."

"Perhaps there should have been additional instruction," conceded Blom finally. Throughout his operational life he had been accustomed to the neutrality of Switzerland rarely being challenged—never having had to confront the sort of terrorism and violence that these men appeared to accept almost as a normal part of their day-to-day operational lives—and he was frightened: frightened of the speed with which they thought ahead of him because of that experience and the assumptions they seemed so quickly able to make. And he was most concerned of all at their attitude toward him, which appeared to be increasingly hostile even from the American, whom he had seen as an ally.

"These reports you talk of?" questioned Charlie. "They're logs, aren't they? Recorded entries and departures, against times. With anything unusual isolated?"

"Yes," said Blom.

"I'd like to see them," said Charlie. "I'd like access to every twenty-four-hour period, from the thirteenth."

Blom opened his mouth to protest, but before he could speak Levy said, "I would like to examine them, as well."

And the American said, "Me too."

"Of course," agreed Blom. "I hope you'll find it a vindication of my people."

"I hope so, too," said Giles.

"I think it would also be a good idea if we had a daily meeting," said Charlie innocently. "Say here, at three o'clock every afternoon? To exchange information and ideas: stuff like that."

Blom looked between Giles and Levy, trying to guess the traitor.

"I think it would be a good idea as well," supported Giles. Damn Langley and their living-in-the-past vindictiveness and hands-off edict against the Englishman. The American decided he couldn't give a damn how or why the scruffy bastard had screwed the Agency. He meant the promises he'd made in the letter to Barbara, but that didn't mean neglecting his career. And his career was very much tied up at the moment with whether or not Clayton Anderson left in a blaze of international glory. And that was the only sort of blaze with which Giles intended to be connected. Charlie Muffin was calling too many shots ahead of the rest of them to be ignored. The man had to be brought aboard, not cast adrift.

So the traitor had been Giles, Blom decided. He would have imagined the Israeli the more likely suspect. He said, "If that is the wish of you all."

"I think it's got merit," said Levy.

Charlie looked at the Israeli, trying without success to gauge from the expression of the man's face what he was thinking. Trying to make it easier for the cornered Blom, Charlie said, "We've not got a lot of time, after all."

"I don't need reminding of that," said Blom.

Never one to let an advantage go, even from a cliché, Charlie said, "So we can see those logs right away then?"

* * *

There were two searchers. The senior supervisor was a balding, paunchy old-timer named Sam Donnelly; the younger was a new entrant still with six months to complete before final graduation. His name was Peter Ball. He was a small, terrierlike man, eager to the point of arrogance, disdainful of advice for the same reason. It was Ball who picked the lock of Charlie's flat, hot with irritation that the instructing Donnelly was able to isolate the barely visible scratch the wire had made against the Yale edge, halfway down. Ball considered it absurd even to imagine that Charlie Muffin would be able to know from it that his apartment had been turned over.

"Jesus!" exclaimed Ball, who always smelled of strong cologne. "This is like one of those medieval places where people lived with their animals!"

"Looks like it could do with a dusting," agreed Donnelly mildly. As the younger man moved forward from the threshold, his foot disturbed a letter among the pile that had built up upon the doormat during Charlie's absence, and Donnelly said sharply, "Careful, you careless bugger!"

Ball stopped, just beyond the accumulated mail, and said, "What the hell's wrong now!"

"Stay there!" ordered Donnelly. "Don't move for a minute. Just listen. This place looks a shithole and maybe it is, but this is going to be the best exercise you've been on, from the moment you started to try to learn your trade. An expert lives here, someone who's forgotten more than it'll take you to memorize in twenty years. So stuff your usual arrogant crap. Watch and listen and learn!"

Ball stood in front of the other man, face afire, unable to conceive the idea of another six months of the man. "So!" he demanded.

"So you've already missed something," said Donnelly. "Two things, in fact. You've failed, even before you've started."

Ball swallowed, angry now at himself. Unable to think of anything else, he said, "What?"

"What have we just come through?" demanded the older man.

Ball sighed. "The door," he said patiently.

"From the outside?"

"Yes." Ball's tone was curious now.

"What's unusual about the inside?"

The younger man looked around for the first time, unable to find the answer. "There's nothing unusual about it," he said.

"Look again."

"I am looking, for Christ's sake!"

"Not hard enough," rebuked Donnelly. "Charlie Muffin is a senior officer in British external intelligence, someone who's worked in security all his life. So where's his security?"

"No internal locks," realized Ball, at last.

"No internal locks," accepted Donnelly. From inside his jacket he took out four rubber wedges of the sort they always put beneath the door of a burgled room to prevent their discovery if they feared the occupant might return, but which both knew would not be necessary today because of Charlie being in Switzerland. "Somewhere—probably in the kitchen—you'll find a set of these, with which Charlie locks himself in at night. Because he knows, like you and I know, that the only way to open a door secured by these is to break it off at its hinges, by which time he would be ready. What else does it tell you?"

"I'm not sure," said Ball, more humbled now.

"That he's not bothered about being burgled because there's nothing here to take. Or more importantly, for us to find."

"You mean you aren't going to bother!"

"Of course I am going to bother," said Donnelly. "It's years since I've had a challenge like this. I'm just pointing out the signs to you. And you still haven't got the second one."

"What?"

Donnelly gestured downward toward the splayed letters. He said, "Which one did you kick?"

"I don't know!"

"You should," said the searcher. "Because one—maybe two—of them is a trap, and at the moment you're falling over the edge."

"What are you talking about now!"

"Tell me the date that Charlie Muffin went to Switzerland. Went without even coming back here," insisted Donnelly.

"I don't know," admitted the younger man.

"You should know," lectured Donnelly. "It was in the report and it was important. It was the sixteenth."

"So?"

"So get down on your hands and knees," ordered Donnelly. "The letter you disturbed, incidentally, was the envelope colored red, the free soap powder offer. But don't touch that yet. Memorize how every letter is displayed on that mat. And then, one by one, lift it. We're going to read and photograph every piece that's there, and having examined it all, we're going to put it back precisely as it was. You understand that?"

"We were always going to do that," said Ball. "What's so important about the sixteenth?"

"The postmark," said Donnelly. "The first thing you do is study the postmark and not just for the point of destination. You look for the date. Allow three days for any delay."

"I don't understand!"

"Anything there prior to the thirteenth will be the snares that Charlie has left," warned Donnelly. "A trained searcher can go through mail without trace, but if he finds it on the mat, the assumption is always that it's arrived after the occupant has left. So there's no need to replace it as it supposedly fell. There'll be at least three envelopes among that pile with dates before the thirteenth. They're the ones that would tell him we've been here."

"Bullshit!"

"You got ten pounds?"

"Yes."

"Put it where your mouth is, against my twenty pounds."

There were, in fact, four. It took them an hour to go through the mail, using the method in which a split piece of bamboo is slipped sideways inside the flap and the contents slowly wound up like a tiny blind, to be extracted without the flap being unsealed. As he handed over his twenty pounds, Ball said, "Seems I'm not the only one who's a bad gambler."

The repeated demands from Charlie's bookmaker were two of the uppermost letters. Donnelly said, "Three hundred quid isn't the end of the world."

"It is if you haven't got it," said Ball.

"That's all there is though," reminded the older man.

Ball straightened gratefully from his squatted position on the floor and said, "What now?"

"Don't relax," advised Donnelly. "What about that table, for example?"

It was in the center of the room into which the front door directly led. Beyond it was the television set and pulled close was an easy chair, the seat sagged, the cushions indented from the last person to occupy it. The table had an obvious flap in its top, the lid to some space beneath, and on that flap was a glass serving as a vase for a single flower, a long dead tulip that had shed its leaves in a haphazard pattern around the base. The water in the glass was dark brown with prolonged use. There was a half empty bottle of Islay malt, the top still off, and a small residue in the bottom of the type of glass handed out at service stations for buying a required amount of gasoline. There were two plates. Upon one was a half-eaten piece of bread, beginning to mildew, and on the other the congealed remnants of a fried meal—rock-hard yellow of an egg yolk and the rind of some bacon. There was also something black and solid, which could have been the remains of some mushrooms. The knife and fork were left as they had been put down, discarded across the plate in a rough cross.

"How on earth can someone live like this!" exclaimed Ball.

"You'd be a fool to think he does," warned Donnelly. "Look at the chair, for instance."

"What about it?"

"There's no way a human body could make the indentation in the seat as well as in the cushion like that, not at the same time," pointed out the searcher. "It's another trap. If you lifted the cushion to see if anything was hidden beneath—which is what we've got to do somehow—the indentation would be disturbed. Just as it would in the cushion, if you looked carelessly beneath that."

"Yes," agreed Ball, with doubtful acceptance. "It would, wouldn't it?"

"What about the flower?"

Ball sniggered a laugh. "Just a dead tulip."

"Nothing strike you as unusual about the petals?"

Ball took a long time, before finally shaking his head.

"Count them," instructed Donnelly. "There are forty, including the five still actually attached to the stem. On your way to work tomorrow go into a florist and ask the name of the tulip with that many petals. It's another trap, laddie. We've got to look to see what's inside that table and again the temptation would be to imagine he would not know how the petals lay, having been away for some time. He's put at least ten in specific, memorized spots."

"What else?" said Ball, almost wearily.

"It's a funny thing," said Donnelly. "But when a person enters a room to find a discarded glass—particularly a glass like that, with just a little drop in the bottom—the instinctive reaction is to pick it up and smell it." From his inside pocket Donnelly took an expanding device, like a pair of scissors without any cutting edge, and put the jaws inside the glass, expanding them so he could lift it. "He'll check for fingerprints when he gets back," said Donnelly. "And see that?" He pointed to a ring beneath. "It looks as if the glass made it, but it's another marker to insure it remains in the same position." He replaced the glass and extracted his lifting tool, offering it to the other man. "Try the whisky bottle and the cap," he suggested. "There'll be rings beneath each."

Ball did and there were.

"Now the plate," ordered Donnelly. "Use the tool like

pliers: it works. Be careful not to disturb the knife and fork, though."

There was a ring beneath the plate and Ball said, "I suppose the knife and fork were particularly placed?"

"Of course," said Donnelly. "The bed will be unmade, when we get to the bedroom. It's much more difficult to search an unmade bed and leave it exactly as it was than it is to turn over one that's neat and tidy. Watch the pillow indentations, too. And any discarded clothes: they're sure to be some. Don't think the pile of washing-up in the kitchen sink is slovenliness either. Or that what's thrown in any of the bins or wastepaper baskets has actually *been* thrown. Be careful of any disarranged curtain or covering. Reposition any books precisely as you find them. Newspapers and magazines, too. And be careful about screws."

"Screws?"

"We'll need to look in the back of the television set and the radio: behind some cabinets and closets, probably," reminded the older man. "Don't dare let the screwdriver slip to score the screw-head. And make sure when you refasten that the crossmark on the screwhead is left in the same position as it was when you undid it."

"Nobody's that careful!" protested Ball.

"Just do as I say," ordered Donnelly.

The bed was unmade and there were clothes scattered on the floor, the sink was stacked with dirt-rimmed cups and glasses and plates, and the dustbins and wastebaskets were full. It took nine hours of uninterrupted searching, and they were exhausted when they finished, despite which Donnelly insisted on a check of everything that had been disturbed, to insure it had been undetectably replaced.

"I can't get over the books on the shelves!" said Ball, as they drove away. "Goethe and Pushkin were in the original. And all the Robert Frost were first editions! All that and then at least a year's supply of *Playboy!*"

"He's a surprise a minute," agreed Donnelly.

"You really think he'll spot the entry scratch?"

"Maybe."

"What about the rest of the search?"

"There's no way we'll ever know, is there?"

"I guess I owe you an apology."

"Forget it," dismissed Donnelly.

"Where the hell did you learn so much!" demanded the younger man admiringly.

"Charlie Muffin taught me," said Donnelly.

It was a full meeting of the committee, with Mikhail Lvov there as well as Berenkov and the KGB chairman.

"A copybook collection?" demanded Lvov. The confident head of the assassination division regarded Zenin's uninterrupted visit to the Bern embassy as a complete vindication of his insistence that the Run Around operation should be continued, and he was making absolutely sure that others more important in the Kremlin came to the same conclusion.

"There was never any doubt about Zenin's professionalism," said Berenkov. "The man is brilliant."

"Sufficiently brilliant to defeat two of the special groups of watchers whom you sent to guard the embassy!" said Lvov.

Kalenin and Berenkov viewed differently the open challenge. Berenkov hadn't until that moment imagined the other man to be the internal threat that he was clearly emerging. Kalenin decided to sit back and let the dispute take its course. He was quite sure about his own ability to survive. He hoped Berenkov was up to it.

"Brilliant," conceded Berenkov cautiously. The better fighter was always careful at the beginning of a contest to study the footwork of his opponent.

"On one side if not the other," said Lvov. "Little point, really, in bothering to send them at all. Certainly no purpose whatsoever in retaining them there, now that Zenin has made the pickup."

"What are your views upon bringing them back, Comrade Berenkov?" asked the KGB chairman, formally.

"I think they should be kept there for a while longer," said Berenkov. He was curious at Lvov's response.

"But for what purpose?" demanded the assassination

chief. "They can take no active or useful part anymore. Not that they took an active or useful part before."

A tendency for overconfidence, gauged Berenkov. He said, "Let's just consider it insurance."

"Against what!" demanded Lvov.

"Isn't that what one always insures against?" replied Berenkov. "The unexpected disaster."

"There is going to be no unexpected disaster," said Lvov.

"I hope not," said Kalenin.

"Not in Switzerland at least," said Lvov, exceeding himself.

Neither Kalenin nor Berenkov responded, each with their own thoughts.

21

With his habitual and trained caution, Vasili Zenin arrived in Geneva early and by train, as the first rehearsal for what would be necessary later. During its final approaches to Geneva, through the outskirts of the city, the Russian gazed from the carriage windows to the streets outside and occasionally below, watching the rush hour traffic and confirming his earlier impression of the uselessness of a car for his escape. The dossier of complaint against the Soviet embassy in general and Yuri Ivanovich Lyudin in particular was going to be very extensive.

From the Cornavin terminal, Zenin walked in the direction against the clogged traffic along the one-way Rue des Terreaux du Temple and on the side furthest from the café he had specified in the unsigned note to Sulafeh Nabulsi. It was just opening, and black-aproned waiters were rearranging stacked chairs around freshly washed pavement tables. Three were pulling the striped canvas canopy from its sprung housing to form a protective roof over the outside area. It was a bright day, despite being autumn, and Zenin hoped the weather would hold so they could later sit at a curbside table: it would be easier to run, if he had to run, from somewhere already out in the open rather than from inside the more easily sealed café interior.

In the Rue Bautte there was a much smaller place, more a bar and *tabac* than a café, already open for early morning workers. On the pavement there were three small tables, each bordered by plastic-ribbed chairs, but Zenin went inside, wanting concealment now. He ordered coffee and from a bench directly against the fronting window looked across at the designated meeting place, studying everything with proper professional alertness. If the note to the woman had been intercepted or found—or if she were not the committed zealot she was supposed to be, but some sort of bait—then that afternoon he would be walking into a trap, a trap at this moment being primed and set.

He watched the waiters individually, intent upon establishing that each moved about the cafe and the tables with accustomed familiarity, with none showing an awkwardness to hint at hurriedly drafted counterintelligence officers. Satisfied all the waiters were genuine, Zenin extended the examination, looking for any buildup of loitering groups of watchers. Or maintenance tents or vans in which they might have been hidden. When he failed to locate any, he sought out parked but enclosed vehicles which could be disguised mobile communication centers from which his encirclement could be coordinated once he got to the cafe. Again there was nothing.

Finally reassured, Zenin left the bar but did not rejoin the Rue des Terreaux du Temple, unwilling to risk association a second time with a street upon which he was later to return for a third. Instead he left the area along the Rue de Mandement, picking up a streetcar at the first available stop to take him to the quais, instinctively checking for pursuit and finding none.

With time to spare before the woman's stipulated departure from the hotel, Zenin strolled along the Bergues, enjoying the unexpected sunshine, and lunched overlooking the island in the middle of the river. None of the training, no matter how realistic, could properly have prepared him for an actual assignment and almost illogically, now that he was involved in one, Zenin was experiencing a sensation of anticlimax. The problem, he recognized, was that the training had been too intense, every hour of every day at Kuchino and Balashikha forced to a degree of tension calculated to take him to within a millimeter of his limit. But the reality—this reality—was nothing like that. Of course there was no relaxation: what he'd done by arriving in Geneva today as early as he had and by carrying out the checks that he had was unnecessary assurance to himself that he was leaving nothing to chance or trusting anything to be as he imagined—rather than knew—it to be. But the reality still lacked the . . . the what? Frenzy was the word that came at once to his mind, momentarily confusing him, but then he accepted it. Frenzied was a fitting description of the training: sabotage instruction at nine, unarmed killing at ten, draining physical exercise at eleven, thirty minute meal break (but not a moment longer) at twelve. And everything resuming precisely at twelve-thirty, murder by untraceable poisons, communication security at fourteen hundred, and . . . Zenin did not bother to recall the next session. What he *could* remember was the physically exhausting, sagging effect of it, of crawling every night into bed sapped of all strength and all adrenaline. This reality was not like that. There had been moments of tension but not many and nothing like the training stress. This had been like . . . no, holiday was not the right word, not like frenzy had so perfectly fitted into his mind, but it was the only description that presented itself. Between the limited highs of the tension, there had been too many long extended troughs of inactivity. How easy was it, he wondered, to become complacent? Not to check someone else's preparation which was supposed to be impeccable or improvise for personal protection upon the rigid patterns choreographed by Moscow? Easy for some, Zenin decided: for most. But never for him. He determined never ever to be lulled into dangerous relaxation. He would create his own tensions, his own adrenaline-pumping strains, maintaining the constant nerve-stretched expectation that something was always about to go wrong, if not this minute, then the next minute, always suspicious, always distrustful. And most important, always safe.

With that determination in mind, Zenin pushed himself up from his table, the bill carefully checked and the required fifteen percent, precise to the centime, added. He retraced his steps back down the quai to cross the Pont de l'Ile on foot before catching another pursuit-checking streetcar not to but near the Rue Barthelemy-Menn. From the drop-off point, once more on foot, he zig-zagged through the streets and roads at times directly away from his destination, finally reaching it by narrowing his perambulations in gradually tightening circles.

Zenin was in place but completely concealed in the Avenue de la Croisette thirty minutes before the time he had given Sulafeh Nabulsi to leave her hotel, early again for the same reason he had been early in the Rue des Terreaux du Temple, one professional searching for another professional's hint of surveillance. And as before, he found nothing. The day had built up to be surprisingly warm, somnolent almost, and the streets were practically deserted under the weight of the sun: insects, confused, milled about the tree against which he waited, so that he had to swish them away with his hand. Zenin realized, abruptly, that the effect of any strong sunlight in his eyes had been something for which no allowance had been made during the Balashikha training, because the Bern embassy insistence had been that there would be none at this time of the year. Something further to check when he installed the rifle in the corner apartment off the Colombettes road.

She left the hotel exactly at the time given, and Zenin immediately recognized Sulafeh Nabulsi from the many photographs he had memorized. The temptation was to study her physically but he refused it, security uppermost in his mind. He let her stride past the junction near which he stood, concentrating for any indication of pursuit upon the hotel exit from which she emerged. There was none, so he transferred his attention to the street itself, for a car pickup, but again no vehicle moved. Zenin eased onto the Rue Barthelemy-Menn, picking her up about two hundred yards ahead. Almost at the moment he isolated her, she jerked suddenly sideways and to the left into the Boulevard de la Cluse, so by cutting left himself into the Rue de Peupliers and hurrying he was already on the Rue de l'Aubepine when she came out onto it, continuously glancing behind her. The check for pursuit was pitifully amateurish but at least she was making an effort. The woman hurried north toward the lake and the Russian frowned, unable to believe she intended trying to cover the entire distance on foot because he knew she would never be able to make the café on

the Rue des Terreaux du Temple in the time he had set out.
She was still darting backward glances and he realized she
was seeking something more than surveillance so when she
hailed the taxi he was on the lookout too, managing to stop
one almost at once. Sure of her destination but not wishing
to make any ridiculous "follow that taxi" demand upon his
driver, Zenin asked for the Quai du Seujet, at its connection
with the Coulouvreniere bridge. He still had the woman's
vehicle in sight when it stopped short of the bridge. Zenin
let his own taxi continue over and then waited, and within
minutes she appeared, hurrying over the footcrossing.

He let her get ahead and fell into step but on the far side
of the road and a long way behind, so that any surveillance
would visibly intrude between them and show up to him.
And at last allowed himself the indulgence of some physical
impression. The black shoulder-touching hair bobbed as she
hurried, and on her frequent, backward-checking half-
turns, which she made without pause, he was aware of her
breasts bouncing with her movement. She wore a khaki-
colored dress, belted, so that it was difficult to know
whether it actually was a dress or a matching skirt and top,
and carried a large handbag, more a briefcase, supported
from her shoulder by a strap. Always, as she walked, she
kept her hand securely over it. Fuller-figured than he had
imagined from the photographs, Zenin decided; most certainly heavier-busted. And not as tall, although that was a
reflection at which he was surprised because he knew her
precise height from the already provided description.

She slowed when she reached the Rue des Terreaux du
Temple, obviously seeking out the café, and then picked up
pace when she identified it. When she reached it, she hesitated again, looking around as if she were expecting a greet-
ing from among the people who thronged the outside area.
When nothing came, she went forward; Zenin smiled,
pleased, when she chose one of the few vacant outside tables. It was far back, close to the café, and well-positioned
to see anyone approaching. Which Zenin did not attempt.
Instead he continued onto the corner of the Rue Bautte from
which he had watched earlier that day, to insure no surveil-

lance had been established in the intervening period. While he watched, he saw Sulafeh Nabulsi take a cosmetic compact from the large case and spend a long time examining her face and putting into place the hair that had become disarranged during her evasive approach from the Rue Barthelemy-Menn.

Zenin allowed ten minutes, alert now not so much upon her but upon anyone or any group getting into position around her. She had almost finished the mineral water she had ordered and was actually looking nervously about her before the Russian moved.

He crossed the street and threaded his way through the outer tables, smiling as he approached her table.

"Hello," he said, still testing. He spoke English.

"I'm waiting for someone," she said.

"Maybe it's me."

"Go away."

"Why so hostile?"

"If you don't go away, I shall call a waiter. Or the management."

"We can talk, can't we?"

There was a waiter three tables away and Sulafeh looked toward the man and made as if to raise her hand, in a summons.

"Why be so difficult?" said Zenin, pleased at her reaction. "Why give me the Run Around?"

She dropped her hand at the code phrase. At first she stared at him quite without expression and then, slowly, she smiled hesitantly. She gestured to the chair on the opposite side of the table and said, "Why don't you sit down?"

Zenin did, smiling back at her. Close up she was very attractive, almost beautiful. The olive skin of her face was perfect and unblemished and despite the compact she wore little makeup, only a suggestion of lip coloring. There was nothing at all around her eyes, which were deep brown, open in apparent innocence and which were studying him with the interest matching that with which he was looking at her. He let his own eyes drop, briefly, to her body, particularly those full rounded breasts, and she knew what he was doing and wasn't offended. The nearby waiter came up and Zenin remembered to order mineral water although he could have explained alcohol away by telling her he was a Christian Palestinian. Sulafeh accepted another drink, and when the waiter left, looked at him expectantly. He said, "Would you have called someone to throw me out?"

"Of course," she said, at once. "I've every reason to be here. We can't risk anyone getting in the way, can we?"

Zenin nodded, believing her. "Very good," he said.

She swallowed, dipping her head at the praise. She said, "I'm being very careful."

"I know."

"How do you know?" she demanded at once.

"I followed you here, all the way from your hotel." He jerked his head to the Rue Bautte. "And then watched for awhile, from over there."

"Why?"

"To make sure that you were alone," said Zenin. "I'm being careful, too."

"I didn't know what to expect," said Sulafeh. "Now, I mean."

"And?"

"I still don't know." She was immediately drawn to him, but was unsure if that was because of his obvious attractiveness or because of what she knew him to be.

"I'm not sure either," said Zenin, which was a lie, but he was content to let her make what she wanted from the ambiguity.

She looked directly at him for several moments, and Zenin held her eyes; a heaviness grew between them. To break the mood, Sulafeh patted the briefcase she had trapped between her leg and the chair support and said, "I've got everything here."

"What's everything?"

"Complete plan of the conference area, with all the rooms and chambers marked and identified. The most up-to-date schedule of the sessions—"

"Which could be changed, of course?" Zenin interrupted.

"I believe they frequently are," she agreed.

"How much warning do you get, as interpreter?"

"Overnight."

"So we'll need to meet every day."

She did not reply at once, looking directly at him again. Then she said, "Yes, we'll have to meet every day."

Zenin smiled at her and she smiled back. He said, "Will that be difficult for you?"

"I don't think so."

Beneath the atmosphere growing between them, Zenin was instantly aware of her doubt. "What is it?" he demanded.

"It's not a problem with the conference arrangements," she qualified. "Until the sessions start, there's very little for me to do."

"What then?"

"A man called Dajani, the other interpreter. He's becoming a nuisance."

"Sexually?" insisted Zenin, openly.

Sulafeh nodded. "He's made a play from the beginning. Hung around the conference area and the hotel." She shuddered. "He's repulsive," she said.

"I can't kill him," said Zenin reflectively. "It would draw attention and we obviously can't risk that."

Although she knew what he was—or believed she knew what he was—the casualness with which he spoke of killing astonished her. At once there was a further, wonderful sensation: the eroticism of it erupted through her and she felt the wetness between her legs. "No," she accepted, her voice uneven. "You can't kill him."

Zenin was conscious of the change in her tone and wondered at it. He said, "Have you slept with him yet?"

"No," said Sulafeh. The wetness was growing at the equally casual and detached way he was now talking of sex, and she wondered if her skirt would be stained when she stood up.

"You might have to, if it's the only way."

Stop it! she thought, as a fresh surge swept through her. She said, "I suppose so."

"Could you do it, if you had to?"

"I can do anything to insure that we don't fail," insisted the woman, striving for control and for the professionalism she was supposed to have. "I just don't want to. Like I said, he's repulsive."

"Like you also said, it's a nuisance," agreed Zenin, reflective again. "I don't like the risk of anything unforeseen."

"There was no way I could have known."

"I wasn't criticizing you." He thought she was flushed and said, "Are you all right?"

"Fine."

"There's no change in the schedule for the commemorative photograph?"

"No," she said.

Zenin gestured toward the bag and said, "Is the site marked there?"

"Yes."

He would have to visit the unseen apartment soon, to insure the sightline was as he needed it to be. For his own enjoyment, he reached across the cafe table, taking her hand. She reached forward to help him, enjoying his feel. "Such a small hand!" he said.

"I don't understand."

"Have you ever fired a Browning automatic?"

It had not been necessary for him to touch her to ask a question like that. "I thought you were trained in the Libyan camps, like I was," she said. Throughout the planning, Sulafeh had been told by cutouts she believed to be Arab, but who were in fact KGB agents like Zenin, that he was a fanatical member of a breakaway faction of the Palestinian militant Abu Nidal group.

"I know the weapons upon which I was trained," said Zenin, the escape easy and still holding her hand. "Not how women were instructed."

"Usually it was Kalashnikov, Chinese as well as Russian," said Sulafeh. "But there were others. Including Browning."

"It's a parabellum: heavy," said Zenin, freeing her hand at last. "You will need to be very close. The recoil could make you fire wide. Soft-nosed bullets, of course. Guaranteed to kill."

Sulafeh felt the sensation growing again, at the return to casual talk about killing, and thought, please no! She did not think she could sustain much more. She said, "Interpreters have to get close; that's their job."

"What about conference security: getting the gun in that day?"

Sulafeh snorted a dismissive laugh. "Ridiculous!" she said. "I've completed the accreditation and got all my passes, and I've made a particular point of becoming known to the security personnel so that they recognize me." She touched the bag. "I've carried that all the time, so that it has become accepted without question, like I am. Not once has anyone demanded to look inside."

"What about metal-detecting devices?"

"They have the hand-held sort, to run over the body. Again, I've never been checked."

"There aren't any electronically governed doors you have to pass through?"

"No."

"Careless," judged Zenin.

"To our advantage," pointed out the woman.

"I'll get you out, you know," said Zenin, in sudden promise. "We'll need to go through everything very thoroughly to make sure you understand, but I've already planned it. It'll work."

"I was told you would," she said. "Look after me," she added.

"Trust me."

"I can, very easily," she said, holding him with another of her direct looks.

There was the need to examine the apartment off the Colombettes road, thought Zenin. But alone. To consider—wildly imagine—taking her there would be madness, contravening all the training: that too intense, too action-packed training he'd earlier thought of so critically. It was part of the tension to want a woman, Zenin knew. Excitement heightens all the senses and all the needs. He'd actually been warned about it—and against it—during that training. But he hadn't believed it until now. He said, "Have you got to go to the conference center any more today?"

Sulafeh shook her head. "I went this morning, to collect the up-to-date schedules."

"What else do you have to do?"

"Nothing," she said. "I left everything open." Sulafeh allowed the pause and then added, "I did not know what you would want."

It would be safer for her to hand over the schedules somewhere less open, he thought. And then he thought it was a very weak excuse. He said, "There is somewhere I have to go. To an apartment."

"Yes," she said expectantly. Ask me, she thought, please ask me.

"Would you come?"

"You know I will."

"I want you."

"I want you, too. Very much."

"It's not far."

"When we leave, would you walk close behind me?"

"Why?"

"There might be a mark on my skirt."

There was and it excited him more. They sat apart in the taxi, savoring a pleasure by denying it to themselves. They did not talk either. He took her arm after paying the cab off in the Rue du Vidollet, and he felt her shiver. They were hurrying when they reached the apartment block, off Colombettes. The vestibule was deserted and so was the elevator—where again they stood apart—and Zenin was sure they entered the apartment unobserved by anyone. Inside neither could wait. He snatched at her and she grabbed back at him, pulling off his clothes as fast as he tried to undress her, and they made love the first time on the floor just inside the entrance, Zenin still half-wearing his shirt. They climaxed almost at once and together, and he left her lying there while he hurriedly explored the apartment to find a bedroom. He led her there, and they made love again, twice, but more calmly now, exploring one another, finding the secret, private spots, each wanting to please the other.

"Wonderful," Sulafeh gasped, the last time. "You're wonderful."

"So are you. Fantastic," said Zenin. He wanted to make love to her again immediately and knew he would be able to. He wondered if his excitement was hardened by realizing that in a few days' time he was going to kill her.

Charlie missed it the first time, picking out the significance only on the second, comparable study of the logs. Determined to be sure of everything, he caught the afternoon train to Bern and walked several times around the streets bordering the Soviet embassy on Brunnadernain, expertly studying all the overlooking buildings to isolate the observation points from which the Swiss watchers would maintain their surveillance. Although official checks were still necessary, Charlie was sure he knew what the answers would be, and he was not mistaken.

"Fuck it!" he said, to himself. "Too fucking late again!"

Back in Geneva, he telephoned David Levy in advance of the Swiss counterintelligence chief, curious to know if the Israeli had spotted the same inconsistency as he had. As a test, Charlie let Levy lead the conversation. The Mossad chief mentioned it at once.

"Have you told Blom yet?" asked Charlie.

"No. Have you?"

"I want to make absolutely sure, from the service people first."

"You're wasting your time."

"It's still got to be done," insisted Charlie. "Has there been any independent contact from the others?"

"Giles called. Said he thinks it's ridiculous to exclude you. He's told Blom, apparently."

Loved at last, thought Charlie. He said, "Did Giles see anything in the logs?"

"If he did, he hasn't told me."

"Do you think they'll accept this as positive evidence that the bastard is here somewhere?"

"No," said Levy at once. "And neither do I. It's proof of something perhaps. But not that he's our man."

"You know what you're all going to do!" demanded Charlie, exasperated. "You're all going to be pissing about trying to convince yourselves nothing's wrong when the shooting starts!"

"I do think we should meet tonight instead of waiting until tomorrow though," conceded the Israeli.

Charlie had been marked by two squads of the specially drafted Soviet watchers when he walked past the embassy on Brunnadernain the second time and positively targeted on the third occasion by both. Between them, the two groups managed five exposures, and the photographs were included in that night's diplomatic dispatch from Bern to Moscow under a priority designation, so that instead of remaining overnight in Dzerzhinsky Square, they were taken at once by special courier to Berenkov's apartment in Kutuzovsky Prospekt.

The courier meant it was official, and normally Valentina would have said nothing, but she was abruptly conscious of her husband's startled reaction.

"Alexei Aleksandrovich!" she exclaimed, alarmed. "What is it?"

"Someone from the past," said Berenkov. He remembered his wife had met Charlie Muffin during the Moscow episode, but decided against mentioning the name.

The special meeting in Geneva was already underway when Berenkov summoned his emergency session in Moscow.

22

"So your people didn't need any specific instruction!" accused Charlie. The rudeness was intentional. He wanted to stir one of them—or more hopefully, all of them—into some sort of reaction.

"I don't think it is as indicative as Charlie does," said Levy. "But it's certainly curious."

"I think so, too," endorsed Giles, pleased he had isolated the inconsistency like the other two.

"There might be an explanation different from that you are reaching," tried Blom. He was burning with impotent anger.

Charlie tossed the log records onto the desk of the Swiss counterintelligence chief and said, "Look at it! The entry of a workman carrying a toolbag is recorded at ten-thirty in the morning. They actually wrote it down, for Christ's sake!"

"I know what they wrote down," said Blom.

"So where's the matching entry of his leaving!" demanded Charlie. "Are you trying to suggest that the Soviets have kidnapped a Swiss workman and have still got him in the embassy?"

"They could have missed the departure," suggested the American. "A workman is a pretty normal sort of arrival and departure, after all."

"That's exactly what it is *not*!" insisted Charlie. "It just seemed so to these watchers and it shouldn't have been. They need their asses kicked! The Russians *never* employ local labor for any work inside their embassies. It's their standard tradecraft to have everything done by Russians: to fly people in from Moscow, if necessary. . . ." He hesitated for effect. Then he said, "And just in case they changed the habit of a lifetime, I checked with every service agency I could think of: telephone, electricity, gas, everyone. There is no record of any call to the Soviet embassy at Brunnadernain. I asked about the past, too. They never get called."

"You think he came out with that mass exit recorded at lunchtime?" asked Levy, referring to his own copy of the watchers' log.

"It's the most obvious answer," said Charlie. He looked at the Swiss intelligence chief. "And your watchers did not think that was significant enough to report specially either, did they?"

"There appears to have been some slackness," conceded Blom, with no choice. "I still think it would be wrong to twist it to fit the circumstances."

"I'm not twisting it to fit any circumstance," argued Charlie. "It's actually got a pattern. He almost beat us by merging into the background in England, and he beat us here by merging into the background again. It was actually a mistake on his part."

"What about a different exit?" said Giles.

"I went to Bern and looked at the embassy for myself," said Charlie, unaware of his own mistake. "They're all covered."

"I think the squad on duty when the workman went in should be interrogated, to see if we can get a description that matches the one we've already got," said Levy.

"It was the pickup," said Charlie, in adamant frustration. "This was when he collected the weapon. Or weapons."

"There's no record on the log of anyone in that lunchtime crowd carrying anything out," said Giles.

"The squads should be interrogated on that, too," said Charlie.

"They will be," promised Blom.

"You've got five days before the Middle East conference begins," reminded Charlie. "The delegation leaders start arriving in the next forty-eight hours."

"So?" said Blom.

"So publish the damned photograph!" said Charlie. "Frighten the bastard off!"

"I don't think anything has happened to change the attitude on that," said the Swiss.

"Suggest it again," urged Charlie, looking to each of the other three men. "And warn the other delegations."

"I won't start a panic," said Blom.

"It's the way to avert one," said Charlie.

"Give me some positive proof," demanded Blom. "Better proof than this."

"By the time you accept it, it'll be too late," warned Charlie.

"I'll raise it again with Jerusalem," undertook Levy.

"I'll play it back, too," said Giles.

"I'm sure the answer will be the same as before," said Blom, confident his security committee would not change their minds.

"If it is, it'll be a mistake," said Charlie. Christ, how he hated working with a committee!

Sulafeh stirred and Zenin shook her gently, fully awakening her.

"We should go," he said.

"I don't want to."

"It's late."

"Can we come here again tomorrow?"

"Yes."

"Every day?"

"We'll see," avoided the Russian. "I think we should leave separately. You first."

"Shall we meet at the same place tomorrow?"

"No."

"Where?"

Zenin hesitated and then said, "The Cornavin terminal. The main concourse."

"What time?"

"Three."

"Make love to me again."

23

Alexei Aleksandrovich Berenkov regarded Charlie Muffin to be his equal, which was an accolade. The Russian had frequently concluded during those long, sleepless, and gradually despairing nights in London's Wormwood Scrubs that no one but Charlie Muffin would have persisted, sifting and checking and cross-checking and then pursuing with the relentlessness of a starving Siberian wolf the labyrinthine maze Berenkov had created for his own protection and which eventually ensnared him. Or behaved, either, as Charlie had after the arrest. Not treating him as a hydra-headed monster, to be looked at like some fairground curiosity through the prison-door hatchway, but treated as that of an equal, professional to professional. It had been a challenge, being debriefed by Charlie. Berenkov still sometimes wondered what the score had finally been, before his release. He'd meant to ask, when they'd met later in Moscow, but the occasion had not presented itself. They'd been fools, the British, to imagine such a man as sacrificial. But to his benefit, Berenkov recognized. If the British had not decided to use Charlie Muffin as the disposable bait in the crossing of the Berlin Wall—and been caught out by the man doing so—Berenkov guessed he could still now be decaying in that damp-walled cell with the stinking pisspot in the nighttime corner and the eight boring hours in the prison library and the one boring hour in the exercise yard and the rest of the time alone with the smell of damp and piss. Charlie Muffin had hardly been his capturer then. Savior in fact. No, that was not correct either. There might have been professional admiration between them, but that was where the feeling ended: where it had to end, as professionals. His repatriation to the Soviet Union in exchange for the British and

American intelligence directors whom Charlie lured into Soviet entrapment in Vienna had been convenient, that's all. He'd been an advantage and Charlie had used him, like he used all advantages. Which was why the man was so dangerous. And why he had to be destroyed. Berenkov reached the conclusion quite dispassionately: again it was professional, not personal. He knew Charlie Muffin would understand that. Were the situation reversed, it was the sort of decision that Charlie would have reached. It was regrettable but necessary. That was why he had not mentioned the man's name to Valentina. She'd liked Charlie; perhaps rightfully considered him to be the man who had restored a husband to her, after so many, too many, years as an espionage agent in the West. Women thought like that. With their hearts rather than with their heads. Men had to think differently.

Berenkov arrived first at Dzerzhinsky Square, of course, but Valery Kalenin was close behind, with such a short distance to travel from Kutuzovsky Prospekt. Berenkov had considered their coming together in the same car but decided upon some time to himself, to consider fully the implications of the Swiss sighting.

"A problem?" demanded Kalenin at once.

Instead of replying, Berenkov handed the other man the set of photographs.

The KGB chief gazed down at them, slowly shaking his head. Then he looked up and said, "Charlie Muffin!"

"They were taken outside the embassy today, in Bern," announced Berenkov.

"How many were there?" demanded the KGB chief at once.

"That's the confusing part," admitted Berenkov. "I checked, obviously. But it was not a concentrated sweep. Just Charlie Muffin. And he was too late. Zenin had already made the pickup."

"I don't understand a fishing expedition," complained Kalenin.

"If the British knew more, there would have been a

buildup," insisted Berenkov. "The Swiss would be swamping the embassy. And they're not."

"Still worth letting it run, then?"

"We've still got the embassy covered," reminded Berenkov. "If there's any sort of change in the surveillance, we can still turn Zenin off at the apartment. I know it's not in the planning and there's a risk of panicking him, but it's always an option for us."

"Charlie Muffin, of all people!" said Kalenin reflectively. Kalenin had posed as the defector bait to lure the English and American Directors to Vienna, and there had necessarily been supposed planning meetings between himself and Charlie.

Berenkov knew the KGB chairman had a professional regard for Charlie Muffin similar to his own. He said, "I know Charlie Muffin. So do you. His being there worries me."

"But you said he was alone."

"How professional were the cells I ran in England and Europe regarded?" asked Berenkov confusingly.

Kalenin frowned across the Dzerzhinsky Square office at his friend, whom he regarded as one of the least conceited people he had ever known. He said, "Magnificent. You know that."

"Charlie Muffin worked virtually alone when he closed me down," said Berenkov. "And what about his coming here after the escape from a British jail?"

"A plant: we know that."

Berenkov shook his head. "The Englishman who was with him and whom we captured admitted everything," he said. "Everything except that. He always insisted Charlie Muffin knew nothing about it."

"But that's how Natalia Fedova discovered there was an attempt at infiltration in the first place!" refuted Kalenin, who had again personally interrogated the woman.

Berenkov, who knew of his friend's involvement, said, "That's what Comrade Fedova insists."

"Are you suggesting Charlie Muffin was working quite separately, on something we haven't realized?"

"I'm suggesting we reopen the file on the whole episode of his being here," said Berenkov.

"It would mean Comrade Fedova was mistaken," said Kalenin, in further reflection.

"Or something worse," said Berenkov.

"Oh no!" said Kalenin, understanding. "That can't be. She was the one who alerted me!"

"Isn't the classic way to avoid suspicion to shift it entirely upon someone else, particularly if that someone else is guilty?"

Kalenin was silent for several moments. Then he said, "I agree the file should be reopened. But personally, by you. I don't want any suggestion of a mistake having been made."

Berenkov nodded, accepting the order and said, "I think we should go beyond a reexamination. I think Charlie Muffin is too dangerous. I think he should be taken out."

Kalenin sat regarding the other man for several moments, considering the suggestion. He said, "You're surely not suggesting he should be killed in Switzerland?"

"Of course not," said Berenkov. "It would attract far too much attention: actually confirm everything. But I think an operation should be devised for something very quickly afterward."

Once more Kalenin did not respond immediately. Then he said, "I admired him. Liked him, too."

"So did I," said Berenkov. "I don't think that should affect our getting rid of him."

"Not at all," nodded Kalenin, in agreement. "But I want to know what he was doing here first. Discover that if you can, before you order it."

Sulafeh Nabulsi felt gripped by an inner warmth, an excitement that would not dissipate and that she did not want to go away. She was scarcely conscious of anything around her on the way back across the city, to the Rue Barthelemy-Menn, switching between taxi and streetcar but not really trying to weave any sort of false trail.

So enclosed was she that she did not hear Mohammed Dajani when he first called out to her in the hotel foyer. She still frowned at him in apparent lack of recognition when he put himself in her path.

"Where have you been?" Dajani demanded.

"Out," she said.

"I've been waiting."

"What for?"

"You. I thought we could explore the city, like we talked about."

It took Sulafeh a great effort to concentrate. "I'm tired," she said. Even to have the man near her was repulsive, after the ecstatic experience of that afternoon.

Dajani's face tightened. "I thought we were going to be friends," he said.

"Leave me alone!" she said, stepping around him. "Just leave me alone!"

The arrogant, career-minded, oversexed bitch needed to be taught a lesson: to learn to whom it was necessary to show the proper sort of deference, recognized Dajani. So she would be taught.

24

The Secretary of State and his wife used the underground link to get from the old Executive Office Building into the White House. Martha Bell wore a startling red suit, which she'd told her husband was an Ungaro. He didn't know the significance but guessed it meant expensive. It usually did when she used designer names like that. The route meant they entered on the basement, working floor of the White House, and Martha enjoyed the respect that was obvious from the staff toward her husband, although of course she gave no indication. She'd hoped they would gather in the Oval Office, which she regarded as the fulcrum of the presidency, and so she was disappointed when they were directed instead to the small drawing room on the ground floor, overlooking the gardens and the fountain. The President and his wife were already there. Anderson came expansively forward, arms spread wide, and kissed her on both cheeks. As he did so, she was aware of the odor of rye on his breath competing with the sweeter smell of his cologne.

"Good to see you, Martha!" he said, boom-voiced as always. "Looking forward to Europe?"

"Very much, Mr. President," she said.

"Going to be a great trip," forecast the man. "A great trip."

Janet Anderson had remained standing by the back of the two easy chairs set on either side of the fireplace. She was wearing a pale lemon two-piece, with a matching hat, and Martha Bell decided it did nothing for her at all: the woman looked washed out and faded, like she always did.

Martha smiled and said, "Hello, Janet" and Janet smiled back and said, "Hello, Martha."

Martha knew by now that such groupings were as formalized as medieval dances. She moved at once toward the other woman, leaving the men by themselves.

"You look wonderful," she said to the President's wife.

"So do you, dear," said Janet Anderson.

"I gather there are some sightseeing arrangements for us?"

"If I can fit them in," qualified the President's wife, wanting at once to establish the gap between them. "I've got a visit to a children's orphanage in Berlin and separate receptions with the Presidents' wives, both there and in Venice."

"I don't think anyone realizes how hard you work," said Martha, in seeming admiration.

"But of course," said the other woman, in apparent recollection. "You're not coming immediately to Venice. After Berlin, are you?"

"Geneva," confirmed Martha, going along with the charade. "And afterward we're going to stay on."

"Stay on?"

"Paris for a few days. Then London . . ." She smiled. "You must miss the freedom, as the President's wife, of not being able to go out without a mob of Secret Service guards? Just wander about a store, like an ordinary person? Poor Janet."

"You learn to adjust," said the other woman tightly.

Across the room, Martha saw her husband refuse a Jack Daniels that early in the day and watched the President add to his own glass and wondered what Anderson was celebrating. Bell caught his wife's attention and gestured her toward him. He said, "We're going in the first helicopter."

So that Anderson and his wife could by themselves get the maximum television and photographic coverage, Martha knew. She let Bell lead the way from the small room, out of the French doors onto the lawn where the naval helicopters were waiting, but halfway toward them, she eased her way through the phalanx of State Department officials to get alongside the man, so that they arrived at the steps together. She timed it perfectly. Bell, who was an inherently polite man, hesitated to make noncommittal replies to the shouted questions from the cordoned-off journalists, and there was the clatter of camera shutters and the sudden yellowing of television lights. It kept up as they mounted the steps and continued when Bell paused at the top, to look back and wave, before ushering his wife ahead of him into the helicopter.

"That'll catch prime time television, won't it?" demanded Martha, as they buckled themselves in for the flight to Andrews Air Force Base.

"Every newscast, this early," agreed Bell.

"Did you see Janet's outfit?"

"Not really." He wondered if it was an Ungaro, too.

"Looks like a dishrag that's been boiled too often."

The helicopter snatched up and went toward the Washington Monument, before turning south. The route took them over the Mall and just to the right of the Capitol building itself. Further away to the right, Martha could make out the traffic-clogged Beltway roped around the city. Poor, ordinary people with poor ordinary lives, she thought.

At Andrews Air Force Base, the boarding procedures were reversed. They had to wait until Anderson and his wife arrived and boarded *Air Force One* first, again surrounded by cameras, this time those of the journalists actually traveling with them to Europe. There was still some camera sound when Bell and his wife followed and the television lights stayed on, but Martha guessed the coverage to be less than it had been leaving the White House.

The interior of *Air Force One* is quite unlike that of a normal airliner. The rear has seats set out in the customary design, for the support staffs and a few selected journalists elevated from the accompanying press plane, but there is a division a little over halfway along the fuselage beyond which the layout is that of a set of luxury hotel suites. Couches line the bulkhead in an outer room, where there are television sets that work through satellite connection. The telephone and communication apparatus also operate through a satellite facility, although separate from that to which the televisions are aligned. The President's private quarters include a sitting room and dining area with couches and easy chairs, a full-sized bed with an adjoining bathroom, and a kitchen in which food is separately prepared. At Anderson's insistence, some of the kitchen space had been modified to accommodate additional wine and alcohol: before takeoff Dom Perignon champagne was being served with the caviar boats. Bell caught his wife's eye and smiled, knowing she would be pleased that every fantasy was being fulfilled.

Anderson was the consummate political communicator. He disdained the caution of seatbelts at takeoff and carried his glass to the rear of the aircraft, thanking the support staff for being with him, as if they had any choice in the matter, and arranging off-the-record background briefings for the political correspondents of *The New York Times*, the *Los Angeles Times*, *Newsweek* and NBC. The pilot was identifying the Chesapeake Bay to their left when Anderson wandered back, empty glass in hand, gazing expectantly for it to be refilled, which it was. "Been keeping the natives happy," he announced to the Secretary of State. "We got things to talk about, Jim?"

"I think so, Mr. President."

Anderson led the way further forward to his inner sanctum, throwing off his jacket and sitting, feet outstretched behind the desk. "Isn't this the damnedest way to travel!" he said.

"Martha enjoys it," admitted the Secretary of State.

"Janet, too," said Anderson. "Martha looks very striking today, incidentally. Janet remarked on it."

"Thank you," said Bell. He hoped the President's wife didn't feel upstaged.

"What's on the agenda, then?"

"The British warning in Geneva hasn't been resolved," said Bell.

"You said . . ." The President stopped, snapping his fingers for recollection. ". . . Giles," he remembered. "You said Giles was on top of it."

"Which is why I'm raising it now," said Bell. "Seems the Englishman there wants to make the running."

"The guy that screwed our people?"

"Yes."

"You asked London what the hell they think they're doing, involving that son of a bitch in the first place?"

"I think Langley has," said the Secretary of State.

"You should do it too," decided Anderson. "What's come up new?"

It did not take Bell long to outline the few developments and the President said, "That all?"

"So far."

"What about beyond Geneva?" demanded Anderson. "Has the CIA thrown out all the nets?"

"Everywhere they could think of," assured Bell.

"And?"

"Not a whisper of confirmation from anywhere that Geneva is the target. Not even a suggestion that Moscow is mounting an operation."

"Would they have expected to get one?"

"They think so."

"And they haven't?" insisted Anderson.

"Not a thing."

"So what have we got that's positive?" demanded the President rhetorically. "Something that can't be checked out, from a Soviet defector to the British. And the pickup, from a Soviet drop, in London. That's all I can see. From then on we spin off into the circumstantial. The sighting aboard the Swissair plane could be wrong, with no connection whatsoever with London. And the mysterious Herr Schmidt at the Bellevue hotel could be any sort of nickel-and-dime crook living in a dreamworld of false identities."

"What about the logged sighting at the Bern embassy?" asked the Secretary of State dogmatically.

"What about it?" came back the President. "Again what provably connects it to anything going on in London?"

It was inconclusive, conceded Bell. Circumstantial, just like the President said. Yet Bell was concerned that Anderson was being overly dismissive. He said, "That embassy sighting might have been more worthwhile if the Swiss had accepted our help."

"National pride, Jim," reminded Anderson. "Would we have accepted Swiss volunteers in Washington, in a similar situation?"

"I would have expected us to do better in a similar situation," said the Secretary of State.

"What's the Englishman suggesting?"

"What he suggested before: publication of the photograph."

"Within an hour of which everyone would be running so fast from Geneva, whether with good reason or not, that there would be scorch marks on the ground behind them," said Anderson.

"I don't imagine it would be possible to continue with the conference," agreed Bell.

"Then no," decided Anderson, positively. "If the evidence was stronger, then we'd have to take it more seriously, but I don't think it *is* strong. . . ." The President paused and said, "What do you think, Jim? Don't take any sort of lead from me. I want your honest opinion."

The Secretary of State did not hurry with his reply. At last he said, "I think you're right, Mr. President. I don't think the evidence is convincing enough."

Anderson smiled, pleased at his friend's support. He said, "And we've already recognized how we can't lose, if something happens, haven't we?"

"I guess we have," said Bell.

"Tell the British to go and suck ass," said Anderson. He allowed a long pause and said, "If I were a suspicious man, which I am not, I could almost be persuaded into thinking that their interfering in Geneva is nothing more than mischief-making. Every time I've met them, I've pegged them as people pissed off at being the world's doorman rather than its policeman."

"I'll let them know how you feel," promised Bell.

Anderson pulled himself heavily from the chair. "Let's go back and join the ladies," he said. "Have a few drinks! This is a triumphal tour, after all!"

It was thirty minutes in the larger, outer cabin, before Martha Bell could be sure of talking to her husband without being overheard. She said, "We saw the departure on television—the White House as well as Andrews! We were on both times!"

"Great," said Bell. Although he had committed himself to the President's opinion back there, he was not completely convinced that the warning should not at least be extended.

"This outfit looked fantastic!" enthused the woman. "Janet was hardly given any air time."

Reminded, Bell said, "You did check about clothes with her secretary, didn't you?"

"Of course I did," assured the woman. "Why did you ask?"

"Just wanted to be sure," said the Secretary of State.

"Darling!" said Martha. "You don't think I'd do anything to embarrass you, do you?"

"No," said Bell. "I don't think that."

"I don't think I've ever been so happy!" she said.

The luncheon hors d'oeuvres were being served aboard *Air Force One* when Barbara Giles disembarked at Washington's Dulles airport from the courtesy bus upon which she had traveled from the city terminal. She wore jeans and a workshirt, but checked three cases holding her good clothes because she wanted to look wonderful every moment of the reunion with Roger. She did not think she had ever been so happy, either.

"No!" erupted Klaus Rainer.

Blom retreated at once from the outrage from the chairman of the Swiss intelligence committee. He said, "I know it is being raised again, by the Israelis and the Americans. I felt you should know."

"It is right that you convened a meeting," said Rainer, regretting now the abruptness of his response. Again, for convenience, they met at the Bundeshaus.

"The Englishman is a nuisance," insisted Paul Leland. "A positive nuisance."

"There certainly seems to be something odd in the man

Schmidt. And the business at the embassy," suggested the third member of the committee, Pierre Delon.

"Nothing that justifies a hue-and-cry of the sort that publication of a photograph would create," rejected Rainer. To the counterintelligence chief, he said, "Is there any investigation—anything at all—that remains outstanding?"

"None whatsoever," assured Blom at once. "Every source we have has been tapped and double-checked. Quite independently of the British, I have worked in complete cooperation with the CIA and the Israeli Mossad and Shin Bet services. And I know they have made every conceivable investigation possible."

"And there has been nothing, from any of them?" said Leland.

"Nothing," said Blom.

"Would you have expected there to be, if this information from London was accurate?" asked Delon.

"Such an operation would have the highest security classification," reminded Blom. "The restriction would be to the smallest committee of men. Nevertheless, I would have thought there might have been some sort of hint."

"I found the debriefing transcript of the Russian, Novikov, very vague," said Rainer.

"My assessment was that he was telling the truth, but that he didn't know enough for it to make sense," said Blom.

"The British themselves admit there are a lot of other European conferences," said Delon. "Have they extended the warning, do you know?"

"I don't know," said Blom. "The man Muffin seems convinced he's right about it being here."

"Based upon what evidence?" demanded Rainer.

Blom shrugged. "What he has so far produced, I suppose."

"We've had, in effect, the resources of three intelligence services—four, if you include the British—which I would suggest is an unprecedented amount of technical and professional expertise," said Rainer. "And as far as Switzerland is concerned, we've come up with nothing more than a few things which appear mysterious, suspicious even, but which might equally well have a perfectly reasonable explanation. I am not for a moment proposing any sort of relaxation in the arrangement for any international gathering on Swiss soil. But I am certainly arguing against anything being made public about this episode."

"I agree absolutely," said Delon at once.

"So do I," said Leland. "We should proceed as we are at present, nothing more."

"I am grateful for the guidance," said the responsibility-avoiding Blom.

"Another thing," said Leland. "I think there should be some complaint to London about the way this damned man has been behaving."

"Absolutely," said Rainer, and there were supportive nods of agreement from everyone else around the table.

Sir Alistair Wilson guessed his deputy's distress from the unusual color of his face, much paler than its usual pinkness, and wondered at the wisdom of granting an immediate meeting. Maybe it would have been better to have delayed it, to let the man better compose himself. The Director stood at the window for comfort and watched one of the more adventurous Whitehall pigeons on an awayday forage for scraps in the street outside. Wilson thought there was a similarity in the way the bird and his deputy walked, with their strange, chest-forward swagger.

"The result of the Charlie Muffin positive vetting?" anticipated Wilson.

"There is still the personal interview to be conducted when he returns from Switzerland," said Harkness defensively.

"But what have you discovered, so far?"

"He owes various sums to bookmakers. Something in the region of three hundred and fifty pounds."

"Yes," said Wilson, unimpressed.

"He hoards pornographic publications in his flat."

"What sort of pornographic publications?"

"*Playboy.*"

"Choirboys can buy *Playboy* on station bookstands,"

pointed out the Director. "I'm sure a lot of them do. Choirmasters, too."

"There is also membership of some disreputable clubs," said Harkness. "Two are solely for after-hours drinking. The third—it's called the Fantail—features women either topless or bottomless. Sometimes both."

"I think it's fair to say, then, that Charlie Muffin isn't gay and likes a drink, don't you?"

"I think it also indicates rather questionable morals," insisted the deputy director.

"I've often thought that an essential requirement for the job," mused the Director. "What about the business over the restaurant bills?"

Harkness's color deepened. "Three establishments have been traced, all within a mile or two of where he lives. All insist the money was genuinely spent. He appears to be well known in each of them."

"I understand, of course, that having embarked upon it, the positive vetting has to be completed, but it would seem to me that Charlie is pretty much in the clear, wouldn't you think?"

"Not in one thing," argued Harkness. "At his grading level, there is no way he could service an overdraft of ten thousand pounds."

"So you're refusing the bank reference?" guessed Wilson.

"I sent the rejection letter this morning," confirmed Harkness.

25

They started drinking in Levy's hotel but at Charlie's suggestion moved from the Bristol almost at once for what turned out to be a pubcrawl. By the time they reached the bar on the Rue du Port, Charlie had walked off and drunk off most of the anger.

"You're wrong, you know. All of you," he insisted.

"So you keep saying," reminded Levy. Like the pub's name suggested, it was a port workers' bar, with no service, so the Israeli carried the brandies back from the counter.

"And me, too," said Charlie, almost in private conversation with himself. "I've got a feeling I've done something wrong, too."

"Like becoming obsessive?" suggested Levy.

Charlie came out of his reverie. "No," he said. "Not that."

"I've got to admit it, Charlie. That's the impression you're conveying. Certainly that's what Blom thinks."

"I don't believe Blom is capable of thinking."

"Charlie!" pleaded Levy. "It hasn't just been the Swiss. The CIA has pulled out all the stops and we've done the same. And you know what your own people have done in England. If one had missed something, another group would have picked it up."

"He's here!" insisted Charlie. "I can feel he's here."

"An intelligence agent doesn't work on feeling," said Levy.

"I do."

"For two weeks Geneva has been a goldfish bowl with not just one but three intelligence agencies staring into it; four, if you include yourself," said Levy. "Okay, so our man—if there is such a man—is a professional, but to stay undiscovered for that long he'd have to be the most professional operator I've ever encountered."

"The Swiss did not—" started Charlie and then stopped. "Into," he said.

Levy looked worriedly across the tiny circular table. "What?" he said.

"Into," repeated Charlie. "That's the mistake. Into."

"You're not making sense," complained the Israeli.

"Wait," said Charlie, excitedly. "Just wait! In fact, I'll get more drinks." He did, bringing them back from the bar, then said, "We picked up the lead in London and we followed it here and we've spent all this time behind him—on the outside, looking in. Don't you see!"

"No," refused Levy, curtly.

"What about inside, looking out? What about someone in one of the delegations?"

Levy shook his head wearily. "We did that: my people. We compared your Primrose Hill photograph with every delegate and every support member and every secretariat. There were a couple of passing likenesses, but checked again they didn't fit."

"Is that all you checked?" demanded Charlie. "Just photographic likenesses? What about backgrounds? Are you telling me, for instance, that you're letting your government leaders close to a group of Palestinian Liberation people— people you term as terrorists—without knowing everything down to the color of their knickers! And the Syrians and Jordanians, for that matter!"

"Of course, we've got files on as many as possible," smiled Levy. "All have committed crimes against us, at some stage or other. That's why we've got combined security, Mossad and Shin Bet. I don't see how it's going to help find your invisible man."

Neither did he, conceded Charlie, but he was reluctant to let the idea go. He said, "We made the London photograph and the dossier available to you. Novikov, too."

"Yes," said Levy doubtfully.

"Britain is not a participant in the conference, so I've got no in-field intelligence backup."

"So what do you want?"

"Access to your files on the visiting delegations."

"I told you we've done that already!"

"Full cooperation: that was our agreement, wasn't it?"

"It would take days!"

"You know how long it takes a trained assassin to kill someone? I hear an expert can get six shots away in the space of sixty seconds."

"You're wasting your time, Charlie."

"It's my time."

"Why not," agreed Levy finally. "It'll take a while to make the copies. I could telephone. While it's being done, we can have another drink."

"Why not?" echoed Charlie. Christ, how he hated working with anyone!

Roger Giles picked out his wife as soon as she emerged through the arrival doors, but briefly she couldn't locate him and her face closed at his not getting to the airport to meet her. And then he called out, and she saw him and her face filled with her happiness.

"I thought . . ." she started.

". . . I know," he said.

"I was frightened the plane would be delayed."

"It wasn't. Guess we were lucky."

They stood at arm's length, each looking shyly and awkwardly at the other, neither knowing what to do. Giles wondered whether to kiss her and decided against it. He didn't want to rush her.

"You look great," he said.

"So do you."

"I'm glad you came."

"I'm glad you asked me."

There was another silence between them and Giles said, "Everything is going to be fine."

"I want it to be," said Barbara. "I want it to be so much."

"I've got a suite at the hotel. Two bedrooms."

Barbara paused and said, "Yes."

On the way into Geneva they spoke very little. Barbara

said she'd brought three suitcases because he'd made it sound like a long vacation, and Giles said that was fine and while he had to hang around at the conference, why didn't she check out the tourist offices and plan an itinerary. She asked if he had any preference for the countries they were to visit, and he said he'd leave it entirely up to her. It all sounded like the polite conversation of two people who did not know each other particularly well.

The American delegation had taken over an entire floor of the President Hotel, and Giles had managed to get a lake-side suite. He had the porter leave her cases in the minute vestibule, avoiding the choice of a bedroom.

Barbara stood at the window of the sitting room and said, "It's absolutely breathtaking."

"I wanted everything to be just right."

"It is."

"I'm going to be tied up while the conference is on, but after that we'll have a month to ourselves."

"That'll be great."

"The restaurant here has got a pretty fantastic view, too. Or we could get room service, if you're tired after the flight."

Barbara turned away from the window, looking toward the other rooms. She said, "I'm not particularly tired, but room service sounds good."

Giles offered her the card but she said, "Why don't you order for me while I freshen up?"

She carried the smallest of the three cases into the bathroom, leaving the other two where they were. The meal had been delivered by the time she came out, wearing a lounging robe he couldn't remember seeing before. It was made of some filmy material and swept down to the floor.

Giles had the table set up in front of the window. Unasked, the hotel had provided a single rose in a stem glass.

"Champagne!" she said, seeing the ice bucket.

"French," he said. "I didn't order much food. I didn't think you would be hungry after eating on the plane."

"I'm not."

"I'm not either."

Giles poured the wine and handed her the goblet and said, "I suppose there should be a toast?"

"I suppose so."

"I can't think of anything that would sound right."

"This isn't proving easy, is it?"

"Maybe we're both trying too hard."

"I thought that was what we had to do, try hard?"

"Me, more than you," he said.

"I want to say something," she said. "Get something straight."

"What?"

"Sleeping apart was stupid. It didn't prove anything."

"No," he agreed.

She looked away from him, out over the lake. She said, "I want to sleep with you tonight . . . be in the same bed, I mean. But I don't want . . . I just want you to hold me, that's all. You know . . ."

". . . I know," he said again.

"You angry?"

"No."

"Like you, I want everything to be right. And particularly that."

"It will be," he said. "I promise you it will be."

26

Potma is not a single prison camp, as it is often described, but rather a string of gulags not even given the authority or doubtful dignity of names but designated instead only by numbers, one to thirty-six. They are identical in construction, a series of pebble-in-the-water concentric wood-planked and wood-slatted barracks, each block separated from the ripple impression of that next to it by razor wire electrified to an instant-touch lethality. Each of the thirty-six are stitched like buttons onto a shirt along the sluggish, mud-brown Potma river from which the penal colony derives its identity. In the warmth of the brief summer its swamps shroud every camp in a waist-high miasma of mist and fog in which the malaria-carrying mosquitoes and the poisonous, horse-killing, man-maiming *moshky* gnats swarm and attack unseen. In the long frigid winter those same swamps turn the entire area into rock-hard tundra so cold that the flesh from a naked foot tears off after less than a minute's contact. The floors of the unheated barracks are, of course, bare earth. As well as thirty-six gulags there are thirty-six matching cemeteries. Over the years, the cemeteries have expanded to occupy more land than the camps that they serve on a daily—and sometimes hourly—basis.

Alexei Berenkov decided there could be greater advantage in conducting the initial re-interrogation of Edwin Sampson in the crushing surroundings of Potma Gulag 28, in which the man had been incarcerated for almost three years and in which he would be flinchingly aware of every penalty for every infraction. Berenkov was in a hurry and wanted the Englishman as immediately cooperative as possible. Bringing Sampson back to Moscow's Lefortovo jail or to the Serbsky Institute, where he had originally been broken, was something to be considered later, if he resisted. Berenkov could not imagine the man resisting, after what had happened in Lefortovo or Serbsky. Not unless his mind had gone, which was always a possibility.

Winter was already waiting, its warnings everywhere, and the helicopter had to fly low over the river to get beneath the cloud base. The machine was heated, and in addition Berenkov was wearing a fur-lined topcoat and a momentarily discarded hat with fur-lined earflaps, but he still shivered at the unrelieved, brittle-sharp greyness below. It was a monotonous moonscape of sameness, without a single break of color as far as the eye could see. At the height at which they were flying it was possible to isolate the individual barracks and sheds, each guarded by control towers and additionally patrolled by foot squads with dogs. Occasionally there was a head-bent line of men shuffling automatonlike from one task to another, escorted by more dog-handling warders. Between every camp, virtually the thread through the button-holes, entwined the river, not mud-brown from where he gazed down but black, the meandering and twisting link between it all.

Berenkov shivered again in horrified revulsion. He had believed English imprisonment appalling, but found it difficult to find a word—or group of words—to describe or even compare it with what he was looking down upon. Not difficult, he thought, impossible. No words or phrase could adequately convey the awfulness of it. He thought of moonscape again: a place where life could not exist.

The pilot banked slightly higher and then circled Potma Gulag 28 and Berenkov saw the welcoming group already assembled, the helicopter landing cross appearing newly painted on a concrete space in an open area in the most outward of the concentric circles. The safest place, Berenkov remembered. The political prisoners were imprisoned in the very center, with the *urkas*, the common criminals, terrorizing and raping and virtually acting as additional warders from their outer, encircling areas, in addition to the official guards. The last ring housed the least violent and so the least dangerous. If conditions could be better here they were better, the guard barracks and officers' quarters more adequately heated, with proper kitchens and proper sanitation. Also—but most importantly—the officers and guards were immediate to the exit for a quick escape in the event of a riot by men too desperate or subhuman to be put down by dogs or machine guns or flame throwers or gas.

Berenkov had a confusion of impressions as he stepped down from the helicopter. The first was of the already biting cold and of ground so frozen that it rang strangely like metal beneath his feet. And then almost at once came another sensation, a memory he'd never wanted to recapture, but more disgusting than he'd ever known in Wormwood Scrubs. It was the stench of the worst sort of imprisonment and was no single smell. It was of decay and filth and rot, of animals and excrement and urine, of living things discarded and too long and too badly dying.

Berenkov tried to cough to disguise the gagging that rose in his throat and almost failed, so that he came near to choking, but fortunately the rotor engines of the helicopter had not completely quieted, so nobody noticed.

"Comrade General!" greeted the camp commandant. He was a colonel named Slepov. He held himself stiffly to attention and actually saluted. Behind the man, Berenkov saw, ranged other camp officers: two majors and three lieutenants.

"Comrade Colonel," responded Berenkov. He did not bother to reply to the salute, nor to address himself to the escorting officers. "Everything is ready?"

"My own office has been made available," said Slepov. Tentatively he moved away from the landing area, inviting Berenkov to accompany him, which Berenkov did.

"That's considerate," said Berenkov.

"You will require some refreshment?" invited the commandant, frightened at the reason for Berenkov's visit and wanting to extend all the protective hospitality possible.

Berenkov still had a foul taste in his mouth from his reaction to the arrival smell, and there was the need for preliminary discussion anyway. He said, "Perhaps something to drink. Flavored vodka, preferably."

"We enjoy pepper vodka in this climate," said Slepov.

"That will do excellently," said Berenkov.

As they approached the officers' quarters, Berenkov was aware of the attention from the outer ring of prisoner barracks, recognizing the professionalism of the institutionalized in which he had once been so expert himself, the ability to react to something as earth-shatteringly unusual as a helicopter arrival but at the same time showing nothing in that reaction to offend or infringe prison regulations to incur any sort of penalty.

The officers' quarters were raised on supports from the freezing ground and almost oppressively warm in contrast to the outside temperature. There were a series of pot-bellied stoves running down the center of the large, outside office block and additional central heating radiators beneath windows, which Berenkov saw were double-glazed and additionally heavily curtained. Slepov's office was carpeted, and an attempt had been made at a conference area to one side, with easy chairs and a couch and a rectangular table. The bottles were already prepared on the table. Slepov poured and Berenkov sank the first drink in one gulp, needing it. It burned through him, warming like it was supposed to do and taking some of the earlier taste from his mouth. Berenkov accepted a second. As Slepov handed it to him, he said, exploring, "It is not often that we have a visit from a KGB general."

"It is only the Englishman, Sampson," said Berenkov, getting the man's fears out of the way at once.

"I have him waiting," said the commandant.

The man started toward the intercom device on his desk but Berenkov stopped him. "Wait!" he ordered. "You have informers in his block?"

"Three," confirmed Slepov.

"Reliable?"

"They know better than not to be."

"What do they report on him?"

"Very little," said Slepov uncomfortably. "He has not formed any particular friendships, certainly nothing homosexual. In the first month of his imprisonment he broke another prisoner's nose, fighting off a rape attempt."

"No boasts?" demanded Berenkov.

"Boasts?" queried Slepov, bewildered.

"There have been no remarks about his succeeding, in whatever his mission was in coming to Moscow?"

"Nothing," assured Slepov. "If there had been, I would have reported it at once."

"Let me see him," ordered Berenkov.

The man with whom Charlie Muffin supposedly fled to Russia, after their KGB-engineered escape from Wormwood Scrubs, was let into the commandant's office within minutes, and Berenkov guessed he had been held in one of the outside offices. Edwin Sampson was wearing a grey canvas prison suit stiff with age and use and workboots around which were wrapped strips of cloth for additional warmth. Both ankles were manacled and linked by a short chain, so that he could only walk with short, scuffing steps, and from the center of that chain extended a longer metal link to another short chain between a set of handcuffs that held his hands, horny with calluses, close together and tight to his waist. His head was shaved bald against lice infestation, and his skin was tight across his cheekbones and chin. The skin was yellowed by exposure, different only where his eyes sank deeply into his head, where it was oddly black. His stance, between the two escorting guards, was stiffly respectful but docile, the attitude of someone determined against any offense that might earn retribution.

To the guards Berenkov said, "Leave him."

The men looked to Slepov, who nodded.

"I want to conduct the interrogation alone," Berenkov said to the commandant.

"Regulations insist—" began Slepov, but Berenkov cut him off.

"Alone," he said again.

Sampson remained quite still in the middle of the room, as if he were unaware of the conversation around him.

Berenkov settled behind the commandant's desk, wanting the indication of its authority. He said, "You are serving a sentence of thirty years?"

"Yes, sir."

"Do you expect the British to attempt an exchange?"

"I do not know, sir."

"But you hope for one?"

Sampson hesitated, unsure how to reply, worried about offense. Eventually he said, "Yes, sir."

"After your arrest in Moscow, you were taken to the Serbsky Psychiatric Hospital?"

Sampson visibly shuddered. "Yes, sir."

"Where you were treated with drugs?" Aminazin to induce shock, Berenkov remembered, from the man's file. Sulfazin, too, which caused a feverish rise of temperature, further to disorient.

There was another shudder from the Englishman. "Yes, sir."

"Listen to me very carefully," said Berenkov. "I want you to comprehend completely what I say. I am going to ask you some questions and you must reply honestly to them. If you do not reply honestly, I shall insure that any exchange approach by the British is permanently blocked, that you remain here for thirty years. I shall further have you taken to Moscow, to be treated again at Serbsky, until I believe the answers you are giving. Do you understand?"

The yellowed face glistened with the perspiration of fear and the manacled hands began to tremble. Sampson said, "Yes, sir. I understand, sir."

"You supplied disinformation to Moscow from a position in British intelligence while you were stationed in Beirut and Washington and attached to European Planning in NATO?" asked Berenkov. This was all in the file too, evidence from the man's Moscow trial, after his confession, but Berenkov wanted to confirm everything.

"Yes, sir."

"To trick the KGB into believing you were a genuine and valuable spy?"

"Yes, sir."

"Your supposed trial and imprisonment in Wormwood Scrubs was a trick, too, wasn't it?"

"Yes, sir."

"For what purpose?"

Sampson moistened his lips, nervous at having to go beyond the brief, obedient replies. He said, "Further to make the KGB believe I was genuine."

"Did you expect them to rescue you from jail?"

"Yes, sir."

"And then what?"

"I was to try to infiltrate the KGB." The man spoke prisonfashion, his wetted lips hardly moving.

"To act as a spy for the British?"

"Yes."

There had been no deviation from anything that had emerged at the trial but Berenkov had not expected it at this stage. The questioning so far had been to lull the other man as much as he could be lulled into the false security of safe answers. From now on the questions and those answers had to be different. "Tell me about Charlie Muffin," he demanded curtly.

Sampson swallowed, his throat visibly moving. "I was put in a cell with him in England. He was serving a sentence for deceiving the CIA, as well as the British. Both Directors into KGB capture."

Still trial deposition, thought Berenkov. And supported by their own records. Which had to be wrong. Would both services have abandoned their directors for some infiltration scheme? He found it difficult—practically impossible—to conceive yet it had to be, if Charlie Muffin was back in British intelligence, which he provably was. It was the moment to remind the man of penalties. Berenkov said, "Remember what I said about an exchange? And Serbsky?"

"Yes, sir."

"Charlie Muffin's imprisonment was a trick too, wasn't it? Part of the same plot, to infiltrate both of you into the KGB?"

Sampson's distress this time was greater than at any time before. The sweat leaked from him, staining through the canvas and shining his face, and he clutched one metal-strapped hand over the other in an effort to control the shaking. He said, "That was the prosecutor's demand at the trial."

"I know," said Berenkov, hard-voiced. "And then you denied it. But that denial was a lie, wasn't it!"

"No!"

The prisoner had twice forgotten the respectful "sir," which he well knew to be a punishable offense, recognized Berenkov. He said, "So tell me about Charlie Muffin."

"He wasn't part of anything: couldn't be. He had to believe I was a traitor, to build up my credibility when I got to Moscow. And he did believe it. I think he hated me."

"Why did he hate you?"

"Because he did not regard himself as a traitor, although that was what he'd been sentenced for being. He always said he trapped the two Directors for their trying to trap him. That it was personal."

The sweat was making black marks on the prison uniform and the respectful address seemed completely forgotten. Berenkov said, "Why did he come with you to Moscow then?"

The pause this time was different than any before. Throat pumping, Sampson said, "Because imprisonment was destroying him."

You poor bastard, thought Berenkov. It was an easy reflection, from his own experiences, despite everything that the Englishman had done or tried to do. He said, "You remember being separated from him, soon after you got to Moscow?"

"Yes," said Sampson. Then, remembering, he added hurriedly, "Sir."

"Do you know what happened to him?"

"From the questioning at my trial I assumed he had been arrested, too, sir."

"He wasn't," disclosed Berenkov. "He escaped, with the help of the British embassy, back to England."

It was not a question and Sampson was too well indoctrinated to respond. Berenkov let the full awareness settle with the other man and then continued. "And he's back in your intelligence service. Operating as an agent."

For several moments there was no response, because Sampson was fighting against any reaction that might get him into trouble but in the end he failed. His head went back and the word came out in a wail. "No!"

"Yes," insisted Berenkov.

For the first time since the interrogation began, Sampson directly fixed the Russian with those hollow eyes. "Why?" he said, wailing still. "How?"

Sampson genuinely knew nothing, Berenkov decided. No man who had undergone the psychiatric interrogation of Serbsky and endured imprisonment here at Potma—and been threatened with a continuation of both—would have risked lying. Who had lied then? There was only the woman, Natalia Nikandrova Fedova. Yet she had been the KGB debriefer who exposed Sampson as the spy he later admitted to being, under that first interrogation. Nothing reconciled, to make any sense. Unless . . . no, that did not make any sense, either. He said, "So you were tricked, too?"

"But why!"

Something else that did not make sense, thought Berenkov. Honestly he said, "I don't know."

"Sir?"

It was unthinkable for a prisoner to make any sort of demand unless he were on the point of complete breakdown. "What?" said Berenkov.

"I have told the truth."

"I believe you have."

"Please, sir, don't submit me again to the Serbsky!"

"I won't," said Berenkov.

"No punishment, please, sir, no more punishment!"

"No," promised Berenkov. "No more punishment."

Later, during the final moments of Berenkov's anxious departure from the camp, Slepov said, "About the prisoner? Is he to be subjected to any special sort of regime?"

"Nothing," ordered Berenkov. "He is to be treated normally." What, he wondered, passed for normality in a place like this?

Vasili Zenin had decided to sleep at the apartment, to examine it fully in the light of the following morning. And he did so very fully indeed, studying the maps and diagrams of the conference buildings and gardens that the woman had provided and calculating from them the sightlines available from the corner window overlooking the entire area. Definitely the sloped lawn would be designated for the commemorative photograph, the Russian determined. The trees he'd feared from ground level might interfere would be no problem, and if there were any winter sunlight, it would be sufficiently to one side not to impair his vision. He needed the accuracy of the rifle sight to assess the precise distance, but he did not think the range to be any greater than four hundred meters, from which he had never missed.

Zenin turned away from the window and saw the disarranged bed through the open bedroom door. A very definite mistake to have brought her back here, he recognized again. But one that had been made and about which there was no benefit in continued recrimination. Sexually, she was one of the most exciting women he'd known and she answered a need, like she would again.

Sulafeh Nabulsi was less than a mile away in the main conference building, taking the care she had shown from the day of her arrival to be recognized by the security guards. She, too, was thinking of what had happened in the apartment. She knew he would get her away after the killing because he had promised he would. They could live together, she decided. It would be wonderful to be his woman.

27

Permanent State Department officials had, of course, organized the President's European trip, advance groups liaising with the host countries in each capital months before, but the planning had personally been that of James Bell himself. It was the Secretary of State who had either approved or vetoed every one of Anderson's public appearances and selected the people whom the man would meet, both publicly and privately. In addition he had insisted upon seeing the drafts and then the finally prepared speeches that Anderson would make at each event and function, determined nothing would be out of place for what he recognized to be the triumphant swan song of his friend's presidency.

Berlin was as successful as Bell intended the entire trip to be. It began with an impressive arrival ceremony, where Anderson was greeted at Tegel airport by the West German president. Together they inspected a guard of honor to the accompaniment of a full band before the President gave the podium speech at which the theme was struck for every address the man was to make: Clayton Anderson, the man dedicated to peace. In the evening the Chancellor gave a glittering banquet to which Martha Bell wore a shimmering silk gown and once more outshone Janet Anderson, whose husband gave his second speech in which he spelled out more directly that the thrust of his two terms of office had been to mediate and solve intractable international problems and remove forever the threat of war which had divided his host country. In the morning—for U.S. consumption—there was the required visit to an American army base to see and talk with troops forming part of the NATO commitment, which once more provided a forum for another speech, in which Anderson looked forward to the time when tensions between East and West had been swept away to make such a commitment and such an Allied force unnecessary. And an even more required visit to the Berlin Wall. It was the best television and photographic opportunity during this stage of the European trip and Bell had devoted great care to it, even arranging for an elevated platform to be constructed for the cameramen and photographers alongside the observation tower, which Anderson mounted to stare grave-faced across the wire and the mines and the automatically-triggered machine guns into a gaunt East Berlin. Here—brilliantly—there was no speech. Anderson was pictured slowly and sadly shaking his head, and he shook his head again to shouted questions from journalists demanding his impression, only allowing himself to be pressured at the moment of entering his car to say that the Wall was a testimony that required no words. There were provisions, of course, for private talks between Anderson and the Chancellor and the preceding briefing session was the first opportunity since the conversation aboard *Air Force One* for the President and the Secretary of State to talk privately and alone.

"You know what I regret, Jim?" mused Anderson.

"What?"

"That Kennedy got in first with his I-am-a-Berliner speech. That would have gone down well today."

"Circumstances have changed, Mr. President."

"Still a hell of a speech," insisted Anderson. "Anything new out of Geneva?"

"Nothing."

"False alarm then?"

"It's looking more and more like it."

"You've got a lot of private reassuring to do in Geneva," reminded Anderson. "I had to lean on Jerusalem more than anyone else to get them to the same conference table as the Palestinians, and I don't want any backlash to pull the Jewish vote at home away from the Party."

"I understand," said Bell.

"I want you to fix up as many meetings as you can with the Israeli Foreign Minister and anyone else you consider necessary," said Anderson. "You tell Cohen and anyone else who needs to be told that however it might look publicly, privately we're still in their corner: always have been and always will be."

"I'll do that," promised Bell.

"You think it would be risky to give an unattributable briefing about that to the important media people?"

"Yes," said Bell, at once. "If it were datelined out of Geneva, it would be instantly picked up by the Arabs. And I'm not thinking primarily of the Palestinians; I'm thinking of the Syrians and the Jordanians. Don't forget, their foreign ministers are going to be there, too."

"I'm not forgetting either that there are more Jews in New York State than in the State of Israel and that the Jewish vote—and the Jewish lobby—is goddamned important," said Anderson.

"An accusation of secret deals and secret protocols could wreck the conference," said Bell, adamantly. "Cause a walkout."

"Okay." The President retreated at once. "But you make sure the Israelis know the score. And make sure, too, that the right word gets relayed back home . . . America, I mean, not Israel."

"There won't be any misunderstandings or ill feelings," assured the Secretary of State.

"Are there any outstanding requests from Jerusalem?"

"There are some aid packages, in total something around half a billion," remembered Bell. "And there are the continuing arms supply agreements: a whole bunch of stuff, missiles, aircraft, things like that."

"Nothing is for nothing," said Anderson decisively. "You let them know I am grateful for the concessions they've made and that they can have what they want. They've my word on it."

"The arms supply might be awkward."

"How so?"

"The keynote is peace, right?" reminded Bell. "We've got Israeli and Arab at last around a conference table, and we're going to provide the Palestinians with a homeland.

Doesn't it look contradictory to take away the reason for fighting with one hand and maintain Israel's war machine with the other?"

Anderson sat with his head reflectively forward on his chest, momentarily silent. Then he said, "One or two commentators could work up quite a head of steam with that scenario, couldn't they?"

"I think it's a positive danger."

Anderson beamed a smile across his hotel suite and said, "I think making you Secretary of State was the best appointment I managed in seven long years of office."

"Thank you," said Bell.

"I tell you what you do," decided Anderson. "Play the arms supply real close: don't say they can't have them and don't say they can either. Just leave the impression that existing contracts and arrangements will go on, uninterrupted. It's something that can be negotiated when the other agreements are hard and fast and can't be reneged on."

"I think that would be best," said Bell.

"Janet tells me you and Martha are taking a vacation, after Venice?"

"Just a short one," confirmed Bell. "Paris and then London—maybe ten days."

"I've got an idea," announced Anderson. "Why don't we try something private, in Venice? With the existing schedule it won't be easy, I know, but something. Breakfast maybe?"

"That sounds fine."

"Still wish to hell I was coming to Geneva."

"There'd be nothing wrong with a different sort of unattributable background briefing, setting out how Geneva was conceived and became a reality," suggested Bell.

Anderson smiled once more. "I've said it once and I'll say it again: getting you on board was the best goddamned decision I ever made. You have a good time in Geneva, you hear. And tell Martha what we're going to do in Venice."

Bell did, as the State Department plane lifted off for the flight to Switzerland.

"What shall I wear?" demanded the woman at once.

"I don't know."

"Maybe I'll buy something in Geneva. They'll have designer houses there, won't they?"

"I would imagine so," said Bell.

Martha gazed momentarily out of the window, clearly able to see the Wall. Then she turned back into the aircraft and said, "Do you think Anderson really appreciates all that you've done for him?"

"I know he does," said the Secretary of State.

The American plane was the last scheduled to land at Geneva's Cointrin airport that day, bringing the leaders of every delegation to the Middle East conference. The Syrian delegation was the first to arrive, followed by the Jordanian group. The Palestinians were personally led by Yasser Arafat, who predictably wore his combat tiger suit. All had cleared the airport before the Israeli plane landed.

There was continuous television coverage throughout the day, but Charlie Muffin ignored it, staring instead at the stacked files provided by David Levy.

"Jesus!" he said aloud, daunted by the self-imposed task. Then he remembered the source of the dossiers and realized he was calling upon the wrong deity.

Giles had left early, while Barbara was still in bed and she remained there, remembering how she had thought of bed when she was a little girl, as a nest in which she could huddle and be safe from any danger or difficulty. Last night had been difficult, although not as she'd thought it might be. She actually believed Roger had been relieved when she'd said she did not want immediately to make love, as nervous about it as she had been. Which he need not have been because she knew he could have made love: she'd felt his arousal almost as soon as he'd put his arms around her and finally kissed her. She wished, almost, that he'd tried. She certainly wouldn't have protested or made to stop him because when they had been close together in the bed, she'd wanted to as well but had not been able to tell him.

When she finally got up, Barbara wandered, still in her nightgown, into the living room. The room service cart had been collected the previous night, but the single rose had been left in its slim vase on a side table. Already it was wilting. Barbara took it from the container and carried it with her to the window, standing with the flower between both hands and cupped just beneath her chin. Pale winter sunlight was silvering the lake, broken in several places by bustling, self-important ferries. Maybe, she thought, she'd take a pleasure trip while Roger had to work. But not today: today she had other more important things to do, like organizing their vacation.

She went toward the bathroom still carrying the rose, deciding always to keep it as the important souvenir it was. She'd press it, like her mother had pressed flowers as mementos of special occasions. Use it maybe as a frontispiece for the album of photographs they'd make of the trip. But then again, maybe not. Maybe she'd keep the rose separate, a private reminder to herself.

After she showered and dressed, she telephoned the car rental agencies to get comparable quotes before going downstairs to the coffee shop for breakfast. After she'd eaten, she got the addresses of the six best travel agencies from the concierge and patiently toured all of them, collecting brochures and catalogues. From the last, she obtained the location of the tourist offices for Germany and Italy and France and then went to each of those as well to pick up official guidebooks and maps. She lunched contentedly alone in a cafe near the Promenade du Lac, flicking through some of the brochures and trying to devise an itinerary. She liked the idea of driving south into Italy and then along the coast into France. From there they could either drive right up to Paris and fly directly home or detour earlier into Germany.

Barbara returned to the hotel by midafternoon and for an hour wrote out different suggestions and routes, each of which she neatly annotated alongside the appropriate page so that it would be easily found when she discussed it later with Roger.

She actually felt quite tired when she finished, stretching up and going again to the window with its view of the lake. Everything was so beautiful, so wonderful. She decided she'd been right in thinking what she had at Dulles airport. She had never been so happy, not even on her wedding day. Somehow, getting back together seemed better than getting married.

28

In Charlie's experience, any assessment by fellow professionals inevitably ranked the Israeli secret services among the top three in the business. Frequently they came out top, likely to be beaten by Russia, America, and perhaps Britain only on the extent and degree of technical intelligence-gathering facilities—particularly satellites—that the others possessed.

Within fifteen minutes of beginning on the background dossiers on everyone involved in the Middle East conference, Charlie, jacket discarded, in his relieved stocking feet and with the sustaining bottle of the Beau-Rivage's best whisky delivered from room service, acknowledged how well deserved the reputation was. Never from any other service—and certainly not his own—had Charlie had access to such well-documented and complete material. Each participant, even the support staffs and secretariats that Levy had talked of, were allocated a separate file, and where that information linked to another person or a group, the dossier was also annotated and indexed to enable instant cross-referencing. And each file was accompanied by a photograph, sometimes several.

"Bloody marvelous," he said admiringly in the empty room.

Just as quickly Charlie formed another opinion: that by himself it was going to be an impossibility to assimilate everything that was there by the scheduled end of the conference, let alone by the beginning.

The most obvious shortcut was not to attempt initially to read the files at all but to conduct upon each a visual photographic comparison against the Primrose Hill print. Even that took a long time because there were so many Israeli pictures and, anxious though he was, Charlie refused to hurry, never replacing them in their folders until he was entirely satisfied there was no fit, able to speed up only when the dossier proved to be that of a woman. The male to female ratio seemed to be about eight to one, perhaps higher.

Charlie felt a spurt of excitement after two hours when he thought he saw a similarity between the London photograph and a man identified as a ministerial aide on the Syrian delegation. It leaked away as soon as he snatched open the file to see the immediate notation that it was one of the likenesses the Israelis had isolated and discounted after fuller investigation. He came upon another man—the deputy press spokesman for the Palestinian party—after a further hour, less excited this time, and found again that it was another that Levy's people had eliminated. It was midday before Charlie completed the checks—finding nothing.

He slumped back in his chair, absentmindedly massaging his foot with one hand, whisky glass in the other, frustrated by another now familiar dead end. Shit, he thought, annoyed not just by the obvious failure. He had, he admitted to himself, made the mistake of forgetting the ability of the Israelis until he was presented with it. Which still did not mean, of course, that he was going to rely on their assessment. And there was a way he could streamline, if not actually shortcut, the examination. The files on the American contingent—which was the largest—could be relegated to last, together with those upon the Israelis, which Charlie was passingly surprised Levy had included. Which left the Syrian, Jordanian, and Palestinian groups, with the Palestinians perhaps being the obvious first choice.

Sighing, Charlie topped up his glass, and was pulling the folders toward him when the telephone shrilled. He was so engrossed in what he was doing that he jumped, startled.

"Cummings," said the British intelligence *rezident*, in immediate identification.

"Yes?" said Charlie, irritated at the interruption.

"There's a summons, from London."

"Something important?" demanded Charlie.

"There's no indication," said Cummings.

Charlie said, "Be a good mate and say you couldn't get hold of me."

"I'll do nothing of the sort," refused Cummings. "And anyway, it's marked Priority Urgent."

He shouldn't have used the phrase good mate, Charlie realized. Cummings might have responded better to good chap or good fellow. He and Witherspoon would have made a fine matching pair, thought Charlie, remembering Witherspoon's reaction to the restaurant receipt request on the day of the Novikov debriefing in Sussex. "Tut, tut! On an open telephone line, too!" rebuked Charlie. He didn't detect the intake of breath but guessed there had been one. Not much of a victory, he thought, unsure why he'd bothered.

"I shall in fact say that the message has been passed on," insisted the other man. "According to instructions."

"Always follow the instructions and stand back after lighting the touch paper," agreed Charlie. "Tell them it'll take me a while."

"I said it's urgent."

"I heard what you said." Prat, he thought.

Charlie did not hurry after replacing the receiver. In fact, he poured himself another drink, looking again at the task before him, considering another way to break it down. Or rather extend it, although the burden would not be his. Was it worth it? he asked himself, sipping the drink. Maybe. Maybe not. Sometimes the British technical facilities were better, he thought again. So why not? Keep the buggers busy and justify their existence, if nothing else. Meant a hell of a lot to carry, though.

Charlie managed the one o'clock train and bought a first-class ticket so he could occupy the first-class dining carriage. He regarded eating on trains—particularly a train traveling through the spectacular scenery outside—to be one of life's true pleasures, and increasingly, there didn't seem to be many of those left any more. The fish was good and the veal excellent, and although he limited himself to half a bottle of wine and only one brandy with his coffee, he guessed the carefully stored bill would add at least five notches to Harkness's blood pressure. If the man knew what he was carrying with him on a train, unescorted and in a briefcase that didn't even have a proper lock, the pressure would probably go off the Richter scale. By now the sneaky bastard would have checked the restaurants he'd listed, Charlie guessed. No good worrying about spilt milk, or to be more accurate, frequently spilled wine. So why the summons? And on a Priority Urgent grading, which was a come-running-and-don't-bother-with-your-trousers demand. He hadn't done anything wrong: nothing that he considered wrong, anyway.

He caught a taxi from the railway station to Thunstrasse and was actually entering the British embassy when what seemed to be all the clocks in the world opened up in competition to be first to chime four o'clock.

"Faster than a speeding bullet," grinned Charlie, as he entered the security section of the legation.

"I told London you'd be here an hour ago," said Cummings.

"Traffic was dreadful," said Charlie.

"They want you at once. The Director himself is waiting."

He appeared to be because Sir Alistair Wilson came on the line immediately when the connection was made to London. The scrambling device at either end whined slightly and gave both their voices a hollow, tinny tone.

"I should have known it was inevitable!" said Wilson. He sounded weary.

"What?" asked Charlie.

"Official complaints. From Washington and from Bern. You've caused another hell of a row. Whitehall is furious."

"I was trying to get them to react!"

"You succeeded," said the Director bitterly.

"They're acting like nothing is going to happen!"

"Maybe nothing is."

Not Wilson as well, thought Charlie, dismayed. He said, "The Swiss have made a cock of it. They haven't wanted to believe it from the beginning."

"I'm pulling you out, Charlie. Tonight."

"No!" protested Charlie. "There's less than thirty-six hours left!"

"No more arguments," insisted the Director. "The decision isn't mine anymore. It's coming from above, from the very top."

Which meant Wilson had got a dressing down from the Prime Minister, Charlie recognized. Bloody nuisance, that. It really gave the man no alternative, unless he pulled a big fat rabbit out of the hat. So what the hell was it? Charlie abruptly remembered the Israeli photographs he'd hauled all the way from Geneva and started to talk with the idea only half-formed. He said, "I think I've got a positive lead."

"What!"

"Photographs," said Charlie. "There are actually two that look good to me. I intended to make contact today anyway and ask for them to be properly compared, technically and against our records."

"Where did you get them?"

A difficult question, Charlie acknowledged. If he admitted they all came from Mossad sources, the Director would know at once they would already have been checked and cleared and realize the delaying tactic. He said, "All over the place. Mostly from delegation spokesmen . . ." To cover himself, he added, ". . . A few from the Israelis."

There was a long silence from the London end. Then the Director said, "You being honest with me about this?"

"Yes," said Charlie comfortably. It wasn't actually a lie that there were photographic similarities.

There was another pause. Wilson said, "If it is positive, there'll be a need to renew the warning, at least. Which means leaving you there, while they're checked. But you listen, Charlie, and don't you even think of choosing to misunderstand what I say. You're to pouch the photographs to London right now. And after that, you are to do nothing but sit and wait until I come back to you. You got that? Sit and do nothing. Go near no one, upset no one, talk to no one. You disobey me just once, by one iota, and I will personally oversee your dismissal. You heard everything I have said?"

"I heard," said Charlie. He'd backed himself into a right

fucking corner this time, he thought, and he wasn't quite
sure why he'd even done it. And less sure what he hoped to
achieve by maneuvering the phony reason for staying on.
Unless it was to say, "I told you so," when it happened.

Cummings was waiting in the office outside the secure
communications room. Charlie said, "There's an urgent
shipment for London. A special pouch. Can you fix it for
me?"

"Of course," said the resident intelligence officer.

Charlie sent all the photographs, even the women,
wanting the unnecessary comparisons to take as long as possible.

The choice of the railway station as a meeting spot was
professionally excellent, crowded with passengers and noise
amongst which it was easy for Vasili Zenin to merge invis-
ibly. With his customary caution he arrived thirty minutes
early. The mistake of taking the woman back to the apartment still nagged irritatingly in his mind, and he determined to deny himself any further relaxation.

He found a slightly raised section near the northern departure gates from which it was possible for him to maintain an elevated watch. As he had been at the restaurant the
previous day, he was alert for any surveillance buildup and,
like the previous day, isolated nothing about which to become alarmed.

Zenin picked out Sulafeh almost as soon as she entered
the vast concourse, immediately curious at the woman's demeanor. She was hurrying and darting birdlike looks around
her, behaving quite differently from the way she had when
he'd followed her from the Palestinian hotel. Zenin's initial
impression was that she herself had spotted someone whom
he'd missed in pursuit. Anxiously he scanned the crowd
around and behind her, letting their planned meeting time
pass while he searched, unable to detect anything.

He still approached cautiously, until the last moment
hiding himself from her, conscious, as he got closer, of her
continued nervous fidgeting. Sulafeh thrust forward when
he let her see him at last, holding out her hand almost in

some sort of plea, her face twisted as if she were in physical pain.

"What is it?" he asked.

"It's not going to work!" she said. "It can't work, not now!"

29

It only took moments for Vasili Zenin to realize the woman's attitude was fueled by anger and not anxiety, but longer to discover the reason because she was so furious that her thoughts and words were disjointed, without any comprehensible thread. He held the hand she offered and talked over her, telling her to stop and become calm, but he had to say it several times before she ceased babbling, her throat moving as if she were literally swallowing the words. As she did so, the tension went visibly from her, so that she seemed to sag in front of him.

Zenin looked quickly around, judging it safe to talk where they were, at least until he got some reason for her attitude, and said, "Okay, but slowly now. Why can't it work?"

"Dajani," she started, the explanation still jumbled. "The other translator; the one I told you about."

"What's he done?"

"He was waiting for me when I got back to the hotel after I left you, and he began the usual stuff. I couldn't stand it, so I told him to go to hell," expanded Sulafeh. "When I got to the Palais des Nations this morning, I was called in by our secretariat Director; his name is Zeidan. He said there were to be some changes to the translation roster. I've been relegated. For everything."

"The photographic session?" demanded Zenin, at once.

"That's why it can't work now," said the woman. "I specifically asked about the ceremony. He said Dajani would definitely lead there. They published this morning for secretariat guidance the positions in which everyone will be standing. I've brought it with me. I shall be at least twenty yards away."

She was right, accepted the Russian. It couldn't work now. He looked around him again, deciding they had been there long enough. And he needed time to think. He cupped her arm in his, conscious of the anger still trembling through her, and said, "Let's go and find a cafe."

Sulafeh fell obediently into step beside him, enjoying his touch, the frustration ebbing away. He'd think of something, she knew. Make it all possible. She felt completely protected—confident, too—now that she was with him.

Zenin took her to the first reasonably sized cafe they encountered, on the corner of the Rue Fendt. There were pavement tables, but he went inside and got a booth in a corner near the bar where they were quite hidden. He felt out, retaining her hand across the table, aware she needed his touch, pressing her fingers against any conversation until they had ordered and the waiter had delivered the drinks— beer for him, red wine for her—and then said, "I want to go through everything. I want to know it all. Why won't it work? How is Dajani involved?"

"Because I asked specifically about that, too," said Sulafeh. "It was always the intention for me to lead the photographic session. I maneuvered for that particular appointment for months, because it was so important. Obviously I reminded Zeidan. He said Dajani came to him this morning. Said it might offend the other Arab delegations to have a woman in such apparent importance. Sexist bastard!"

The operation had always been structured for the aftermath to be more important than the actual killing, and the cornerstone of that structure was the woman's involvement. Zenin knew that whatever an unknown man named Dajani had done was almost immaterial. The one consideration was to get Sulafeh Nabulsi within apparent killing distance of the assembled delegations because the Palestinians had to be blamed. He said, "There is no possibility of persuading . . ." He stopped, searching for the name. ". . . Zeidan," he resumed, remembering. "No possibility of persuading Zeidan to reverse the change?"

"None."

"Is he someone else who's tried to get you into bed?"

Sulafeh hesitated, finding the conversation more difficult than before because of what had happened between
them now. Reluctantly she said, "Yes."

"Have you?"

"No."

"Would it work?"

She wished so much he hadn't asked like that, as if he
were talking about some other woman and not her. She
said, "There's not enough time."

"No," he agreed, his voice distant, his thoughts quite detached. "There's not enough time . . ." And then he stopped,
smiling, coming back to her. "Time!" he said. "There's not
enough time!"

Sulafeh regarded him curiously. She said, "I'm sorry. I
don't understand."

"There are only two of you, as translators? You and this
man Dajani?"

"Yes."

"How long did your selection take?"

"Me, about six months. Him, I don't know."

"And there's been a long preparation?"

"Of course," said Sulafeh. "We've had to memorize the
position papers and familiarize ourselves to recognize the
delegation spokesmen, for the translation to be simultaneous." Now she smiled at an irony by which she imagined
he would be amused. "And we had to be acknowledged acceptable, by everyone attending."

Zenin continued smiling but at his own hardening resolve to solve the problem, not what she regarded as amusing. He pressed her hand again but more sensually this
time. "If anything happened to Dajani, there would not be
enough time to prepare a replacement, would there? You'd
have to be restored to the original arrangement?"

"No," she agreed, with slowly growing awareness. At
once came the caution, mixed with the memory of her excitement. "But when I told you Dajani could be a nuisance,
you said you couldn't risk attention by killing him."

"I'm not thinking of killing him," said the Russian. "Just
removing him."

"Could you do it? So that it wouldn't create a problem, I mean?" asked Sulafeh, feeling that coveted excitement stir again.

"Yes," said Zenin. "I could do it. But I'll need your help."

"It would be a pleasure," she said, a remark as much for her own benefit as to reassure him.

Zenin's earlier street-by-street movement about the city equipped him well to know best where to look. He wanted narrow roads as little used at nighttime as possible, so it had to be the old part of the city. It meant crossing the river so they took a taxi to the Pont de l'Ile, where Zenin paid it off to go the rest of the way on foot. They went slowly along the Rue de la Corraterie toward the Place Neuve, Sulafeh contentedly holding onto Zenin's arm with no idea of the purpose for the reconnaissance but blissfully content just to be with him. The need was for a meeting place with only one possible approach, and Zenin had to go beyond the Place, near the university park, to find it, a narrow, winding cul-de-sac with alleyways off and a striped-awning bistro at its top. The length of possible vision was important, so while he remained out of sight in the shadows, Zenin sent the woman right up to the bistro, ostensibly to study the menu, while he edged back to the last point from which the necessary signal would be discernible. He was completely concealed in one of the bordering alleys when she returned, and he set the test, pleased that she obviously could not see him until he reached out to stop her.

"I don't understand what I am supposed to be doing," Sulafeh protested.

"You will," assured Zenin. "It's perfect."

"What do I do now?"

"You telephone your hotel and speak to Dajani," instructed Zenin. "You say that you're sorry about your rudeness last night. That you want properly to apologize and that you'd very much like to explore the city with him."

"What!"

Zenin ignored her surprise. "Tell him that you've found a discreet bistro." Zenin stopped, nodding beyond her. "Arrange to meet him there and be precise about the time."

Again Zenin stopped, looking at his watch. "Two hours from now. You arrive early to get one of those outside seats with a view of this road. I don't know what the bastard looks like, so I'll need a signal to go with the physical description you're going to give me. I shall be concentrating entirely upon you. The moment that you see him, put your napkin to your lips: that will be the signal."

"What then?"

"You wait for five minutes, then pay for your drink and walk back along this cul-de-sac. I'll pick you up as you pass."

"What are you going to do to him!"

Zenin detected the thickness of anticipation in her voice and looked at her curiously. He said, "Remove him as a problem, like I said."

"Can I see you do it?"

"Of course not. You can't be identified as being involved."

"Afterward then!"

"No," he refused.

"Please!"

"I said no."

"Tell me about it later then, at the apartment?"

Zenin hesitated and said, "In all the detail that you want." He'd never known a woman excited in this way before.

They went back out onto the busier Place Neuve and Sulafeh called the Barthelemy-Menn hotel from a bar. Zenin leaned against the bar, drinking the pastis he'd bought to justify their use of the telephone, apprehensively aware of the uncertainty of Dajani being there and not even relaxing when he saw her obviously in conversation because it could have been with another member of the delegation.

She was smiling when she came back toward him, and he said, "Well?"

"He promised not to be late."

He relaxed then, answering her smile. "I hope he won't be."

He offered dinner but she said she was too tense to relax

over a meal, so they had another drink and left with an hour to spare before the arranged meeting. To avoid being conspicuous in the confined cul-de-sac, Zenin led her into the park and she pulled herself closer to him and asked him if he could guess what she wanted to do, here and now on the grass, and he said he could but they would have to wait until later, back at the apartment. Instead he took her again through everything he wanted her to do and made her repeat it to insure that she completely understood. Then he had Sulafeh provide as detailed a description as she could manage of Mohammed Dajani, querying and probing to add to it when she protested there was no more to describe because he knew there would be, under questioning, which there was.

Sulafeh got a curbside seat in the bistro half an hour before Dajani was due to arrive, and carefully following his instructions, she dabbed her lips with her red-checkered napkin after the first sip of her wine, as an insurance that the signal was still visible now that it had become darker and a rehearsal for later. Zenin saw it perfectly. He pulled into the blackened alleyway, vaguely aware of distant sounds: a radio and a child crying. The crying went on for a long time and became more and more distressed, and the assassin thought how cruel it was to abandon a child like that. The cul-de-sac was comparatively busy, but the alleyway in which he waited remained deserted and unmoving, and Zenin decided again it was an excellent choice.

Tonight would be the last night she would be able to return with him to the apartment, Zenin realized—the last night that they would make love, in fact. The following day he had to retrieve the rifle from the Bern garage and set it up in the Colombettes apartment to carry out the full rehearsal, strapped into the harness. He didn't want her back there, once he'd assembled everything. She'd been an interlude, an enjoyable way of filling in the time, but after tonight it would be over. A pity, in some ways; she really had been incredible in bed. Possibly the best he had ever known.

He remained constantly alert to the time, clearing his mind of any outside reflection and concentrating entirely upon Sulafeh Nabulsi fifteen minutes before the Palestinian was due to arrive. Which was fortunate, because the man was early.

Warned of the approach by the napkin signal Zenin turned away, looking directly into the street, recognizing Dajani at once. Dajani was as fat and unattractive as the woman had described him. Zenin's attention went immediately beyond, to anyone around his victim, seeing at once that his luck was holding. At that moment the cul-de-sac was deserted.

Dajani went to hurry by and Zenin guessed the man would be able to see Sulafeh, apparently waiting. As the Palestinian drew level, Zenin grabbed the man at the shoulder to jerk him abruptly off balance and pulled downward so that Dajani spun into the mouth of the alley. Zenin saw the man's mouth open, the beginning of a cry, and cracked upward with the heel of his left hand, but insufficiently hard enough to kill, as he'd killed Barabanov in that final test. All it did was drive Dajani's mouth closed and jarred his head backward. Zenin had the man's coat lapels in both hands now, hauling him into the darkness and bringing his knee up into the man's groin in the same movement. Dajani stumbled at the moment of contact, and Zenin missed. He still caught the man in the groin, so the breath grunted from him in agony, but not at the breaking point so Zenin hauled him upward and kneed him again, this time conscious of the pelvis cracking. As Dajani doubled up, Zenin chopped against the carotid artery in his neck, not hard enough to kill, but sufficient to render him deeply unconscious.

There was a dip in the alley wall to accommodate some drainage pipes, and Zenin dragged the slumped man into the alcove. He pulled the heavy gold watch from the man's wrist and went quickly through his pockets to make it appear like the robbery that he intended the police to record. There was some accreditation identification for the conference, and this Zenin was careful to throw down nearby, the action of a thief frightened to discover whom he had mugged.

He was at the entrance when Sulafeh reached it.

"Where?" she said, trying still.

"Come on!" the Russian insisted, urging her away.

"Let's get back to the apartment then, quickly!"

"We're not finished yet," cautioned Zenin.

They walked fast, but without any obvious, attention-attracting haste back down the Rue de la Corraterie to the bridge and a public telephone kiosk that Zenin had isolated when they crossed earlier. He said, "The secretariat Director, Zeidan? Is he staying at your hotel?"

"Yes," she said, curiously.

Zenin nodded toward the telephone. "Call him," he ordered. "Say you had an appointment tonight with Dajani but he did not turn up. Ask him if he knows where Dajani is."

"Why?"

"To maintain your absolute, unknowing innocence," said Zenin. "This way you are a worried colleague who has been stood up. If you don't bother to raise what is later going to become an alarm, there might be some suspicion."

She smiled up at him. "You're very clever, aren't you?"

"Careful," he qualified.

Sulafeh was very quick, and when she came back to the Russian, she said, "Zeidan thought there must have been some misunderstanding. He asked what I was going to do." She hesitated pointedly. "I said I was going to eat by myself and then look around the city; that I might be late getting back. Which I want to be."

Zenin did not bother to look at what he'd taken from Dajani's pockets until he got back to the apartment and when he did, he laughed.

"Dajani's a careful man, too," he said. "Look! Condoms!"

"We're not going to need those, are we?" said Sulafeh.

Alexei Berenkov reread completely the interrogation transcript and the trial record of Edwin Sampson after his return from Potma and created for himself more uncertainties than he discovered answers. It was Kalenin's turn to eat with them, which gave Berenkov the opportunity to discuss it informally while Valentina was discreetly and customarily busying herself in the kitchen.

"Sampson is adamant that Charlie Muffin had no part in his attempted infiltration," insisted Berenkov. "I threatened him with interrogation at the Serbsky again and said I would block any release approach from the British. He still maintained his story."

"You believe him then?"

"Yes," said Berenkov simply.

"So where does that leave us?"

"With Natalia Nikandrova Fedova," said Berenkov, simply again.

"She was adamant, too," remembered the KGB chairman. "At the trial she said she followed Charlie Muffin to the GUM department store and saw him meet Sampson there after they had been debriefed and separated from each other here. There was nothing she said that varied at all from what she told me the night Charlie Muffin escaped—the night she raised the alarm."

"I've read the transcript," said Berenkov. "She was hardly questioned, because of Sampson's confession of guilt."

"There was no need."

"Maybe that was an oversight."

"Are you inferring some sort of collusion between the woman and Charlie Muffin!" said Kalenin. "Suggesting in fact she's a spy, in place?"

"There was an affair, wasn't there?"

"Which she intentionally cultivated, according to her testimony. She was suspicious of him, despite his successfully passing the debrief. It enabled her to maintain a constant watch on the man."

"Very praiseworthy!" said Berenkov.

Kalenin frowned at the obvious doubt. He said, "There has never been any reason to doubt that Natalia Nikandrova is not a loyal member of the debriefing section of the KGB."

"Until now," said Berenkov.

As he spoke, his wife came into the room, carrying the

coffee and brandy. Valentina said, "You look as if you're plotting!"

"I think Alexei is," said Kalenin.

"Maybe others have in the past," suggested Berenkov.

30

Charlie reckoned he'd done bloody well, complying to the letter with the Director's instructions. He'd gone near no one, upset no one and talked to no one, except to room service for a meal and a bottle of wine when he got back from Bern. The only thing he had not done was to sit and do nothing because that was clearly daft. Instead he worked steadily and without interruption—apart from the brief meal and even then he read on—through the Israeli dossiers, determined to absorb as much as possible despite the size of the task. By nine he had gone through the Palestinian and Jordanian backgrounds and stopped because the words were blurring before his eyes, exhausted concentration aching through him. Deciding that it was a deserved reward for effort, Charlie went back to room service and ordered brandy, two large ones because it seemed a waste to bring the waiter all that way with just one.

The more detailed examination completely confirmed his initial impression, Charlie decided, feeling the brandy warm through him: the Israeli files could not be faulted. Every Arab investigation was painstakingly detailed. In the case of the Palestinian and Jordanian records, what Israel considered terrorist links were individually itemized along with the incidents and events supporting those allegations, all of which were set out in a chronological arrangement. When such people were picked out, there was a red marker on the cover of the folder and top-sheet assessment of that person. In every instance the judgment was that none of them any longer represented risk or danger.

Charlie found no difficulty accepting that view, despite the skepticism of a man who never completely admitted the vice-versa logic of night following day. After all, the major-

ity of commonwealth leaders jostling to get as close as possible to the Queen during those London conference photo-
calls had Foreign Office records identifying them as
independence-fighting villains who in their time had
danced around demanding the demise of the British monar-
chy.

He was wasting his time, Charlie reluctantly decided.
He was creating work to convince himself he *was* working.
Whatever or wherever the lead, it was not going to come
from this filing clerk's nightmare. Of which, objectively,
he'd already been aware, from the comparable pictures.
Where then? He didn't know. And he didn't like not knowing and he didn't like the impotent frustration he'd felt, ever
since this sodding job began. In fact he liked nothing at all
about any of it. If he were honest—which he always was
with himself, if sometimes not with other people—Charlie
accepted it was easy to understand the doubt everyone else
was showing. Because he *had* nothing. His own doubt
wormed its way into his mind, disconcertingly. Had he got
it wrong? Clutched too eagerly at a mistaken identification
and really wasted his time, spending days running around
like a blue-assed fly in quite the wrong place? He liked the
prospect of that least of all.

Although he would have been surprised if they had managed it so quickly, Charlie lifted the telephone when it rang,
expecting it to be Cummings with a come-and-get-your-
wrist-slapped order from London for conning them with the
photographs. But it was the barrel-toned Levy, the man's
voice echoing into the room.

"How's it going?" demanded the Israeli intelligence
chief.

"Slowly," conceded Charlie. He was not talking to anyone else, he thought in self-defense; Levy was talking to
him.

"Thought I might have heard from you."

"Why?" demanded Charlie, immediately hopeful there
might have been a development of which the other man
wrongly imagined him to be aware.

"Believed we were going to keep in touch," said Levy.

"I've come up with nothing," admitted Charlie. The persistent problem, he thought.

"This is the house phone," disclosed Levy. "I'm downstairs. How about a drink?"

Charlie looked at the file copies and remembered his impression about work for work's sake and said, "Why not?" What Sir Alistair Wilson didn't know wouldn't hurt him.

Levy was already at the bar, bulged over a stool, shirt open beneath his jacket, the tangle of hair visible at the neck and along the thick wrists extending beyond his sleeves. He shifted slightly for Charlie to join him, indicating the brandy snifter. Charlie nodded in acceptance.

"Well," said Levy. "Everybody's here."

"I'm not interested in everybody. Just one person."

"He's a ghost, Charlie."

"We'll see." Charlie wished there had been more conviction in his voice.

"You looked at the dossiers?"

"Not all," admitted Charlie. "A lot."

"And?"

"Impressive," praised Charlie.

"But leading us nowhere?"

"Yes," agreed Charlie. "Leading us nowhere."

"I warned you."

"It was something I wanted to do myself."

"No real purpose in your staying any longer, is there?"

"That's what London thinks," revealed Charlie. "There have been complaints from the Swiss. And the Americans."

"You've been pretty outspoken," said the Israeli.

"I've been honest," insisted Charlie. About the important things at least, he thought.

"They've got tender feelings, Charlie, tender feelings."

"A bullet in the head leaves it pretty tender, too."

"So are you going back?"

"They've agreed to my staying on for a while," said Charlie, noncommittal. "No idea for how long." He gestured to the barman for more drinks, and the man approached the unkempt couple with ill-concealed disdain.

Fuck you, thought Charlie. It's your tip you're gambling with, sunshine.

"It's a bastard when a seemingly good start comes to nothing, isn't it?" said Levy, professionally sympathetic.

"Happened to you much?"

"From time to time," said Levy.

Charlie was unsure whether the man was being honest or carrying on with the sympathy. He said, "Any more separate meetings with Blom?"

Levy smiled and said, "How did you guess?"

"Psychic," said Charlie. "What was it about?"

"It was private, just Blom and myself and some foreign minister people who came in with our leaders this afternoon," said the Mossad chief. "Blom gave the assurance on behalf of his government that they'd done everything they could."

"And you didn't call him a liar!"

"He'd done his best."

"Bollocks!" rejected Charlie.

"*His* best, I said," reminded Levy.

"So aren't you worried?"

"We've got a pretty good security record, Charlie."

"Usually on your own ground. This is an away match."

"So was Entebbe." The Israeli beckoned the reluctant barman and said, "Two more." He paused and then added, "And a smile."

The barman managed one, just.

There wasn't any functional purpose in his staying on, Charlie conceded. Even in the embassy communication room he'd been unsure why he'd bothered with the photograph bullshit, apart from the hope of some later I-told-you-so satisfaction. And after the afternoon and evening in his hotel room and the self-honesty that he had been foolishly avoiding, he was increasingly doubtful about that. So he'd been a damned fool, putting himself into a position from which he couldn't maneuver without Sir Alistair Wilson realizing he'd been conned. It was a mistake and it angered Charlie when he made mistakes, like it angered him to lose face when others had the I-told-you-so satisfaction.

He said, "Blom say anything about a meeting tomorrow?"

Levy nodded at the persistence. He said, "He's offered Giles and me a full tour of the entire conference area. So we can satisfy ourselves about the on-the-ground security arrangements."

"What about me!"

"You weren't mentioned. Britain isn't a participant, remember?"

"Would you support me if I asked to tag along?"

"I wouldn't have any objection."

"What do you think Giles would say?"

"No idea," said Levy. "Why not ask him?"

"I will," said Charlie determinedly.

"You'll have to wait until the morning," advised Levy. "The Americans have got a reception tonight; everyone's there."

"Why aren't you?"

Levy grinned sideways. "Somehow I never learned how to drink champagne with my finger stuck out. And I always drop those little biscuit things covered with congealed mayonnaise and last week's shrimp."

They lay side by side, damp with each other's perspiration and totally exhausted by sex, unable to love anymore. It was Sulafeh who moved first, reaching sideways for his hand, linking their fingers.

Cautiously she said, "You haven't told me about afterward?"

It had been an oversight not to have gone through the charade, Zenin acknowledged. He said, "I was leaving it until tomorrow. What time do you think you can get away from the Palais des Nations?"

"Noon," she said at once.

"We'll do it then," he promised. He'd already decided to return to Bern after she left that evening and stay overnight in the retained room at the Marthahaus, to enable his collection from the garage to be early the following morning. Zenin was confident he would be able to complete most of the setting up before he had to meet her. Anything that remained could be finished off in the late afternoon or evening.

"And then we'll come back here?" she asked eagerly.

"No."

She shifted slightly, looking more directly at him. "Why not?"

There was no real reason, Zenin accepted. He'd just felt it better that she did not see the assembled rifle. He said, "There are things I have to do here. Arrangements to make."

"How would I interfere?"

"It's the way I want it," he said. He'd never spoken to her harshly and was conscious of her flinching.

"Of course," Sulafeh said, retreating at once.

"There'll be time, afterward," he said carelessly, not wanting to alienate the woman.

The happiness flooded through her, washing away the immediate hurt at the way he had spoken. It was only natural that he would start becoming tense as the time got close. Sulafeh said, "I've so much wanted to hear you say that. So very much."

For a brief moment the Russian could not understand what she was talking about and then he realized. Improvising awkwardly, he said, "It will be wonderful. I promise."

"Where will we go?"

"I haven't decided yet," he avoided. "Let's get the mission over first."

"Of course," she agreed again. Emboldened, she said, "But you do mean it, don't you? About our staying together?"

"You know I do," said Zenin.

"I want to say it," she blurted, with the shyness of a young girl. "I love you."

She looked at him expectantly, so Zenin answered, "I love you, too."

31

As the senior intelligence controller guarding the American delegation, Roger Giles spent almost the entire day in and around the banqueting rooms at the President Hotel in which the reception was to be held, formulating and supervising all the security arrangements and coordinating with Brigadier Blom, who personally supervised the Swiss input.

For the first time, it gave Giles the excuse to dictate rather than defer to the Swiss intelligence chief, and he utilized it fully, ordering that all the hotel staff involved in the catering and employed on the floor occupied by his delegation should be vetted by his own officers. He insisted on some of them being stationed in the kitchen as apparent workers and on more being dressed as waiters and hotel employees to mingle among the guests during the actual event. Further, disguised again as hotel staff, he deployed more of his own people throughout their permanent floor. If the Secretary of State or any of the senior officials were a target, Giles considered a professional more likely to attempt to penetrate their official but temporarily deserted quarters and lie in wait than make any sort of frontal assault at the crowded reception.

In the diplomatic pouch from Washington, he'd had flown in electronic equipment adapted by the CIA's technical division from the hand-held metal detectors used at airports. The devices were smaller but more sensitive than those in commercial use, capable of being carried in a man's pocket and of triggering an alarm within a ten-meter radius of any metal object the size of a knife and certainly the size of a pistol or grenade. Giles issued these to ordinarily dressed officers, who were to circulate among the guests, as well as to those disguised as waiters. Also from the technical division came X-ray machines once more adapted from airport equipment. With the agreement of the hotel management and of the brigadier, he installed these unseen in the closets to be used as cloakrooms, with instructions to the operators that all deposited baggage should be screened against a bomb being left to explode when the reception was at its height.

Giles was also specific in the orders he issued to every officer, particularly in the use of specialized weaponry he handed out to some whom he individually selected for a specified function. The normal operating procedure on such foreign operations was initially a halt-and-explain demand to any suspicious person, with the drawing and firing of a handgun understood to be a last resort. Giles decreed there should be no delay. If any of them—and especially those stationed at all times within a five-meter radius of the most senior officials—detected the approach of anyone by whom they were alarmed, they were to shoot immediately, with no preliminary challenges.

His final briefings were to those agents individually selected. To each was issued a further consignment from the CIA's technical division, the adaptation this time of the sort of stun grenades developed by the Israelis against aircraft hijacking. Each man was given two of the grenades, together with earplugs to defeat their function and enable him to remain conscious afterward. If there was any sort of concerted attack by a terrorist group, Giles ordered that the grenades should be exploded irrespective of the temporary unconsciousness they would cause everyone, the essential requirement only the immobilizing of the attackers before they could commit any outrage. Giles's final instruction was that those protected by the earplugs should insure that every attacker was completely neutralized before bothering to summon any medical assistance for the unconscious guests.

The senior and supervising agents all had their linked communication earpieces and throat microphones, connected not just to each other in the reception area but also on their accommodation floor above as well.

As a matter of courtesy, Giles involved the Swiss intelligence chief throughout the security preparations. Just before the reception began, Blom said, "So you are still taking the British warning seriously?"

"I take my job seriously," said the American diplomatically.

"I thought to work effectively stun grenades needed a confined space like an aircraft fuselage?" queried Blom.

"They do," agreed Giles. "Our training is that the best way to defeat an assassination is to deflect it. If anything happens, I'm gambling on the grenades being sufficient to disorient, to give our people time to block off the attack and get some shots in themselves."

"I'm sure it will all be unnecessary," said Blom, confidently.

"I hope it is," said Giles sincerely.

Giles had chosen to put himself at all times close to the Secretary of State, the assistant Secretary of State, and the American ambassador to Switzerland. It placed him initially near the receiving line, so he saw Barbara the moment she entered. She moved swiftly along the line, seeing him when she was halfway along and smiling. She approached him hesitantly and said, "Is it all right if I stand with you?"

"Talk to any other guy and I'll break his legs," said Giles. It had seemed natural that she should come—he'd wanted her to be with him—but Giles thought suddenly of what would happen if there *were* an attack.

He got her a glass of champagne from a genuine passing waiter and she said, "So this is what you call work!"

"There's a lot of mental strain," he said, trying to match her mood, pleased at her lightness.

"Isn't that thing in your ear uncomfortable?"

"You get used to it."

"Martha Bell is more attractive in person than in all the newspaper pictures."

"She works hard at it."

"That sounds as if you don't like her."

"I don't know her." Giles spoke, never looking at her but all around, not at his agents but carrying out his own surveillance. He said, "Don't think I'm ignoring you."

"I know you're not."

"I'm afraid this is how it's going to be for the next few days."

"I expected it," she said. "I thought I might take a trip on the lake tomorrow. There's an afternoon cruise."

"Sounds good," said Giles. "I'm going to be tied up longer tomorrow than I have been today."

"I can wait," said Barbara. She paused and said, "Until tonight, at least."

Giles looked fully at her for the first time, smiling. "You sure?" he said.

"Very sure," she said.

"Wonder what everyone around us would think if they knew what we were talking about!" he said.

"I don't give a damn about everyone around us."

"Right now I wish I didn't have to, either."

"Let's not rush away when the conference finishes," Barbara suggested. "Why don't we stay on, so you can rest up after all this nonsense? Properly plan."

"Fine," agreed Giles. "Whatever you say." He talked looking away again, studying the room, which was how he saw one of the staff members from the Secretary of State's office approaching, as the receiving group broke up and started to circulate around the room. The man's name was Dawes, he remembered, from that afternoon's introduction, or maybe it was Hawes. A head-thrust-forward, eagerly smiling young man, prematurely balding and awkward because of it.

"Hi, Roger!" he greeted. He was the sort of State Department careerist who always remembered names, even given ones.

"My wife, Barbara," introduced Giles.

"Ma'am," said the man, politely, and with further politeness saved Giles the embarrassment by introducing himself. "John Hawks," he said, offering his hand.

Close, decided Giles. And his job was not diplomacy, just keeping its practitioners safe. He said, "Everything going well?"

Hawks did not respond at once, making what appeared

a head jerk of apology to Barbara first. Then to Giles he said, "The Secretary wants to see you. He's been allocated an anteroom near the entrance."

"I know," said Giles, immediately worried that the five appointed members of James Bell's personal security team would do something silly like remaining outside the room instead of going into it with the man. To Barbara, he said, "I've got to go."

"Of course you have," said the woman. "Why talk about it?"

As he hurried away, Giles heard Barbara start a conversation with Hawks by saying, "Did you know my husband breaks legs?" and grinned. There were two members of the bodyguard team outside the door when Giles reached it, but when he entered the room, he saw with relief that the other three had accompanied Bell inside.

"Looks like you're taking good care of me here, Roger," greeted Bell.

Remembering names appeared to be a familiar trick, thought Giles. He said, "That's what we're here for, Mr. Secretary."

"Sort of what I wanted to talk about," said Bell. He looked beyond Giles, to the other three and said, "I'd welcome a little privacy, boys."

The room was obviously one that Giles had examined, but he looked around it again. There was only one door, which he knew was already guarded, and from the discussion with Blom, he also knew the area outside the window was sealed off by police guards. He turned to the three agents, all of whom were looking at him expectantly. Giles said, "Okay. Stay right outside."

As the men filed out, Bell said, "Tell me something. If you hadn't given the word, would they have ignored me?"

"Yes, sir," said Giles at once.

"Even if I'd ordered it?"

"Yes, sir," repeated Giles.

Bell grinned. "Not able to look after myself, eh?"

Giles was glad of the other man's reaction. He smiled,

too, and said, "The theory is you may have other things on your mind to distract you."

Bell waved Giles to the settee, alongside which bottles were arranged on a tray and said, "Care to join me?"

"Very much," said Giles. "But have you ever seen how wide someone shoots after a couple of drinks?"

Bell poured his own, nodding, and said, "You're making me feel real safe."

"That's what I'm supposed to do."

"So okay," said Bell, seating himself on a facing chair. "I've had briefings from the Director and I think I've seen all the field reports you've sent, but I want it from you personally. We got any sort of a problem here?"

"I honestly don't know," replied Giles. "It certainly looked like we had, at the beginning. And there have been one or two odd things since. But it's just . . ." Giles paused, looking for the right expression. ". . . just wisped away; come to nothing."

"What about the Schmidt thing?"

The Secretary of State had certainly read the papers, thought Giles. He felt comfortable with the man. He said, "That was one of the odd things. It could have been mistaken identity at the hotel. Or half a million other explanations."

"The Swiss responded properly?"

Giles hesitated. Striving for diplomacy in such diplomatic surroundings, he said, "I'd like to have seen one or two different approaches in places."

"So they haven't!"

"They haven't wanted to believe it could happen," said Giles.

"What have you guys done independently?"

"Used every asset we've got here. Turned over every mattress and looked under every bed. And come up with absolutely nothing."

"The Israelis?"

"The same," assured Giles. "We've been liaising, obviously."

"Tell me about the Israelis," insisted Bell. "You got any

feedback about how they feel? About the conference itself, I mean?"

Giles shrugged. "Levy—he's their security coordinator—hasn't expressed any opinion. Not that I would have expected him to; it's not our job."

"The President's worried," disclosed Bell. "Feels assurances are necessary. You're the senior guy here, supposed to be getting the whispers. You hear anything, anything at all, I want you to tell me, you understand?"

"Of course, Mr. Secretary."

"I've a feeling you've got the handle on everything, Roger. That there aren't going to be any problems."

"I hope you're right, Mr. Secretary." As he spoke, Giles realized it was the second time that day he'd had exactly the same sort of conversation and said exactly the same sort of thing.

Barbara left before the reception ended, and Giles had to wait until all the senior officials were safely in their own suites and rooms, with relief guards on duty outside each, before he could join her. She was waiting in bed, wearing the lounging outfit of the previous night. There was a book closed on the bedside table, and the spectacles she needed for reading were on top in their case.

She saw him look and said, "I couldn't concentrate."

"I'm sorry I was so long. There was a lot to do."

"You don't have to keep apologizing."

"Can I get you anything?"

"Just come to bed."

As he undressed, she did too, slipping her shoulders out of the lounging suit and finally taking it off under the covers. He'd forgotten how large and firm her breasts were, and he felt a jump of excitement. She saw it and smiled. She came easily to him and there was none of the nervousness either had feared. They were old friends, knowing each other's ways, comfortable with each other without the need to impress. They climbed the hill together, reached the top at the same time, and afterward held each other tight on the descent, completely happy.

"Haven't we been bloody fools?" she said.

"Not any longer," he said.

Charlie Muffin was very frequently in the thoughts of Natalia Nikandrova Fedova. It had been a bizarre interlude—one that could have ended in disaster for her—but she had no regrets. Not about the involvement, at least, dangerous though it had been. Sometimes, suddenly awake in those lonely, empty nights or during the weekends now that Eduard no longer came home from college, she wondered how it would have been if she'd done what he'd begged and fled with him back to England, after she'd discovered he was not a genuine defector. The reflection never lasted long. Eduard's father had abandoned him; it was unthinkable she could have done the same, although her abandonment would have been for love and not like her husband's, for any passing tart prepared to lift her skirt.

Natalia wished there could have been a reminder, a photograph of Charlie or some inconsequential souvenir of their brief months together. But it was safer that there were none: certainly not a photograph. She'd avoided suspicion, by strictly following Charlie's instructions to report him to her KGB bosses after the minimal time possible to let him reach the embassy, but knew she would always have to remain cautious, never properly able to relax. A photograph would still have been wonderful. Would he still look the same, rumpled and messed up, which she had learned to recognize as a carefully cultivated demeanor to deceive people into thinking he was as sloppy as he appeared? Would his hair still stray like straw in the wind? Would he still drink but never really get drunk, another act? Would he still enjoy reading aloud, like he'd read aloud to her, revealing to her things about books she'd imagined she'd known but never really understood? Would he still laugh at himself, more than other people laughed at him? Would he have met . . . Natalia abruptly stopped the last question, one she never wanted to confront. There was no reason why he shouldn't have become involved with someone else, she told herself objectively. Quite understandable if he had. What there had been between them was over, forever, could never be recovered. Natural, then, that he should make another sort of life. If he had, Natalia hoped—reluctantly hoped—that Charlie was happy. It would be nice to imagine, as she often did imagine, that Charlie sometimes thought of her, too.

At that moment Charlie Muffin was not thinking of her. Alexei Berenkov was, though.

32

Vasili Zenin continued to set his planning around traffic congestion, actually using the early morning rush hour into Geneva to lose himself, just one of a thousand cars and a thousand men arriving for a day's work. He utilized the parking lot at the railway station again, for the same reason, but on this occasion it had the additional advantage of being a place where people were expected to be seen with luggage.

He took the gun case from the trunk but did not set out at once for the Colombettes apartment. The rush hour had served its purpose, but he did not want to arrive at the block with the crush of workers on their way to the lower floor offices. Instead he went into the station to arrange his escape train for the following day. There was still some last-minute timing to coordinate—timing which was impossible until today's tests—but there was a local departure for Carouge at twelve forty-five, which he thought was possible. As a failsafe, there was a train for Thonon at one. Zenin purchased separate tickets from separate windows and decided it was still too early to quit the station. He bought a coffee and croissant in the cafeteria, carrying out a personal test when he lifted the cup to his lips. This near to the final moment and there was still not the slightest shake in his hand, he decided, satisfied.

It was nine-thirty when he left the station, choosing the already reconnoitered route that connected with the Avenue Giuseppe Motta, transferring the case from hand to hand every so often to balance the weight, instinctively alert to everything around him but confident he was unobserved.

He slowed when he cut off the Colombettes Road, wanting his entry to be precisely right. It meant hesitating fur-

ther, to let a group of people enter the block, and allowing
a full minute to pass before entering himself. There were
only two girls in the foyer, talking animatedly as they
waited for the elevator. Zenin passed them, sure he remained unobserved, and climbed the stairs to the second
floor before summoning a lift himself. It arrived empty and
he managed to reach the top floor without it being stopped
by any other passengers on the way up. He emerged cautiously onto the residential corridor. There were sounds from
behind apartment doors but the walkway was deserted.

Zenin hurried now, practically running, pushing into his
own apartment and closing the door quickly behind him.
Directly inside he remained for a moment with his back to
it, releasing the pent-up breath. A completely successful entry, he told himself in further congratulation. He held his
hand up. Still no shake, and that despite having carried the
heavy bag so far.

He bent to it, taking out first the three rubber wedges he
had bought in Bern, together with the workman's overalls.
Still stooped, he jammed them firmly between the bottom
of the door edge and the floor, totally securing the place
against any sudden, unexpected entry, actually testing the
door to be sure they worked. He then carried the bag over
to the chosen window but did not immediately take anything further from it. Instead—standing back so that he
would not be visible with the net-curtaining pulled aside—
the Russian went again through the sightline to the spot
where the commemorative photograph was to be taken,
wanting to be sure he had chosen the right window. He had.

The already assembled rifle was the first thing Zenin
took from the bag but without any specific attention at this
stage, wanting to get to what lay beneath. He took out the
tripod, extending its legs and fitting the securing hinges to
the bottom of each, but did not try to screw the hinges to
the floor. He maneuvered the rest into a trial position and
took up the rifle from the chair upon which he had laid it.
The grooved bolt, three inches beyond the trigger guard,
slid smoothly into the swiveled receiving disc on the tripod
head, and experimentally Zenin swung the rifle around a

wide arc, covering not just the window through which he intended shooting but also one to the left. Fitted with the sound suppressor, the barrel was too long, needing to extend through the window. All right on the day, but not now, Zenin decided, removing it and laying it alongside. He crouched over the rifle, reaching forward to make a minute adjustment to bring the stadia into line, and was at last able with the sight magnifier accurately to calculate precisely at four hundred and twenty meters the distance from the window to where the photograph was to be taken. An easy shot, he thought. Several easy shots, he corrected.

Zenin checked his watch and then squinted up. There was hardly any sun now, but there could be the following day, and at the time scheduled for the photograph, it would be shafting in dangerously across his vision. Deciding a protective shift was necessary, he eased the tripod closer to where the wall jutted out into the room. It put him close to the buttress, but not close enough to interfere with his ability to swing the rifle, and the sightline was in no way impaired.

Zenin made several more tests before marking the position of the tripod feet and then lifting the entire assembly away from the window, he jabbed into the floor the initial entry points for the screws. To make the fixing easier, he took the rifle off its base, arranged the three feet into position, and screwed the bolts through the hinges with hard, positive twists of the screwdriver. Finished, Zenin squatted back, shaking the tripod with both hands. It was absolutely rigid.

For a few moments he rested contentedly, enjoying at last some definite activity. He replaced the rifle on the tripod, sighting once more to be sure, and then took the leather harness from the case. It was an elaborate fitment, a buckled and belted vest, and one with which he was not altogether happy. Certainly it succeeded in its purpose, literally attaching him to the weapon so that he became part of it, but so complete was the attachment that it was not easy to extricate himself. At Balashikha his best time had been four minutes and Zenin considered that too long. It would be necessary to rehearse and practice again today because it formed part of the schedule necessary for the escape train.

Zenin took off his jacket, put it across the back of the chair on which he had earlier rested the rifle and slipped into the harness. It had been tailored to fit him and did so perfectly. It was without sleeves but complete, front and back, to provide the base for the necessary straps which connected with the rifle. The front zipped up, from waist to neck, and there were two cross-straps to prevent it sliding around his body. Zenin closed both, shrugging, as he had earlier with the rifle, to make himself completely comfortable before taking up the straps to connect him to the rifle and tripod. There were four, three at different lengths to link with specific rings on the rifle—one near the tip of the muzzle, one where the barrel met the butt, and the last on the butt itself—and the fourth the longest of all, to connect him to the tripod. He attached all of them, tugging and testing each one as he did so, needing only slightly to adjust that to the tripod. The vest welded him to the weapon, so that they were one entity, and Zenin gazed through the sight yet again, swinging it along an imaginary line of people as he would the following day, knowing that it was impossible for him to miss. Indulgently he pressed the trigger of the unloaded weapon, once, twice, three times, hearing the greased click of the hammer hitting home, pulling back himself every time as the M21 would kick when the bullets were fired. Dead, he told himself; all dead. But not just three: five was the instruction for the maximum chaos. He wondered if he would maintain his one minute, ten second average. He supposed the woman would get at least one, so the score could go as high as six.

Reminded of timings, Zenin twisted, awkwardly restricted, and took from his wrist the heavily calibrated watch, placing it on the convenient chair where it would always be in view. As he did so, he depressed the button to start the second hand, then bent over the rifle again. He aimed, fired, and edged the weapon slightly at each shot, as he would have to the following day. On the fifth occasion, he snatched a look at the watch to fix exactly the position of the moving hand.

And then started his release. He unbuckled himself from the tripod first, then the rifle, moving from butt to muzzle. As the last strap fell away, he jerked up to free himself from the leather vest. Zenin continued the zipping-down movement as the fitment came off, snapping off the timing. Four minutes, thirty seconds, he saw, disappointed. It had to be a month since he'd last practiced. On the second attempt he only clipped ten seconds off the first test and just a further five on the third run-through. For several moments he paused, panting and wet with the on-off effort, gazing down at the discarded vest. Should he discard it, literally? Zenin was confident he could hit every time without it, and as he'd told the woman, all he needed was to hit because the shock factor of the hollow-nosed bullets insured it would be fatal, wherever the wound.

But all the training had been conducted wearing it, he reminded himself, in balancing argument. And it absolutely guaranteed the accuracy that would be necessary after the first or second shot, because by then the panic would have erupted.

Sighing, Zenin zipped and buckled himself into the vest yet again, rehearsing and adjusting and rehearsing and adjusting, not satisfied until he had achieved the Balashikha minimum of four minutes on three consecutive occasions.

Physically aching, Zenin slumped onto an easier chair, away from the rifle and the tripod, but staring fixedly at them, the harness crumpled alongside. One minute ten seconds to fire off the shots, four minutes to disentangle himself, a minute to the door—putting on his jacket as he moved—and six minutes to quit the building, allowing for the two minutes it had usually taken on his test departures for the elevator to get to the top floor and descend again. Twelve minutes, ten seconds. During that time he was sure there would be nothing but panic at the Palais des Nations, no one knowing what was happening or from where, milling about in confused pandemonium. And there was the woman as the decoy, the person whom all the security forces were supposed to believe responsible, not immediately troubling to search further. Zenin smiled at his calculation. He decided he could allow as much as a further three minutes to get clear of the apartment and he already knew how long it would take for him to walk briskly but unhurriedly to the railway station. Easily enough time for the Carouge train. Later that day, after getting rid of Sulafeh, he would drive the Peugeot there, so it would be waiting when he arrived.

The orders were that he should abandon the car, against the risk of Swiss intelligence carrying out some car rental sweep after the killings and ensnaring him in the net, but now that he had evolved his method of escape, Zenin doubted the necessity. He'd leave the final decision until later, but the Russian saw no reason why he should not return the vehicle on the due date and leave the country quite ordinarily. But not by air, initially. He'd wait a day or two—not in Bern but somewhere else, Zurich perhaps because it was conveniently north—and then cross the border into Germany by train. He had no need for an airport until Amsterdam, for the connection back to Moscow, so Zenin thought he might continue by rail right into Holland. But not in one journey. He'd break it in Germany: Munich, maybe. He'd never been to Germany and considered he would deserve a short vacation, after it was all over. And it would not strictly be an indulgence. His training was to work in the West, so the more exposure he got in the different countries the better he would be able to carry out the assignments.

Aware of the appointment with Sulafeh, Zenin shifted at last, going back to the gun case still containing the Browning with which she was to be supplied. Her obvious excitement by violence concerned him. She could not be relied upon to have it today, he determined. It would have to be a last minute hand-over. There was the need anyway for them to meet briefly on the actual day in the event of there being schedule changes, so it could be done then.

Zenin closed the bag and arranged the harness more tidily over the rifle like a dust cover. He carefully pulled the already concealing curtains and looked briefly around the apartment, making sure he had forgotten nothing, before removing the wedges from beneath the door. He stared uncertainly at them for a moment, realizing that by not using them he could reduce by at least thirty seconds—maybe a whole minute—the time it would take him to leave the apartment after the shooting. Something else to be decided on the day, he thought, putting them neatly side by side on the table.

Zenin was customarily early at the cafe on the Rue de Coutance he had given the woman as a meeting place, wanting his usual satisfaction that it was safe, not approaching it until he saw her arrive without any pursuit—and unflustered like she had been the previous day—and settle herself at a window table.

She smiled up eagerly when she saw him approach, reaching out for his hand to pull him down into the chair opposite.

"It worked!" she announced at once.

"Tell me."

"All hell was breaking loose when I got back to the hotel last night," said the woman. "Some passerby had found Dajani in the alley. His accreditation, too, so it didn't take long for the police to notify the delegation. They even interviewed me!"

"The police?" said Zenin.

"There was no problem," she said reassuringly. "They just asked me what the arrangement was and I said we were going to dine as colleagues but that he did not turn up. Zeidan sat in on the interview and confirmed that I had called, asking about Dajani." She smiled. "I agreed last night that having me call him was clever, didn't I?"

Her coquettishness irritated him. "Was it only the police?" he demanded.

Sulafeh retreated, as she always did. She said, "Of course, darling! It was just routine?"

"How routine?" he persisted.

"Just like I said it was. Zeidan confirmed that I had called. He said that he thought it had been a misunderstanding and didn't bother to do anything. That he hadn't worried about it until they, the police, arrived."

"How much questioning was there about what you were doing?"

"None," insisted Sulafeh. "I said that after telephoning I went to another cafe, had a meal, walked around Geneva and then went back to the hotel. Where I found the police waiting for me."

"Did they ask which cafe?" said Zenin, realizing another possible oversight.

"No."

"Or for any proof of your eating there?"

"They don't suspect me!" insisted Sulafeh in weak defiance. "They're putting it down to a street mugging: embarrassing in the circumstances, maybe, but just a mugging."

Why hadn't he thought of the need to identify a cafe other than the bistro! Because he'd become sexually involved and failed to be as objective to the degree of removed sterility to which he had been trained. No more, Zenin determined. And never again.

"What else?" he asked.

Sulafeh sniggered, coquettish again. "Guess what Zeidan said afterward?"

"What?" responded Zenin, forcing the patience.

"He said there was no possibility of bringing anyone else in to replace Dajani," recounted Sulafeh. "That he was sorry if there had been any misunderstanding between us and that he had the greatest admiration for me as a linguist. And that he was sure I could take over the sole responsibility, demanding though it might be!"

Zenin forced the cynical laugh. "So it worked," he said.

"I am back where I should be for the picture session," she announced proudly. "It's all right now."

Zenin relaxed, just slightly. "Good," he said, distantly. "Very good." Now everything could work, as it was designed to work. It would be all right, like she said.

"The police told me something during the interview," announced Sulafeh.

"What?" said Zenin again, feeling the tension rise.

"About Dajani," she said. "Do you know what you did to him? You broke his pelvis."

"Did I?" said the Russian, in apparent innocence.

"He really won't need those condoms again for a long time, will he!"

Zenin realized the direction of her conversation and did not want to follow it. He said, "Does the translator change involve anyone at the conference?"

She shook her head. "It was made public today at the Palais des Nations, on an adjustment of representation order. There was no reaction whatsoever, apart from a few ridiculous expressions of sympathy for the randy bastard."

It seemed he had got away with it, thought Zenin. He said, "We'll need to meet tomorrow for you to tell me of any last minute changes."

"When do I get the gun?" she demanded eagerly.

"Then."

"Why not today?"

"Too dangerous," he refused. "There could be a spot check, even though you've made friends with the security people. Someone could go through your room. Better to leave it until the very last moment."

"I have to be at the Palais des Nations by eight-thirty."

"It will have to be before."

"Shall I come to the apartment?"

"No!" said Zenin, too anxiously. He'd taken his last chance with the woman. From this moment on it was distancing time. Less forcefully, not wanting to upset her, he said, "I told you yesterday we've got to protect the mission. Nothing else matters now until that is all over."

"We've still got to make arrangements for afterward," she said.

"One step at a time," Zenin insisted, thinking. The railway station was an obvious meeting place but they had used that almost too much; and it was the route he had chosen for his escape, so it would definitely be wrong to be seen there with her. A hotel then. He said, "Do you have a list of the delegation hotels?"

"Yes," she said, bending to the large briefcase and handing it to him.

Zenin ran through the list, from the Beau-Rivage and the Des Bergues and the President and the Bristol and then smiled up. "On the Quai Terretini there's the Du Rhone. It's on the way you will take from your hotel to the conference. I will be in the foyer, at seven."

"What do I do?"

"If there are any changes to the schedule, just hand me the sheets."

"The gun?"

"And I'll give you the gun," promised Zenin patiently.

"And afterward?"

"You've got a city map?"

"I bought one the first day."

"Memorize where the Rue de Vermont connects with the Rue de Montbrilliant," instructed Zenin. "There will be immediate panic when the shooting starts. Get away from the garden and out of the international area at once. And go to that connecting point."

"I understand," said Sulafeh intently.

"I will already be waiting there. The car is a blue Mercedes, numbered 18-32-4. You got that?" said Zenin. The Peugeot was brown, the number was 19-45-8 and it would anyway be at Carouge, awaiting his arrival off the train.

"Blue Mercedes, license number 18-32-4," Sulafeh recited, trustingly.

"Where would you like to go?" asked the Russian.

"I don't care," she said. "Anywhere, as long as it's with you."

Playing the part, Zenin reached across the table, covering her hand with his. "You're going to be," he promised.

"Please let's go to the apartment now," she said. "I want you!"

"I thought you wanted the gun, just as much," said Zenin, the excuse already formulated.

"I don't understand," said the woman.

"The weapons aren't here in Geneva," lied the Russian.

"I've got to get them. There isn't time for the apartment today."

Zenin walked from the cafe to collect the car from the railway terminal, relieved to be away from the claustrophobia of Sulafeh's attention. He took the southern route out of the city, the lake grey and stretched away to his left, picking up the Carouge signpost almost at once. This time tomorrow, he thought, it would all be over. He was beginning to feel excited: excited but not nervous.

David Levy made the demand as soon as he entered the office of Brigadier Blom in the Geneva safe house. Roger Giles was already there and said he thought it was a good idea as well.

"I've arranged the tour for the security services of the participating countries," said Blom stiffly. "That's all."

"What harm would it do for Charlie Muffin to come along?" asked Levy.

"He has no cause or reason to be there."

"Or not to be, by the same token," pointed out the American. "I'd actually like him along."

"So would I," said Levy. "We're all convinced it's a false alarm. Let's show him the protection is more than adequate, whatever happens."

Charlie responded at once to Blom's telephone call, nodding as the man extended the invitation.

"Thought you'd never ask," said Charlie.

33

They swept up to the Palais des Nations in Blom's official car and were gestured straight through the crisscross barriers and on into the conference complex. The vehicle stopped at the front entrance, where another man in uniform who was never introduced saluted the brigadier smartly and nodded to Levy, Giles, and Charlie, all of whom nodded back.

"Central control first," announced Blom.

The uniformed man led them into the main building and along a wide, sweeping corridor where other uniformed security guards were obvious and very visible. One group was actually looking through a bag being carried by a woman into one of the side offices as they went by. There was an average of two men in each group carrying hand-held metal detectors.

The control room was on the second floor, its entrance guarded. The man came smartly to attention, opening the door as they approached for them to enter unhindered. It was a large, circular room, its walls lined in serried rows with television monitors in front of which sat operators manipulating banks of camera adjustments and sound switches. The camera placings inside the huge conference chamber insured no part of it was unobserved. The corridor along which they had earlier walked was also well-covered, as well as the entry area where the delegation leaders would be received. Externally the cameras were clustered over the entrance area, so that every section of the approach was displayed, and further cameras were installed around the building to give practically a complete view of the grounds outside. The special area where the commemorative photographs were to be taken had a separate camera grouping, supplying three different monitors with visibility almost as good as that in the conference room. Blom handed each of them the final, definitive conference schedule.

Charlie accepted it, but did not look at it. Instead he asked, "If any of these operators see something suspicious, what is the system for them to raise any alarm?"

Blom's unidentified aide indicated telephones in front of each operator and said, "They are direct lines to security control."

"Does security control have a matching monitor system?" demanded Charlie.

"No."

"So a verbal description has to be given of whatever appears suspicious, and where it's happening has also got to be verbally described?" persisted Charlie.

"Each man—the operator here and the security supervisor in their section—work from identical, grid-divided maps," came in Blom. "The location is instantaneous: the system has been extensively practiced and works very satisfactorily."

"How long, from the moment of picking up a telephone in this room, until someone from security gets to the designated spot on the map?" asked Levy.

Blom looked to the assistant, who hesitated. Then he said, "Five minutes."

A guess if ever he'd witnessed one, thought Charlie. He said, "You think you'd have five minutes, in a real security emergency situation?"

"No doubt you've got a superior suggestion," said Blom sarcastically.

"What about a sound alarm, a klaxon?" said Charlie. Was it all a waste of time? he wondered. Or might it just stir some reaction? Whatever, he supposed he had to try, if only for his own satisfaction.

"A klaxon has no other practical benefit beyond making a noise and alarming people without letting them know where the danger is," rejected Blom.

"Making a noise has a very practical benefit," disputed Charlie. "It makes your villain run." He nodded to the other two security chiefs next to him. "And they don't need initially to know where the danger is: just that there *is* danger and that they'd better throw a cordon around the people they're supposed to be protecting."

"This is a system that has been perfected over a number of years and never found to be wanting," insisted Blom.

"How many potential security disasters has it averted?" asked Giles.

"There have been a number of alarms," said Blom.

"False alarms or real alarms?" asked Levy.

"Fortunately there has never been a real danger," conceded Blom.

The American appeared to be coming over like Levy, thought Charlie. How much real pressure was either prepared to exert, though? He said, "So it's never been properly tested in real circumstances. Just practice and false alarms?"

"I've not the slightest doubt it will work as it is designed to do in any real situation," said Blom. He paused, looking directly at Charlie. "Which we've yet to confront," he added.

Any discussion with Blom was like making rude faces at himself in the mirror, thought Charlie. He said, "Is this it? Just this television surveillance and the physical security checks?"

"All the bomb checks have been carried out. Every member of every support staff has been vetted," assured Blom.

"That wasn't what I was immediately thinking about," said Charlie. "Do you intend having aerial surveillance, from helicopters, while the conference is on?"

There was the briefest of pauses. Blom said, "There is a helicopter provision within the complex."

"Will there be helicopters in the air?" asked Giles, coming out even more strongly with demands upon the Swiss.

"If it is considered necessary," conceded Blom.

"While we're talking about it, what about air space?" said Levy.

Blom experienced yet again that stomach-sinking sensation of things moving away too quickly for him to be able to grasp. "Air space?" he asked weakly.

"Is the entire overflight area being closed to commercial aircraft?" asked the Israeli.

"It will be," promised Blom, with increasing discomfort.

Charlie indicated the group of screens showing the approach and entrance areas and said, "Five manholes, I've just counted them. Are they sealed?"

Once more Blom looked to his assistant, who responded with a shoulder-shrugging gesture of uncertainty.

Charlie said, "The sewers must extend out beyond the boundary into the city. It would be the obvious and perhaps the easiest way for anyone to get in undetected."

"Why bother to get in?" asked Levy.

Charlie looked to the screen again and nodded in agreement. "You're right," he said to the Israeli. "With the area swept and declared clean, all that's necessary is to clamp explosive devices beneath those manhole covers and set them to detonate when the cars of the delegation leaders pull up for the official arrival. No one would survive."

Blom swallowed and said, "All the manholes will be checked and then sealed. And the sewer lanes secured against any human entry at the complex boundary until the conference concludes."

It had not been a waste of time, decided Charlie. In fact it had been very worthwhile. He said, "Can we look outside?"

It was a more subdued Swiss intelligence chief who led the group into the gardens, deferring to the assistant unnecessarily to point out the cameras feeding the control room they had just left. Giles made a point of identifying manholes as they made their way through the sidecourts and surrounding gardens—picking up two in the gardens where the photograph was to be taken—and at Blom's urging, the aide made notes on a small pocket pad for them to be sealed.

At the gardens Charlie stared around, starting to isolate the overlooking buildings, when Levy announced, "I wasn't happy with our entry this morning."

Charlie turned back to the group as Giles said in agreement, "We weren't checked."

"The car was recognized to be official!" insisted Blom.

"The cars carrying all the delegation leaders will be official," pointed out Levy. "My people are going to sweep our vehicles before we set out each day and I know the Americans will do the same. But what if someone were to attach a bomb to one of the other delegation cars in some hotel parking lot overnight? And again, time the explosion?"

Charlie was glad Levy had brought it up, sparing him the need.

"It could cause a bottleneck," protested Blom.

"I think it would be justified," said Giles. "And the congestion could be eased by opening up more than one entry point and covering it with more men."

"Possibly with sniffer dogs," encouraged the Israeli.

"Yes," admitted Blom. "It would possibly be a good idea." He started back toward the conference block, physically anxious to get away from the concerted pressure. They were playing games, all of them, each trying to prove who was the best counterinsurgency expert. Damn the scruffy, ridiculous, posturing Englishman who'd started it all! Blom was glad the Swiss protest had been made to London. He could not understand why the man had not been withdrawn. Certainly it had been a mistake letting the other two persuade him into letting the man accompany them on the security tour. The final satisfaction was going to be his, of course, when the conference ended and all these fantasy precautions were going to be shown to have been quite unnecessary.

There was a moment of uncertainty among them back at the entrance where Blom's car was waiting, and Giles said, "My people picked up something about an attack on a member of the Palestinian secretariat?"

Blom's face tightened perceptibly. "It is not a matter for us," he said. "It is a police investigation."

"What happened?" asked Charlie curiously.

"Street crime: a mugging," said Blom. "A member of the Palestinian translator staff. Mohammed Dajani."

Long-time Arafat supporter, Charlie remembered from the Israeli files. Identified as a moderate and advocate of negotiation, certainly with no marked involvement in what Jerusalem regarded as terrorism. Charlie said, "Have your people talked to him?"

Blom sighed. He said, "This is not something into which to start reading significance. I have personally seen the full police report. He was attacked last night, near the university. Unfortunately quite badly injured: a broken pelvis. But it was a robbery, pure and simple. He lost a watch and a quantity of money."

"What about any sort of documentation to have gained access here?" demanded Levy.

Blom smiled, happy for the first time with a question. "Precisely why the evidence was submitted to me," he said. "There were some accreditation documents found near him. There's been the most detailed check with what was found and what remained in his hotel room. Nothing whatsoever is missing." Blom saw the disappointment on the faces assembled around him. "As I already told you," Blom said, continuing to enjoy himself, "it is a regrettable street crime, nothing more."

"How many people involved in the attack?" asked Charlie.

"He thinks only one, but he's not sure."

"Description?" pressed Giles.

"There was absolutely no street lighting; he saw nothing."

"It wouldn't seem to have any significance," agreed Levy. "Not with all the documentation remaining intact."

"I am glad you agree with me," said Blom.

It was Giles who resolved the impasse about what to do next, inviting everyone into the American secretariat section where American security had established their headquarters. Blom declined, remarking heavily that there were further arrangements he had to make, but Charlie and Levy accepted.

Giles had a separate but necessarily cramped office very close to where the conference was to take place. Everything appeared temporary, a snakes' nest of telephone, teleprinter, and television cables across the floor of the outside rooms and a lot of people looking lost, trying to remember where their assigned places were. From a desk drawer Giles produced a bottle of Jack Daniels and apologized for only having two glasses. Charlie said he was happy with the cup.

"Well?" said Charlie. It was nice to be admitted at last, but he was unsure how genuine was their acceptance.

"I think we closed a few doors that were too wide open," said Giles.

"I don't have any authority to interview Dajani," said Charlie. He looked at Levy. "And I guess it would be difficult for you, as well." He turned to Giles. "Don't you think it might be an idea to investigate the attack yourselves?"

"For what?" said Levy. "According to Blom, the man didn't see anything."

"According to Blom, there's no danger!" said Charlie, conscious as he spoke of the look which passed between the two other men. In full awareness, he said, "So you would have suggested all the tightening up today even if there hadn't been any warning!"

"That's our job, Charlie," said the Israeli.

Being patronized was something that pissed Charlie off the most and he thought it was close to happening here. So much for acceptance. He said, "You don't think it's worth looking at independently? You're the people talking about doors that have been left too wide open."

"I think it's been checked out," said Levy.

"I don't believe it's anything to get spooked about," agreed the American.

"Believers in coincidence!"

"Don't make a monster out of every shadow, Charlie!" pleaded Levy. "The poor bastard was mugged. The one thing that would have made it suspicious—the loss of any conference documents—didn't happen!"

"Like nothing else is going to happen," accused Charlie. Cunts, he thought. He was still thinking it three hours later when Alexander Cummings reached him at the Beau-Rivage from the Bern embassy.

"You're to come right away," ordered the British intelligence *rezident*. "London says it's important."

Back and forth like a fiddler's elbow, thought Charlie.

Alexei Berenkov had studied all the interrogation transcripts and the records of the trial evidence and reviewed yet again his own interview with Edwin Sampson. And acknowledged that the only conclusion possible was that which Kalenin had reached: that Natalia Nikandrova Fedova was a loyal and dedicated KGB intelligence officer whose brilliant intervention had prevented Sampson infiltrating the Soviet service.

And he refused to accept it.

Berenkov had survived in the West for so long by refusing ever to believe the obvious—intrigued during the debriefing after his capture to realize it was also a precept of Charlie Muffin's—even when it was supported by incontestable fact.

The need was to uncover something which did contest the facts. Because Natalia was attached to the First Chief Directorate and subject to his authority, it was easy for Berenkov to know at all times where she was, enabling his squads to enter her apartment without any fear of discovery. The searchers went in first, under Berenkov's strict instructions that nothing should be disturbed for her to realize her apartment had been burgled, and after them, the technical experts went to work. There were two video cameras installed, both with fish-eye lenses capable of recording the activities throughout the entire room, one in the main bedroom and another in the living room. The encompassing lenses were the size of pinheads and fitted high in the ceiling coping in both places. The audio equipment was not put actually into the telephone, where Natalia might have discovered it, but installed as an additional wire alongside the regular lead-in line. An extra microphone was fixed as a valve to a small portable radio, which usually appeared to be kept in the kitchen but which she sometimes carried from room to room, particularly to the bathroom in the mornings.

Berenkov hoped the break would not take long: Charlie Muffin was a problem that should be eradicated as quickly as possible.

34

"It could be nothing," cautioned Sir Alistair Wilson, over the echoing, scrambled line. "But I think it's sufficient for a warning."

"What?" demanded Charlie.

"The two men didn't match," said the British Director. "But another picture did."

"With the man in Primrose Hill!"

"No," declared the Director. "With a picture you sent of a woman described as Sulafeh Nabulsi."

Charlie frowned in the secure communications room of the Bern embassy, striving for recall. "The translator," he said, remembering.

"We didn't have a name, until your picture. All there was in our terrorist files were two other photographs, both blurred and indistinct. With the assessment that she was a fanatic," said Wilson.

"A positive match?"

"The technical physiognomy comparison suggests it's the same person and two of our expert visual examiners here agree."

Charlie's mind was far ahead of the conversation. Levy and Giles might believe in coincidence—his word, Charlie recalled—but he didn't. So what connection was there between an apparent street attack on one translator with the Palestinian party and this sudden discrepancy with another? Charlie was sure the Israeli dossier on the woman had not recorded any terrorist connections at all, like it had with some of the others. Aged thirty-four, he remembered further. Single and a language graduate from the University of Jerusalem. Her father had been listed as a doctor, practicing in Ramallah; her mother, dead. There had even been a number of teaching appointments he could not recall, apart from their having been in Lebanon and Egypt. And from the University of Cairo there had been a further language degree. As the memories returned, Charlie had the most important recollection. The Israeli material had been indexed, with function descriptions of everyone. Now that Dajani had been incapacitated, Sulafeh Nabulsi was not just another translator: she was the only translator. Charlie, a man of hunches, felt a familiar tingle: he had not felt it for far too long. He said, "What have we got on her?"

"Practically nothing, like I said," reminded Wilson. "The name even came from you. One of our photographs was supplied from Egypt. She's very much in the background of the Sadat attack. The other is from Lebanon. It was taken at a mass funeral of guerrillas who died in an Israeli air attack on Marjayoun in the south."

"Why the insistence that she's a fanatic?"

"What information there is with both pictures describes her as belonging to the Fatah Revolutionary Command," said Wilson. "That's the most extreme of the Palestinian factions. It's led by Abu Nidal who, according to the Foreign Office, has pledged his followers utterly against the accord being worked out in Geneva."

"None of this is in the Israeli dossier," disclosed Charlie.

"I'm not prepared to be definite about it," said the Director, cautioning again. "I'm sending some stuff first thing tomorrow morning and I want you to warn Blom that it's coming. Nothing has changed about our role. Which means your role. We're advising. Nothing more."

"Of course."

"I mean it, Charlie."

"I understand," assured Charlie, easily. He'd gone through the routine of fuzzy pictures with Blom and been patronizingly tolerated by Giles and Levy, just in case he came up with something they'd missed—which they had with this—and now it was time to return to normal, Charlie Muffin's normal. Working by himself.

"Anything new from your end?" inquired the Director.

The attack upon Dajani lifted the London information

from the curious to the suspicious. Yet Sir Alistair himself acknowledged that the Nabulsi photographs could mean nothing. No purpose just yet then in crying wolf, Charlie thought, in self-justification. Easily again he said, "Not a thing."

"What's the security like?"

"Better than it was."

"Seems like it might have been a good idea for you to stay on, after all," said Wilson.

"Could easily be."

"I said advisory, Charlie!"

"I heard." To cover his ass he would eventually need to advise as ordered, but the problem with trying to be a one-man band was playing the trumpet and the trombone at the same time as banging the drum. Charlie said, "Any objection to Cummings coming back to Geneva with me?"

"Why?" demanded Wilson, the surprise obvious.

Every cloud turns out to have a silver lining in the end, thought Charlie. He said, "The Swiss complained, don't forget. It might be better if he were involved, as the local man whom they know and have worked with before."

There was a long silence from London. Wilson said, "Involved with what?"

"Liaison," said Charlie. He hoped this part of the conversation didn't continue much longer because there weren't many words left before he fell over the edge.

Wilson spoke slowly, spacing the delivery, wanting Charlie to understand every nuance. He said, "Strictly speaking, I disobeyed higher authority by not bringing you home."

"Yes," said Charlie shortly.

"Now there seems to be an excuse. Just."

"Yes," repeated Charlie.

"This conversation—everything I've said—is being recorded at this end."

"I know," said Charlie. "It's automatic."

"It's a protection device, to insure accuracy," said the Director. "Don't forget it, will you?"

"No," promised Charlie. "I won't forget."

There was another discernible pause. "Have Cummings, if you think it's necessary," conceded the Director.

The Bern *resident* suggested driving back to Geneva in his own car and Charlie readily agreed, wanting to be cocooned with his thoughts. There was a need to be careful, he accepted; despite the experts' assessment, the identification could still be mistaken. And the Dajani assault really could be coincidence, although he didn't personally believe in coincidence, space ships, ghosts, or that the world was round. That long-absent sensation wouldn't go away, though: that tingle of anticipation, the gut feeling that at last something was going right after so much going wrong. Inside looking out, he'd told the Israeli. There would obviously have been the need for someone on the inside. Christ, he'd been slow, not thinking of it before! Still not too late: almost, but not quite.

"I still don't know what I am supposed to be doing," protested Cummings beside him. "What this is all about?"

Charlie told the other man as much as he felt necessary, editing completely the restrictions imposed upon him by their director in London, realizing as he talked that it would be an advantage to have a car. Beside him Cummings listened in increasing discomfort, physically shifting in his seat. Cummings had felt safe in Switzerland. It was one of the easiest postings in the service, a place where nothing ever happened and where his role had previously been to transmit between Bern and London low-level intelligence judged so unimportant by both that neither side minded the other knowing. Which was how he wanted to continue, acting out the role of a special postman, enjoying the overseas allowances and the embassy cocktail parties and avoiding anything and everything which might upset the status quo. Like this, he recognized worriedly.

"I don't believe it!" he said.

"Millions don't."

"What do you want me to do?"

"Sit in my hotel room and drink Harkness's whisky until it comes out of your ears," said Charlie. He felt cheerful— ebullient—at finally having a pathway to follow.

"What?"

"I need a contact point—a number and a person I know will be there when I call. Just leave the bathroom door open when you pee so that you'll hear the phone."

"Why?"

"There'll be a need to tell the Swiss." And I hope the time, Charlie thought, remembering Wilson's injunction.

"Why not tell them now?"

"Because we don't know enough to tell them anything yet." Which was a lie and could get him hanging by his balls from the ceiling hook if it all went wrong and Wilson launched an inquiry.

"What are you going to do?" asked the man.

"See what the second-class hotels of Switzerland are like," replied Charlie nebulously. "And I'll need this car, incidentally."

"I'm not sure about that," protested Cummings.

"It's a department car, isn't it?"

"Yes."

"And we're in the same department, aren't we?"

"Mr. Harkness is very strict about office property," reminded Cummings.

And don't I know it, thought Charlie. He extended his hand across the vehicle, so that Cummings could see his fore and middle fingers tight together. "Dick and I are like that," he said.

"Is that his name, Dick?" said Cummings. "I never knew."

Dick was very much the man's name, reflected Charlie. "Richard," he said. "One of the best."

"I thought you said 'fucking Harkness' that day at the embassy," accused Cummings.

"Joke!" said Charlie. "You don't really think I'd call the deputy director that, do you?"

"I suppose not," said Cummings. "You will be careful of it, won't you?"

"Look after it like it was my own," assured Charlie.

He escorted Cummings up to the room at the Beau-Rivage and actually ordered a bottle of whisky, taking a quick nip himself, and said: "Okay. Just wait for my call."

"How long?" asked Cummings.

There was no way he could make the assessment because he had no idea what was going to happen, Charlie accepted. "The formal session starts at noon tomorrow," said Charlie. "If you haven't heard from me by eleven-thirty, press every button you can find."

"I should know where you're going to be."

"The hotel where the Palestinians are staying, off the Barthelemy-Menn."

"How do you know you'll get a room?" asked Cummings, clerk-like.

"One of their guests is in the hospital with his balls in a bandage," said Charlie confidently.

It was almost midnight when Charlie approached the night desk. As he signed in, Charlie said casually, "Too late to call Miss Nabulsi tonight, I suppose? Two-o-eight, isn't it?"

"Three-forty-nine," corrected the nightclerk, turning to check the key on the hook. "She appears to be in her room."

"I'll wait until tomorrow," said Charlie. "What time does she usually leave?"

"Depends," said the man, consulting a ledger. "But tomorrow she's booked a call for six."

"Thanks," said Charlie, surprised how easy it often was with just a little bit of knowledge. And then thinking in immediate contradiction that it was about time things became easier. Charlie didn't bother to undress, just removed his Hush Puppies to stretch his feet out before him on top of the bed, his back supported against the headboard. Should he have told the others, instead of trying to go it alone? he wondered, in rare second thoughts. No, he decided, in immediate reply. Time enough to bring them in if there were no contact and he was wasting his time: the failsafe was established with Cummings, after all.

Charlie left the hotel at five-thirty, using the fire exit on the ground floor to avoid the informative clerk of the previous night, shivering in the early morning mist that spilled over from the lake to cloak everything in wet, clinging greyness. To have started the engine to get the heater working would have created telltale steam from the exhaust so he remained hunched in the front seat, arms wrapped around himself, occasionally leaning forward to clear the condensation from the window so that his observation of the hotel was unobstructed.

"Hurry up, my love," Charlie said in the empty car. "It's bloody freezing!"

It was as if she had heard him. Sulafeh Nabulsi left the hotel precisely at six-thirty, hurrying down the step and setting off in the direction of the Avenue de la Roseraire with her head deep into the collar of a yellow topcoat, which Charlie isolated immediately as a marker. He waited until she had almost reached the junction before starting the car and edging forward, switching the heater on to full before the engine was really warm enough.

He reached the connection just in time to see her entering an early morning taxi, which took off toward the L'Arve river, and Charlie let the distance increase between them because the roads were practically deserted, making him too obvious. The taxi made a right turn onto the Rue de l'Aubepine, heading into the center of the town, and Charlie let a newspaper delivery van intervene between them, head craned to his left to keep her vehicle in view around the obstruction.

Charlie was alerted to its stopping just before the sweep of the Carrefour Pont d'Arve by the sudden glare of brake lights and managed to halt with Cummings's car still hidden by the van. As he hurried forward, Charlie passed a sign warning that parking was prohibited at all times and said softly, "Sorry, mate."

Charlie paced himself about one hundred yards behind the woman, grateful that the city was gradually awakening around them and that the streets were becoming fuller. The yellow coat was very visible, and in the better, growing light he saw that she carried a large, briefcase-type bag slung from her shoulder by a looped strap.

He had to close up when he saw the size of the junction, nervous of losing her at the controlled crossings of the converging streets, able to let the gap grow again when she regained the Avenue Henri Dunant. Sulafeh started obviously to try to clear her trail when she reached the cluster of cross streets. It was amateurish and caused Charlie no problems whatsoever. Rather, it pleased him because he immediately saw it as the confirmation that he'd got it right and that she was heading for some encounter that should not be taking place. Always, despite the dodging, she continued north, either on the Dunant avenue or the parallel Rue Defour. Charlie felt the first twinge of protest from his feet and winced, knowing it would get worse: it always did.

She did something clever that he did not expect when they reached the river, going down the Quai Motrices but then suddenly doubling back upon herself. Had he not been one hundred yards behind, sure of her from the coat, they would have come practically face to face and he would have had to continue on, risking her getting away. As it was, he was able to pull into a newsstand on the corner and study the selection until she unknowingly passed him. She seemed to stop bothering after the maneuver, striding across the Coulouvreniere bridge and going immediately right, when she reached the quai.

Charlie guessed at the Rhone hotel before she entered it, hurrying so that he was only twenty yards behind when she went through the doors. It meant he was too late to see Zenin place the package containing the Browning into her briefcase.

"Any change?" said the Russian.

"No."

From the perfect concealment of the telephone booth into which he had pulled, Charlie made the immediate identification from the Primrose Hill photograph. Got you, you bastard, he thought. Charlie was reaching out for the receiver to alert Cummings when he realized the man was making his way out of the hotel. It would have to be later, Charlie decided.

They had made love before Giles got up and Barbara lay languorously in bed, still warm from it, watching him dress. She said, "I don't think I'll bother with the boat trip after all. Maybe tomorrow."

"They're televising part of the ceremony live," said Giles. "Why don't you watch?"

"I might," she said.

35

Charlie thought many things, all too quickly, the predominant reaction that the bastard had beaten him immediately, the underlying realization that he was up against an absolute professional, which he supposed he'd always known but which had been put out of his mind by the euphoria of actually finding the Russian.

From the Rhone hotel Zenin strode directly across the quai to where the lake cruise boats were assembled, like bustling ducks at feeding time. Charlie, as far behind as he felt it safe to risk, saw the man appear to study the posters setting out the various trips and then board the leading cruiser, a shiny blue double-decker. At the top of the steps he turned at once, leaning on the rail and gazing back onto the quayside.

"Shit," muttered Charlie, in reluctant admiration. The position meant the Russian had a complete view of everyone boarding—and possibly following—behind him. And he *was* studying everyone, Charlie saw. And who studied back, in return, covering himself as best he could by pretending to read a restaurant menu displayed in a glass case, about twenty yards away. The physical description that the experts had created from those snatched photographs was very accurate. So, too, was the impression of the immigration official at London airport: the Russian appeared to hold himself in readiness, a very fit man, tensed always to move. The face, which Charlie could see for the first time, was dark-skinned—like the picture had recorded—but lean and narrow, which it hadn't. The skin seemed stretched over high cheekbones beneath the jet black hair he'd known about. Definitely not Slavic, Charlie judged. Maybe one of the southern republics.

What was he going to do! There was a haphazard line of early tourists straggling aboard the cruiser, but they actually looked like tourists, carrying cameras and guidebooks. The fact that he was not would possibly register at once with a cautious man, Charlie decided. By itself it would mean nothing, but it would isolate him from the rest, mark him out for attention. Could he risk letting the cruiser go, hoping to follow in the next? Ridiculous, Charlie dismissed at once. He did not know because he could not chance going to the departures board to find out but he guessed the sailings were staged, possibly as far as an hour apart. So a boat that left an hour later returned an hour later. By which time the Russian could be God knows where. Wait then, until he got back? Ridiculous again. Once more he didn't know, without checking, but Charlie guessed there would be several stops around the lake, at any one of which the Russian could disembark.

He had to get aboard, Charlie accepted reluctantly. Try to disguise himself as much as possible among a holiday group, avoid the risk of eye contact and bury himself as quickly as he could. Except there did not appear to be a convenient holiday group. Instead, sailors came down the ramp and began their cast-off preparations, and Charlie acknowledged he had only minutes to move and that he'd buggered it up by waiting because his hurried arrival now would attract even more attention from the Russian still at the top of the steps.

Charlie actually started to move when he saw Zenin do the same, just managing to pull himself instead into one of the restaurant chairs, half turned away from the ship. Brilliant, congratulated Charlie, absolutely and utterly brilliant. He saw the Russian gesturing down the ramp to the company officials, indicating his watch as if there were some time difficulty making him change his mind, but then turned to watch the sailing. The maneuver meant the Russian had not been particularly interested in who boarded anyway, just in anyone attempting a panicked departure after him, providing positive proof of pursuit. With the Russian's back to him, Charlie jerked up from the table to avoid getting trapped there with an order, aware of the nervous perspiration across his back. He'd escaped by a whisker. Charlie was accustomed to out-professionalizing everyone and didn't like being matched this close.

Zenin took his time, scouring the deck rail for any obvious, frustrated attention but Charlie saw the beginning of the turn and anticipated the direction, so that he was able to start out ahead of the Russian. Following from the front rather than from the rear is the most difficult method of surveillance, disliked because of the obvious risk of losing the target even by experts able to do it, but it is correspondingly difficult to detect. Which was not the only reason Charlie tried it. He was piqued at coming so near to being caught out and wanted his own private challenge. Careful, laddie, he told himself in immediate warning. Pride doesn't come into it and this isn't a game.

He picked up the Russian behind him in the brief reflection from the glass of a kiosk display and then later from the pane in an angled doorway. Charlie could not risk going further than about ten yards along the main road when he reached the bridge, in case the Russian continued to follow the river line along the quai, but the halt was necessary anyway because it was time to change his appearance as much as possible. He slipped out of his topcoat, which he no longer needed, and reversed it so that the lining was uppermost and visible. He chose the complete concealment of a newsstand, where revolving racks of cards, magazines, and newspapers were set out onto the pavement. Further to appear different, if his presence had passingly registered with the Russian, Charlie bought a copy of *Le Monde* and the sort of guidebook he had been lacking back there on the quai, arranging both visibly in his left hand and held across his body.

Able safely to look directly backward from the protection of his card racks, Charlie saw Zenin come up from the waterside but hesitate, looking directly backward himself, the outward action of an innocent man admiring the view of the lake, in reality the protective action of a superbly

trained operator, not content with the steamer avoidance,
refusing to relax for a moment.

Again Charlie set off slightly ahead of the other man, realizing almost at once that the indulgence of this sort of surveillance would have to end. Ahead the road split into two
major highways and off each ran a warren of smaller avenues and streets, a dream evasion labyrinth for someone as
good as the Russian.

Charlie walked just into the Rue des Terreaux du Temple
where Zenin had staged one of his meetings with Sulafeh
Nabulsi, glad of the immediate department store with its
wide, deep corridor entrances. Although he expected the
Russian still to be around the corner, Charlie thrust in with
the apparent determination of someone intending to enter
the store, only halting at the shadowed bottom and turning
for the man to pass.

Ten o'clock, Charlie saw. Remembering his interrupted
effort to contact Cummings from the Rhone hotel, he realized he needed a telephone. Still a little time, though; thank
Christ for the failsafe. He edged forward as soon as he saw
the Russian go past the entrance, not intending to follow
any closer but wanting to pick him out at once, seeking a
marker. Why the hell couldn't he be wearing something that
stood out, like the woman, instead of the nondescript, ev-
eryday grey! Charlie didn't bother to answer his own fatu-
ous question because the answer was too obvious. His feet
ached, a solid, thumping ache. He wasn't happy.

And he grew unhappier. Never, in any pursuit at any
time in the past, had Charlie been opposed by such a man.
There was not a tradecraft trick the Russian did not employ.
In a cafe on the Rue des Terreaux du Temple, Zenin ordered
coffee, but just as Charlie reached the telephone booth to
make contact with Cummings, he jerked up without drinking it, staging another of his hurried departure tricks like he
had with the ferry. He got on a streetcar at one stop, feigned
disembarkation at the next and finally got off at the second
stop, making Charlie run to catch it and stand sweating
more than before, frightened of detection. At the railway
station he milled among passengers on the concourse, join-

ing a line so that Charlie actually thought he was going to board a train but then hurried away to a lavatory on the first floor. He stayed inside a very long time—far longer than any natural necessity—and Charlie fought back the tensed inclination to hurry in after the man to insure he had not escaped through another exit, unable either to risk the increasingly urgent telephone call because the telephone booths were too far away to use and still maintain the proper watch at the same time upon the lavatory entrance.

Deciding they had served their minimal use, Charlie dumped the newspaper and the guidebook and put his topcoat back on, although he didn't need it. He was damp with effort. Which was still not enough, he acknowledged. He'd been so preoccupied just keeping up that he had not properly recognized what was happening until now, when there was a moment literally to stand still. And he'd even admired the tradecraft, failing properly to see it for what it was! This was no ordinary caution. This was the twisting and weaving of an ultimate professional doing what an ultimate professional did just before the focus of his mission, going through every motion to remain undetected. One awareness followed another. Despite all the dodging and the backtracking, they had been drawing inexorably closer all the time to the Palais des Nations.

So the assassination was actually planned for today!

The realization brought a fresh trickle of apprehension and Charlie scrubbed the sleeve of his coat across his forehead, looking again toward the faraway telephones. It had been a mistake, trying to go it alone. He needed more people, a squad at least. There should have been proper, technical communications and necessary warnings, not just to those who had been involved so far but to the other unwitting delegations. And his having finally located the Russian should not have been allowed to run, like he was being allowed to run now. The difficulty of any proper charge could have been ignored. The Russian should have been swept up and held, until the conference was over and the danger with it. Ten-thirty, Charlie saw, from the station clock. Time was getting tight, too tight. Should he abandon the Russian, worry only about a warning? There was still Cummings to provide that, whatever happened. Blom would not be able to keep everything under wraps, once the woman was seized. So everyone would be alerted, the protection made absolute. And Charlie wanted the Russian. After all the ridicule and condescension, he wanted to bring the bastard in and destroy the entire Soviet operation, not just half. He'd stay with the Russian, Charlie decided. Cling to him like shit to a blanket until the man stopped moving and he could lead Blom right to him.

Charlie actually started, as if he were surprised, when the Russian emerged from the lavatory, making at once for the steps leading down to ground level. Charlie set out in renewed pursuit, conscious at once that the man was moving faster and with more positive direction than before, striding around Cropettes Park into the Leonard Baulacre avenue. Twice Charlie was aware of him checking his watch, appearing no longer concerned about being followed. They seemed to be heading absolutely northward now, without any attempted evasion, directly toward the Palais des Nations. Convinced he was safe from any surveillance, the Russian had abandoned any further precautions, which represented a victory. There began a bubble of satisfaction in Charlie that popped abruptly, unformed. He'd fucked it up! The awareness crowded in upon him, sickeningly. He'd been wrong—horrifyingly, stupidly wrong—relying upon an imagined failsafe of eleven-thirty, with the conference not convening until noon. He'd forgotten the photographic session: all that stupid posturing for posterity! Charlie looked at his own watch. An exposed, targetable photographic session that began in precisely seventeen minutes!

They turned off the Rue du Vidollet onto the Avenue Giuseppe Motta, Charlie searching desperately for a telephone box or a policeman. Why were there never either about, when you wanted one, like the joke said! Almost at once, ahead, the Russian went off the major highway and Charlie hesitated, unsure. Why hadn't the man continued straight onto the Palais des Nations? Because he had almost arrived at wherever he was heading, idiot, Charlie told himself.

Charlie risked getting closer, only twenty yards behind when the Russian turned into the small road off Colombettes. Charlie stood at the corner, watching, feeling another small spurt of satisfaction when he saw the man enter the building. Gotcha! he thought again.

Charlie practically ran forward himself, hesitating only at the entrance, but the Russian had already entered the elevator. Charlie didn't need to see the indicator needle heading to the top floor, because he'd already worked out the building's location and its overlooking vantage points into the conference complex.

Inside the foyer Charlie looked desperately around, seeing the travel agency in the corner. He threw open the door and said to the startled clerk who looked up, "A telephone! For Christ's sake, where's a telephone?"

There was a wall clock facing him. Fourteen minutes, he saw.

The assembly was strictly regimented, rehearsed over several days by the support groups, so there was no confusion. The Israeli group formed one edge, with the American delegation creating the buffer as they did within the conference building. Then came the Palestinians, followed by the Jordanians and finally the Syrians. The delineation was very positive in the front, with the leaders, but less formal among the aides and secretariat. Sulafeh Nabulsi stood less than ten feet from her victim, the briefcase containing the Browning no longer hanging from her shoulder but held in front of her, her hand already partially inside.

36

Vasili Zenin hesitated immediately inside the apartment, looking at the neatly positioned rubber wedges and recalling his uncertainty during the escape preparations. Unnecessary and time-delaying, he decided positively. A hindrance, in fact. He continued on, taking off his jacket as he went, throwing it over the chair that remained in position from his weapon assembly and crouched before getting into the harness to bring the photographic gathering in the faraway garden into view through the image magnifier. Practically assembled, he saw. All very neat and orderly. Lining up like targets, in fact. The Russian smiled at his own joke, slipping into the leather vest and zipping it tightly beneath his chin. He secured the cross-straps but did not attach himself at once to the M21. Instead, attachments trailing from him, Zenin pulled the curtaining tightly to one side and then lifted the bottom half to loop it through the sash of the adjoining window, so that it was completely out of the way. He raised the chosen window as far as it would go, giving him a gap about a meter and a half square and swiveled the rifle on its tripod mounting to point directly through it. Still in front of the M21, Zenin screwed on the sound suppressor which made the barrel protrude through the open window and snapped the magazine of hollow-nosed bullets into place. The guns of Israeli security would be loaded with the same, he knew. And so was the Browning carried by Sulafeh Nabulsi.

Four minutes to go, he saw, clipping the muzzle strap onto its ring. Timing was vital now, because Sulafeh had to move first. Zenin fastened the last strap to the tripod, hugging the stock into his shoulder, knowing that familiar sensation of the weapon being an extension of him, not something apart. The grouped-together statesmen were very clear through the sight. Zenin could see the American Secretary of State, Bell, with Arafat quite close. Mordechai Cohen, the Israeli Foreign Minister, was talking earnestly to someone just behind him and Hassani, the Jordanian minister, was trying, but failing, to catch the attention of someone in the Syrian group alongside.

Zenin brought the rifle into line, sighting perfectly upon his first kill, breathing easily, quite relaxed. Zenin saw the gathering start to come formally together, everyone turning toward the camera, and realized the photographic assistant just intruding into the bottom of his magnified circle was warning them the session was soon to begin. Not much longer now, thought the Russian.

Charlie Muffin stared impatiently at the floors lighting up and then going blank on the indicator board as the elevator climbed upward with agonizing slowness, driving his right fist into the palm of his left hand in his impatience, willing it to go faster. Cummings was probably right, he realized, in further frustration. Blom and Giles and Levy would all be out there, somewhere around the picture session and impossible to contact immediately. But there'd surely be a radio contact, to Blom at least! Some way of reaching the man. No klaxon alarm, Charlie remembered. And he remembered Blom's words: *a klaxon has no other practical benefit beyond making a noise and alarming people.* Exactly what they fucking well needed! Any noise! Any alarm! Anything as a warning!

So what the hell did he think he was going to do, all by himself! Charlie didn't know. The conversation with Wilson and Harkness came back to him with crystal clarity, the experts' opinion that calculating stature against build the Russian was toned to a muscle-hardened fitness, a fitness that the airport immigration officer had remarked upon and which had been Charlie's impression, looking up from the quayside a few hours earlier. Charlie's feet were agony now, and he was panting with exertion and conscious of the stomach bulge over the inadequate trouser belt. And he acknowledged that in a one-to-one physical contest he'd stand as much chance of winning as a virgin saying no at a sex maniacs' convention where they'd all been on the booze. The trained-to-kill-in-every-way Russian would literally beat the shit out of him. And that just as a beginning. So what the hell was he going to do, he thought again, as the elevator sighed at last to a halt at the top.

The photographic assistant came officiously forward, rearranging the positions very slightly to make sure no one would be obscured, and Zenin sighed at the delay. He'd isolated Sulafeh through the magnifier, appreciating how close she was and keeping the sight on her for the very moment she moved. She couldn't miss, not from there. Or be intercepted, until it was too late. Come on! he thought, come on! The assistant edged backward again and Zenin brought the gun against his shoulder once more, his finger shifting from the safe, no-shot hold beyond the guard to the trigger itself, taking up the imperceptible slack. Time! Zenin said, in mental conversation with the woman. It's time!

Charlie's indecision was fractional, no more than seconds, when he emerged from the elevator. The outside of the building—and the area it overlooked—was vivid in his mind. He went at once to his left, seeing that the corridor was straight and ended blind, which meant the far end door and still to the left had to be the place. It would be a corner window, of course, a choice of shot. He still had not decided what he was going to do. He'd been trained to fight, you put your foot there and I put my hip there and whoops, over you go, and a karate chop for luck, like it was in all those spy films. Except that he'd always put his protesting foot in the wrong place and got his stance wrong and invariably ended up flat on his ass with the instructor asking what the hell he thought he was doing. What about a weapon, then? Charlie had been as bad with a gun as he had been in unarmed combat, never able to stop his eyes from squinting shut against the bang, invariably blowing leaking holes in all the backing sandbags but rarely managing to hit the paper square and even more rarely the rings outlined upon it. And it was anyway a meaningless run of thought because he didn't have a gun in the first place.

There was only distraction. He had to surprise the man, deflect the attack. Anything, until the Swiss got here. Hurry, he thought. For Christ's sake, hurry!

Zenin saw the woman's hand come out of the briefcase, the heavy handgun clutched before her. It became an odd, slow-motion sequence: there she was, out in the open and completely visible to everyone, with a gun raised in her hand and they all appeared unaware, still smiling at the camera, all holding their poses. He saw the faintest puff of smoke and the jerky recoil, as she fired. Only then—and still slowly—did the stances begin to break but by that time Zenin was firing, moving easily with the rifle's kick.

Charlie was at the door when the sound came, not an explosion but the fart of a silencer, and he knew it immediately, like he knew immediately that he was too late. He pushed against the door, not expecting it to give but it did, so quickly that he actually stumbled into the room, off balance.

The rifle farted again.

Everything registered instantly with Charlie. He saw the Russian turned practically away from him, attached to the rifle by the complicated professional harness and knew without having to look that it had been the photographic session and that there'd already been two shots and that the man had concentrated so much that despite the sound, the Russian was first unaware of his entry.

And then there was the compressed hiss of a third shot.

"NO!" That's all there was, just a yell. Distract and deflect, nothing more. Certainly Charlie did not anticipate the reaction.

From the Russian there was no pause or hesitation, no surprise or fear. Zenin moved instantly and smoothly, trying to swing the rifle on its revolving stand around into the room to fight off whatever the intrusion, and Charlie saw the movement and thought, fuck it, I'm dead. He actually hoped it wouldn't hurt.

But the gun would not completely swing. The silencer

extension caught the edge of the window frame, jarring Zenin against the buttress he'd chosen to shield himself against the light. He swung again, harder this time, but still it was too long and again he rebounded off the wall extension. Trapped inside the harness, Zenin strained back, trying to bend the tripod away from its floor mountings to complete the movement and kill Charlie.

And Charlie realized the man's helplessness.

He'd actually been half turned, hopelessly to run. Now he jerked back, dashing instead toward the man and lashing out with his fist when he reached him, wincing with the pain that shuddered up through his fist and into his arm when he connected just below the Russian's left eye. There was another desperate jerk against the rifle and another collision with the buttress and Charlie properly knew it for the first time, snatching out for the rifle barrel with the hand that was not numbed.

Zenin saw what Charlie intended and tried to brace himself against it but was so restricted by the leather vest there was no way he could stop it happening, just initially reduce the force of impact by stressing his feet against the floor and that only briefly. Charlie hauled the rifle back and forth, as if he were working a pump handle, battering the Russian encased at the other end against the sharply edged wall. The barrel was high now, far away from its target, and twice before the breath was driven from his body and he lost consciousness, Zenin fired, trying to frighten Charlie's grip away from the barrel. But Charlie did not let go, working it back and forth and back and forth, smashing the gradually weakening man into the buttress. Even when Zenin hung in apparent unconsciousness, blood smearing the wall and floor, Charlie did not stop, needing two hands against the barrel now and stopping, exhausted, only when the Russian became such a dead weight that he could not move him any more.

For several moments Charlie slumped where he was, actually bent over the rifle from which Zenin now lolled backward, mouth open, snorting his unconsciousness. Charlie gulped at the air from the open window, vaguely aware of the scream of approaching police sirens, gradually conscious of the panicked scene far away, too far away properly to distinguish. And then he saw the magnified sight, only inches from his face.

Experimentally Charlie pulled at it, isolating the restraining screw. He undid it, slid the sight from its housing and pulled himself up against the tripod, still needing its support. He used the sight like the spyglass it was, needing to adjust it only slightly.

He was perfectly able to see the blown-apart, bloodsplattered body of James Bell being lifted onto a stretcher, American security men needlessly ringed around the dead Secretary of State, handguns drawn. They appeared to be standing over another body, too, and as Charlie watched, medics lifted it onto a stretcher. Before they fully covered it with a blanket, he saw it was Roger Giles, but only part of the man because the left side of his body wasn't there anymore. There was a third body from which everyone seemed to be standing back and Charlie adjusted the magnifier, better to see it, not sure until it was also lifted onto a stretcher. There was a huge, gaping hole in the side of Sulafeh Nabulsi's body, to the left again like it was with the American security chief, but not quite so extensive because the hit had not been so direct.

Charlie swept the area, back and forth, trying to see if there were anymore dead or injured, stopping abruptly when he identified David Levy. The Israeli delegation had already been hustled away to safety and the intelligence chief was looking calmly about him, standing apart from all the other scurrying security officials. And then, suddenly, Levy turned and looked directly up at the window from which Charlie was watching, as if it would be possible for one to see the other.

The final answers to the final questions flooded in upon Charlie, who pulled himself up unsteadily from his halfkneeling position. He lowered the spyglass but remained staring at the scene he could no longer properly see, realizing fully just how wrong he had been.

"Oh you bastard," he said, quietly at first. Then, more loudly, "You bastard!"

Charlie became aware of running feet and shouting and moved away from the still unconscious body, not wanting wrongly to become a target by association for some trigger-happy policeman.

But it was Blom who came into the apartment first, pistol drawn. The white-haired, pink-featured man stared around, halting at the sight of Zenin still strapped to the rifle.

"Satisfied now?" asked Charlie.

Barbara Giles had taken her husband's suggestion to watch the opening ceremonies of the conference live on television and Martha Bell watched, too, because she always did when James was doing something publicly, so they both saw their men gunned down at the very moment it happened.

Aloud, Barbara said, "No, please no! I want to love you!"

Aloud, Martha said, "What's going to happen to me?"

Both women, of course, were in shock.

On the Rue Dancet, where Charlie had hours before abandoned Alexander Cummings's office car, the traffic cop attached the second penalty ticket and made a note in his book to summon the towing service if it wasn't moved in the next hour. Arrogant foreigners with their damned diplomatic plates believed they could do what they wanted and get away with it, but the law said he could penalize them and so he would.

37

"Bastard!" yelled Charlie, again.

"Why so upset?" demanded Levy mildly.

"You knew! You fucking well knew!" accused Charlie. He was tight with anger, fury shaking through him, relieved only that he was at least able to confront the Israeli security man. Charlie had been frightened he would be too late. Blom had delayed him, seeking a full briefing so that he in turn could provide a complete explanation to the Swiss Security Committee and the Federal cabinet, so by the time Charlie got to the Bristol hotel, the Israeli leaders, like all the other delegation heads, had already flown away from Geneva and the cancelled conference, each unwilling fully to accept the Swiss assurances that there was no risk from an ongoing assassination conspiracy.

"I don't know what you're talking about," said Levy, still mildly. They were alone, just the two of them, in Levy's hotel room. There was no indication that the man was packing to leave.

"Bull!" said Charlie. "You led me by the nose, all the time. And I fell for it! When I talked of a possible attempt that first day, you weren't surprised. You argued against any public warning, despite it being the obvious thing to do! You actually questioned me, after letting me have the files, to make sure I hadn't discovered anything! And then tried to encourage me to quit!" Charlie came breathlessly to a halt. "You even distracted me, when we got to where the photographs were going to be taken. Until I saw you look up, it didn't register that it was inconceivable you would not have known Sulafeh Nabulsi for what she was!"

"Dangerous woman," agreed Levy. "Very dangerous."

He poured brandy, Remy Martin, into two glasses and offered one. "Have a drink, Charlie," said Levy. "Calm down."

Charlie accepted the glass but didn't drink at once. "The dossier on her was complete bullshit, wasn't it!" he demanded. "Phony from start to finish."

"Everyone can make mistakes, even the Israeli service," said Levy.

Charlie shook his head, refusing the evasion. "You knew all about her and what she might do," he insisted. "Learning from me—from the British—of some Soviet involvement confirmed it all for you!"

"We were grateful for the warning," said Levy.

"You made me look a fool," said Charlie. "A fucking idiot!"

"No, I didn't, Charlie," argued the Israeli. "You worked it all out, so that doesn't make you a fool. And it might not become public knowledge because of the need to protect your identity, but within the trade you're a hero. Even to the CIA, who tried to kill you themselves once."

He'd realized how the Israelis had checked him out, too! remembered Charlie, further annoyed. He said, "People got killed!"

"Unfortunate," said Levy. "Now look at what you've got. You're the man who made it possible for the Swiss to seize a provable Soviet agent and publicly show the world the link between Moscow and Arab terrorism. It's a coup, Charlie. Enjoy your reputation."

"Christ, it was clever," said Charlie. "Pressured by America to take part in a conference including Palestinians with whom you're committed never to become involved, you allowed a fanatic to be part of their delegation knowing there'd be some outrage to wreck everything: wreck it for years."

"The positive Russian intrusion was a bonus," allowed Levy. "If you had not got him, it would have been put down to a lone Palestinian assassin. And when the rifle was eventually found, the suspicion would have been of American, not Soviet involvement."

"Why did Russia become involved?"

"Moscow doesn't want peace in the Middle East," said Levy. "Certainly not peace orchestrated by Washington and an American President. Syria would have ceased being a client state, for a start."

"Doesn't Israel want peace?"

Levy smiled, adding to both their glasses. "It's an odd fact, but Israel exists better as a cohesive society with a . . . what is it you British call it? A Dunkirk spirit?"

"There's got to be more in it than that."

"The American administration was backing away from us," disclosed Levy. "There were private assurances that the aid would continue, as well as the arms supply, but we had our doubts. This way everybody wins. Anderson is the man who came closer than anyone else to achieving peace, Russia is exposed as the villain, and we go on getting all the American support we ask for."

"Weren't you frightened she'd move against one of the Israeli delegates rather than the American Secretary of State?"

"That was always the biggest risk," admitted Levy. "She wouldn't have succeeded, of course. We were always ready."

"Your people shot her?"

"Of course," said Levy. "But there's more than one wound, apparently. Seems like the Russian had orders to kill her, as well. The same bullets as we used: they tried to think of everything."

So they *had* expected someone to die. Charlie said, "What do you imagine the American reaction would be if they ever learned you'd allowed their Secretary of State— and a protective CIA man—literally to be led like a lamb to the slaughter?"

"Proof, Charlie, where's the proof? This conversation never took place. You know that."

"Bastard!"

"You already said that," reminded the Israeli. "Let's just say that this time I won."

Like fuck, thought Charlie.

The preliminary inquiry had been in one of the small committee chambers of the Praesidium building of the Kremlin, and afterward Berenkov and Kalenin drove back to Dzerzhinsky Square in the same car, the KGB chairman's Zil. They traveled with the curtains drawn and the separating window raised between themselves and the driver.

"They were right," said Kalenin. "It's an unmitigated disaster."

"It was a wise precaution for Comrade Lvov to be so openly acknowledged as the architect of the entire operation," said Berenkov. "And personally regrettable for him to be recognized as the strongest opponent of it being cancelled."

"We'll have to deny Zenin, of course."

"He carried nothing connecting him to Russia," said Berenkov.

"What if he confesses?"

Berenkov shook his head. "His entire training is against that."

"I'd feel happier if he were eliminated."

"It would be difficult in jail. And a lot of people would regard it as confirmation of his being a Soviet agent if he were killed," suggested Berenkov.

Kalenin nodded, accepting the argument, looking expectantly toward the yellow-stucco front of the approaching KGB headquarters. He said, "There's still the British."

"Yes," agreed Berenkov.

"There's no way of assessing how much they know?"

"Absolutely none."

"The greatest uncertainty then?"

"I'm afraid so."

"What about Charlie Muffin?"

"It was definitely him," disclosed Berenkov. "Remember we stepped up the intercepts to the British embassy here?"

"Of course."

"We managed a computer break on one of the codes we had not previously been able to read," said Berenkov. "Charlie Muffin sent queries concerning Novikov to a man here called Gale. We had not positively identified Gale as the *rezident* at the embassy, so it was a double bonus."

"You are right," said Kalenin. "Charlie Muffin has to be eliminated. He's a recurring nuisance."

"I'm handling it personally."

"Have you devised a way yet?"

"Not yet," conceded Berenkov. "I'm considering one possibility."

"No more mistakes," warned Kalenin. "It would not be wise if either of us were associated with another mistake." It was fortunate, Kalenin thought, that he possessed all those incriminating biographies of so many men in positions of power and importance.

"I won't make any move until I'm sure," said Berenkov.

"You liked Charlie Muffin, didn't you?" said Kalenin, aware of the background of his friend, like he was aware of all the other backgrounds.

"He was a very clever operator," said Berenkov.

"Regrettable in some ways that he has to be removed."

"Unavoidable," said Berenkov.

38

The polygraph test was the final part of Charlie's positive vetting, and he entered the technician's room, satisfied that so far he had done pretty well. He'd know soon enough, he supposed. The appointment with the Director was scheduled for that afternoon. He was wearing the bank interview shirt that he'd had laundered at the Beau-Rivage.

"Long time since I had one of these," he said to the technician.

"You know the rules then?" He was a doleful, long-faced man so accustomed to uncovering human frailties that he could no longer be shocked.

"Yes or no answers to everything with a lot of sexy stuff at the beginning to see if I'm telling the truth," said Charlie. "Tell you what, why don't we try to speed things up a bit? I've masturbated since I was nine, try to get my leg over as often as possible, and I've never had a homosexual relationship but I've always been curious."

The man sighed wearily. "Let's just do it my way, shall we?"

Charlie let himself be hooked up to the sensors that would monitor his sweat, pulse, and heartbeats and said, "Whenever you're ready."

It took two hours. Throughout Charlie sat quite relaxed, Hush Puppies extended before him, his legs crossed at the ankles, part of his mind not concentrating upon the examination but what he still wanted to do about Switzerland. That afternoon's appointment was at Sir Alistair Wilson's demand, but if it had not come, Charlie would have sought a meeting anyway. He hoped Wilson would agree. What was the greater spur, he asked himself objectively. His hurt pride or his offended sensibilities over what had happened in Geneva? It didn't really matter. Getting the Director's approval was all that mattered. Charlie was damned if he was going to be beaten.

Charlie was almost surprised when the test ended. As the technician unhooked him, Charlie said, "How did I do?"

"Well enough," said the man.

"Mum always said that honesty was the best policy," said Charlie.

"I'm not impressed," said the man. "Why don't you save the independence bullshit for elsewhere?"

Assholes, thought Charlie. His inclination was to go to the pub at lunchtime but he resisted it, remaining instead in his office to complete his Swiss expenses, smiling at the confetti of receipts and bills he had amassed. Keep Harkness happy for hours, he thought. Charlie squinted through the opaque glass, trying to see if Witherspoon were in his office. It appeared to be empty. Charlie wondered if the man had been switched back to Novikov or put on something else: school crossing traffic warden, for instance.

Charlie arrived at the Director's office on time and was admitted at once, immediately conscious of something being different but not initially able to recognize what it was. And then he became aware that the room was devoid of roses.

Wilson saw Charlie looking curiously around the room and said, "Green fly."

"Sorry to hear it," said Charlie.

"Causing havoc," said the Director.

"I've heard that it does."

"Some of the stems will die." The Director, at the windowsill, leaned absentmindedly downward, massaging his stiff leg.

"Sorry," said Charlie again, unable to think of anything else.

"It's Islay malt, isn't it?" said the Director, limping toward the drinks cabinet, enclosed behind a bureau door.

"For preference," accepted Charlie.

"Never could acquire a taste for whisky," said Wilson,

with the sadness of someone confessing a failing. "Pink gin man, myself. The Russian isn't saying anything, you know."

"I didn't expect him to."

"The photograph of Koretsky's surveillance that day in Primrose Hill is a positive link to Moscow," said Wilson. "And there is the corroborative affidavit from Novikov."

"We'd have to move against Koretsky, if he were identified as the London *resident*," reminded Charlie.

The Director nodded. "That's the bugger: means MI-5 would have to spend a lot of time identifying his replacement. But the Cabinet feeling is that causing as big a sensation in Switzerland as possible is worth the sacrifice."

"Probably," concurred Charlie.

"If you hadn't got him, the whole thing would have been put down to a suicide assault by a Palestinian zealot. There would not have been any proof of Soviet involvement because all the hollow-nosed ammunition flattens out and is impossible to differentiate forensically." Wilson hesitated and said in begrudgingly professional acknowledgment, "You've got to give them credit. The bloody Russians are nothing if not devious."

"There was a second plot," announced Charlie abruptly. "Or maybe it was the first, I don't know. The Israelis set the whole thing up. Let the woman run, to wreck everything. Whether the Russians had been involved or not really wouldn't have mattered a damn."

Wilson turned, the whisky bottle suspended over Charlie's glass, but not pouring. He said, "I think you'd better explain that."

Charlie did, not once trying to disguise or gloss over his own mistakes. By the time he finished, Wilson was nodding. He finished making the drinks, handed Charlie his glass and said, "Cheers."

"Cheers," responded Charlie.

"Levy admitted that?"

"Yes."

"Bastards!"

"That's what I said. Several times."

"Despite everything, you still did well," praised the older man.

"I want to do something more."

"What?"

Charlie told him, in as much detail as he'd given in the earlier explanation, and when he finished, Wilson said, "Why?"

"Why not?"

"There's no benefit for us," protested the Director objectively.

"Yes, there is," disputed Charlie. "Levy was right, saying that I was the flavor of the month with the CIA. It would make them more grateful: not to me personally, but to the service as a whole."

"Maybe," said Wilson doubtfully.

"People died," said Charlie. "People needn't have."

"No," accepted Wilson. "No, they didn't have to let it go to that extreme."

"So can I go to Washington?"

Wilson gazed for several moments down into his glass, like a fortune-teller trying to forecast an event from the arrangement of tea leaves at its bottom. Then he looked up and said, "Why not? Let's strengthen the bonds of Atlantic friendship."

"Thank you," said Charlie.

Wilson put his glass down positively on the desk in front of him and said, "You passed your positive vetting."

"I'm grateful for your telling me so soon," said Charlie.

"You were worried?"

"One never likes having one's honesty and integrity doubted."

"Were you surprised that one was ordered?"

"Such decisions are always at the discretion of senior management," said Charlie, feeling safety in formality.

Wilson sat in silence, observing Charlie over the rim of his glass. He said, "You made application for a bank overdraft—for ten thousand pounds?"

"Yes," agreed Charlie cautiously.

"Harkness has refused to provide the necessary reference."

"Oh," said Charlie.

"And you've been passed over in the last two grading assessments?"

"Yes, sir."

"I've written a memorandum today correcting that," said the Director. "You're upgraded, with backdated effect from January 1. The salary increase is five thousand pounds a year."

"Thank you, sir." Charlie was uneasy.

"I want you to tell me something."

"What?"

"Do you think I am a stupid man?"

"I don't understand, sir."

"Do you think I am a stupid man?" insisted Wilson.

"No, sir."

"Good," said the Director. "Now I am going to tell you something. I think you knew that any overdraft application like that needed a reference and that it would be referred to the deputy director. I think you knew regulations automatically required an investigation and a vetting procedure, which would declare you one hundred percent clean. I think you knew that I would be involved in discussions upon it and that during those discussions the oversight of your promotion would become known to me. You got anything to say about that?"

"No, sir."

"You never wanted a bloody overdraft in the first place, did you? You were playing the silly buggers, making sure I got to know you'd had a rotten deal."

"Still nothing to say, sir."

"Don't you ever try a trick like that again, Charlie. I don't care who else you try to con—and I know you con everybody—but don't you ever try it again with me, you understand?"

"Yes, sir."

"Now get out!"

"Yes, sir." All in all, decided Charlie, descending to his

own office on the lower level, it really hadn't been a bad day. Not a bad day at all.

The bodies had been kept in Geneva for the necessary autopsy and forensic examination and Clayton Anderson re-routed his return from Venice personally to escort the coffins and the widows home to the United States.

There was a full military guard of honor when the coffins, both draped with the Stars and Stripes, were loaded aboard the aircraft and the President stood with head bowed, his arms around Martha Bell and Barbara Giles. During the days of medical delay, Martha had managed to buy a black mourning suit and a black hat, complete with full veil. Barbara wore one of the grey dresses she'd bought for the holiday she was now never going to have. The escorting press corps had remained with the presidential party, of course, and the television pictures were relayed live by satellite back to America for the main evening news.

Anderson ushered both women ahead of him onto the aircraft, personally seeing that they were seated and telling both that if there was anything they wanted, anything at all, they just had to ask.

The President was in the rear of the aircraft before it cleared Swiss air space, giving unattributable briefings to selected correspondents about a renewed American commitment to combat international terrorism and the unquestionable Soviet links with that terrorism. He also gave *The New York Times* and *Newsweek* front page and cover stories on his regret that a settlement to the Palestinian problem in the Middle East appeared impossible to resolve, despite every effort he had made.

In the front of the plane Martha Bell turned to the woman alongside and said, "Don't you just love *Air Force One*!"

Barbara looked back and said, dully, "What?"

"This plane, *Air Force One*? Isn't it magnificent?"

"Yes," agreed Barbara, disinterested. "Very nice."

39

Harry Johnson had taken over the rear room of the Brace of Pheasants for his farewell party, which had been going for an hour before Charlie arrived. The place was full of noise and smoke and men, few of whom knew each other and who were too professional to propose introductions. Johnson's wife was with him, a wisp-haired, sharpfeatured woman wearing a hat decorated with cherries. She had a confused expression, never before having met her husband's friends and seeming surprised he had so many.

Charlie insinuated himself to the bar and was told they were still drinking off Johnson's kitty, so he chose a pint of beer, not wanting to deplete it too much too quickly.

The retiring watcher saw Charlie as he turned back into the room and shouldered his way forward, beaming.

"You made it!" said Johnson. "That's great."

"Promised I would," reminded Charlie.

"All over now," announced Johnson. "No more leaking doorways or aching hemorrhoids from sitting too long on cold seats."

"Looking forward to it?"

"Can't wait," said Johnson. "I got a Rotavator as a farewell present."

"A what?"

"It's kind of a digging machine. I've taken over more allotment."

"No more peas out of a tin, eh?"

"What about you, Charlie? You looking forward to retirement?"

"Long time yet," said Charlie uncomfortably. No, he thought, he wasn't looking forward to retirement. Harry had a wife with a funny hat and a small holding to grow his own vegetables. What did he have to look forward to when it was time to go? Nothing, he thought. There was a huge difference between working alone and being alone.

"Still feel bad about that last bit of business," said Johnson.

"Water under the bridge now."

"I know you can't tell me, but I'd like to know it worked out."

"It worked out," assured Charlie.

"I'm glad, really glad," said Johnson. "Not a lot in our line of work ever really works out, does it?"

"Not a lot," agreed Charlie.

"Get down to Broadstairs at all?"

"Broadstairs?" queried Charlie, bewildered.

"That's where we're going to be living most of the time." Johnson turned, gesturing to the woman in the hat. "That's the wife, Beryl. We'll be in the book, so if you're ever down that way, give me a bell. Don't want to lose touch completely with the old crowd."

"Sure," promised Charlie emptily. Johnson didn't want to go, Charlie realized. Funny how it was always the same, everyone bitching and moaning for years, counting days and weeks off the calendar until the time came, and when it did, they nearly all wanted to hang on.

"Don't forget now," urged Johnson, knowing Charlie would never come.

"I won't," promised Charlie.

"I'd better get back to the missus."

"Sure."

"Keep safe, Charlie."

"Always."

Charlie got himself another pint and was edging away from the bar to make room for someone else when he felt a hand on his arm and a voice said, "Wondered if I'd see you here."

Charlie turned, smiling in immediate recognition. "How are you doing, Sam?"

"Fine," said Donnelly. "You?"

"Can't complain."

"Looks like a good party?"

"With luck," said Charlie. "You do it, Sam?"

The man who had searched Charlie's apartment nodded and said, "Did you pass?"

"Kisses on both cheeks," said Charlie. "Thanks for the warning, though."

"Couldn't make it too obvious," said Donnelly. "Junior kid picked the lock to leave the scratch."

"It was pretty clumsy."

"He's still learning," assured the other man. "He'll get better."

"He needs to."

"I took over inside," disclosed Donnelly. "How did I do?"

"Failed," declared Charlie.

"I can't have!" disputed Donnelly.

"The bathroom cabinet," said Charlie. "After you searched it, you closed it: people always do. It was ajar when I left."

"Shit!" said the searcher.

"It wasn't much," said Charlie encouragingly.

"It hasn't got to be, has it?"

"Hope your young trainee wasn't offended by the place."

"He thought it was a pigsty."

"Did you tell him why?"

"I tried to."

"Tell him again, so he doesn't forget."

There was a commotion at the door at the entry of the kiss-o-gram girl. She wore a long black cloak which she discarded as soon as she was inside. She was quite naked apart from a miniscule G-string and a garter belt supporting fishnet stockings. She arranged herself on Johnson's lap with her breasts thrust into his face and there was raucous cheering and explosions of camera flashes. Beryl blushed and looked away.

"I think her tits are bigger than that October centerfold you've got," said Donnelly contemplatively. "Not much. Just slightly."

"Prefer the centerfold though," said Charlie.

"Younger," agreed Donnelly. "Certainly firmer. Have you really read all those books you've got?"

"Most of them," said Charlie.

"What about another drink?"

"One for the road," agreed Charlie.

"Not staying long then?"

"Got to be up early in the morning," said Charlie. "Plane to catch."

"You lead a marvelous bloody life in your division, don't you?" said Donnelly. "Bet you haven't had a shitty job for years."

"Can't remember the last time," said Charlie.

All the arrangements had been made between London and Washington at Director-to-Director level, even to the timing of the appointment. Charlie caught a flight that got him into Dulles by noon, determined against being late. He actually drove past the CIA headquarters at Langley on his way into the city, curious if his reacceptance by the Americans would ever be complete enough for him to be received there. He doubted it. There would still be a long way to go.

He had been at the Hay Adams for thirty minutes when his telephone sounded, precisely on time.

"Jesse Willard," said a strong Southern voice. "I'm downstairs in the lobby."

"Shall I come down?" asked Charlie.

"I'll come up," said Willard.

The hotel had been the CIA choice, Charlie knew. His room would have been swept for electronic surveillance, then bugged again. The CIA officer was a tall, bony man whose handshake hurt. "Can I offer you anything?" invited Charlie.

"Just what you came here to tell us," said Willard briskly.

Charlie considered it almost overly melodramatic. When in Rome, do as the Romans do, he thought. He said, "Did you know Giles?"

"I'm in charge of the division he worked in," said the American.

The Agency was definitely taking it seriously, realized

Charlie. Which was good. He said, "He was sacrificed. Your Secretary of State, too." Dramatic enough? he thought.

Willard made no outward reaction, except to pause. Then he said, "Do you know what you're saying?"

"Of course."

"Can you prove it?"

"Not sufficiently."

"How much?"

Instead of replying directly, Charlie said, "You can manipulate a lot of media outlets, can't you?"

"Yes."

"And you've got receptive congressmen on Capitol Hill?"

"Some."

"Then enough," said Charlie. From his briefcase he took the Israeli folder and said, "You'll need this. The Novikov stuff, too."

The *Washington Post* led with the first story a week later. It was picked up by *The New York Times* and all the major television networks by the following day, when the outcry erupted in both the Senate and the House of Representatives.

David Levy was summoned to the Israeli Foreign Minister's office on the day the Israeli government was forced into issuing a public apology, admitting mistakes. And promising an investigation.

There had been nothing, Berenkov acknowledged. The bugging devices in the apartment of Natalia Nikandrova Fedova had recorded the perfectly innocent activities of a divorced woman with a teenage son who telephoned regularly from college and the round-the-clock visual surveillance had failed to discover anything at all suspicious about her behavior. And her KGB work as a debriefer was beyond criticism.

She still had to be the key. Berenkov was convinced of it.

40

There was a table at the side of Mordechai Cohen's office with newspapers and magazines in several languages heaped upon it, disordered where they had been read and discarded.

"Have you seen them!" demanded the Israeli Foreign Minister.

"Nearly all," said Levy. He guessed it was politics time.

Cohen picked up one at random, *France Soir*, and said, "Look at that headline: 'The Shambles of Israeli Security.'" The man snatched up another, the current edition of *Newsweek*. "'The Slaughter that Could and Should Have Been Avoided,'" he read aloud.

"It's very bad," conceded Levy, going along with the charade.

"Do you know how bad?" asked Cohen rhetorically. "At best we're being made to look an incompetent laughingstock. At worst Conre are private demands being made from the American State Department for a full explanation. According to our Washington embassy, a lot of congressmen are openly doubting that it was a mistake at all. There's a groundswell growing to block any further aid. At this morning's Cabinet meeting, the conclusion was that the whole thing has backfired. Disastrously."

"I'm very sorry," said the intelligence chief.

"Are you sure it was the Englishman?"

"It has to be," said Levy. "I gave him the phony biography."

"Why!"

"To deflect him," said Levy. "I wanted to bury him in paper."

"Why didn't you get the damned thing back!"

"I never thought he'd use it. Certainly not like this," admitted Levy. Sadly he remembered, "And he said I'd made him look a fool."

"Now it's been reversed," said the Foreign Minister. Pointedly he added, "In your case, publicly."

"Yes," accepted Levy tightly.

"Has there been any count of the number of times you have been openly named?"

"Quite a lot," said Levy. "About thirty, worldwide."

"Israeli intelligence personnel are expected always to remain anonymous."

Levy did not reply.

Cohen said, "I'm sorry."

Still Levy did not speak.

"The Cabinet meeting also decided that a gesture was necessary beyond the formal expression of regret," disclosed the Foreign Minister. "Something to placate the Americans . . ." Cohen paused and said, "I know it was my instruction, but if I go, it will be confirmation that there was prior government awareness, and that will make everything worse rather than better."

At last Levy responded. He said, "I would like it to be a resignation, not a dismissal."

"Of course," accepted the Foreign Minister.

"Thank you," said Levy.

"I really am sorry," said Cohen.

"When?"

"Immediately."

"Ironic, isn't it?" said Levy. "Charlie Muffin actually called me a bastard!"

Epilogue

Natalia Nikandrova Fedova came with just the slightest hesitancy into Berenkov's office, surprised at his standing politely to greet her, which was a Western courtesy, not Russian. Charlie used to embarrass her at first by doing it.

"I was told to report to you, Comrade Berenkov?"

"Natalia Nikandrova," smiled the man. "I am evolving a mission; a very special mission. One in which you are to be involved."

"Yes?"

"Concerning an Englishman," said Berenkov, intent upon her. "Someone you once knew."

"Someone I knew?"

"Charlie Muffin."

She blushed, just slightly, but enough. It had been there all the time and he hadn't realized it, thought Berenkov. But he did now. He knew the way to make it all work, too.

B
in
V
b
w
C
c
H
re